MUROS
WITHIN MAGICAL WALLS

The Case of the Cemetery Girl

A GRAPHIC NOVEL BY
PAOLO CHIKIAMCO & BORG SINABAN

TUTTLE Publishing

Tokyo | Rutland, Vermont | Singapore

"Books to Span the East and West"

Tuttle Publishing was founded in 1832 in the small New England town of Rutland, Vermont [USA]. Our core values remain as strong today as they were then—to publish best-in-class books which bring people together one page at a time. In 1948, we established a publishing office in Japan—and Tuttle is now a leader in publishing English-language books about the arts, languages and cultures of Asia. The world has become a much smaller place today and Asia's economic and cultural influence has grown. Yet the need for meaningful dialogue and information about this diverse region has never been greater. Over the past seven decades, Tuttle has published thousands of books on subjects ranging from martial arts and paper crafts to language learning and literature—and our talented authors, illustrators, designers and photographers have won many prestigious awards. We welcome you to explore the wealth of information available on Asia at **www.tuttlepublishing.com**.

Published by Tuttle Publishing, an imprint of Periplus Editions (HK) Ltd.

www.tuttlepublishing.com

Copyright © 2022 Periplus Editions (HK) Ltd.

LCCN 2022943397

ISBN: 978-0-8048-5556-3

First edition
25 24 23 22   5 4 3 2 1

Printed in China   2210EP

Distributed by

North America, Latin America & Europe
Tuttle Publishing
364 Innovation Drive,
North Clarendon,
VT 05759-9436, USA
Tel: 1 (802) 773 8930
Fax: 1 (802) 773 6993
info@tuttlepublishing.com
www.tuttlepublishing.com

Asia Pacific
Berkeley Books Pte. Ltd.
3 Kallang Sector #04-01
Singapore 349278
Tel: (65) 67412178
Fax: (65) 67412179
inquiries@periplus.com.sg
www.tuttlepublishing.com

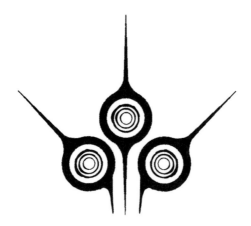

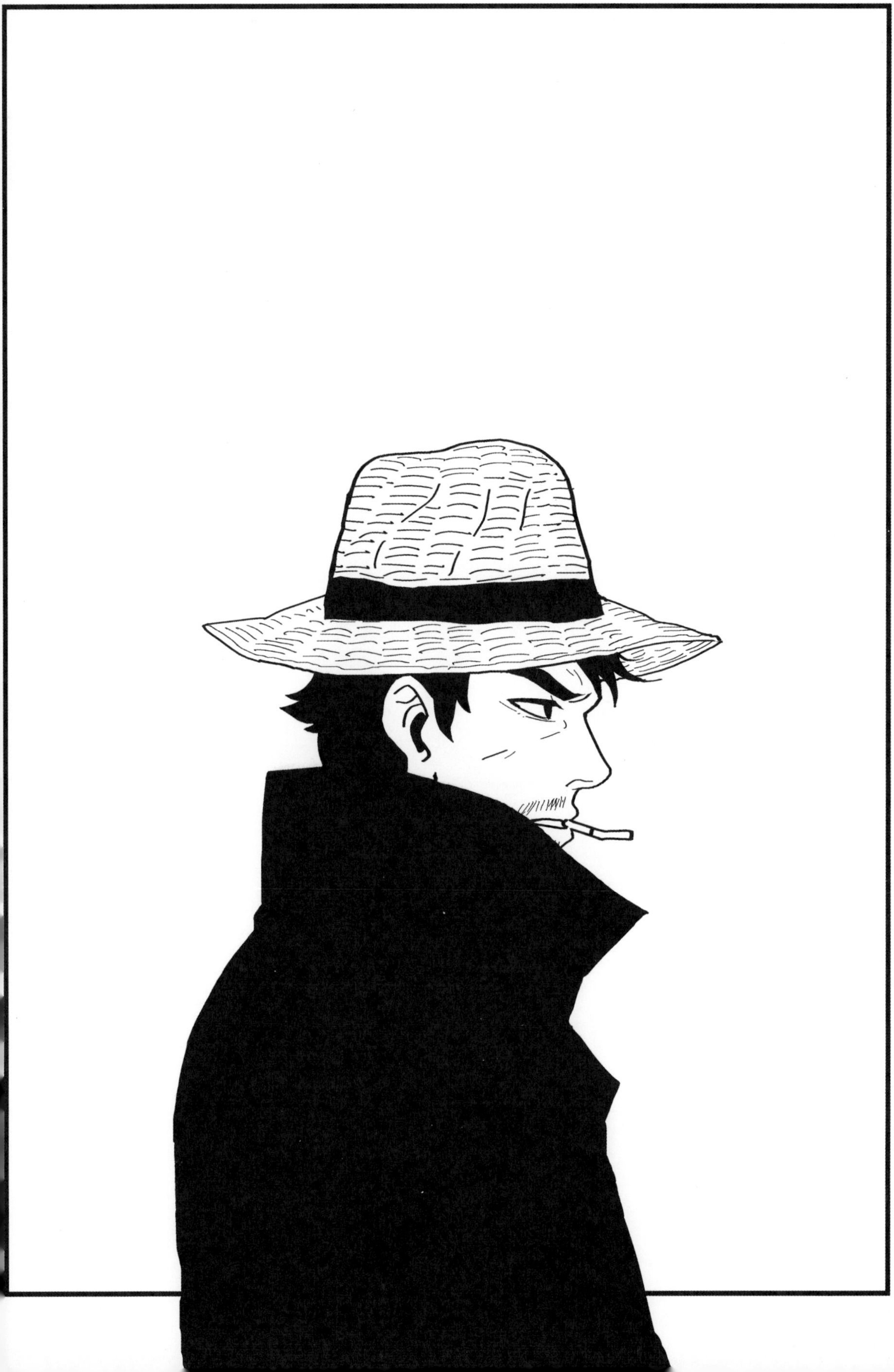

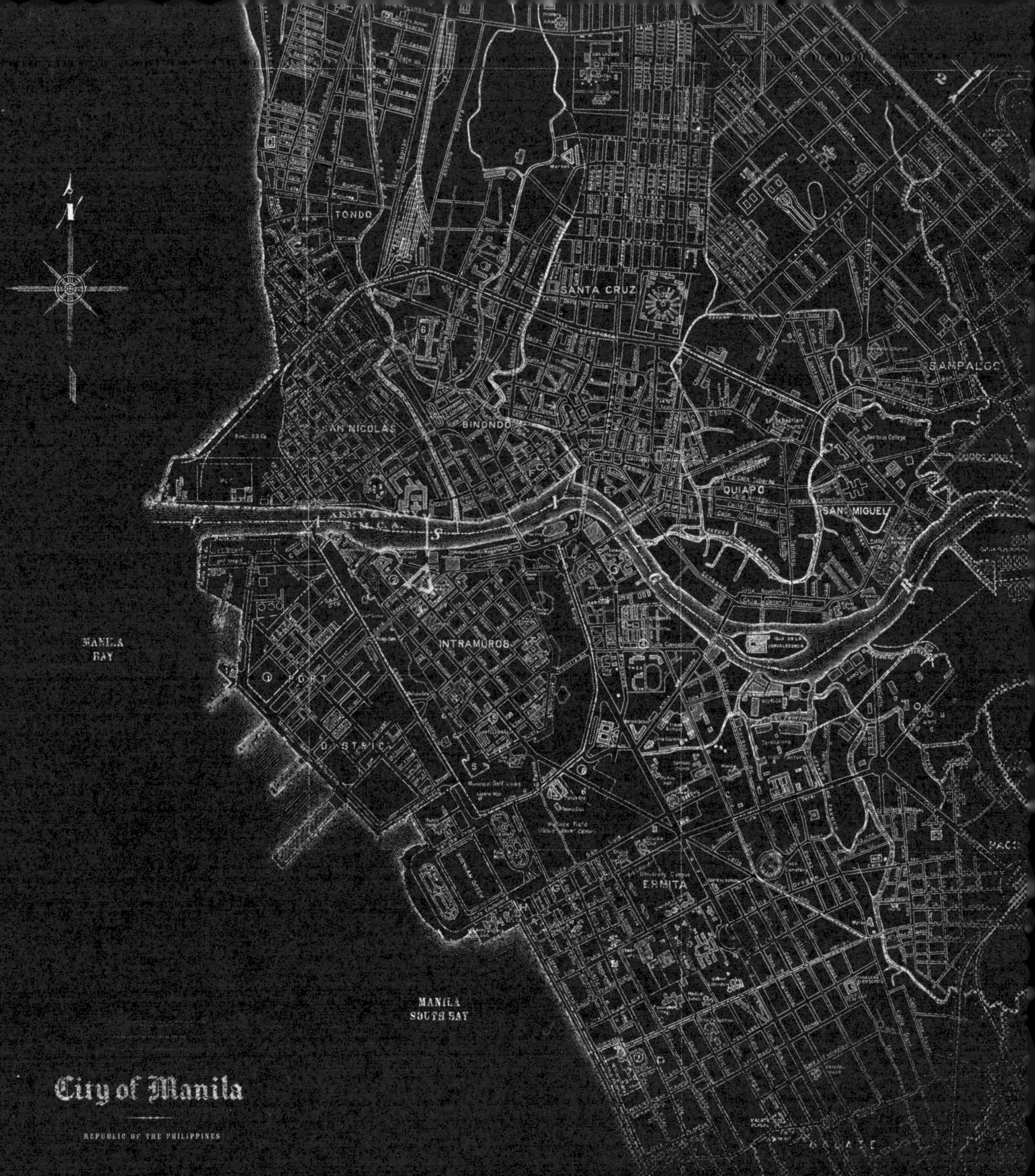
TONDO
SANTA CRUZ
SAMPALOC
SAN NICOLAS
BINONDO
QUIAPO
SAN MIGUEL
MANILA
BAY
INTRAMUROS
PORT
DISTRICT
ERMITA
MANILA
SOUTH BAY
City of Manila
REPUBLIC OF THE PHILIPPINES

THE CASE OF
THE CEMETERY GIRL

CHAPTER I

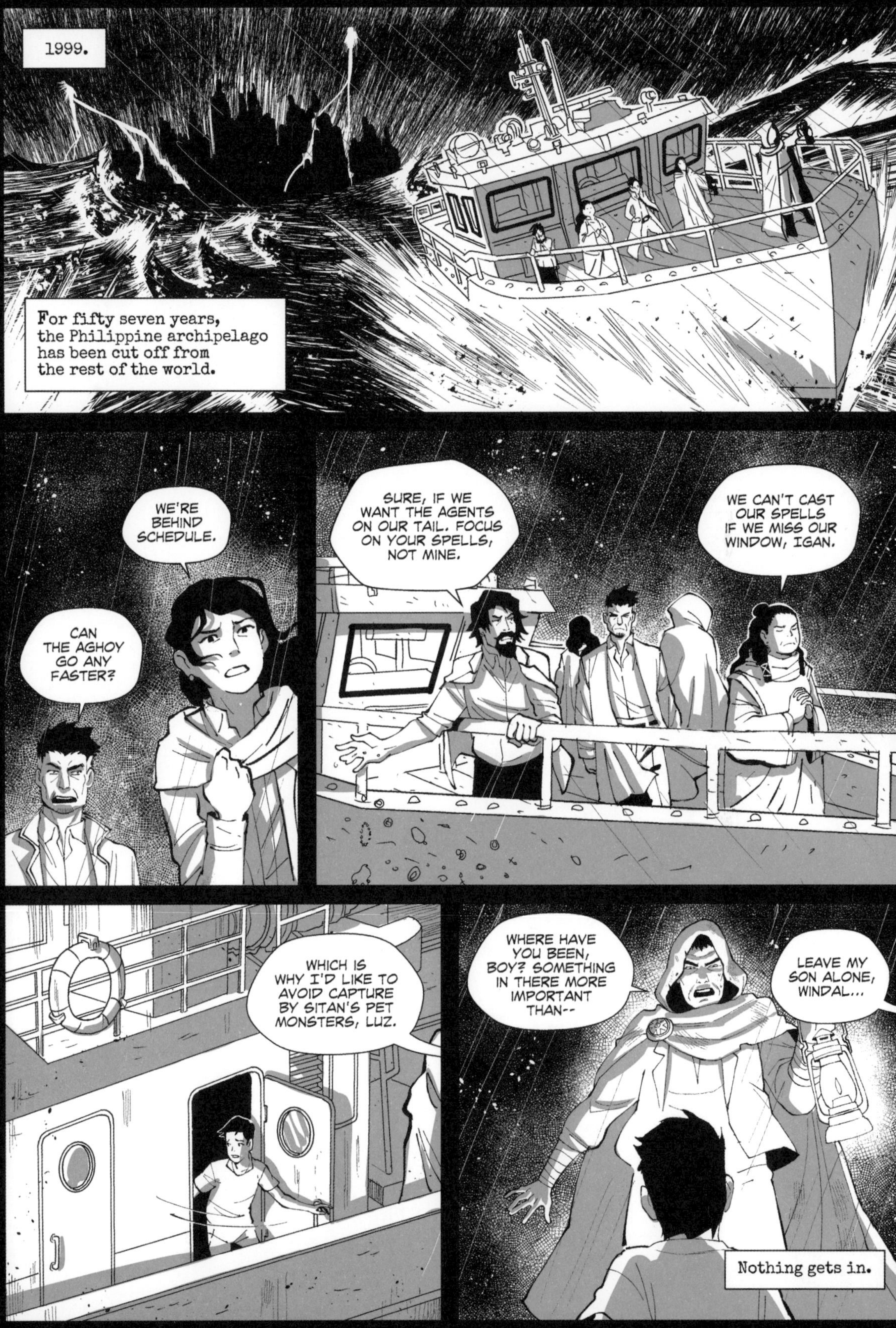
1999.
For fifty seven years, the Philippine archipelago has been cut off from the rest of the world.
WE'RE BEHIND SCHEDULE.
CAN THE AGHOY GO ANY FASTER?
SURE, IF WE WANT THE AGENTS ON OUR TAIL. FOCUS ON YOUR SPELLS, NOT MINE.
WE CAN'T CAST OUR SPELLS IF WE MISS OUR WINDOW, IGAN.
WHICH IS WHY I'D LIKE TO AVOID CAPTURE BY SITAN'S PET MONSTERS, LUZ.
WHERE HAVE YOU BEEN, BOY? SOMETHING IN THERE MORE IMPORTANT THAN--
LEAVE MY SON ALONE, WINDAL...
Nothing gets in.

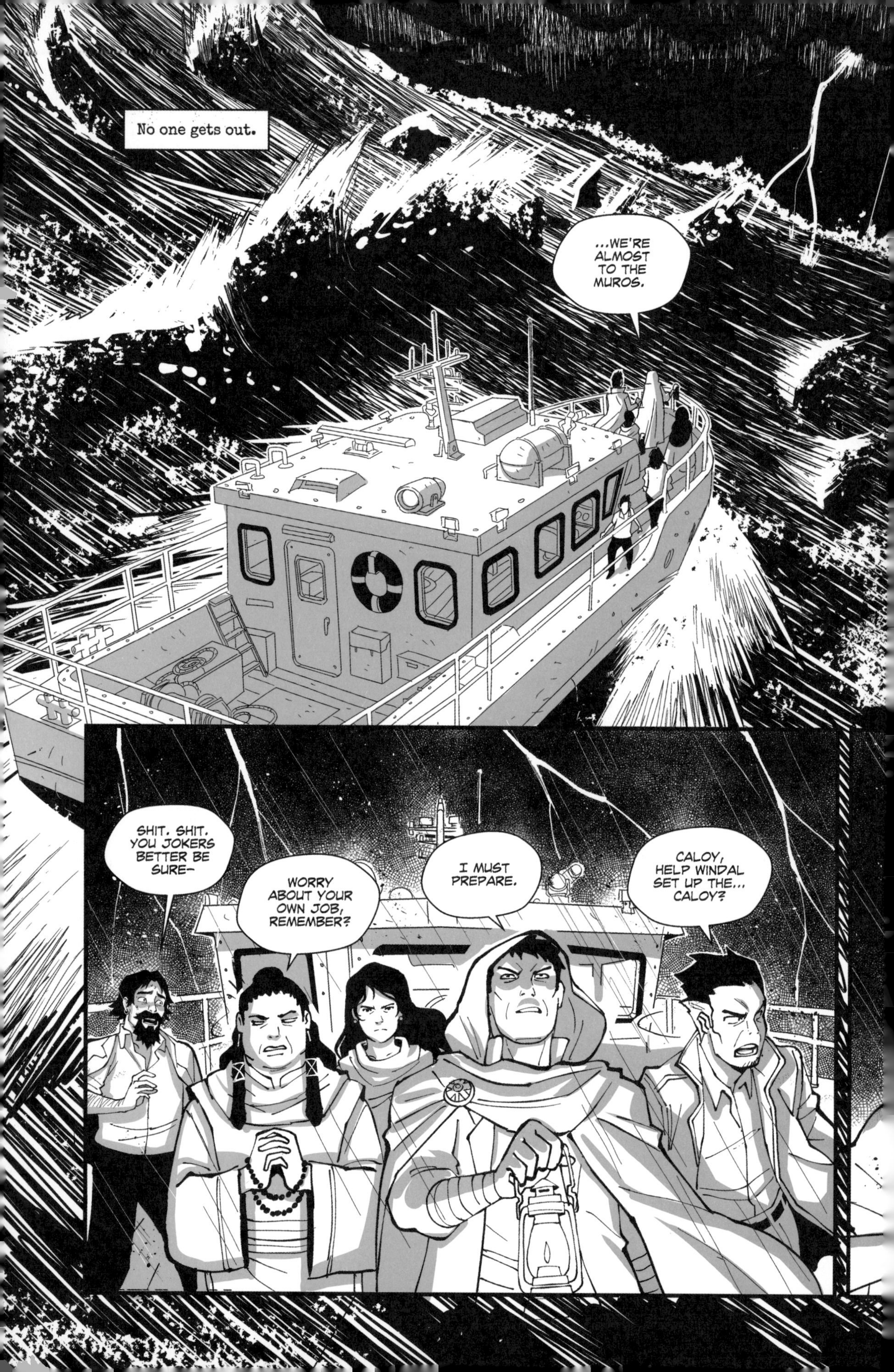
No one gets out.
...WE'RE ALMOST TO THE MUROS.
SHIT. SHIT. YOU JOKERS BETTER BE SURE-
WORRY ABOUT YOUR OWN JOB, REMEMBER?
I MUST PREPARE.
CALOY, HELP WINDAL SET UP THE... CALOY?

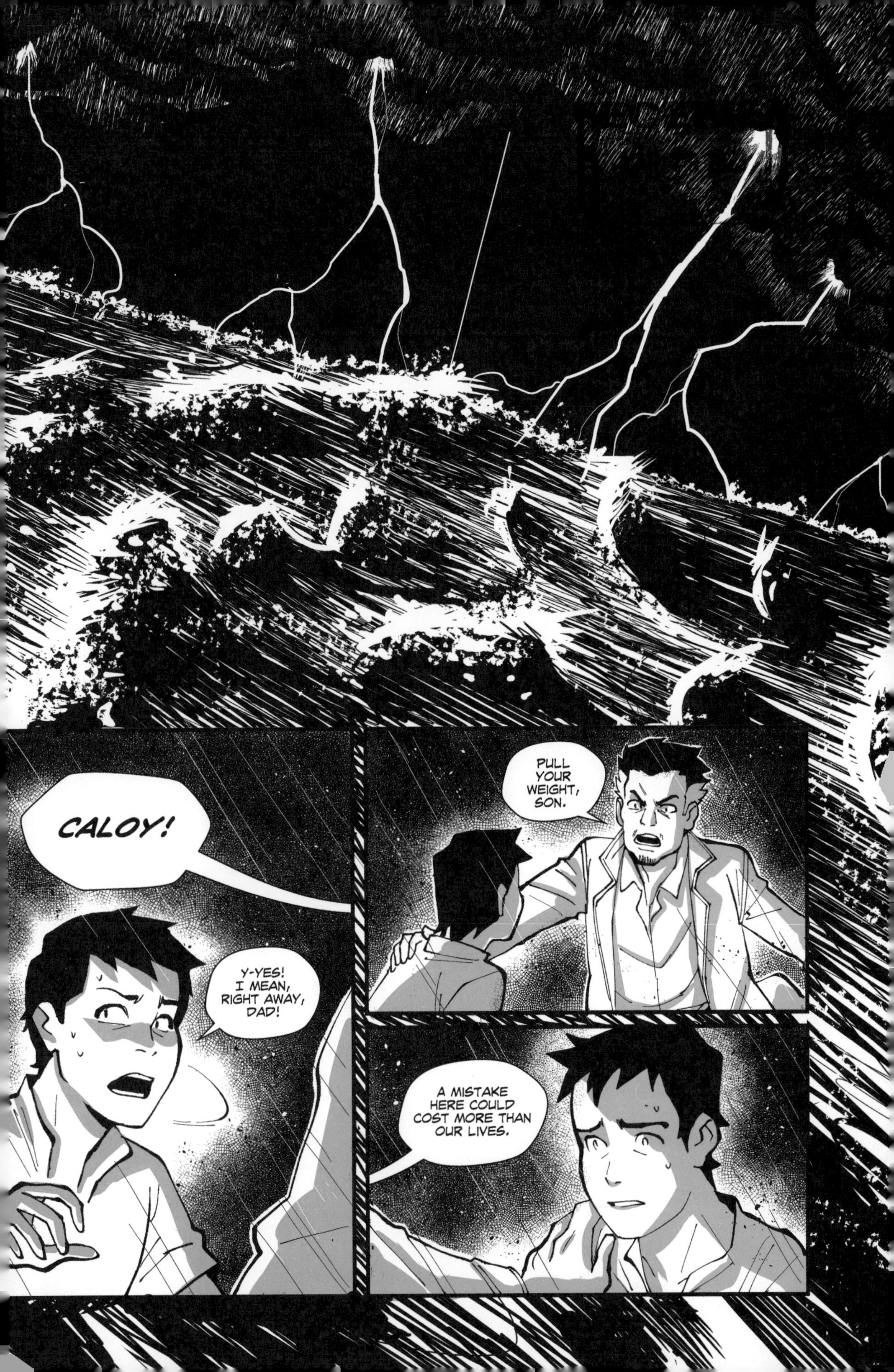
CALOY!
Y-YES! I MEAN, RIGHT AWAY, DAD!
PULL YOUR WEIGHT, SON.
A MISTAKE HERE COULD COST MORE THAN OUR LIVES.

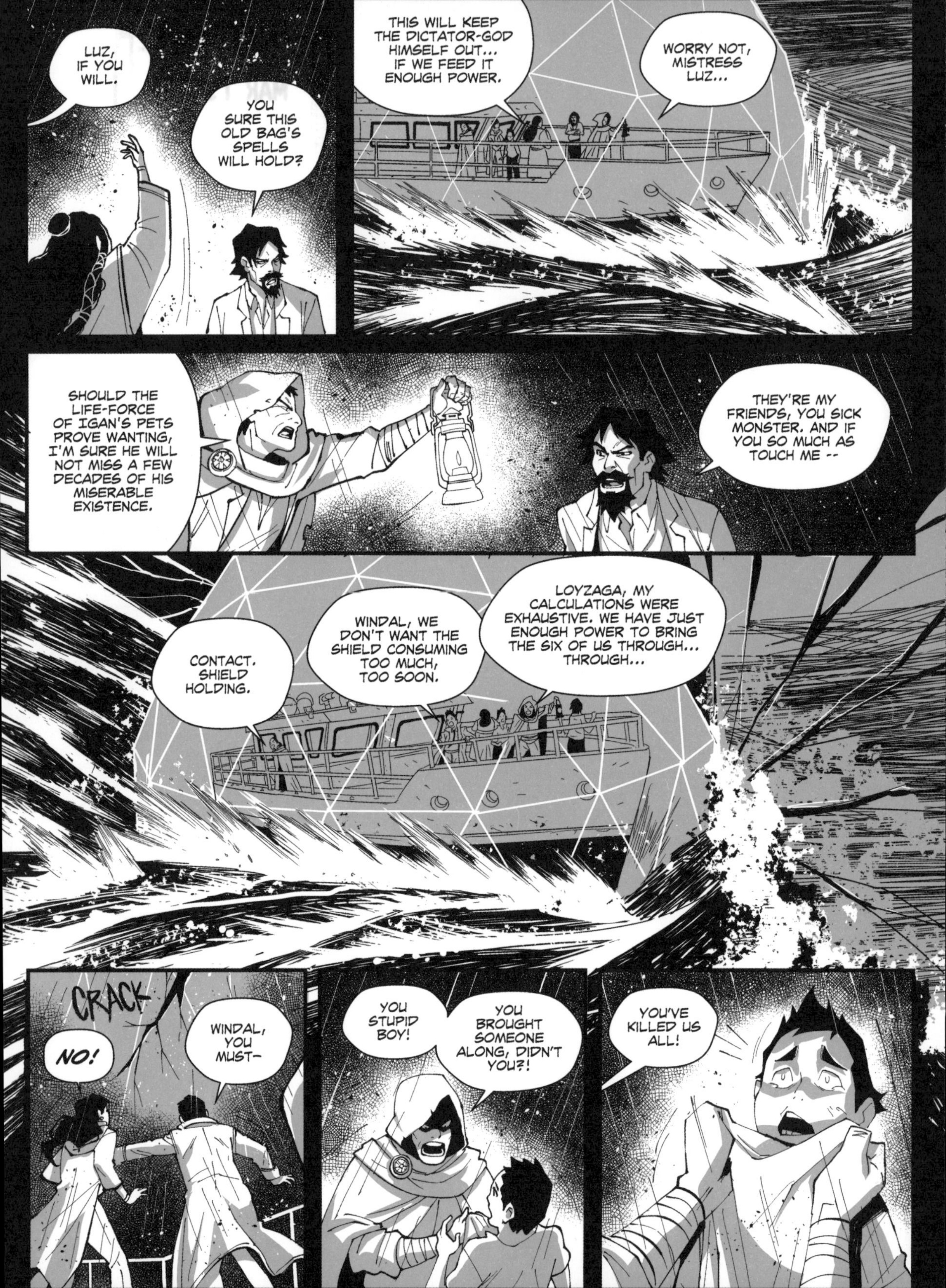
LUZ, IF YOU WILL.
YOU SURE THIS OLD BAG'S SPELLS WILL HOLD?
THIS WILL KEEP THE DICTATOR-GOD HIMSELF OUT... IF WE FEED IT ENOUGH POWER.
WORRY NOT, MISTRESS LUZ...
SHOULD THE LIFE-FORCE OF IGAN'S PETS PROVE WANTING, I'M SURE HE WILL NOT MISS A FEW DECADES OF HIS MISERABLE EXISTENCE.
THEY'RE MY FRIENDS, YOU SICK MONSTER. AND IF YOU SO MUCH AS TOUCH ME --
CONTACT. SHIELD HOLDING.
WINDAL, WE DON'T WANT THE SHIELD CONSUMING TOO MUCH, TOO SOON.
LOYZAGA, MY CALCULATIONS WERE EXHAUSTIVE. WE HAVE JUST ENOUGH POWER TO BRING THE SIX OF US THROUGH... THROUGH...
CRACK
NO!
WINDAL, YOU MUST-
YOU STUPID BOY!
YOU BROUGHT SOMEONE ALONG, DIDN'T YOU?!
YOU'VE KILLED US ALL!

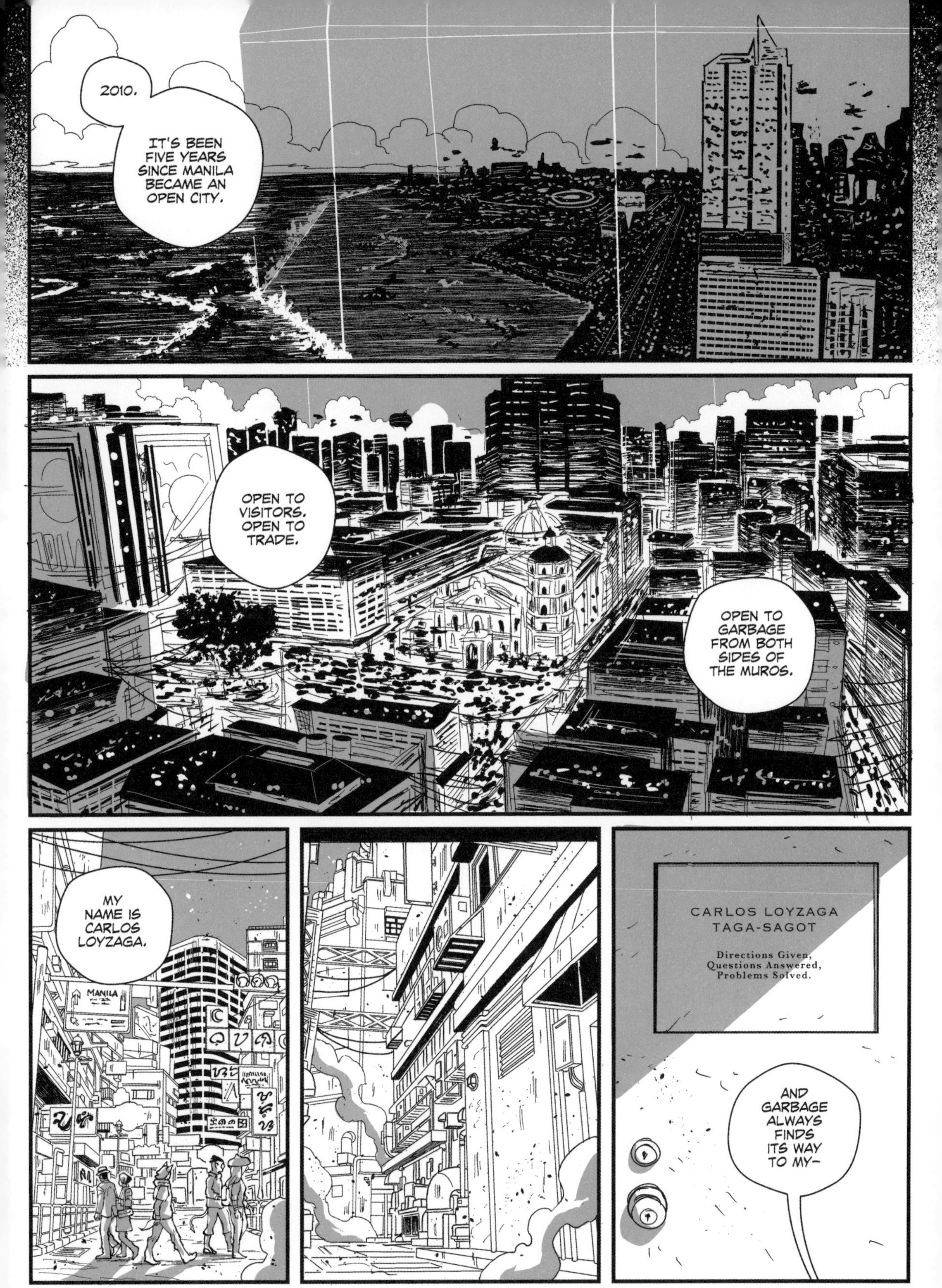
2010.
IT'S BEEN FIVE YEARS SINCE MANILA BECAME AN OPEN CITY.
OPEN TO VISITORS. OPEN TO TRADE.
OPEN TO GARBAGE FROM BOTH SIDES OF THE MUROS.
MY NAME IS CARLOS LOYZAGA.
MANILA
CARLOS LOYZAGA
TAGA-SAGOT
Directions Given,
Questions Answered,
Problems Solved.
AND GARBAGE ALWAYS FINDS ITS WAY TO MY–

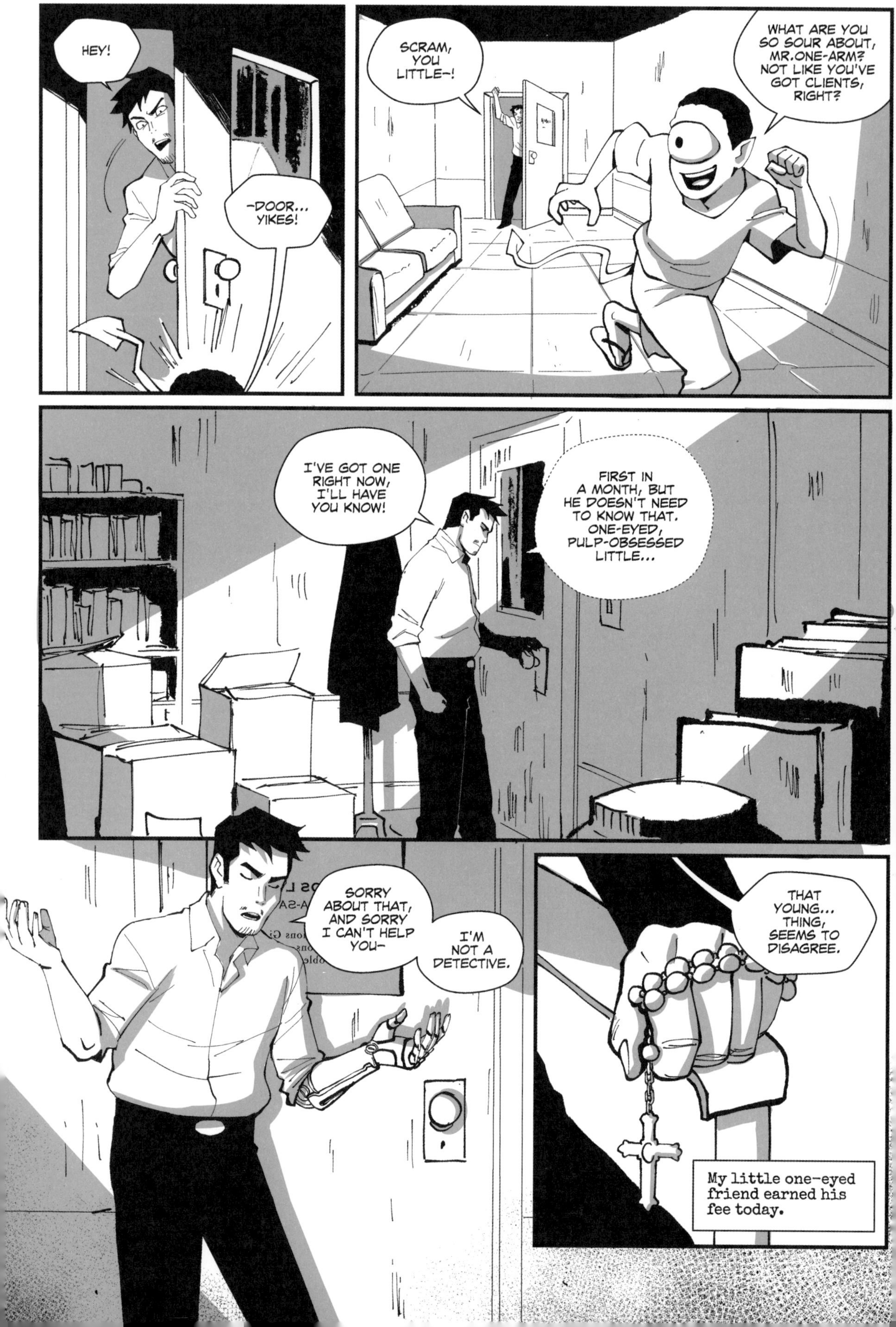
HEY!
-DOOR... YIKES!
SCRAM, YOU LITTLE-!
WHAT ARE YOU SO SOUR ABOUT, MR. ONE-ARM? NOT LIKE YOU'VE GOT CLIENTS, RIGHT?
I'VE GOT ONE RIGHT NOW, I'LL HAVE YOU KNOW!
FIRST IN A MONTH, BUT HE DOESN'T NEED TO KNOW THAT. ONE-EYED, PULP-OBSESSED LITTLE...
SORRY ABOUT THAT, AND SORRY I CAN'T HELP YOU-
I'M NOT A DETECTIVE.
THAT YOUNG... THING, SEEMS TO DISAGREE.
My little one-eyed friend earned his fee today.

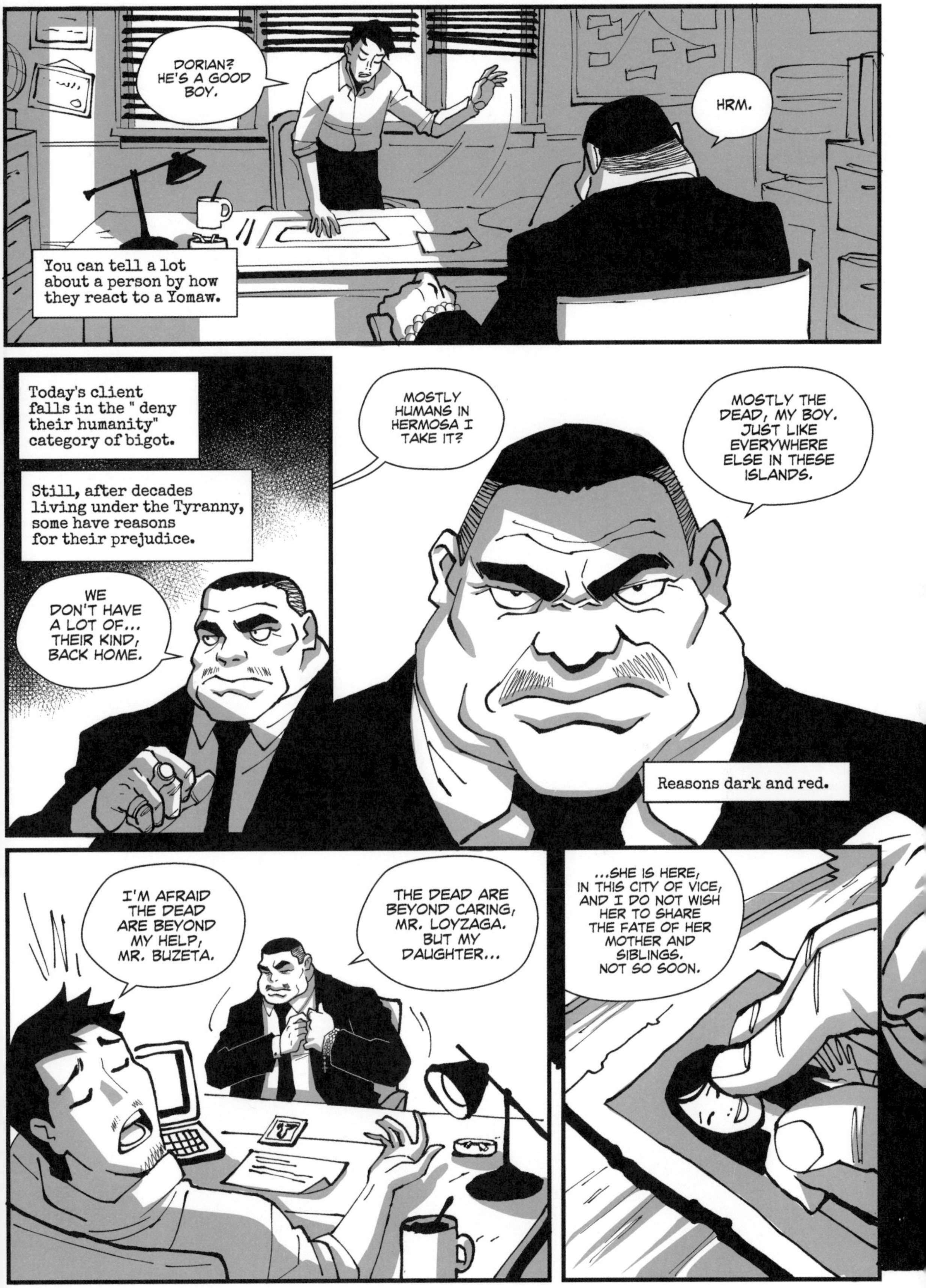
DORIAN? HE'S A GOOD BOY.
HRM.
You can tell a lot about a person by how they react to a Yomaw.
Today's client falls in the " deny their humanity" category of bigot.
Still, after decades living under the Tyranny, some have reasons for their prejudice.
MOSTLY HUMANS IN HERMOSA I TAKE IT?
WE DON'T HAVE A LOT OF... THEIR KIND, BACK HOME.
MOSTLY THE DEAD, MY BOY. JUST LIKE EVERYWHERE ELSE IN THESE ISLANDS.
Reasons dark and red.
I'M AFRAID THE DEAD ARE BEYOND MY HELP, MR. BUZETA.
THE DEAD ARE BEYOND CARING, MR. LOYZAGA. BUT MY DAUGHTER...
...SHE IS HERE, IN THIS CITY OF VICE, AND I DO NOT WISH HER TO SHARE THE FATE OF HER MOTHER AND SIBLINGS. NOT SO SOON.

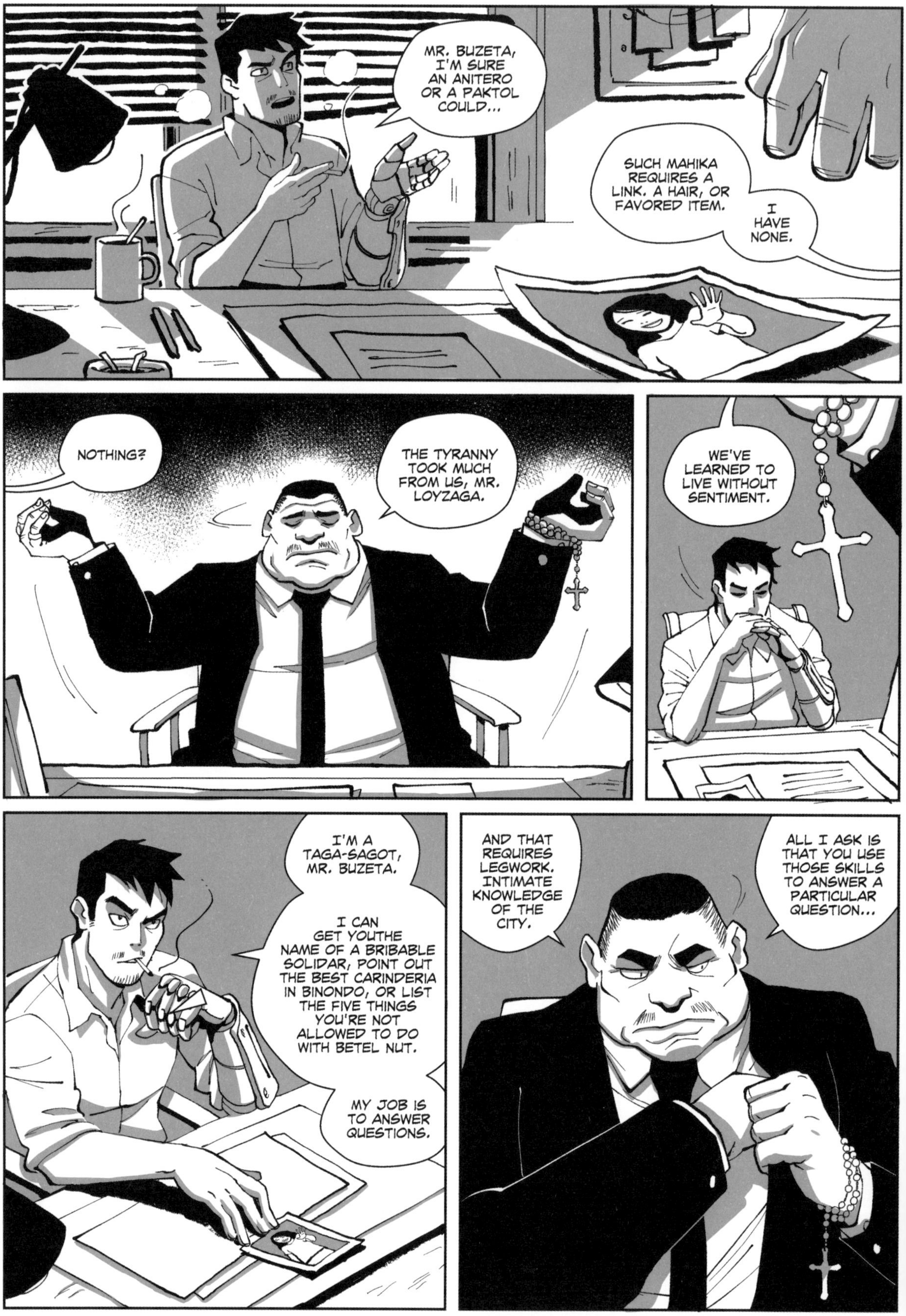
MR. BUZETA, I'M SURE AN ANITERO OR A PAKTOL COULD...
SUCH MAHIKA REQUIRES A LINK. A HAIR, OR FAVORED ITEM.
I HAVE NONE.
NOTHING?
THE TYRANNY TOOK MUCH FROM US, MR. LOYZAGA.
WE'VE LEARNED TO LIVE WITHOUT SENTIMENT.
I'M A TAGA-SAGOT, MR. BUZETA.
I CAN GET YOUTHE NAME OF A BRIBABLE SOLIDAR, POINT OUT THE BEST CARINDERIA IN BINONDO, OR LIST THE FIVE THINGS YOU'RE NOT ALLOWED TO DO WITH BETEL NUT.
MY JOB IS TO ANSWER QUESTIONS.
AND THAT REQUIRES LEGWORK. INTIMATE KNOWLEDGE OF THE CITY.
ALL I ASK IS THAT YOU USE THOSE SKILLS TO ANSWER A PARTICULAR QUESTION...

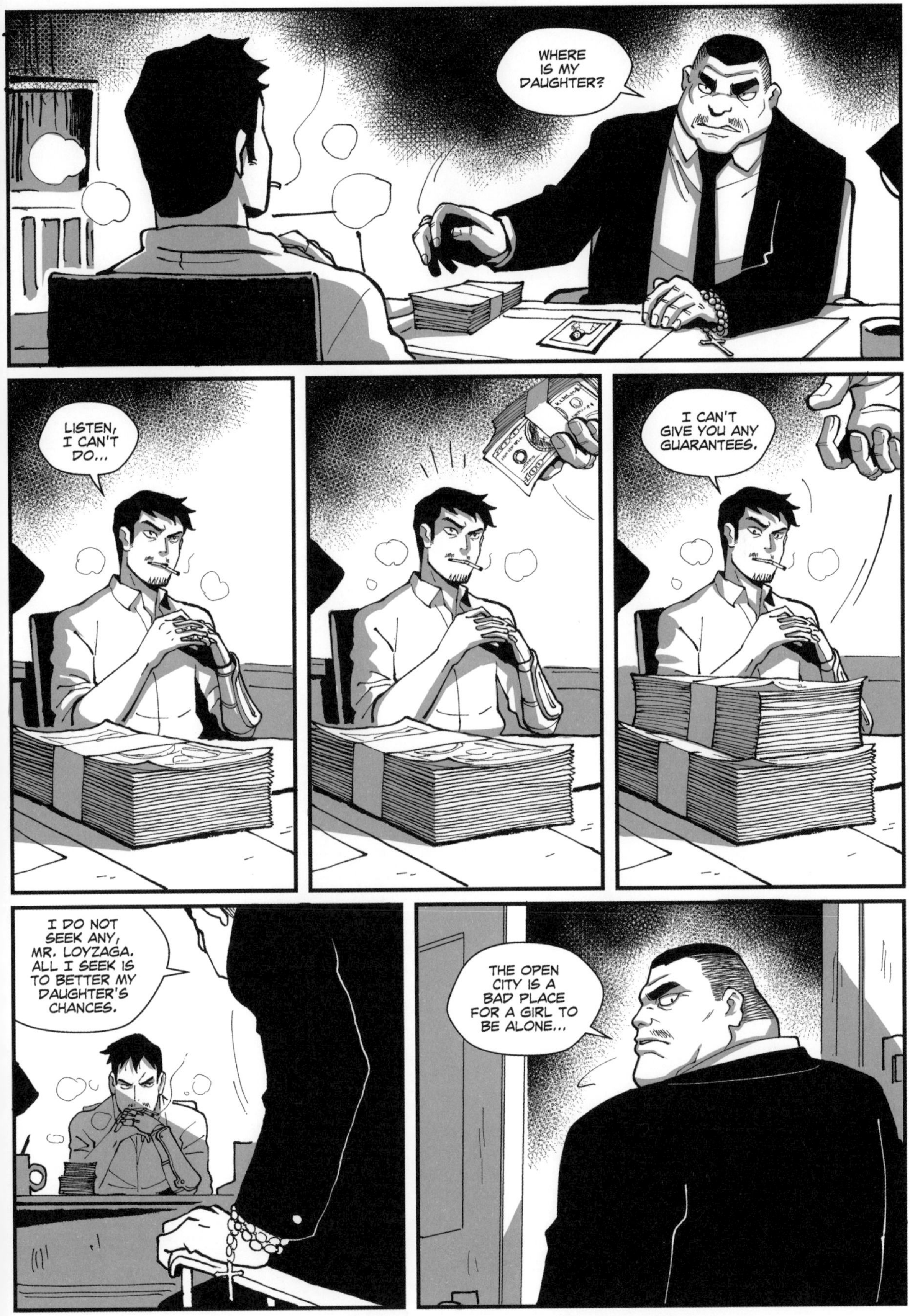
WHERE IS MY DAUGHTER?
LISTEN, I CAN'T DO...
I CAN'T GIVE YOU ANY GUARANTEES.
I DO NOT SEEK ANY, MR. LOYZAGA. ALL I SEEK IS TO BETTER MY DAUGHTER'S CHANCES.
THE OPEN CITY IS A BAD PLACE FOR A GIRL TO BE ALONE...

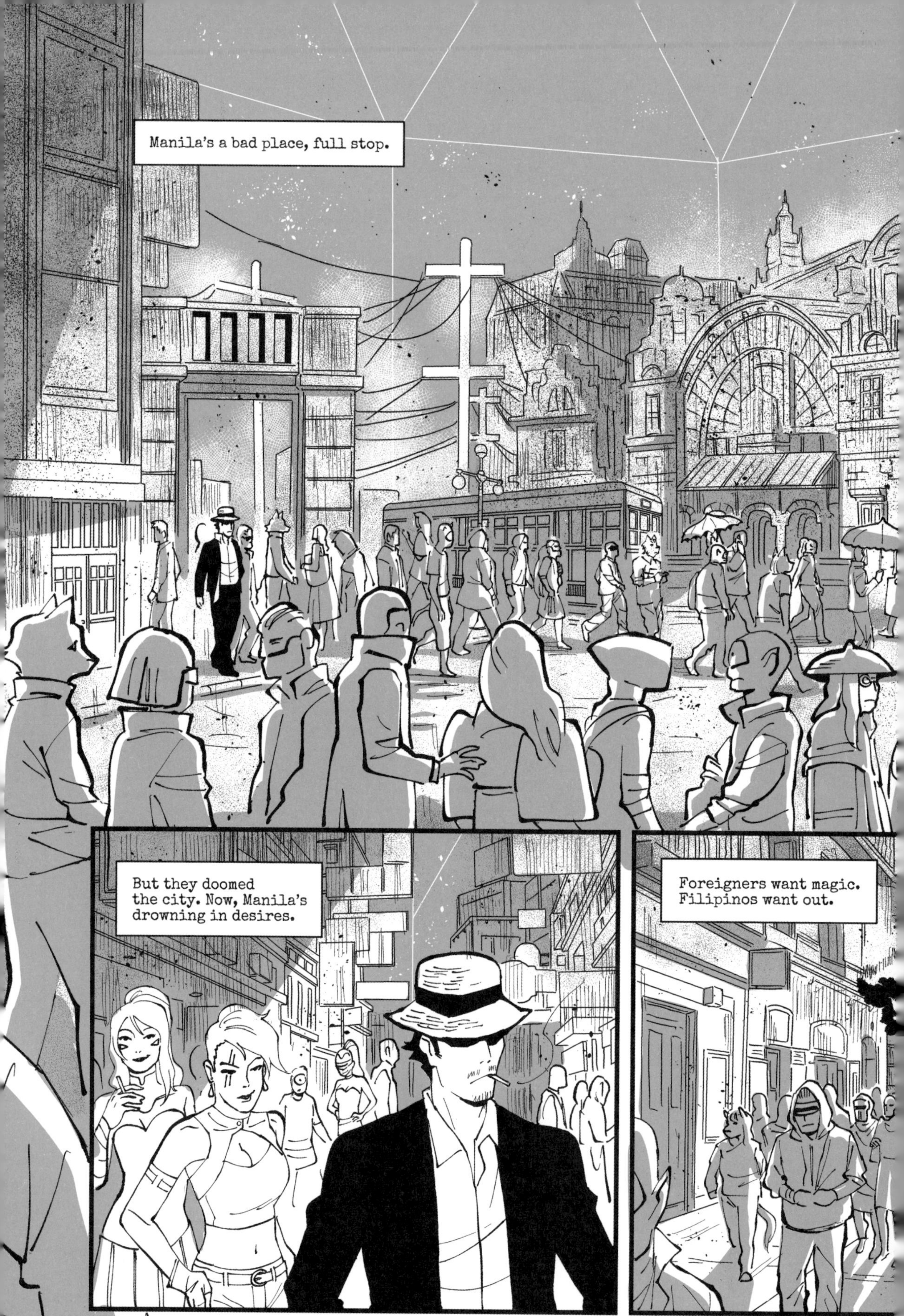
Manila's a bad place, full stop.
But they doomed the city. Now, Manila's drowning in desires.
Foreigners want magic. Filipinos want out.

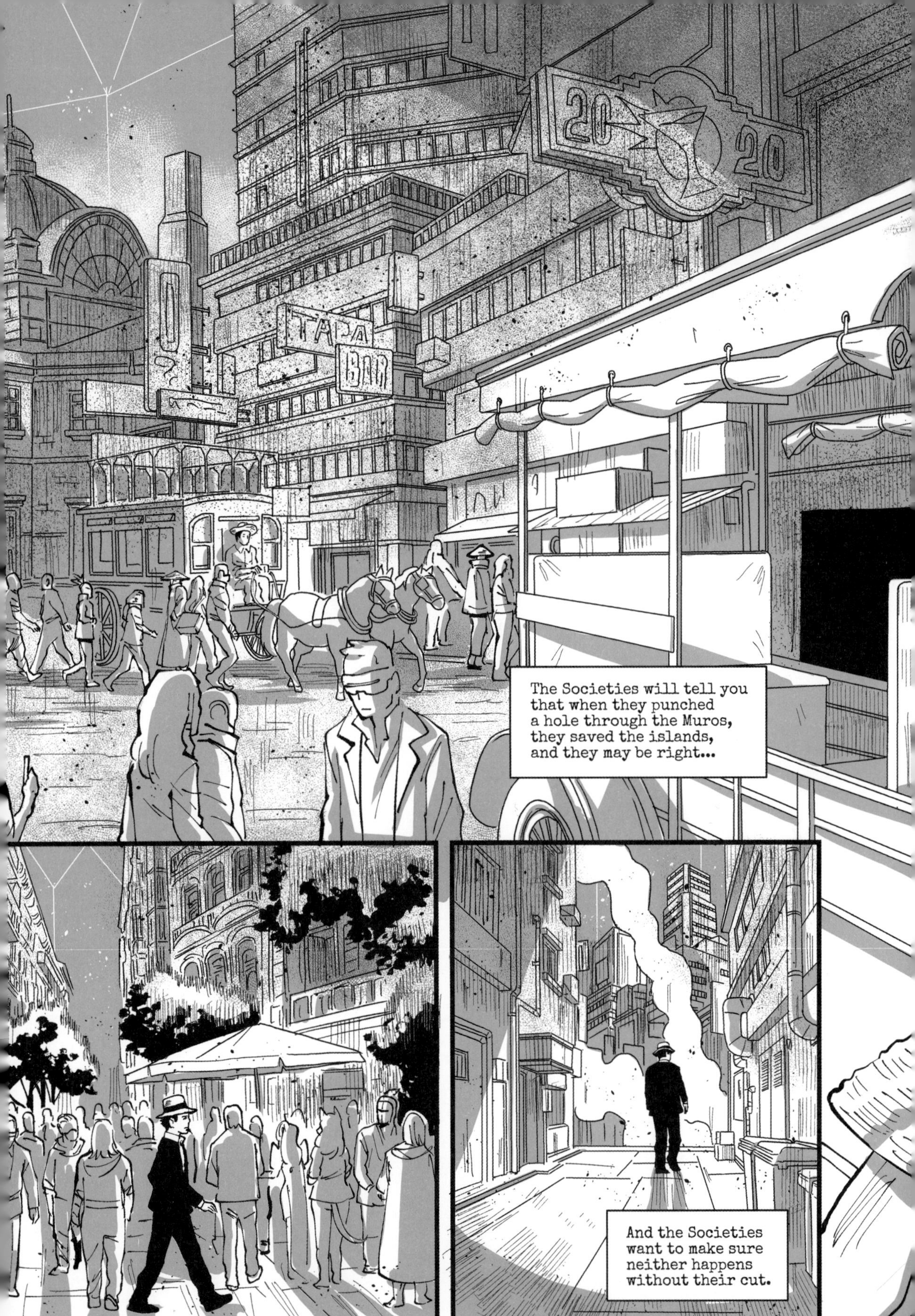
20
20
TAPA
BAR
The Societies will tell you that when they punched a hole through the Muros, they saved the islands, and they may be right...
And the Societies want to make sure neither happens without their cut.

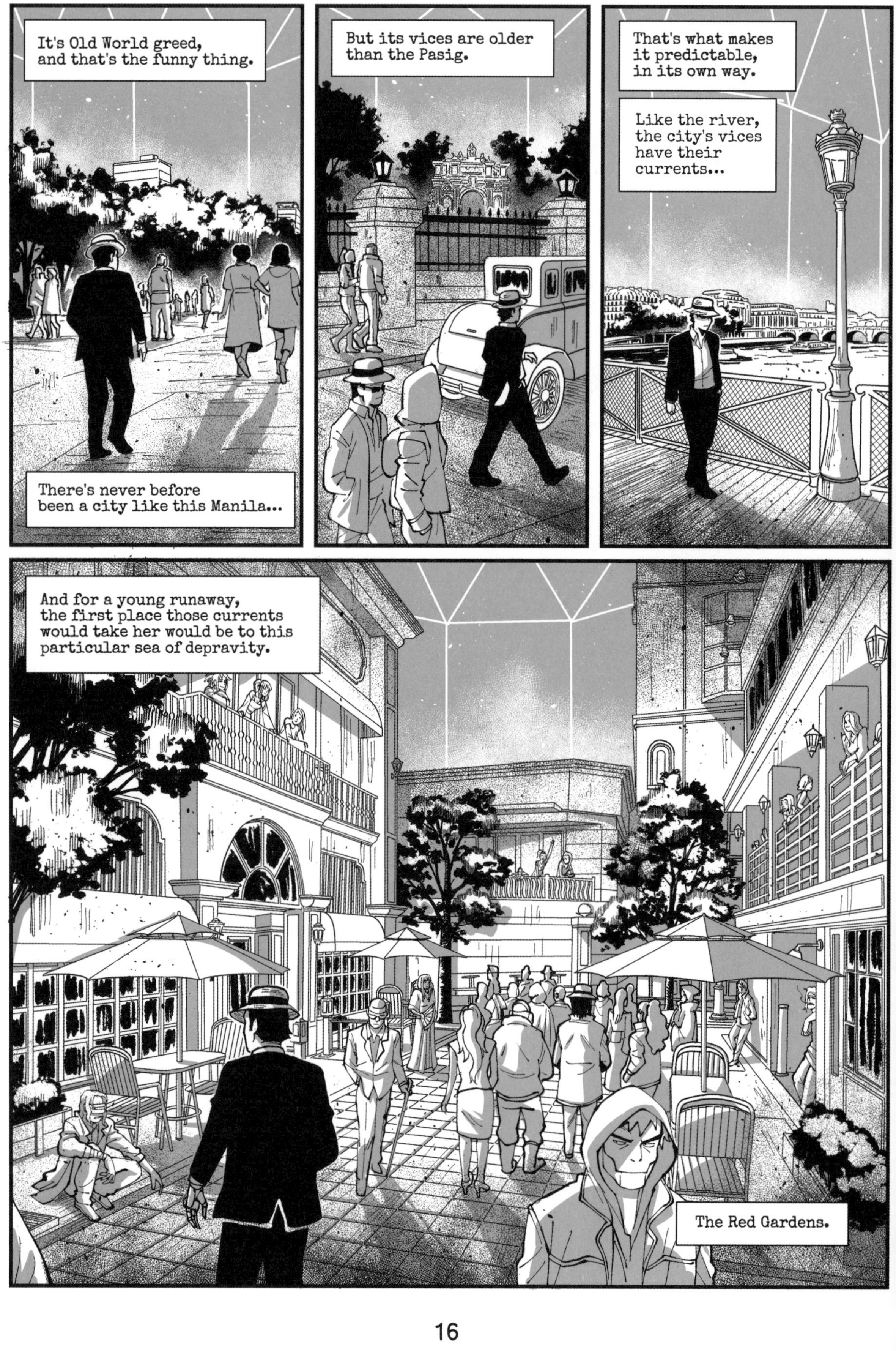
It's Old World greed, and that's the funny thing.
There's never before been a city like this Manila...
But its vices are older than the Pasig.
That's what makes it predictable, in its own way.
Like the river, the city's vices have their currents...
And for a young runaway, the first place those currents would take her would be to this particular sea of depravity.
The Red Gardens.

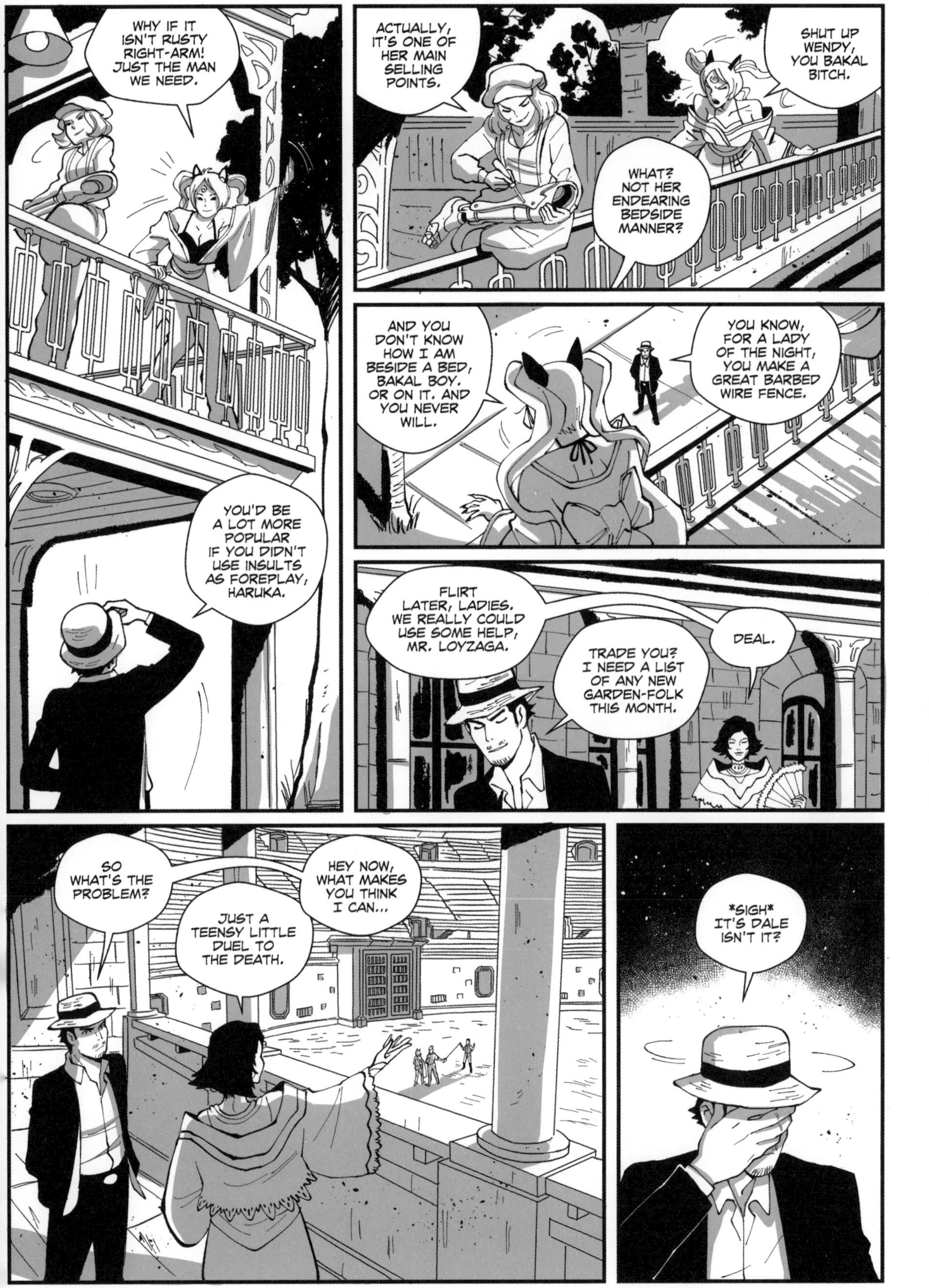
WHY IF IT ISN'T RUSTY RIGHT-ARM! JUST THE MAN WE NEED.
ACTUALLY, IT'S ONE OF HER MAIN SELLING POINTS.
SHUT UP WENDY, YOU BAKAL BITCH.
WHAT? NOT HER ENDEARING BEDSIDE MANNER?
AND YOU DON'T KNOW HOW I AM BESIDE A BED, BAKAL BOY. OR ON IT. AND YOU NEVER WILL.
YOU KNOW, FOR A LADY OF THE NIGHT, YOU MAKE A GREAT BARBED WIRE FENCE.
YOU'D BE A LOT MORE POPULAR IF YOU DIDN'T USE INSULTS AS FOREPLAY, HARUKA.
FLIRT LATER, LADIES. WE REALLY COULD USE SOME HELP, MR. LOYZAGA.
DEAL.
TRADE YOU? I NEED A LIST OF ANY NEW GARDEN-FOLK THIS MONTH.
SO WHAT'S THE PROBLEM?
HEY NOW, WHAT MAKES YOU THINK I CAN...
JUST A TEENSY LITTLE DUEL TO THE DEATH.
SIGH IT'S DALE ISN'T IT?

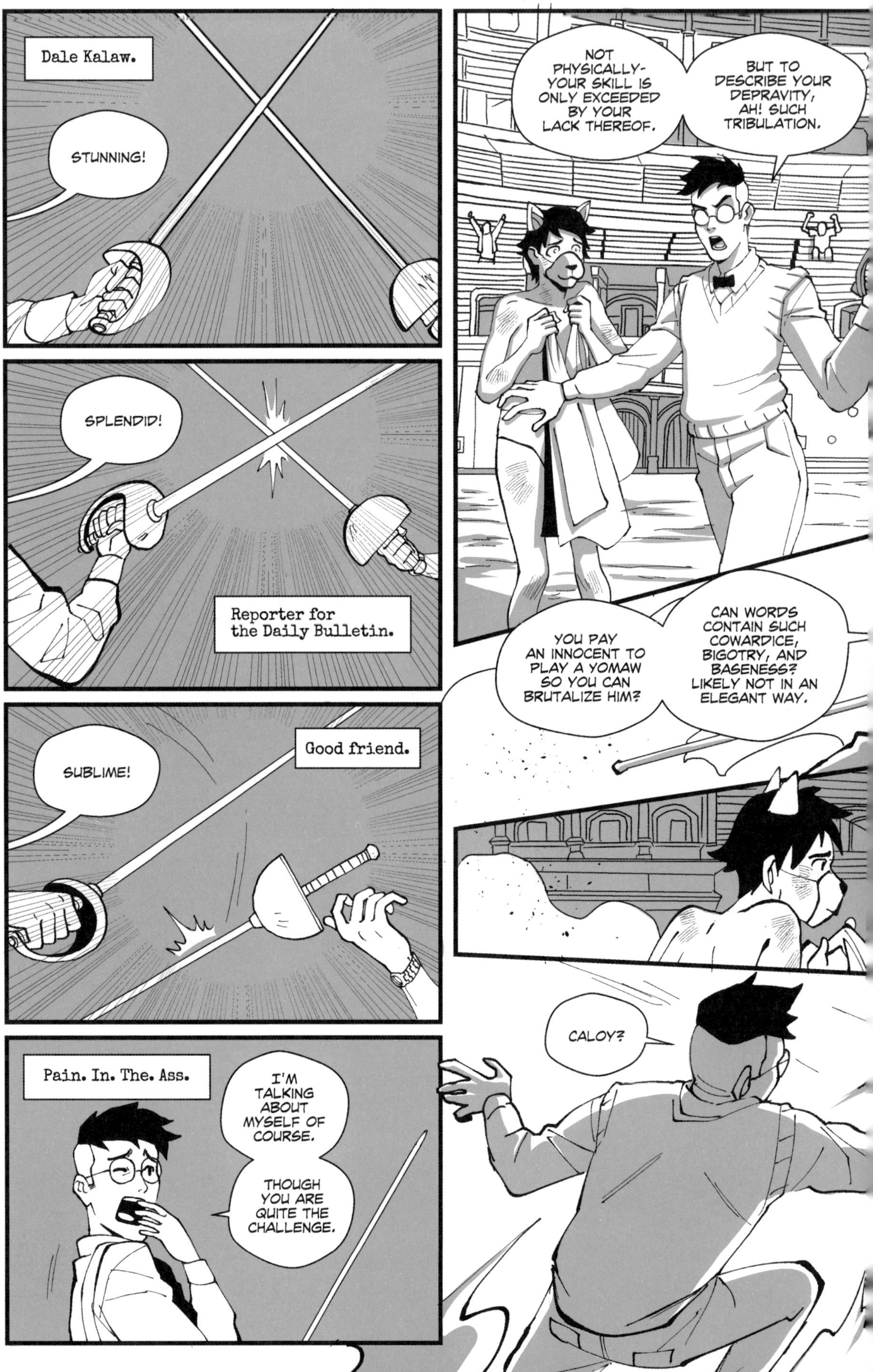

Dale Kalaw.
STUNNING!
SPLENDID!
Reporter for the Daily Bulletin.
SUBLIME!
Good friend.
Pain. In. The. Ass.
I'M TALKING ABOUT MYSELF OF COURSE.
THOUGH YOU ARE QUITE THE CHALLENGE.
NOT PHYSICALLY- YOUR SKILL IS ONLY EXCEEDED BY YOUR LACK THEREOF.
BUT TO DESCRIBE YOUR DEPRAVITY, AH! SUCH TRIBULATION.
YOU PAY AN INNOCENT TO PLAY A YOMAW SO YOU CAN BRUTALIZE HIM?
CAN WORDS CONTAIN SUCH COWARDICE, BIGOTRY, AND BASENESS? LIKELY NOT IN AN ELEGANT WAY.
CALOY?

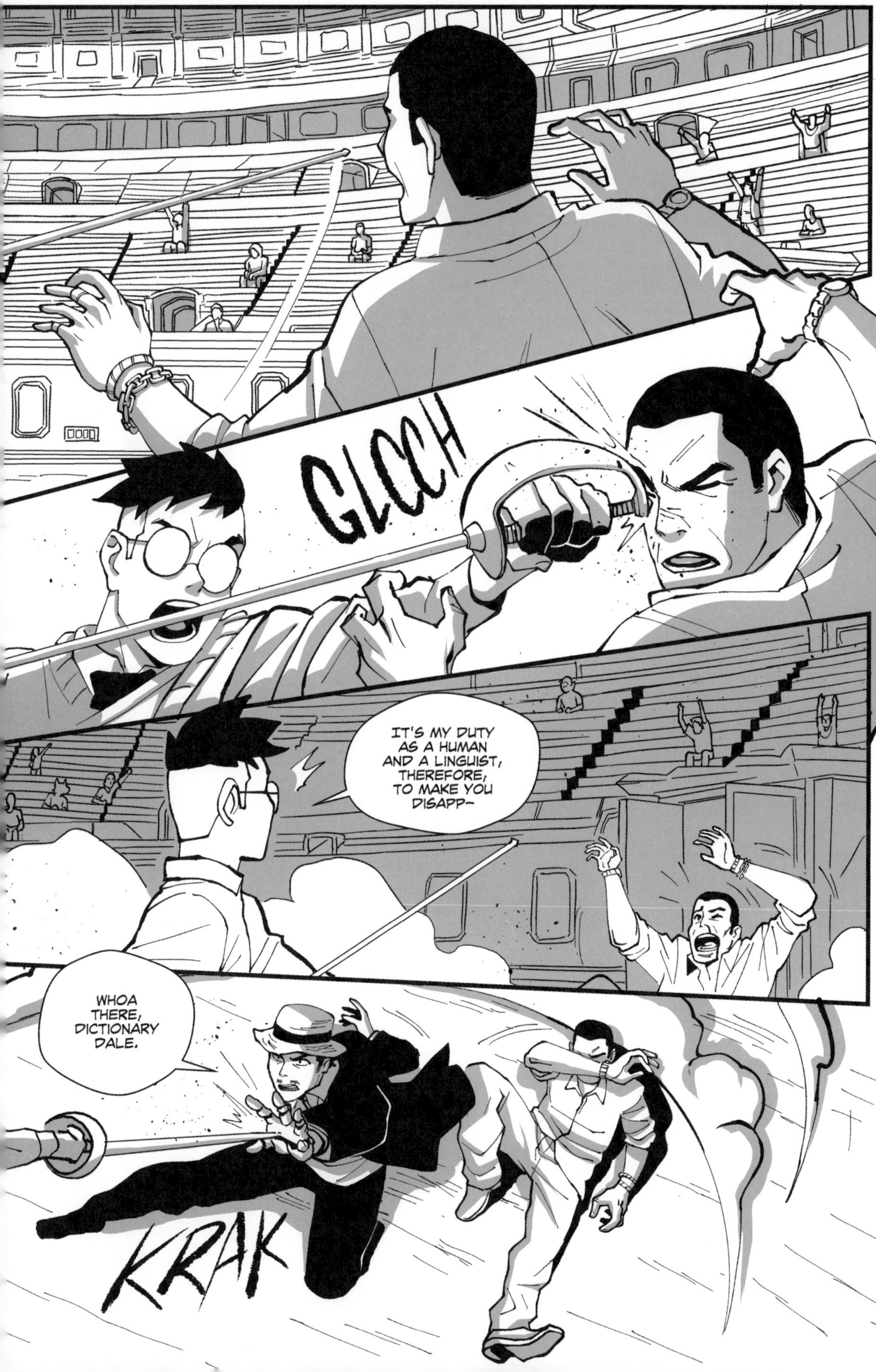
GLOCH
IT'S MY DUTY AS A HUMAN AND A LINGUIST, THEREFORE, TO MAKE YOU DISAPP-
WHOA THERE, DICTIONARY DALE.
KRAK

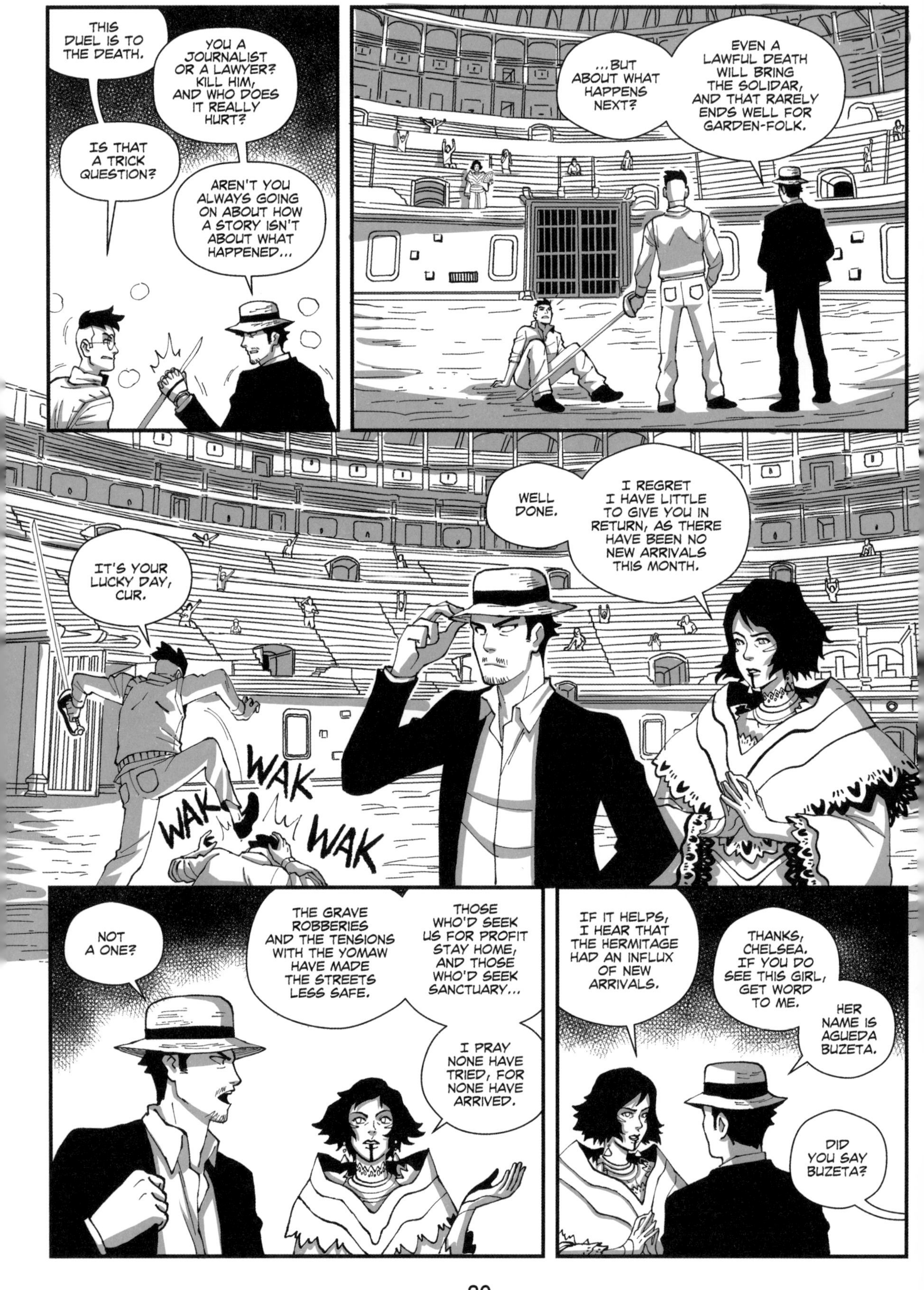
THIS DUEL IS TO THE DEATH.
YOU A JOURNALIST OR A LAWYER? KILL HIM, AND WHO DOES IT REALLY HURT?
IS THAT A TRICK QUESTION?
AREN'T YOU ALWAYS GOING ON ABOUT HOW A STORY ISN'T ABOUT WHAT HAPPENED...
...BUT ABOUT WHAT HAPPENS NEXT?
EVEN A LAWFUL DEATH WILL BRING THE SOLIDAR, AND THAT RARELY ENDS WELL FOR GARDEN-FOLK.
IT'S YOUR LUCKY DAY, CUR.
WAK
WAK
WAK
WELL DONE.
I REGRET I HAVE LITTLE TO GIVE YOU IN RETURN, AS THERE HAVE BEEN NO NEW ARRIVALS THIS MONTH.
NOT A ONE?
THE GRAVE ROBBERIES AND THE TENSIONS WITH THE YOMAW HAVE MADE THE STREETS LESS SAFE.
THOSE WHO'D SEEK US FOR PROFIT STAY HOME, AND THOSE WHO'D SEEK SANCTUARY...
I PRAY NONE HAVE TRIED, FOR NONE HAVE ARRIVED.
IF IT HELPS, I HEAR THAT THE HERMITAGE HAD AN INFLUX OF NEW ARRIVALS.
THANKS, CHELSEA. IF YOU DO SEE THIS GIRL, GET WORD TO ME.
HER NAME IS AGUEDA BUZETA.
DID YOU SAY BUZETA?

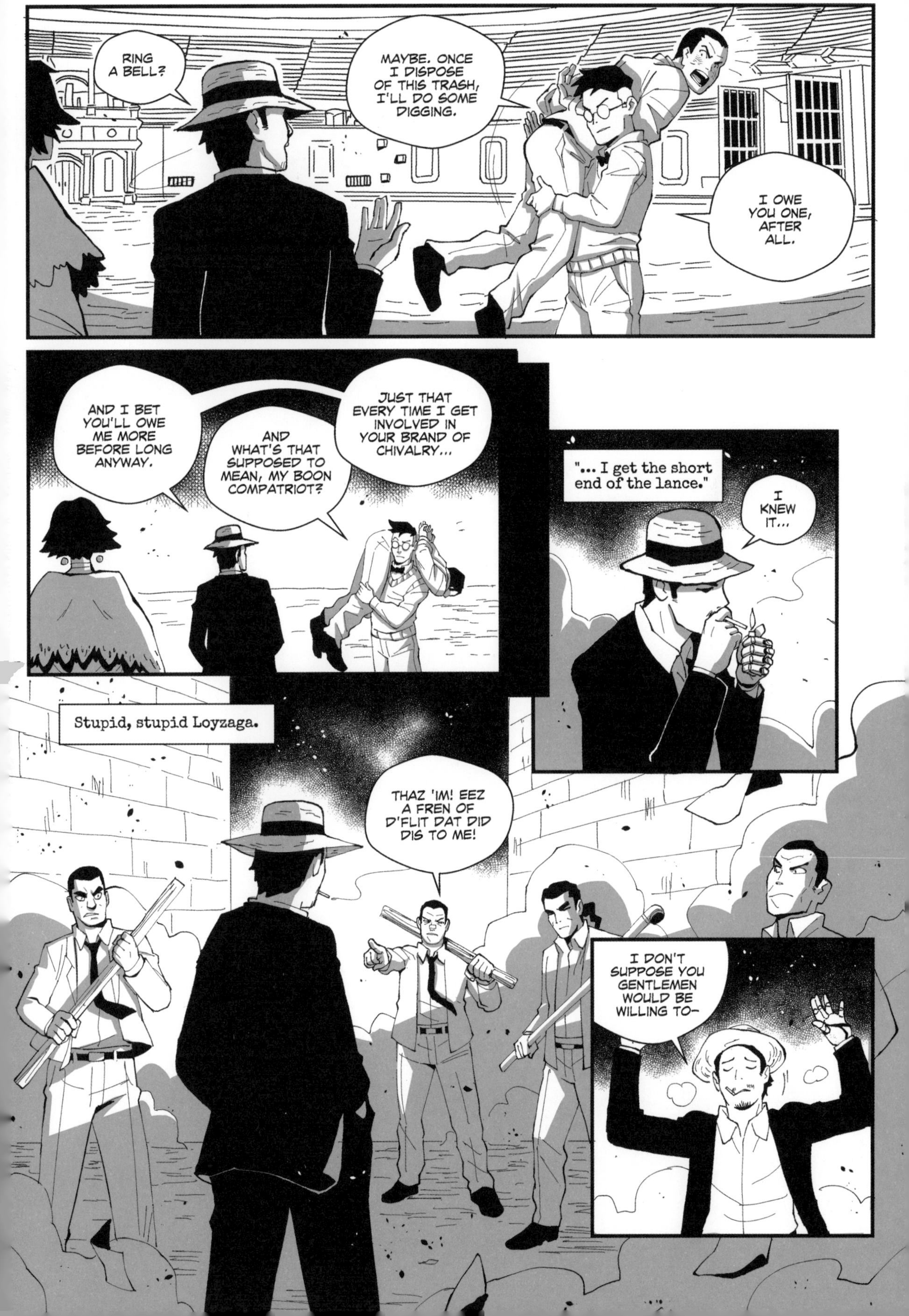
RING A BELL?
MAYBE. ONCE I DISPOSE OF THIS TRASH, I'LL DO SOME DIGGING.
I OWE YOU ONE, AFTER ALL.
AND I BET YOU'LL OWE ME MORE BEFORE LONG ANYWAY.
AND WHAT'S THAT SUPPOSED TO MEAN, MY BOON COMPATRIOT?
JUST THAT EVERY TIME I GET INVOLVED IN YOUR BRAND OF CHIVALRY...
"... I get the short end of the lance."
I KNEW IT...
Stupid, stupid Loyzaga.
THAZ 'IM! EEZ A FREN OF D'FLIT DAT DID DIS TO ME!
I DON'T SUPPOSE YOU GENTLEMEN WOULD BE WILLING TO–

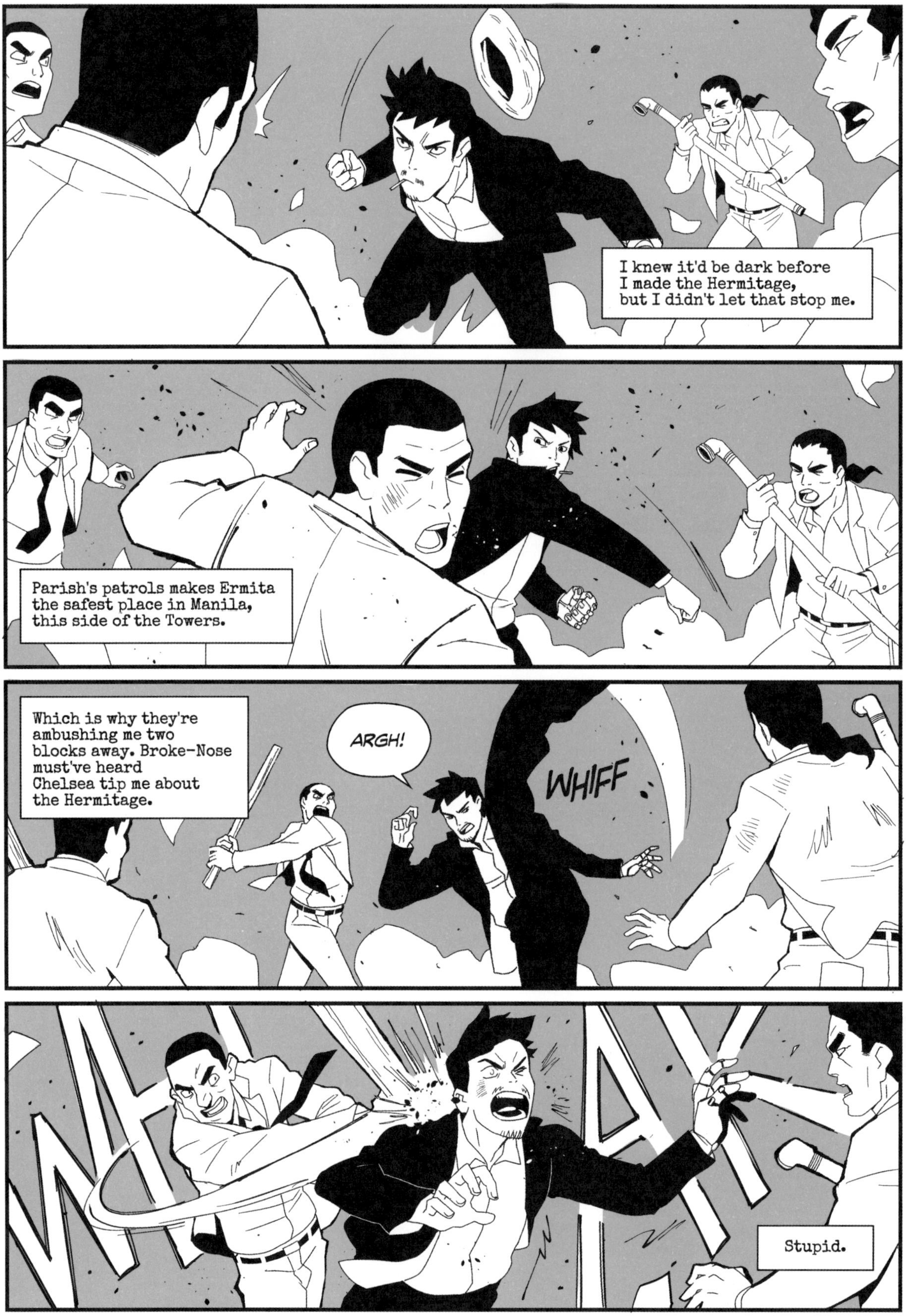
I knew it'd be dark before
I made the Hermitage,
but I didn't let that stop me.
Parish's patrols makes Ermita
the safest place in Manila,
this side of the Towers.
Which is why they're
ambushing me two
blocks away. Broke-Nose
must've heard
Chelsea tip me about
the Hermitage.
ARGH!
WHIFF
Stupid.

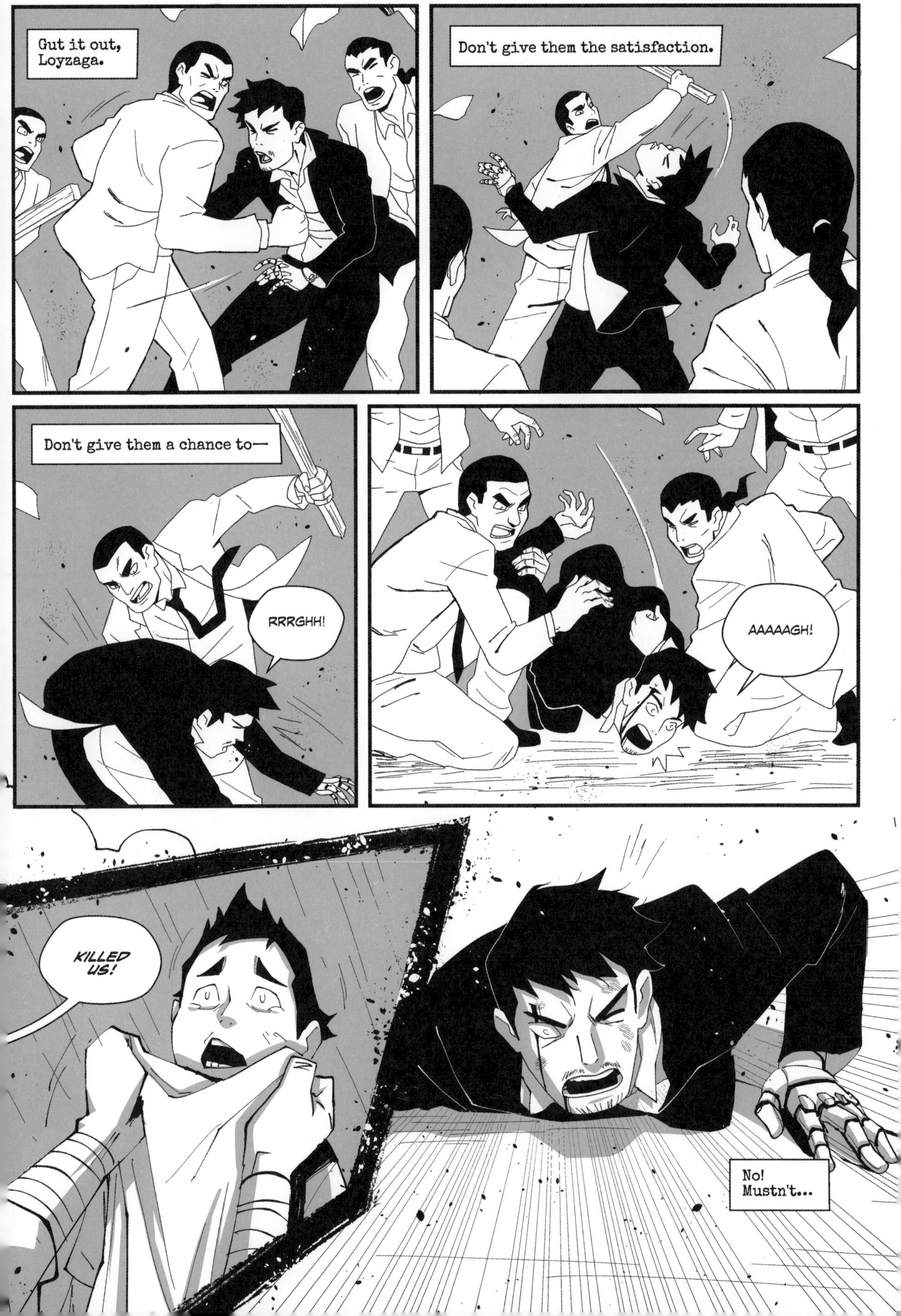
Gut it out, Loyzaga.
Don't give them the satisfaction.
Don't give them a chance to—
RRRGHH!
AAAAAGH!
KILLED US!
No! Mustn't...

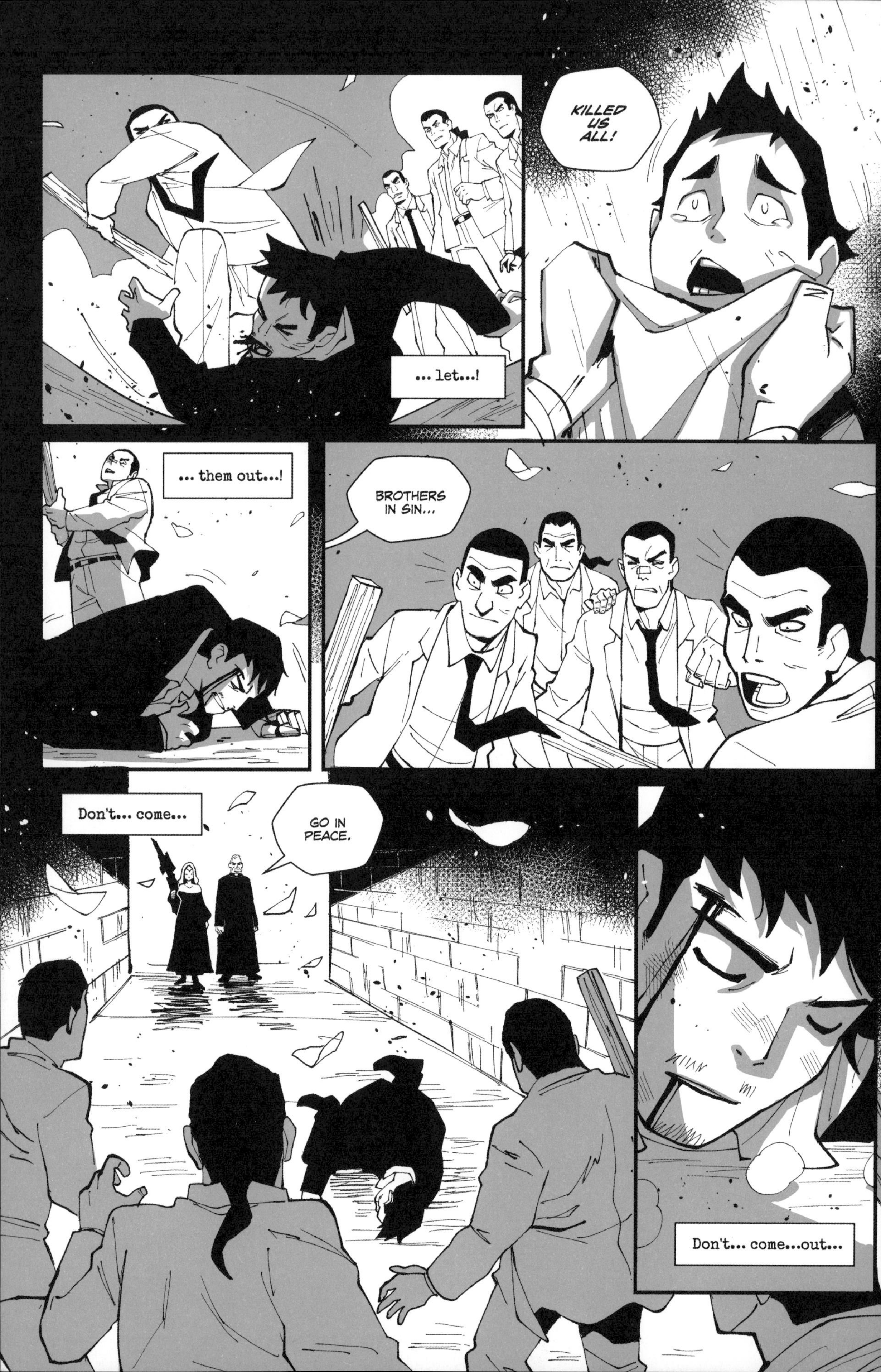
... let...!
KILLED US ALL!
... them out...!
BROTHERS IN SIN...
Don't... come...
GO IN PEACE.
Don't... come...out...

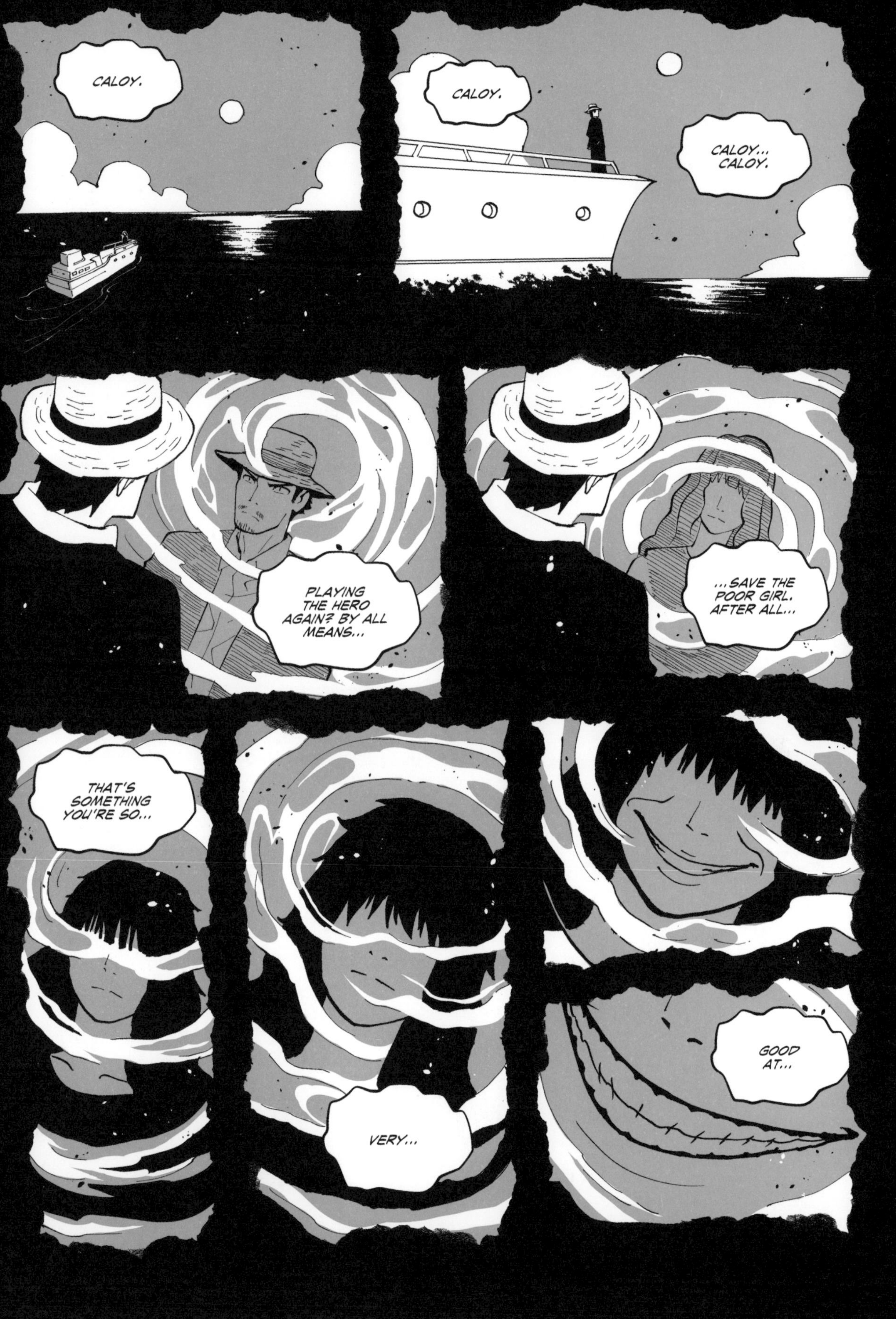
CALOY.
CALOY.
CALOY... CALOY.
PLAYING THE HERO AGAIN? BY ALL MEANS...
...SAVE THE POOR GIRL. AFTER ALL...
THAT'S SOMETHING YOU'RE SO...
VERY...
GOOD AT...

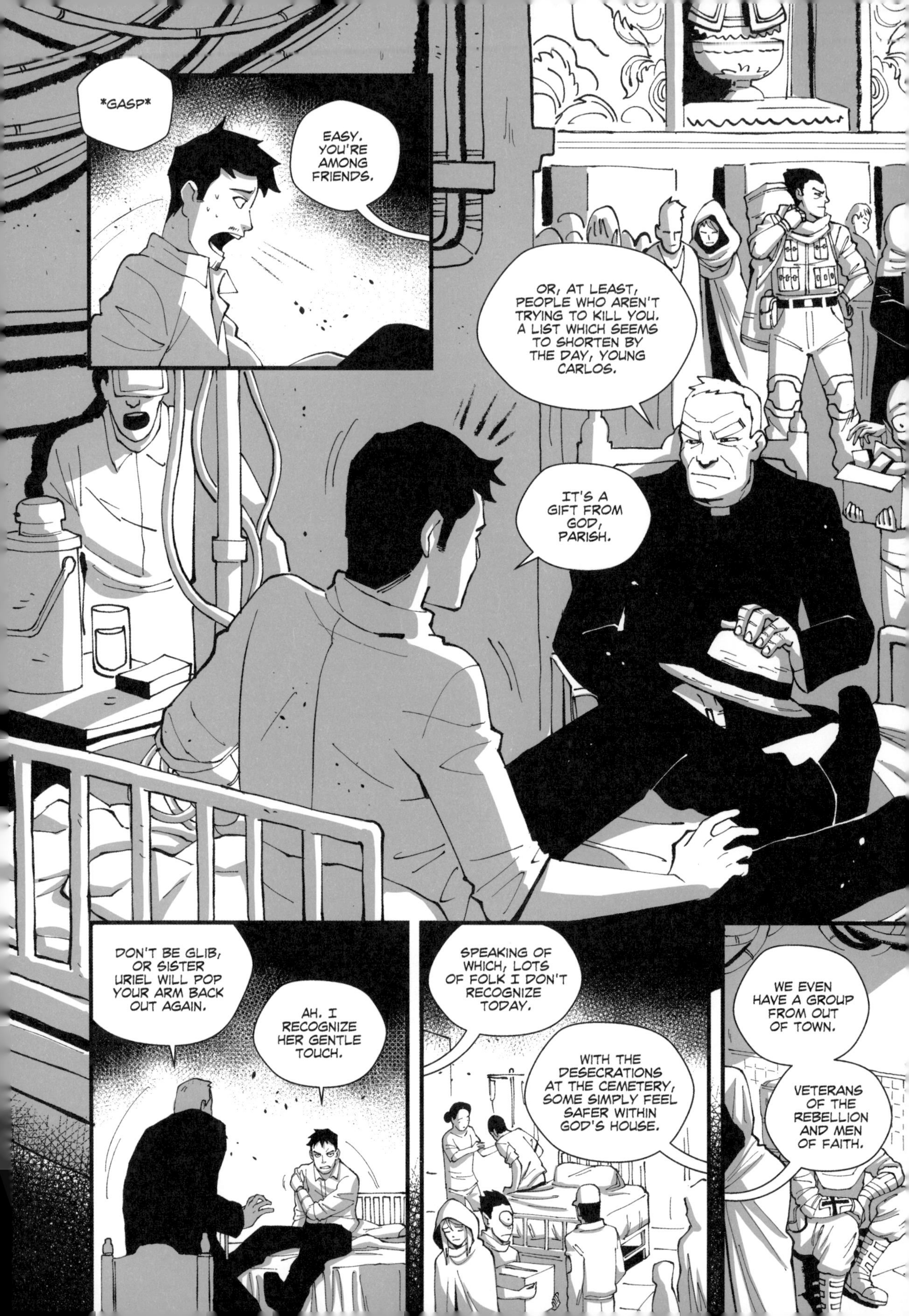
GASP
EASY. YOU'RE AMONG FRIENDS.
OR, AT LEAST, PEOPLE WHO AREN'T TRYING TO KILL YOU. A LIST WHICH SEEMS TO SHORTEN BY THE DAY, YOUNG CARLOS.
IT'S A GIFT FROM GOD, PARISH.
DON'T BE GLIB, OR SISTER URIEL WILL POP YOUR ARM BACK OUT AGAIN.
AH. I RECOGNIZE HER GENTLE TOUCH.
SPEAKING OF WHICH, LOTS OF FOLK I DON'T RECOGNIZE TODAY.
WITH THE DESECRATIONS AT THE CEMETERY, SOME SIMPLY FEEL SAFER WITHIN GOD'S HOUSE.
WE EVEN HAVE A GROUP FROM OUT OF TOWN.
VETERANS OF THE REBELLION AND MEN OF FAITH.

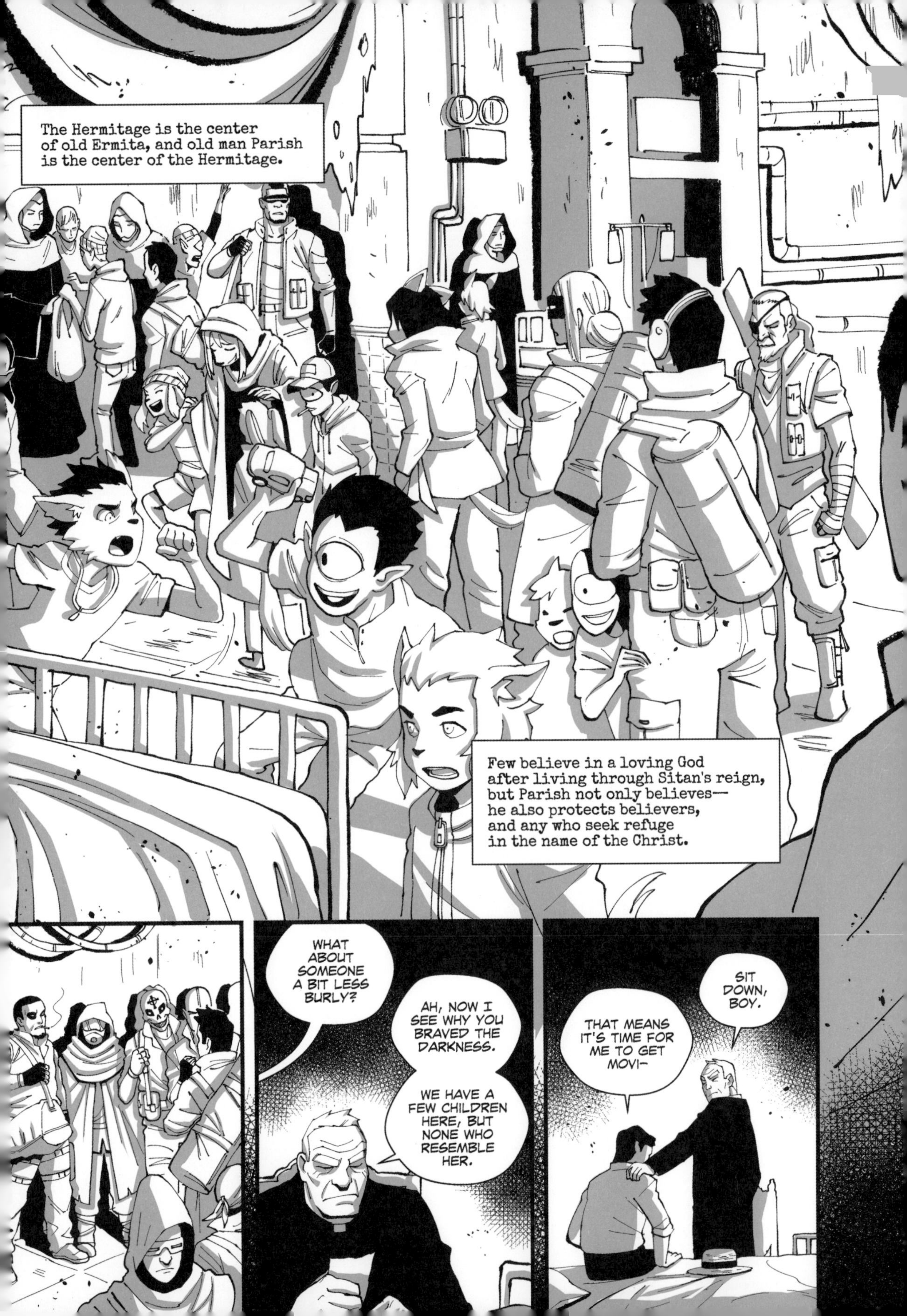
The Hermitage is the center of old Ermita, and old man Parish is the center of the Hermitage.
Few believe in a loving God after living through Sitan's reign, but Parish not only believes— he also protects believers, and any who seek refuge in the name of the Christ.
WHAT ABOUT SOMEONE A BIT LESS BURLY?
AH, NOW I SEE WHY YOU BRAVED THE DARKNESS.
WE HAVE A FEW CHILDREN HERE, BUT NONE WHO RESEMBLE HER.
THAT MEANS IT'S TIME FOR ME TO GET MOVI—
SIT DOWN, BOY.

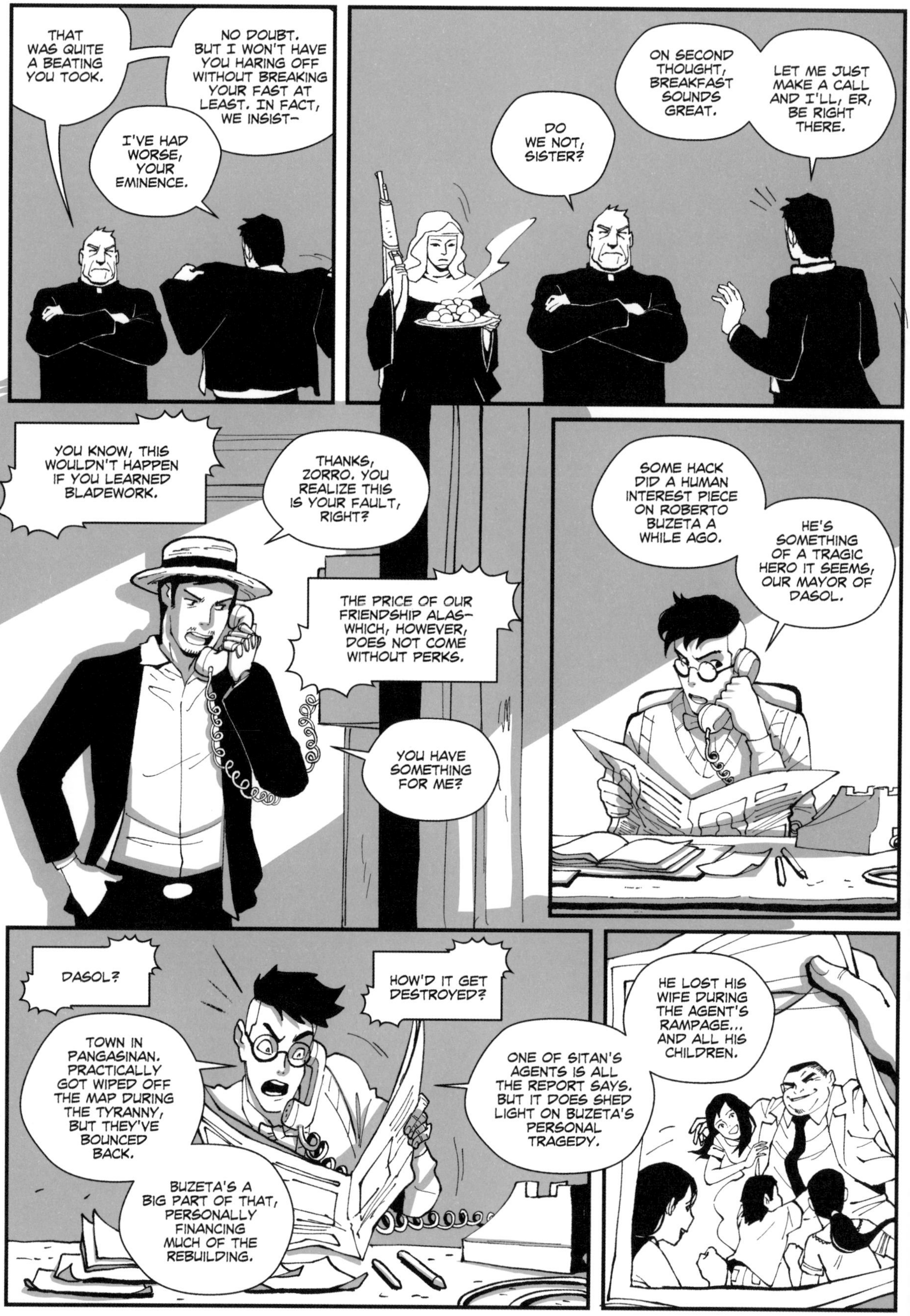
THAT WAS QUITE A BEATING YOU TOOK.
I'VE HAD WORSE, YOUR EMINENCE.
NO DOUBT. BUT I WON'T HAVE YOU HARING OFF WITHOUT BREAKING YOUR FAST AT LEAST. IN FACT, WE INSIST-
DO WE NOT, SISTER?
ON SECOND THOUGHT, BREAKFAST SOUNDS GREAT.
LET ME JUST MAKE A CALL AND I'LL, ER, BE RIGHT THERE.
YOU KNOW, THIS WOULDN'T HAPPEN IF YOU LEARNED BLADEWORK.
THANKS, ZORRO. YOU REALIZE THIS IS YOUR FAULT, RIGHT?
THE PRICE OF OUR FRIENDSHIP ALAS- WHICH, HOWEVER, DOES NOT COME WITHOUT PERKS.
YOU HAVE SOMETHING FOR ME?
SOME HACK DID A HUMAN INTEREST PIECE ON ROBERTO BUZETA A WHILE AGO.
HE'S SOMETHING OF A TRAGIC HERO IT SEEMS, OUR MAYOR OF DASOL.
DASOL?
TOWN IN PANGASINAN. PRACTICALLY GOT WIPED OFF THE MAP DURING THE TYRANNY, BUT THEY'VE BOUNCED BACK.
BUZETA'S A BIG PART OF THAT, PERSONALLY FINANCING MUCH OF THE REBUILDING.
HOW'D IT GET DESTROYED?
ONE OF SITAN'S AGENTS IS ALL THE REPORT SAYS. BUT IT DOES SHED LIGHT ON BUZETA'S PERSONAL TRAGEDY.
HE LOST HIS WIFE DURING THE AGENT'S RAMPAGE... AND ALL HIS CHILDREN.

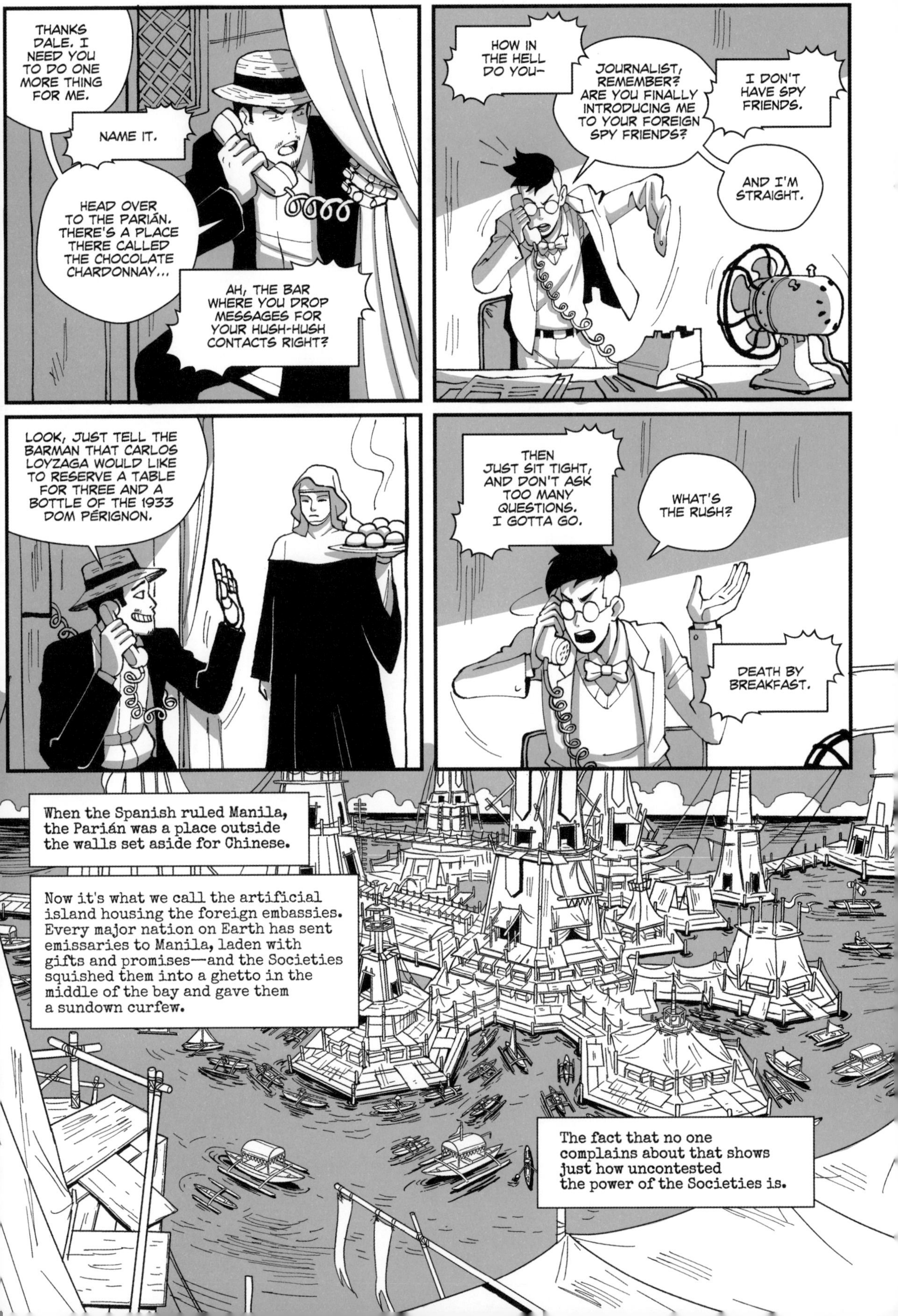
THANKS DALE. I NEED YOU TO DO ONE MORE THING FOR ME.
NAME IT.
HEAD OVER TO THE PARIÁN. THERE'S A PLACE THERE CALLED THE CHOCOLATE CHARDONNAY...
AH, THE BAR WHERE YOU DROP MESSAGES FOR YOUR HUSH-HUSH CONTACTS RIGHT?
HOW IN THE HELL DO YOU—
JOURNALIST, REMEMBER? ARE YOU FINALLY INTRODUCING ME TO YOUR FOREIGN SPY FRIENDS?
I DON'T HAVE SPY FRIENDS.
AND I'M STRAIGHT.
LOOK, JUST TELL THE BARMAN THAT CARLOS LOYZAGA WOULD LIKE TO RESERVE A TABLE FOR THREE AND A BOTTLE OF THE 1933 DOM PÉRIGNON.
THEN JUST SIT TIGHT, AND DON'T ASK TOO MANY QUESTIONS. I GOTTA GO.
WHAT'S THE RUSH?
DEATH BY BREAKFAST.
When the Spanish ruled Manila, the Parián was a place outside the walls set aside for Chinese.
Now it's what we call the artificial island housing the foreign embassies. Every major nation on Earth has sent emissaries to Manila, laden with gifts and promises—and the Societies squished them into a ghetto in the middle of the bay and gave them a sundown curfew.
The fact that no one complains about that shows just how uncontested the power of the Societies is.

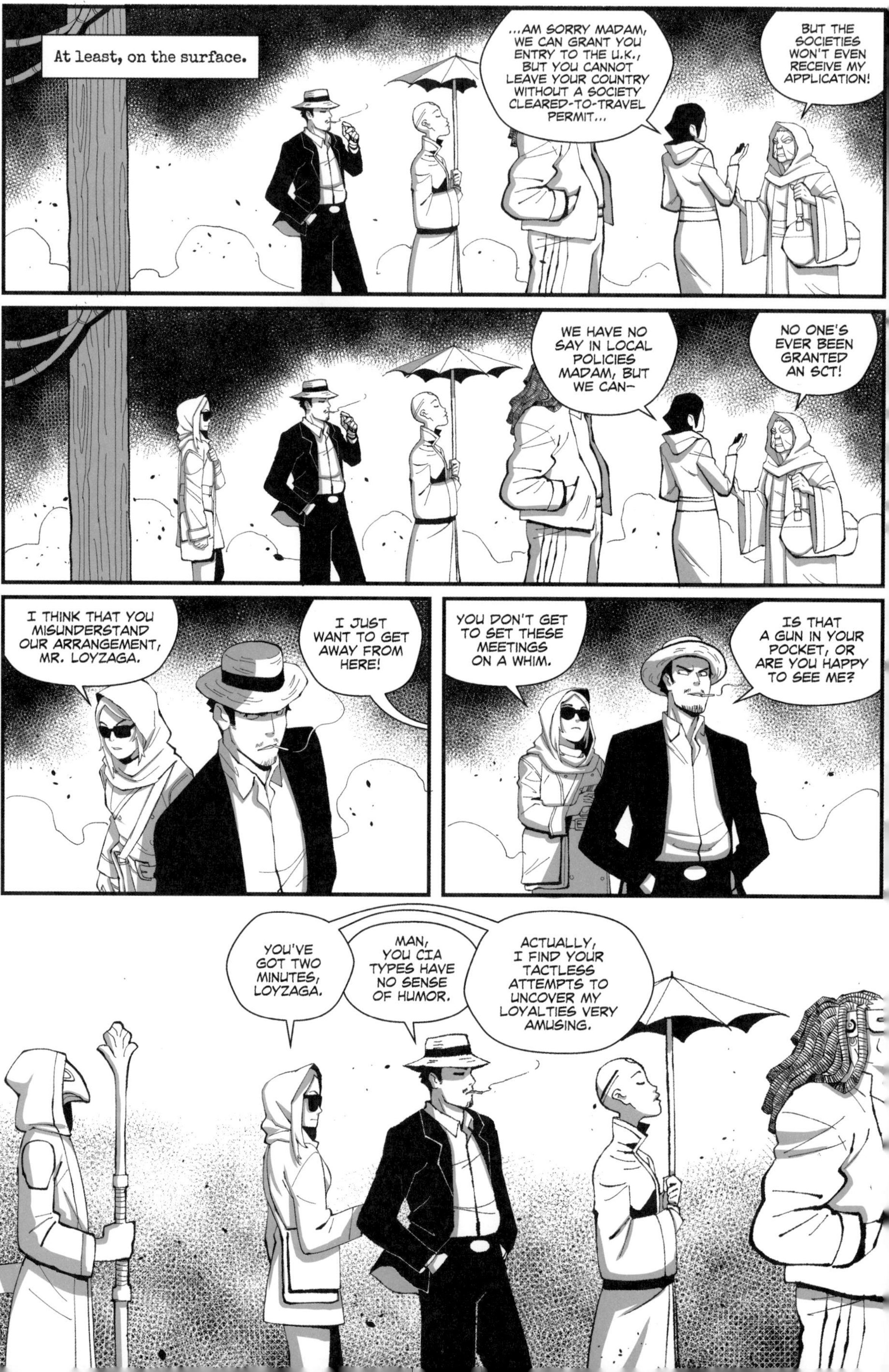
At least, on the surface.
...AM SORRY MADAM, WE CAN GRANT YOU ENTRY TO THE U.K., BUT YOU CANNOT LEAVE YOUR COUNTRY WITHOUT A SOCIETY CLEARED-TO-TRAVEL PERMIT...
BUT THE SOCIETIES WON'T EVEN RECEIVE MY APPLICATION!
WE HAVE NO SAY IN LOCAL POLICIES MADAM, BUT WE CAN–
NO ONE'S EVER BEEN GRANTED AN SCT!
I THINK THAT YOU MISUNDERSTAND OUR ARRANGEMENT, MR. LOYZAGA.
I JUST WANT TO GET AWAY FROM HERE!
YOU DON'T GET TO SET THESE MEETINGS ON A WHIM.
IS THAT A GUN IN YOUR POCKET, OR ARE YOU HAPPY TO SEE ME?
YOU'VE GOT TWO MINUTES, LOYZAGA.
MAN, YOU CIA TYPES HAVE NO SENSE OF HUMOR.
ACTUALLY, I FIND YOUR TACTLESS ATTEMPTS TO UNCOVER MY LOYALTIES VERY AMUSING.

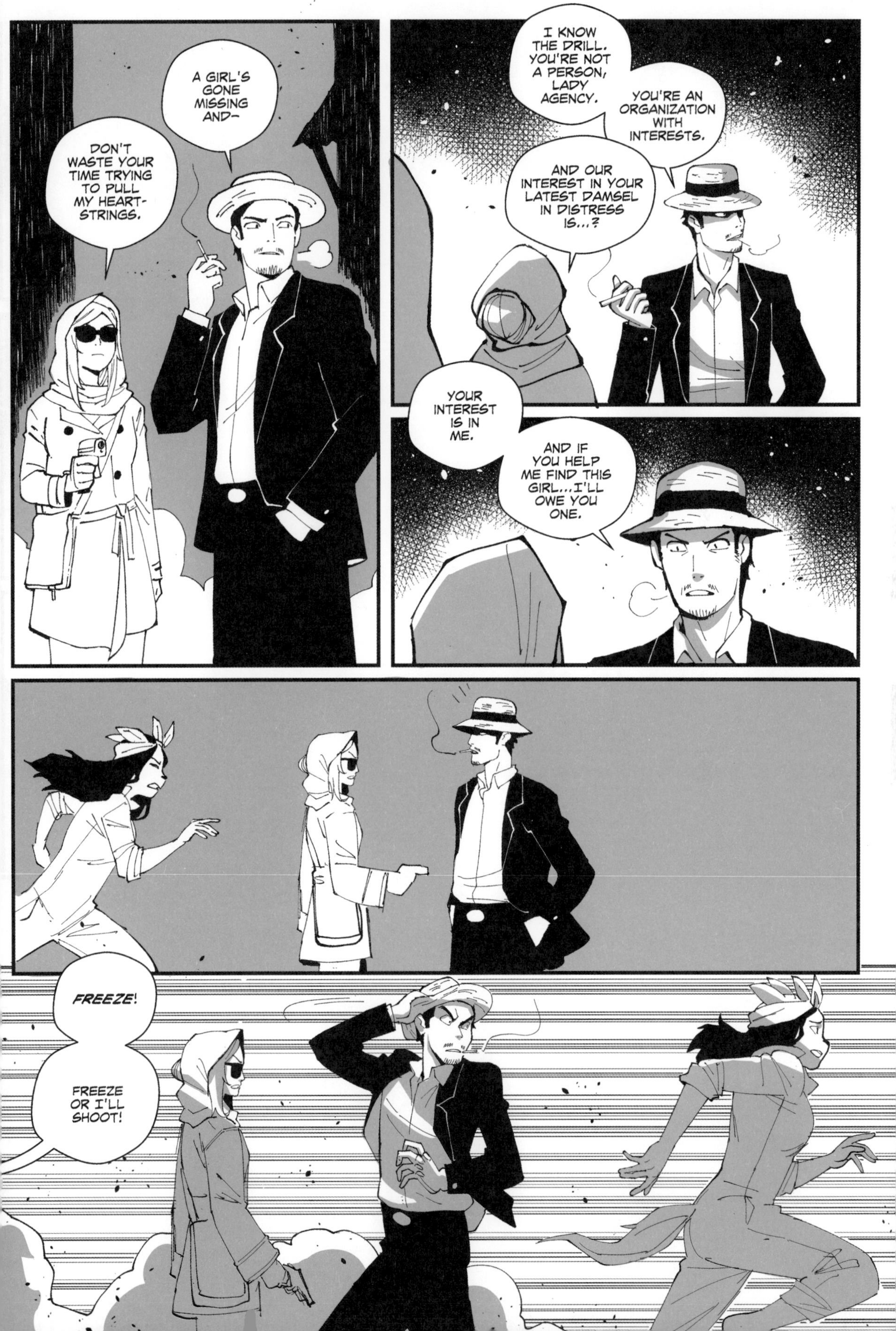
A GIRL'S GONE MISSING AND–
DON'T WASTE YOUR TIME TRYING TO PULL MY HEART-STRINGS.
I KNOW THE DRILL. YOU'RE NOT A PERSON, LADY AGENCY.
YOU'RE AN ORGANIZATION WITH INTERESTS.
AND OUR INTEREST IN YOUR LATEST DAMSEL IN DISTRESS IS...?
YOUR INTEREST IS IN ME.
AND IF YOU HELP ME FIND THIS GIRL...I'LL OWE YOU ONE.
FREEZE!
FREEZE OR I'LL SHOOT!

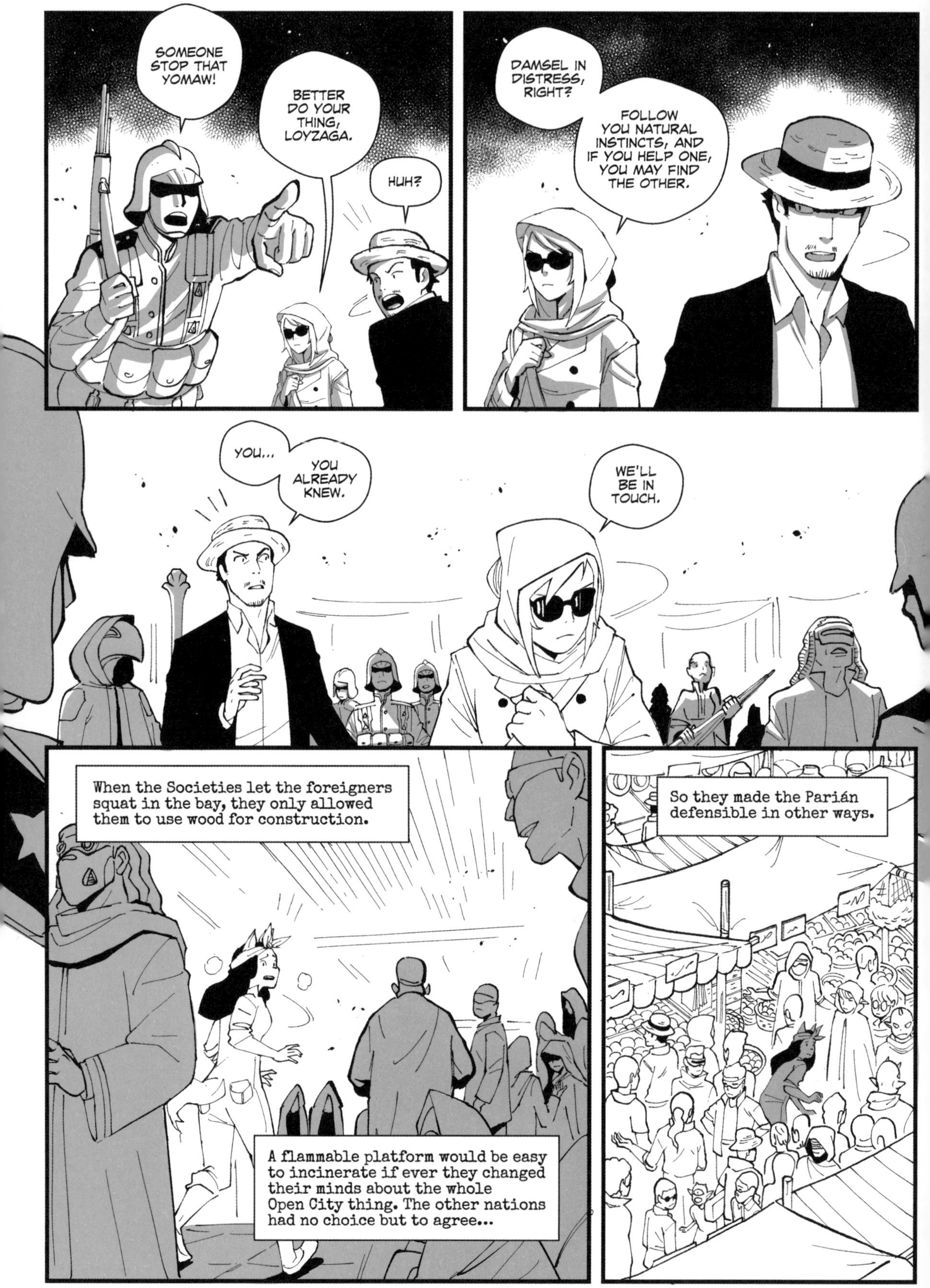
SOMEONE STOP THAT YOMAW!
BETTER DO YOUR THING, LOYZAGA.
HUH?
DAMSEL IN DISTRESS, RIGHT?
FOLLOW YOU NATURAL INSTINCTS, AND IF YOU HELP ONE, YOU MAY FIND THE OTHER.
YOU...
YOU ALREADY KNEW.
WE'LL BE IN TOUCH.
When the Societies let the foreigners squat in the bay, they only allowed them to use wood for construction.
A flammable platform would be easy to incinerate if ever they changed their minds about the whole Open City thing. The other nations had no choice but to agree...
So they made the Parián defensible in other ways.

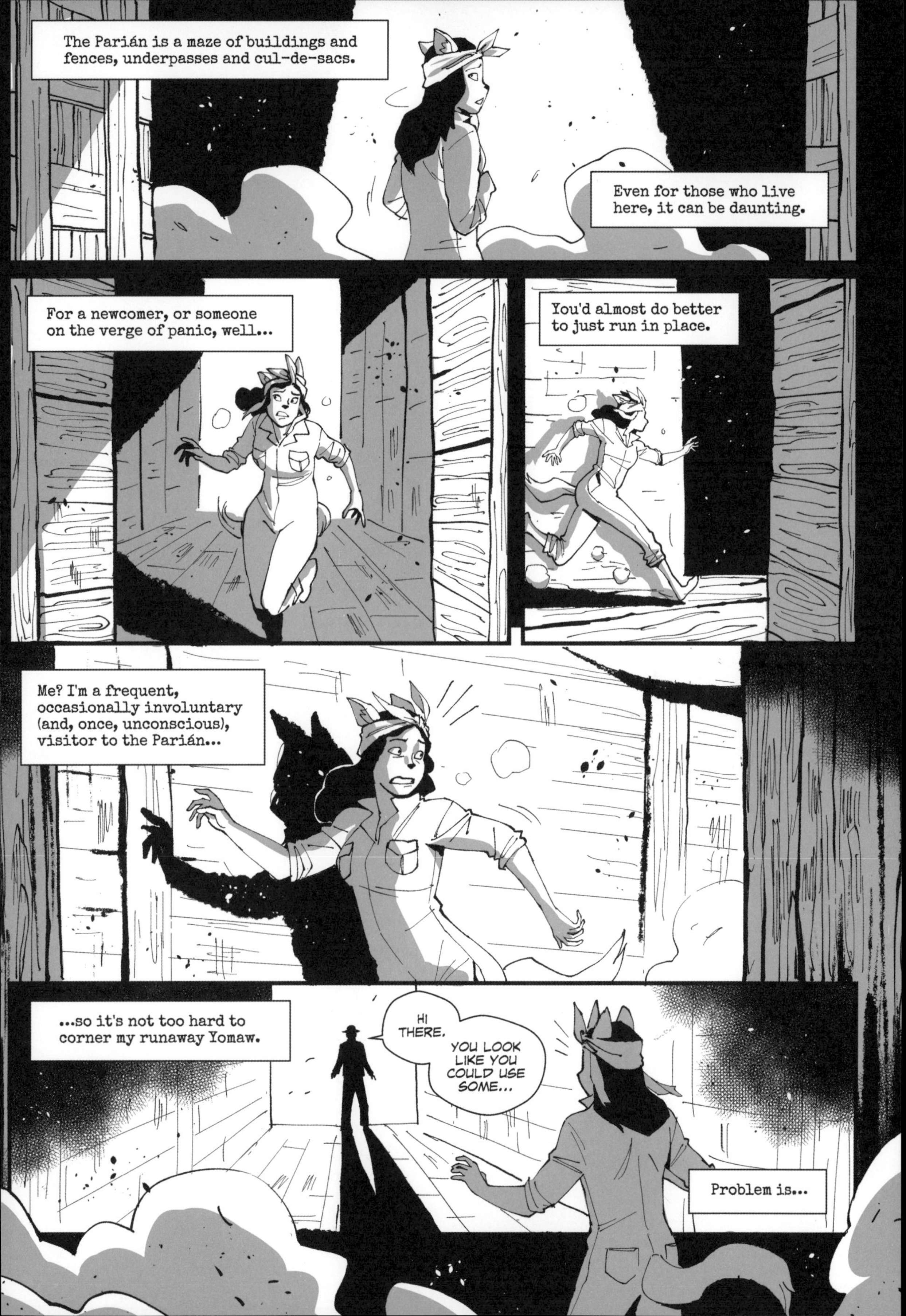

The Parián is a maze of buildings and fences, underpasses and cul-de-sacs.
Even for those who live here, it can be daunting.
For a newcomer, or someone on the verge of panic, well...
You'd almost do better to just run in place.
Me? I'm a frequent, occasionally involuntary (and, once, unconscious), visitor to the Parián...
...so it's not too hard to corner my runaway Yomaw.
HI THERE.
YOU LOOK LIKE YOU COULD USE SOME...
Problem is...

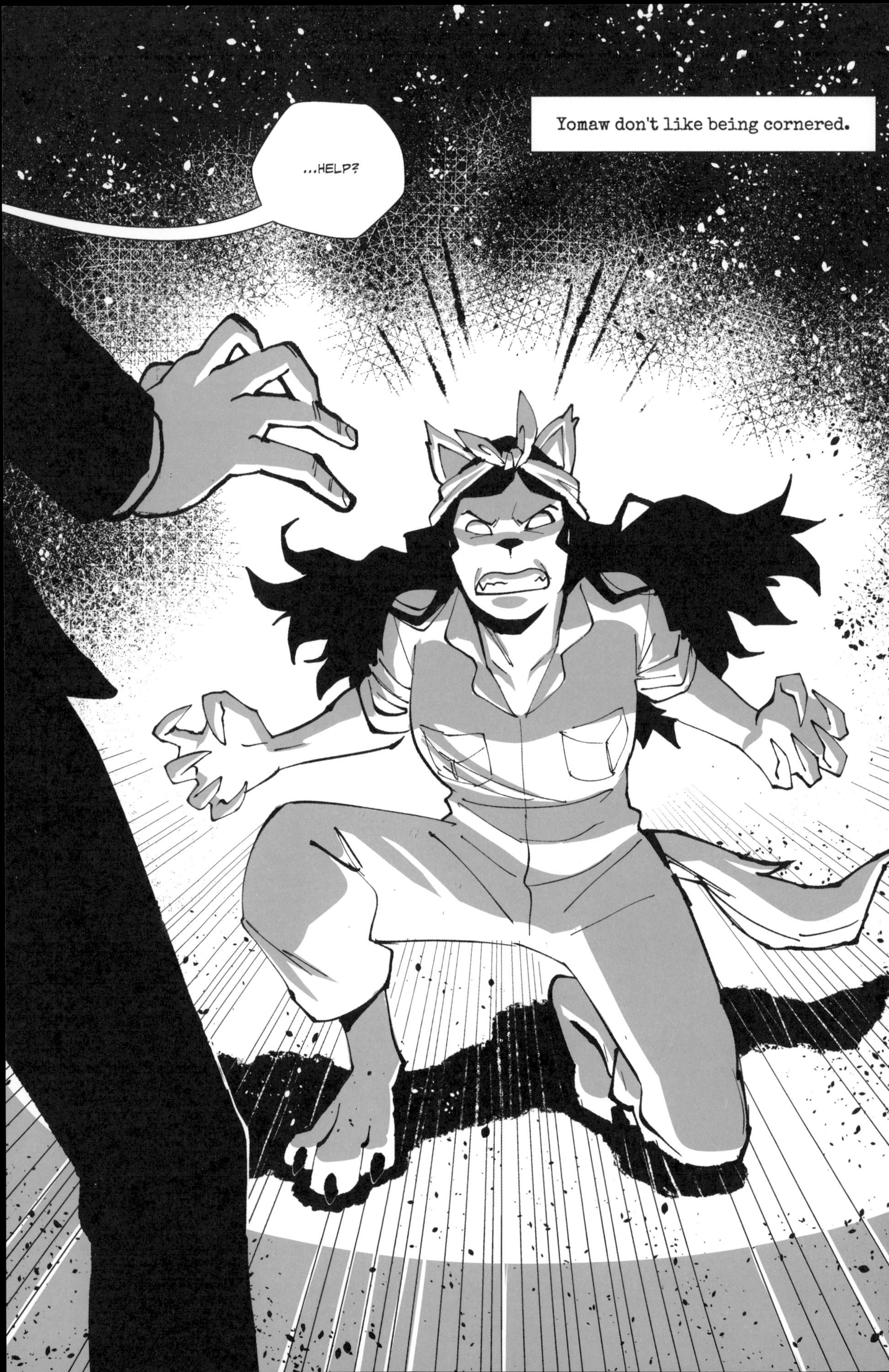

Yomaw don't like being cornered.
...HELP?

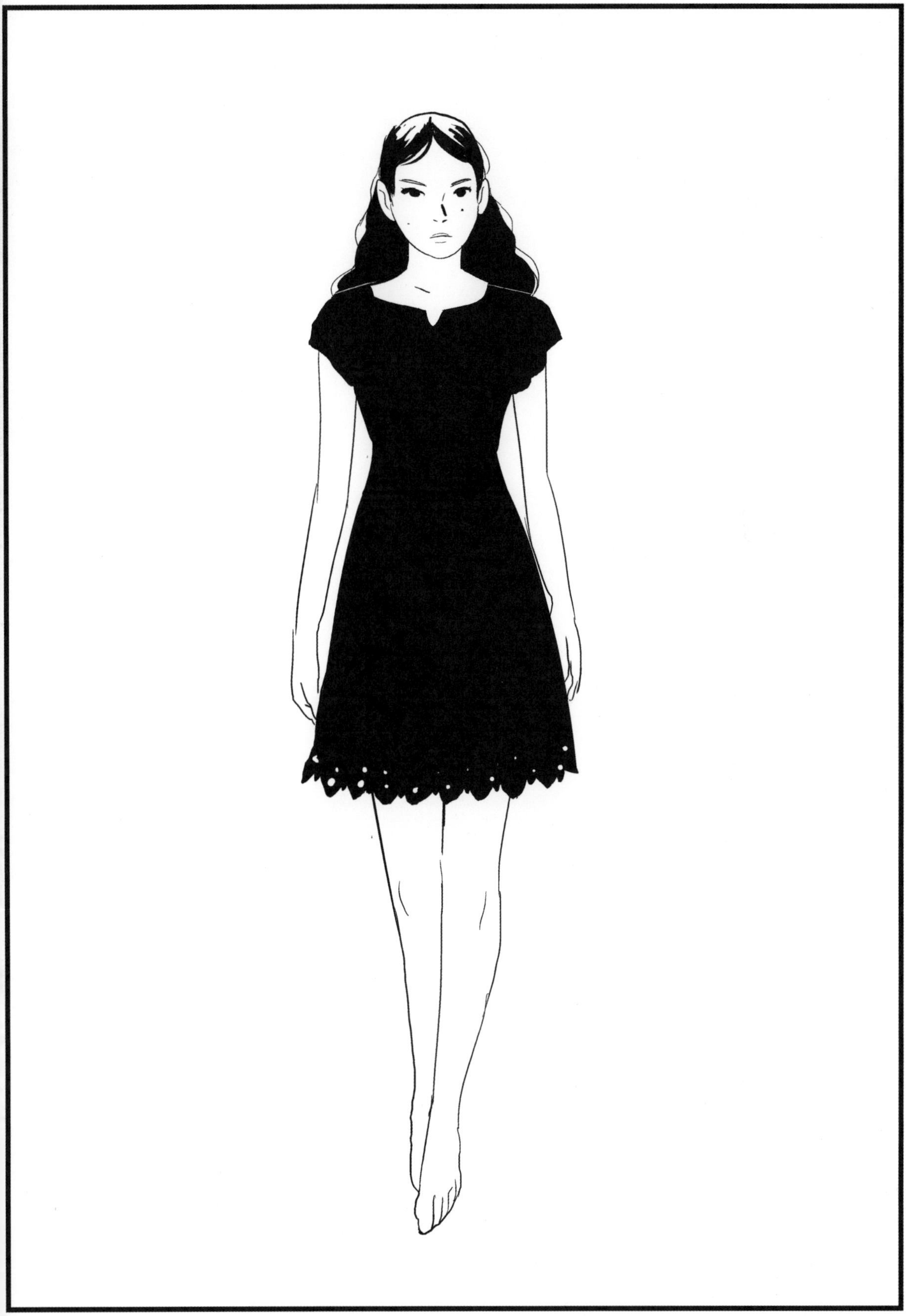

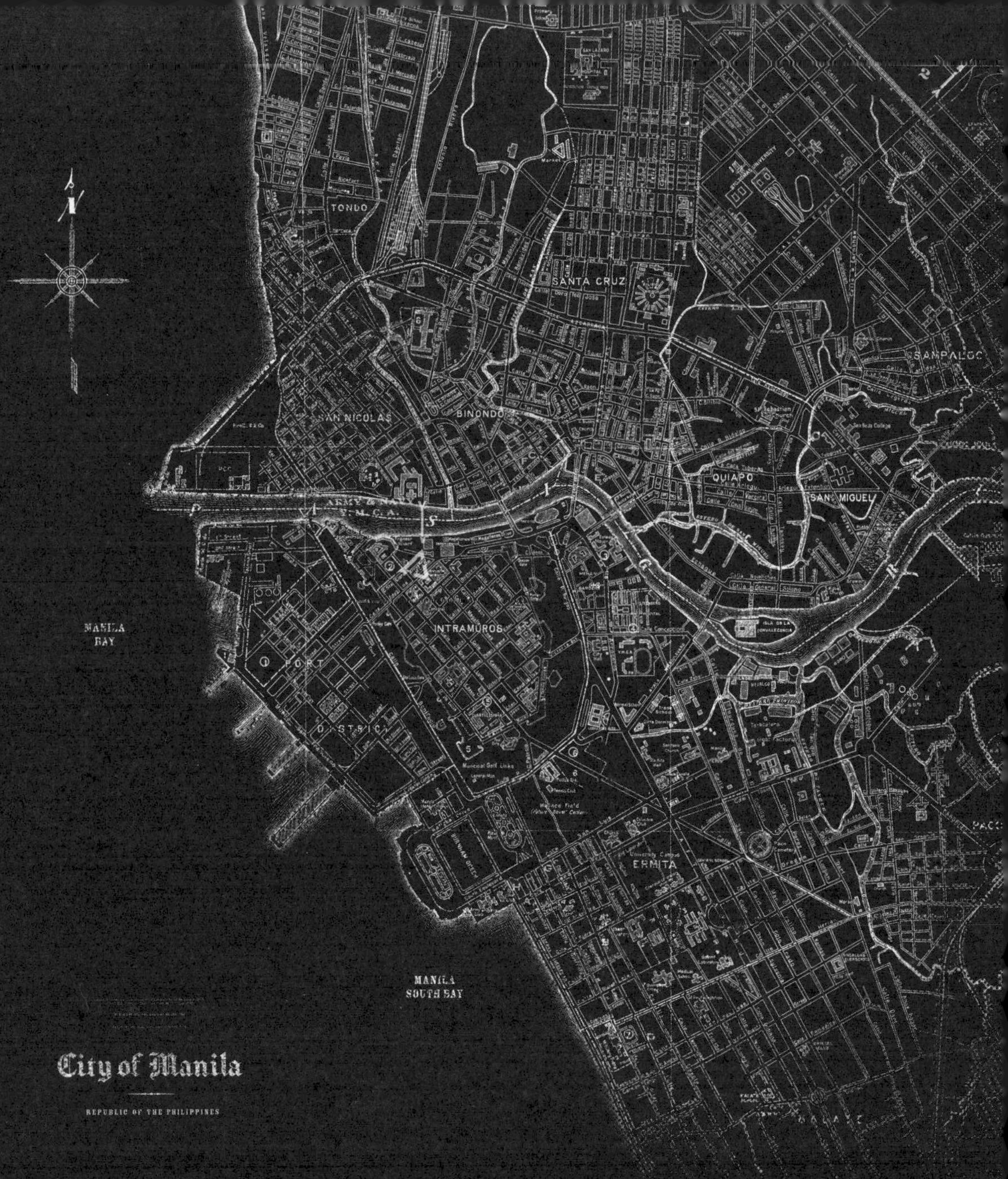
TONDO
SANTA CRUZ
SAN NICOLAS
BINONDO
QUIAPO
SAN MIGUEL
INTRAMUROS
PORT
DISTRICT
ERMITA
MANILA
BAY
MANILA
SOUTH BAY
City of Manila
REPUBLIC OF THE PHILIPPINES

THE CASE OF
THE CEMETERY GIRL

CHAPTER II

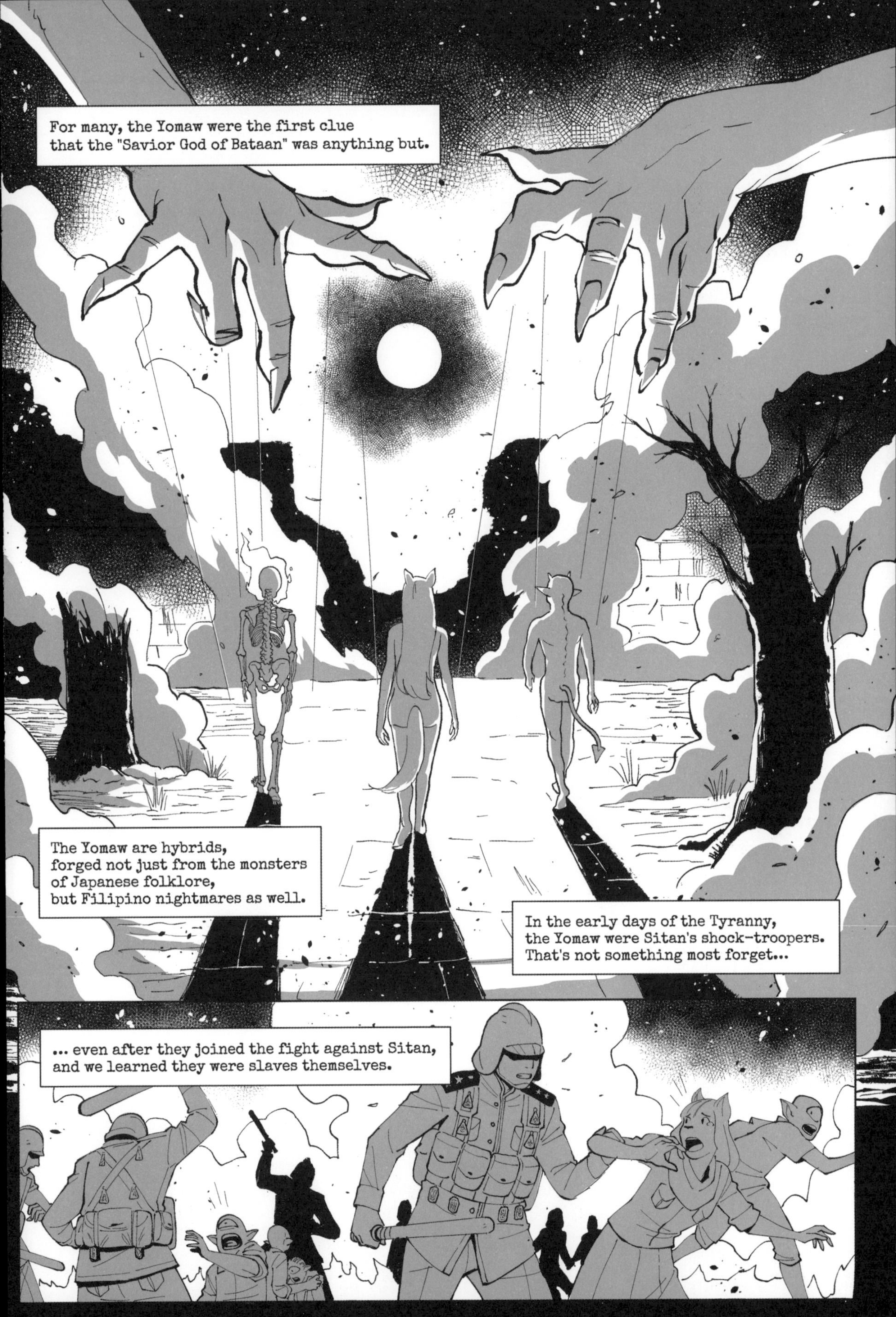
For many, the Yomaw were the first clue that the "Savior God of Bataan" was anything but.
The Yomaw are hybrids, forged not just from the monsters of Japanese folklore, but Filipino nightmares as well.
In the early days of the Tyranny, the Yomaw were Sitan's shock-troopers. That's not something most forget...
... even after they joined the fight against Sitan, and we learned they were slaves themselves.

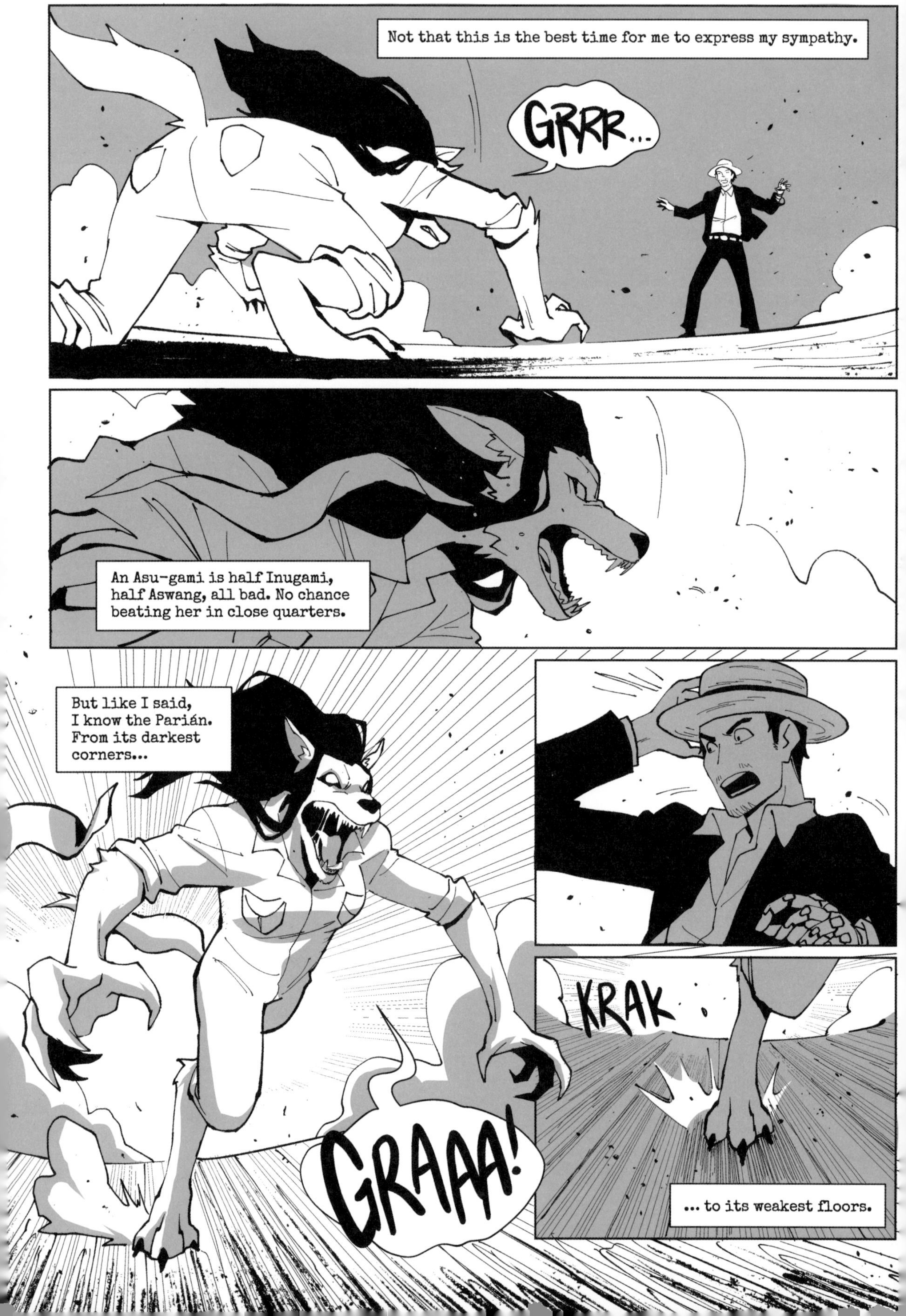
Not that this is the best time for me to express my sympathy.
GRRR...
An Asu-gami is half Inugami, half Aswang, all bad. No chance beating her in close quarters.
But like I said, I know the Parián. From its darkest corners...
GRAAA!
KRAK
... to its weakest floors.

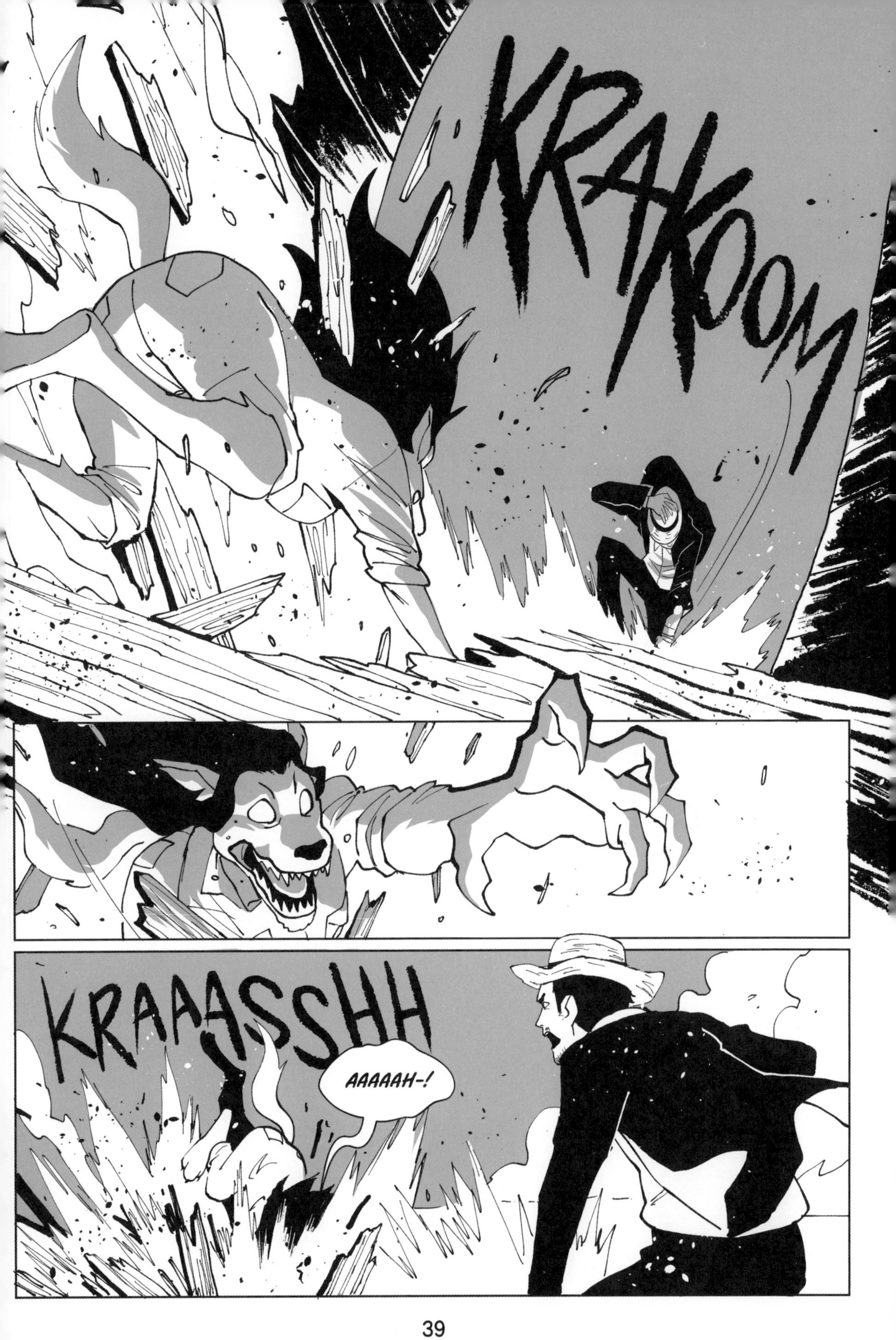
KRAKOOM
KRAAASSHH
AAAAAH-!

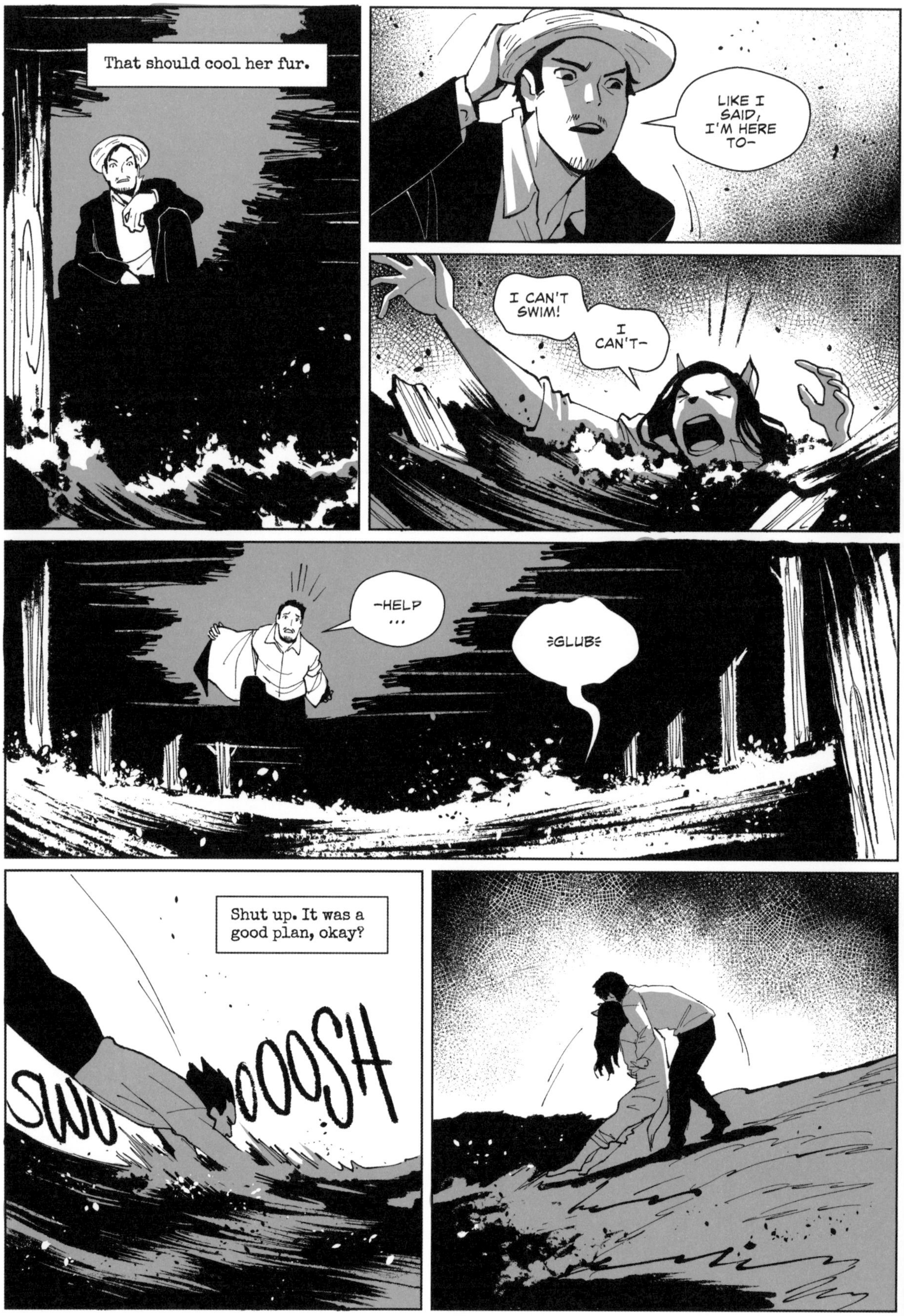
That should cool her fur.
LIKE I SAID, I'M HERE TO–
I CAN'T SWIM!
I CAN'T–
–HELP ...
GLUB
Shut up. It was a good plan, okay?
SWOOOOSH

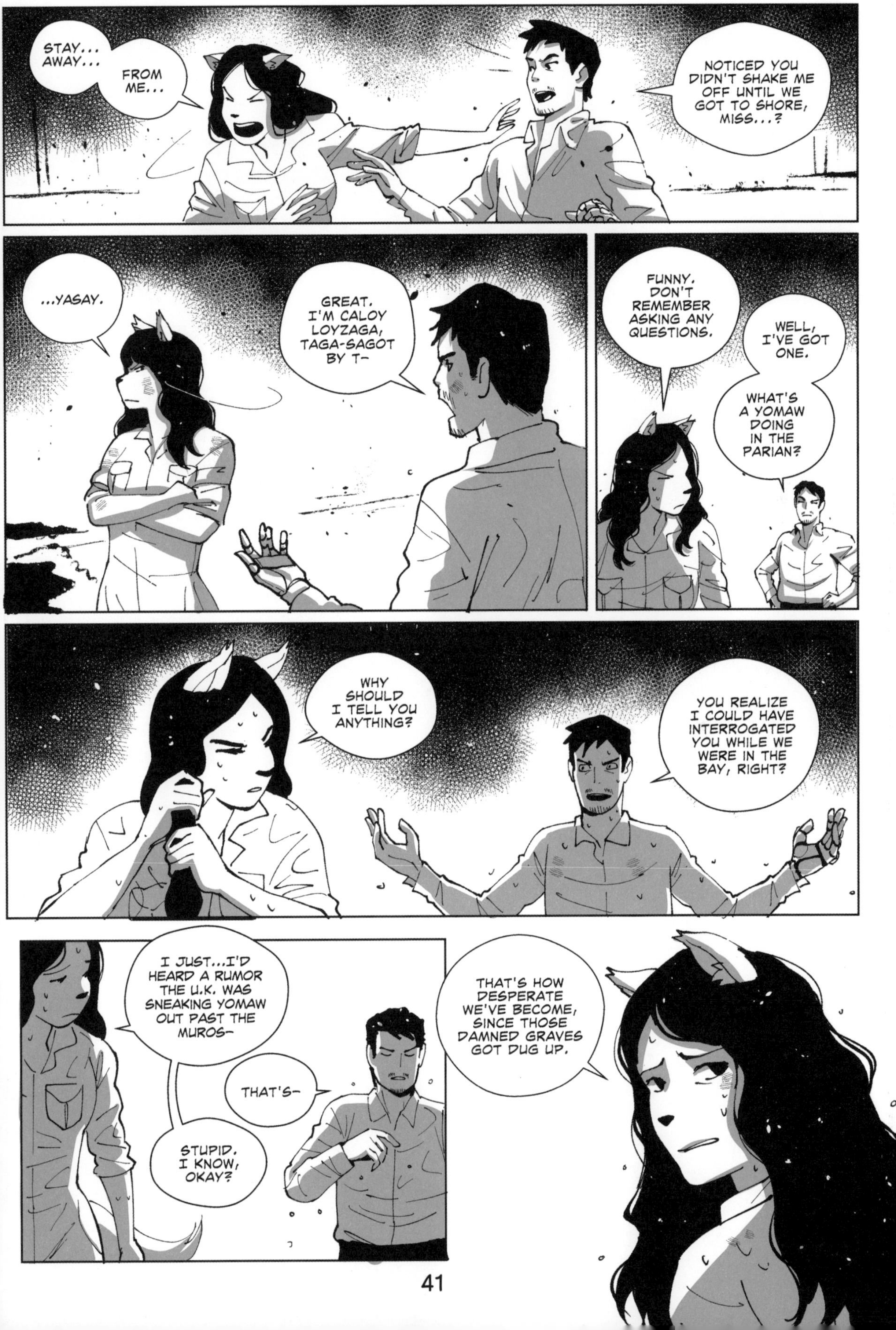
STAY... AWAY...
FROM ME...
NOTICED YOU DIDN'T SHAKE ME OFF UNTIL WE GOT TO SHORE, MISS...?
...YASAY.
GREAT. I'M CALOY LOYZAGA, TAGA-SAGOT BY T-
FUNNY. DON'T REMEMBER ASKING ANY QUESTIONS.
WELL, I'VE GOT ONE.
WHAT'S A YOMAW DOING IN THE PARIAN?
WHY SHOULD I TELL YOU ANYTHING?
YOU REALIZE I COULD HAVE INTERROGATED YOU WHILE WE WERE IN THE BAY, RIGHT?
I JUST...I'D HEARD A RUMOR THE U.K. WAS SNEAKING YOMAW OUT PAST THE MUROS-
THAT'S-
STUPID. I KNOW, OKAY?
THAT'S HOW DESPERATE WE'VE BECOME, SINCE THOSE DAMNED GRAVES GOT DUG UP.

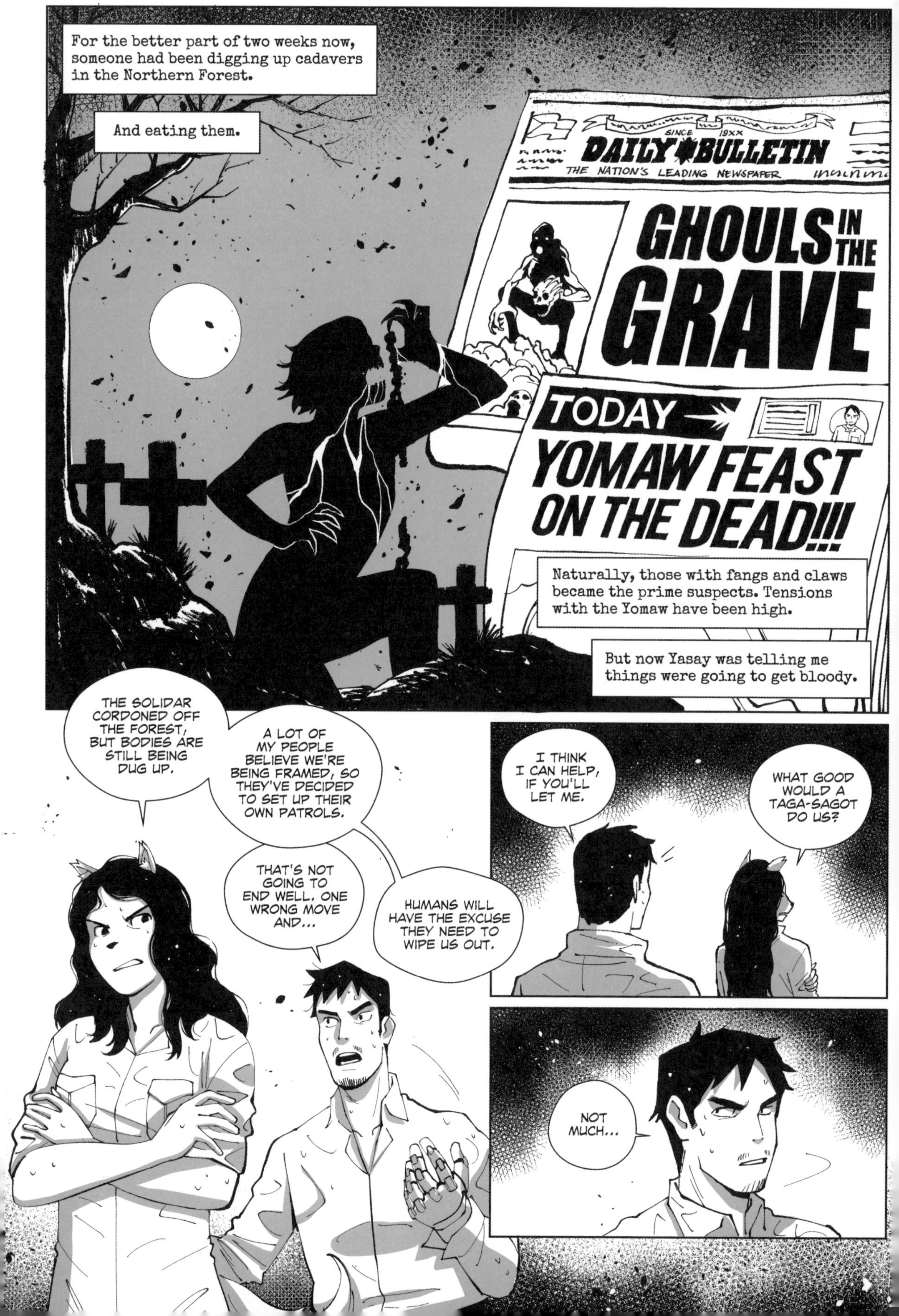
For the better part of two weeks now, someone had been digging up cadavers in the Northern Forest.
And eating them.
SINCE 19XX
DAILY BULLETIN
THE NATION'S LEADING NEWSPAPER
GHOULS IN THE GRAVE
TODAY
YOMAW FEAST ON THE DEAD!!!
Naturally, those with fangs and claws became the prime suspects. Tensions with the Yomaw have been high.
But now Yasay was telling me things were going to get bloody.
THE SOLIDAR CORDONED OFF THE FOREST, BUT BODIES ARE STILL BEING DUG UP.
A LOT OF MY PEOPLE BELIEVE WE'RE BEING FRAMED, SO THEY'VE DECIDED TO SET UP THEIR OWN PATROLS.
THAT'S NOT GOING TO END WELL. ONE WRONG MOVE AND...
HUMANS WILL HAVE THE EXCUSE THEY NEED TO WIPE US OUT.
I THINK I CAN HELP, IF YOU'LL LET ME.
WHAT GOOD WOULD A TAGA-SAGOT DO US?
NOT MUCH...

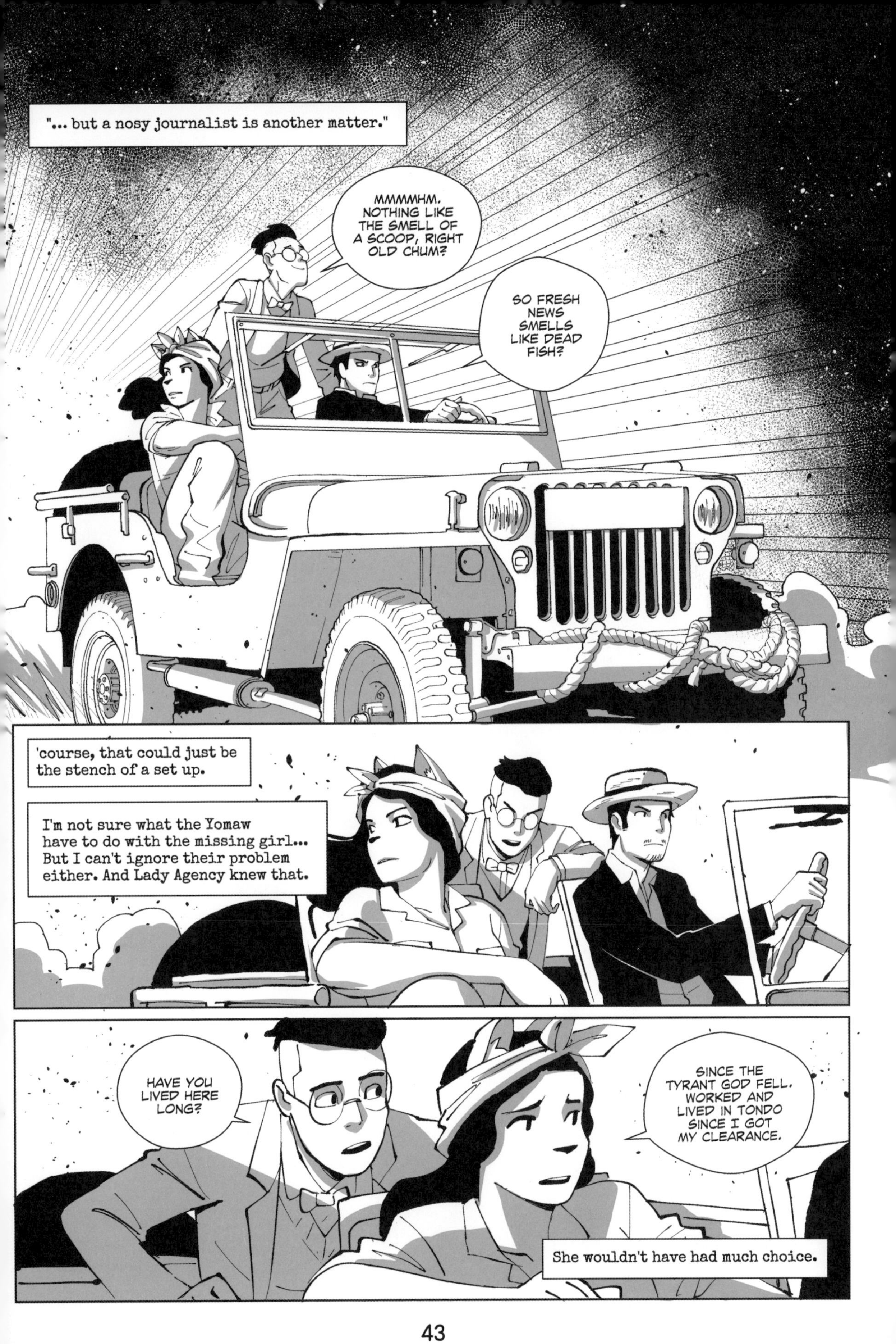
"... but a nosy journalist is another matter."
MMMMHM. NOTHING LIKE THE SMELL OF A SCOOP, RIGHT OLD CHUM?
SO FRESH NEWS SMELLS LIKE DEAD FISH?
'course, that could just be the stench of a set up.
I'm not sure what the Yomaw have to do with the missing girl... But I can't ignore their problem either. And Lady Agency knew that.
HAVE YOU LIVED HERE LONG?
SINCE THE TYRANT GOD FELL. WORKED AND LIVED IN TONDO SINCE I GOT MY CLEARANCE.
She wouldn't have had much choice.

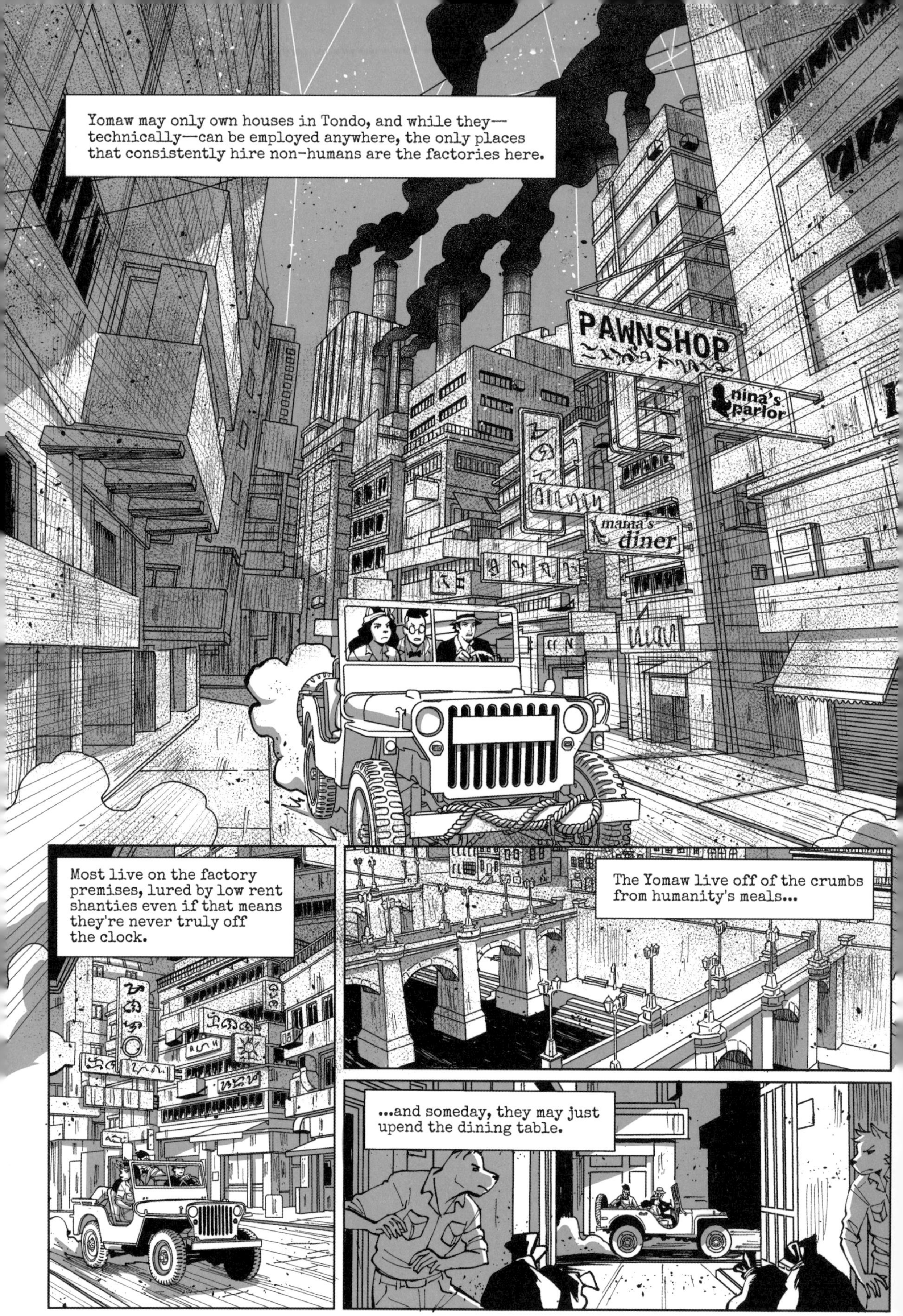
Yomaw may only own houses in Tondo, and while they—technically—can be employed anywhere, the only places that consistently hire non-humans are the factories here.
PAWNSHOP
nina's parlor
mama's diner
Most live on the factory premises, lured by low rent shanties even if that means they're never truly off the clock.
The Yomaw live off of the crumbs from humanity's meals...
...and someday, they may just upend the dining table.

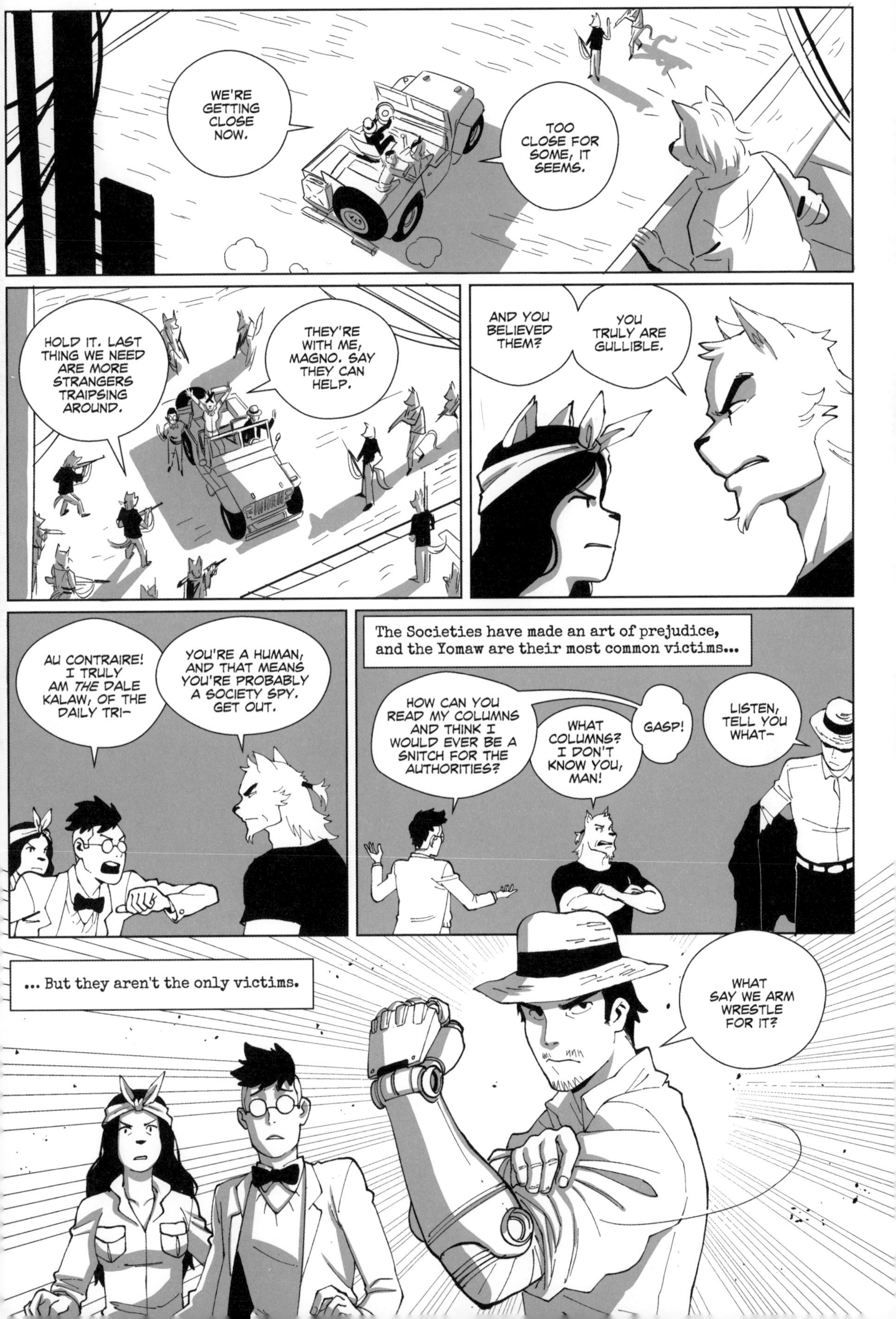
WE'RE GETTING CLOSE NOW.
TOO CLOSE FOR SOME, IT SEEMS.
HOLD IT. LAST THING WE NEED ARE MORE STRANGERS TRAIPSING AROUND.
THEY'RE WITH ME, MAGNO. SAY THEY CAN HELP.
AND YOU BELIEVED THEM?
YOU TRULY ARE GULLIBLE.
AU CONTRAIRE! I TRULY AM *THE* DALE KALAW, OF THE DAILY TRI-
YOU'RE A HUMAN, AND THAT MEANS YOU'RE PROBABLY A SOCIETY SPY. GET OUT.
The Societies have made an art of prejudice, and the Yomaw are their most common victims...
HOW CAN YOU READ MY COLUMNS AND THINK I WOULD EVER BE A SNITCH FOR THE AUTHORITIES?
GASP!
WHAT COLUMNS? I DON'T KNOW YOU, MAN!
LISTEN, TELL YOU WHAT-
... But they aren't the only victims.
WHAT SAY WE ARM WRESTLE FOR IT?

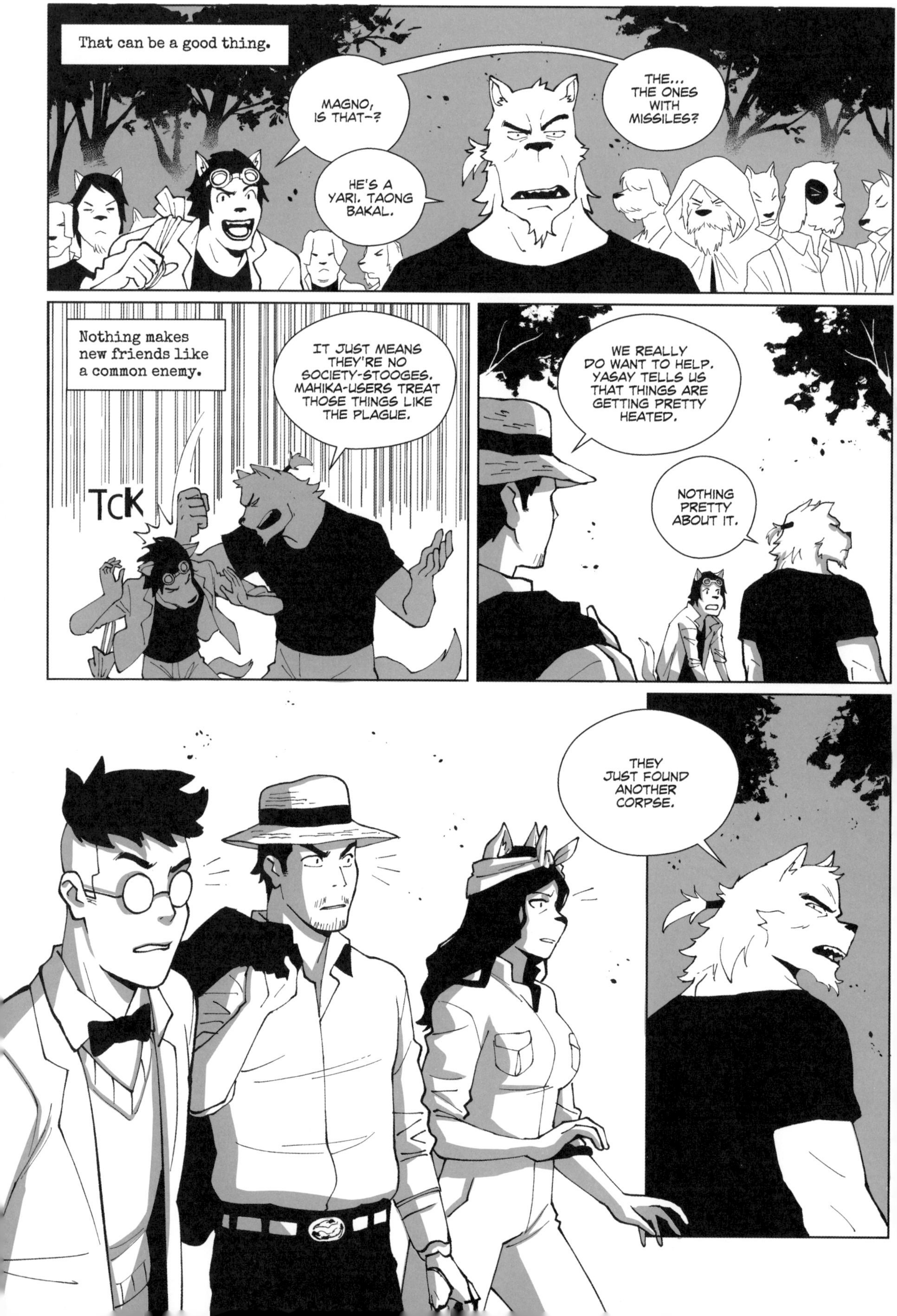
That can be a good thing.
MAGNO, IS THAT—?
THE... THE ONES WITH MISSILES?
HE'S A YARI. TAONG BAKAL.
Nothing makes new friends like a common enemy.
IT JUST MEANS THEY'RE NO SOCIETY-STOOGES. MAHIKA-USERS TREAT THOSE THINGS LIKE THE PLAGUE.
TCK
WE REALLY DO WANT TO HELP. YASAY TELLS US THAT THINGS ARE GETTING PRETTY HEATED.
NOTHING PRETTY ABOUT IT.
THEY JUST FOUND ANOTHER CORPSE.

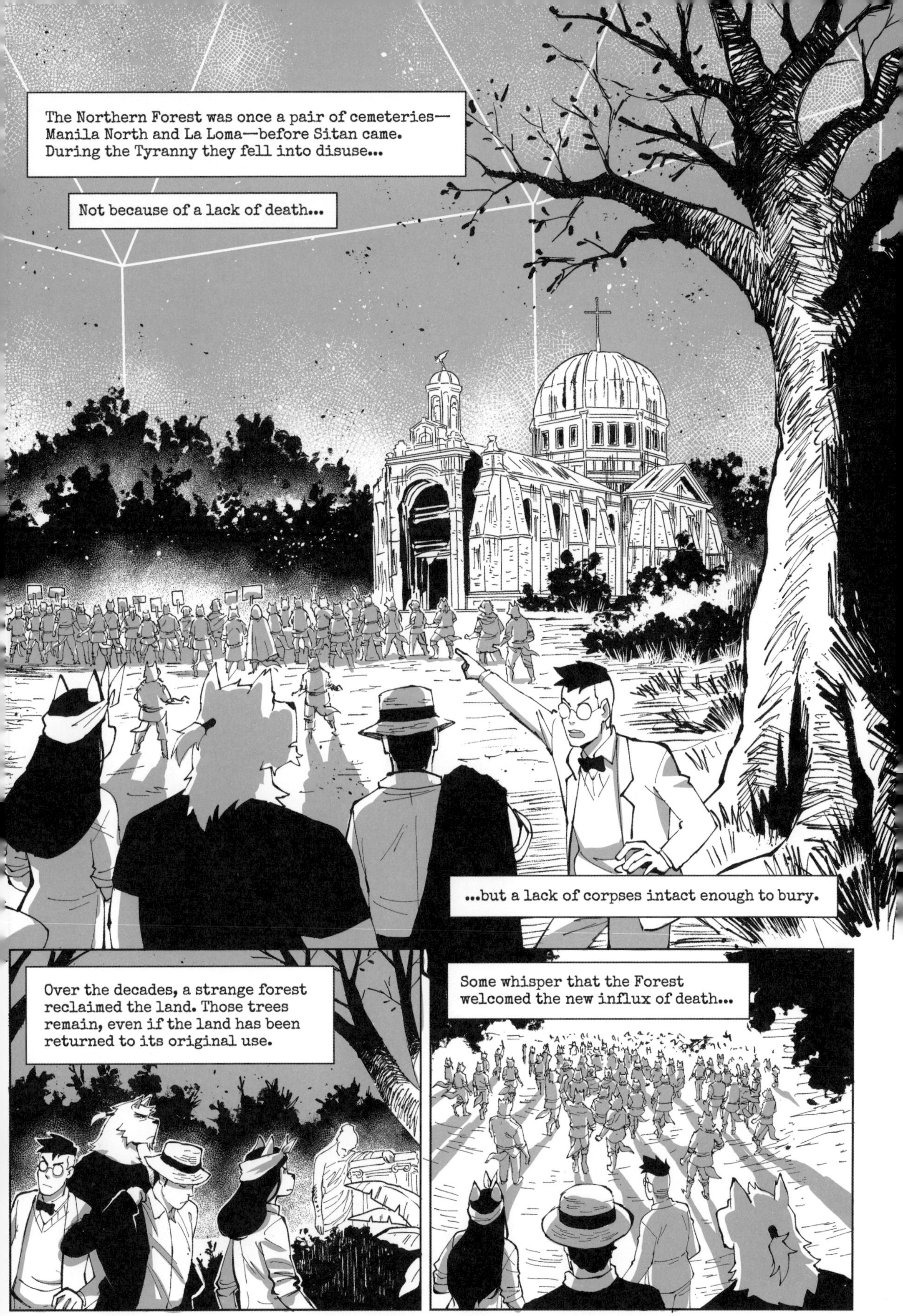

The Northern Forest was once a pair of cemeteries—Manila North and La Loma—before Sitan came. During the Tyranny they fell into disuse...
Not because of a lack of death...
...but a lack of corpses intact enough to bury.
Over the decades, a strange forest reclaimed the land. Those trees remain, even if the land has been returned to its original use.
Some whisper that the Forest welcomed the new influx of death...

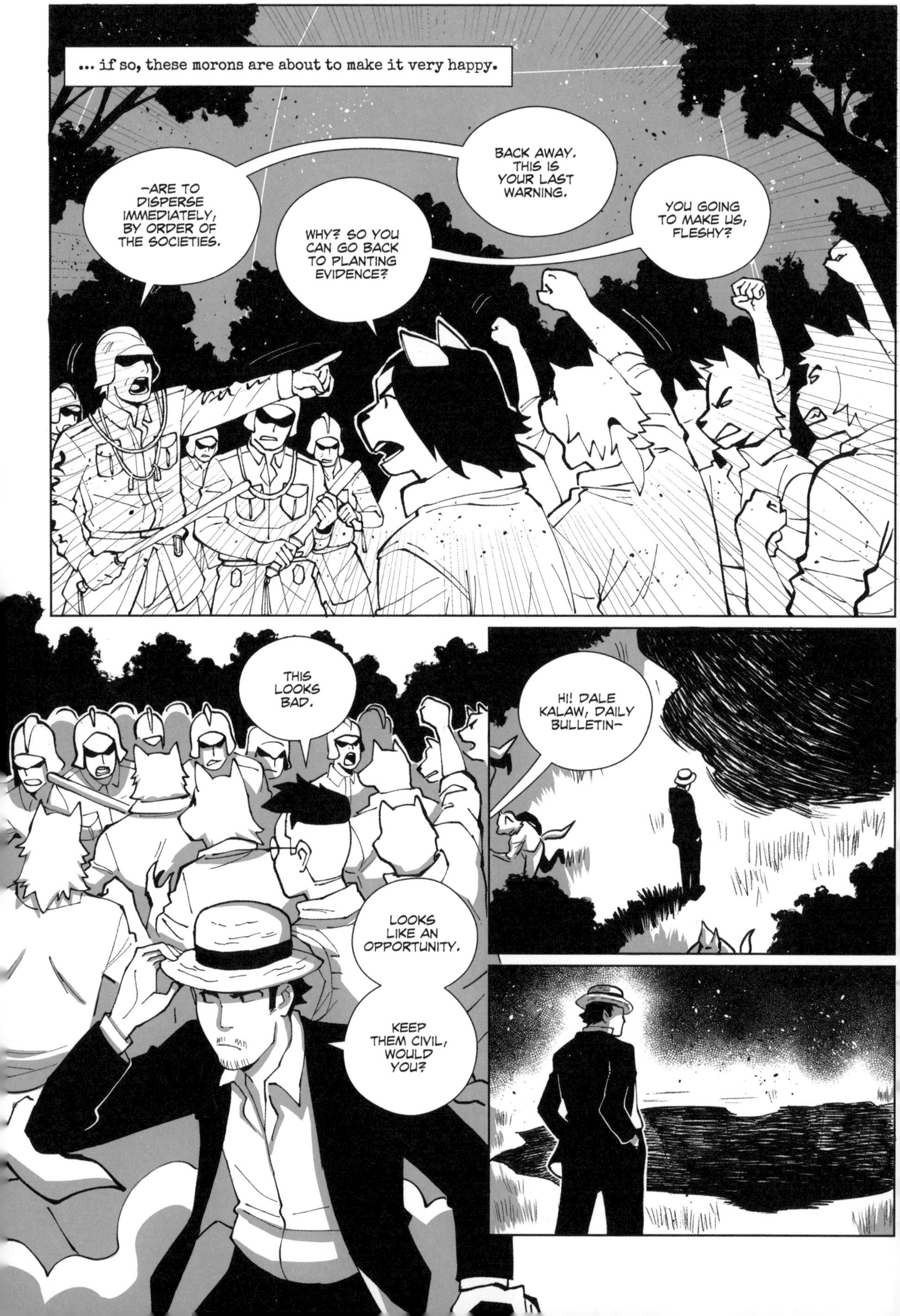
... if so, these morons are about to make it very happy.
-ARE TO DISPERSE IMMEDIATELY, BY ORDER OF THE SOCIETIES.
WHY? SO YOU CAN GO BACK TO PLANTING EVIDENCE?
BACK AWAY. THIS IS YOUR LAST WARNING.
YOU GOING TO MAKE US, FLESHY?
THIS LOOKS BAD.
LOOKS LIKE AN OPPORTUNITY.
KEEP THEM CIVIL, WOULD YOU?
HI! DALE KALAW, DAILY BULLETIN-

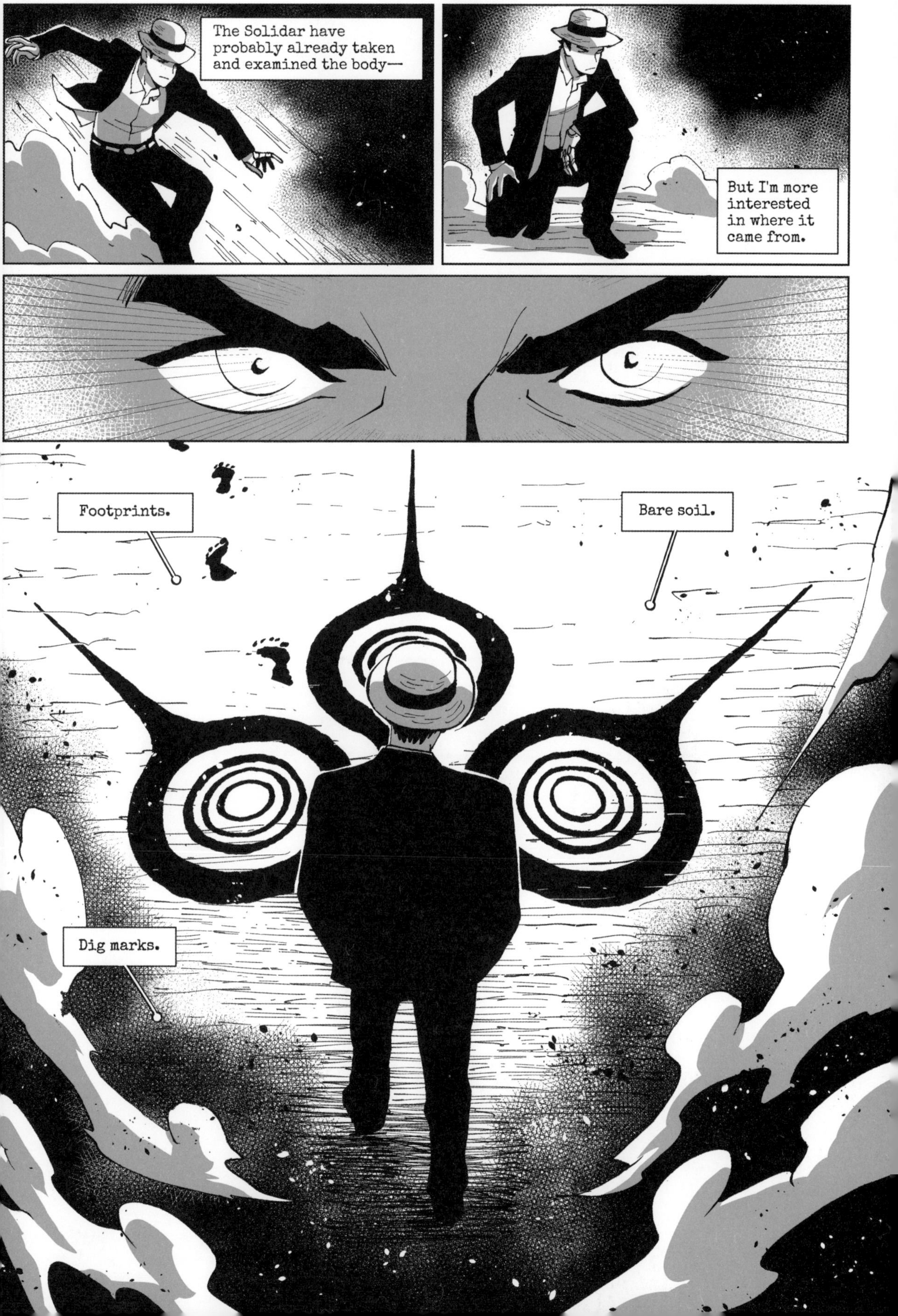
The Solidar have probably already taken and examined the body—
But I'm more interested in where it came from.
Footprints.
Bare soil.
Dig marks.

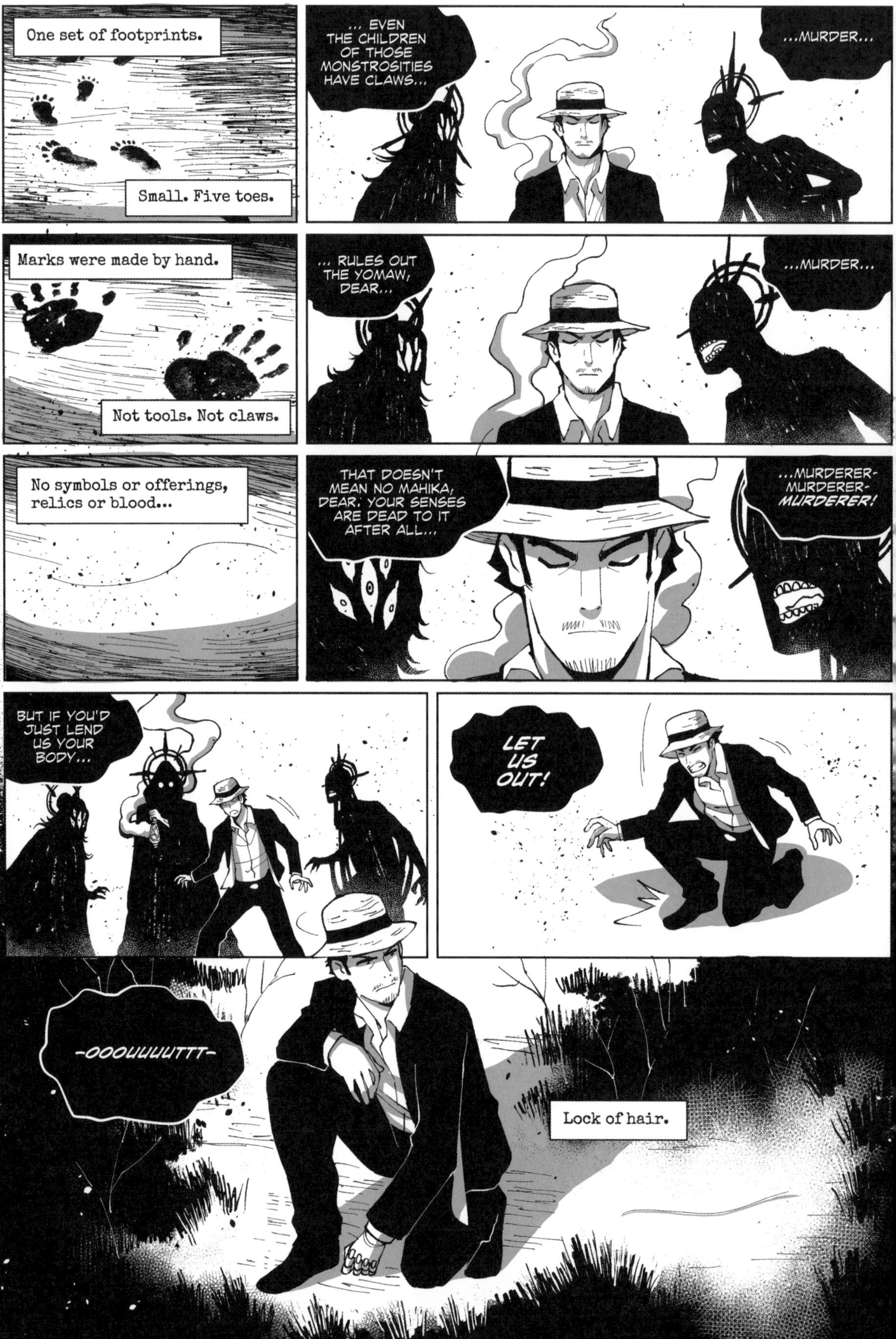
One set of footprints.
Small. Five toes.
... EVEN THE CHILDREN OF THOSE MONSTROSITIES HAVE CLAWS...
...MURDER...
Marks were made by hand.
Not tools. Not claws.
... RULES OUT THE YOMAW, DEAR...
...MURDER...
No symbols or offerings, relics or blood...
THAT DOESN'T MEAN NO MAHIKA, DEAR. YOUR SENSES ARE DEAD TO IT AFTER ALL...
...MURDERER-MURDERER-MURDERER!
BUT IF YOU'D JUST LEND US YOUR BODY...
LET US OUT!
-OOOUUUUTTT-
Lock of hair.

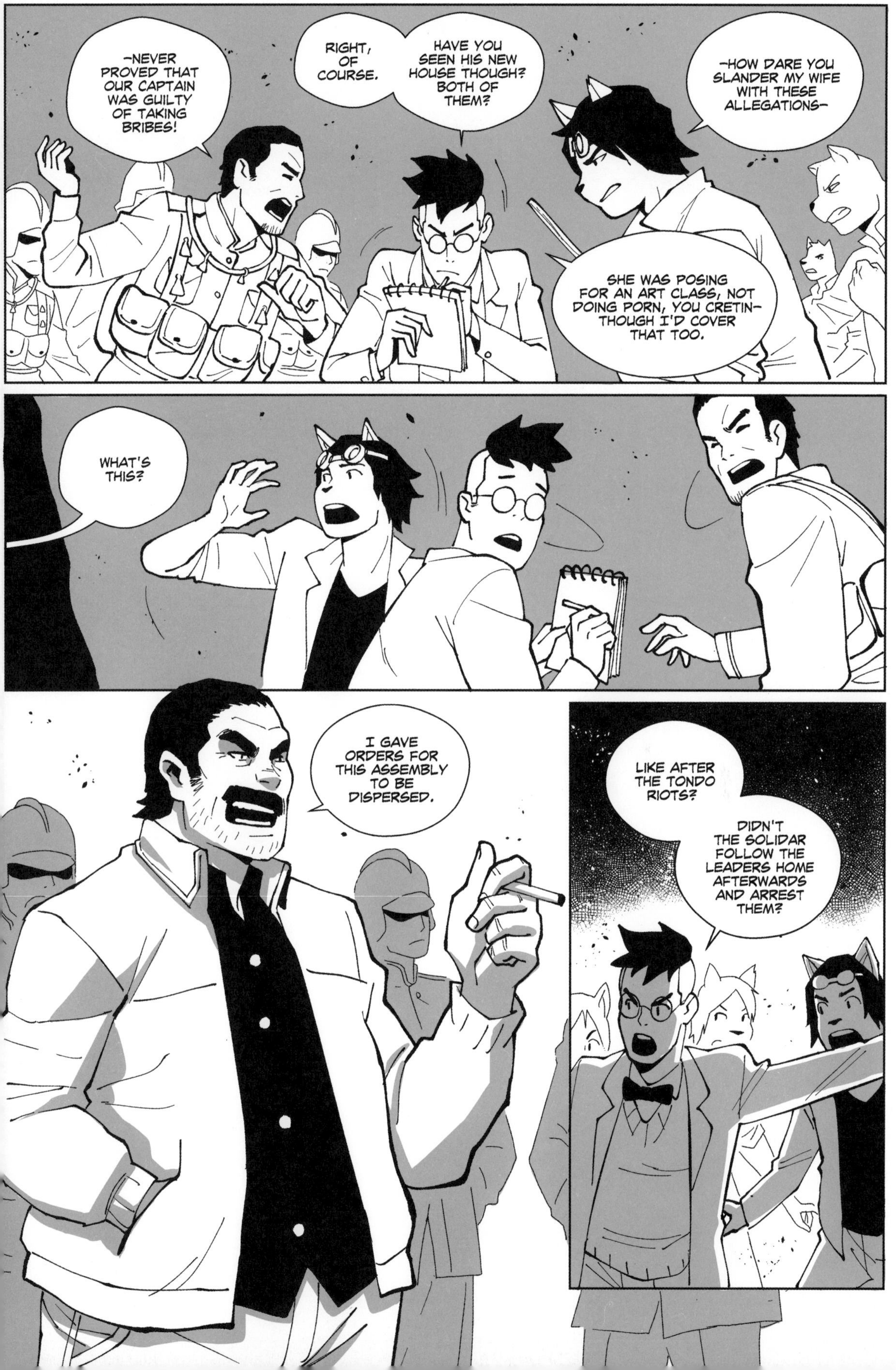
-NEVER PROVED THAT OUR CAPTAIN WAS GUILTY OF TAKING BRIBES!
RIGHT, OF COURSE.
HAVE YOU SEEN HIS NEW HOUSE THOUGH? BOTH OF THEM?
-HOW DARE YOU SLANDER MY WIFE WITH THESE ALLEGATIONS-
SHE WAS POSING FOR AN ART CLASS, NOT DOING PORN, YOU CRETIN-THOUGH I'D COVER THAT TOO.
WHAT'S THIS?
I GAVE ORDERS FOR THIS ASSEMBLY TO BE DISPERSED.
LIKE AFTER THE TONDO RIOTS?
DIDN'T THE SOLIDAR FOLLOW THE LEADERS HOME AFTERWARDS AND ARREST THEM?

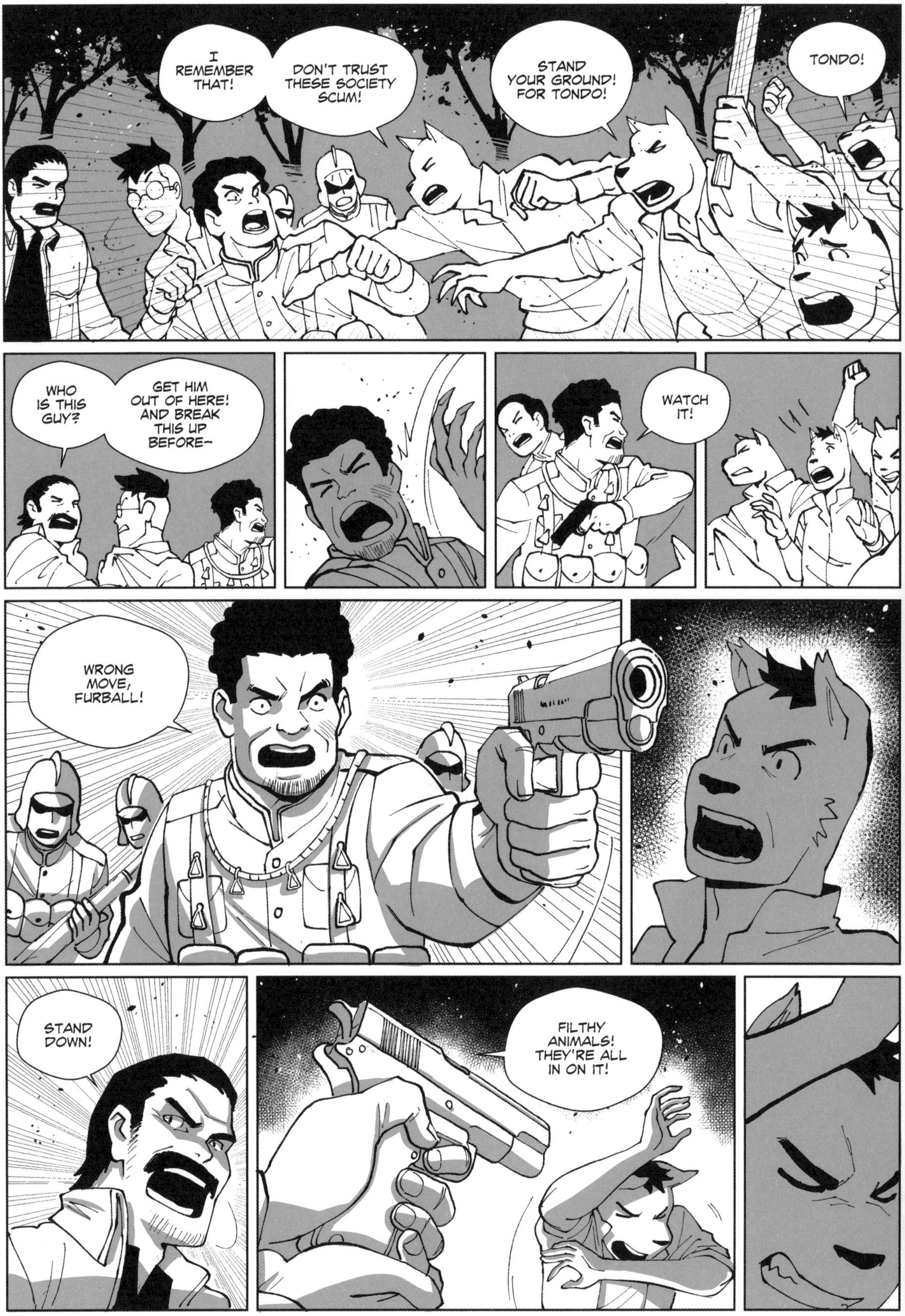
I REMEMBER THAT!
DON'T TRUST THESE SOCIETY SCUM!
STAND YOUR GROUND! FOR TONDO!
TONDO!
WHO IS THIS GUY?
GET HIM OUT OF HERE! AND BREAK THIS UP BEFORE–
WATCH IT!
WRONG MOVE, FURBALL!
STAND DOWN!
FILTHY ANIMALS! THEY'RE ALL IN ON IT!

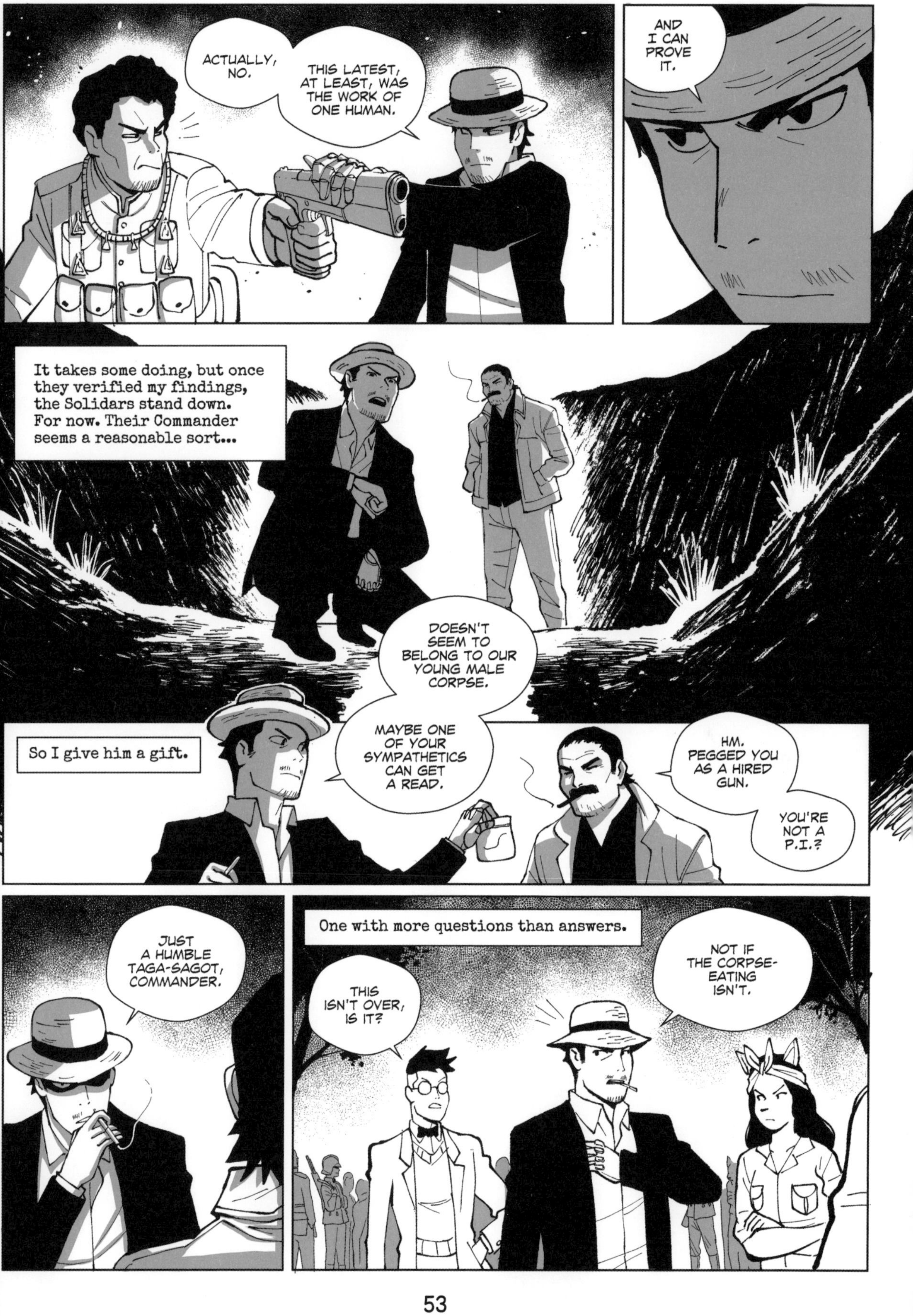
ACTUALLY, NO.
THIS LATEST, AT LEAST, WAS THE WORK OF ONE HUMAN.
AND I CAN PROVE IT.
It takes some doing, but once they verified my findings, the Solidars stand down. For now. Their Commander seems a reasonable sort...
DOESN'T SEEM TO BELONG TO OUR YOUNG MALE CORPSE.
So I give him a gift.
MAYBE ONE OF YOUR SYMPATHETICS CAN GET A READ.
HM. PEGGED YOU AS A HIRED GUN.
YOU'RE NOT A P.I.?
JUST A HUMBLE TAGA-SAGOT, COMMANDER.
One with more questions than answers.
THIS ISN'T OVER, IS IT?
NOT IF THE CORPSE-EATING ISN'T.

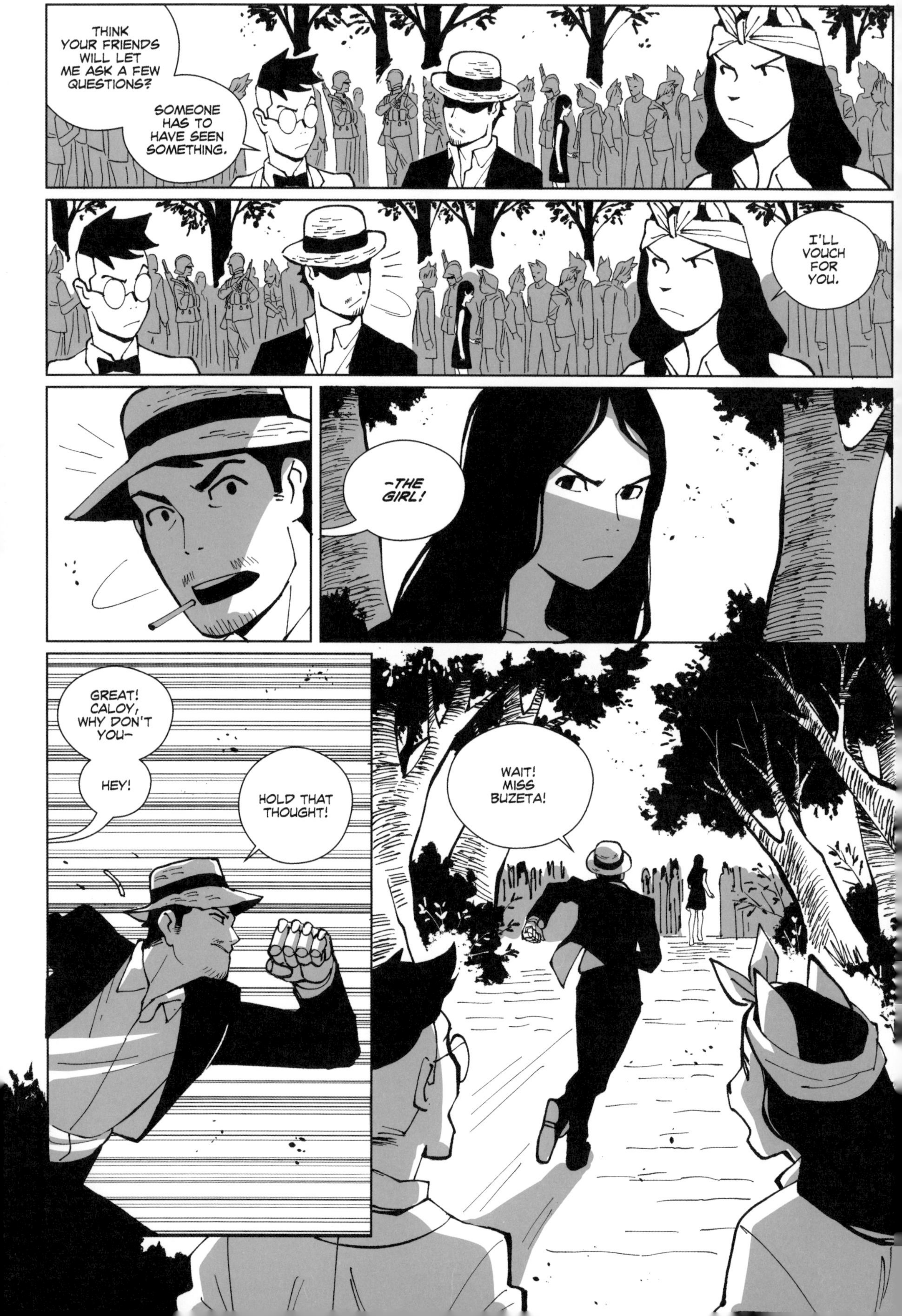
THINK YOUR FRIENDS WILL LET ME ASK A FEW QUESTIONS?
SOMEONE HAS TO HAVE SEEN SOMETHING.
I'LL VOUCH FOR YOU.
-THE GIRL!
GREAT! CALOY, WHY DON'T YOU-
HEY!
HOLD THAT THOUGHT!
WAIT! MISS BUZETA!

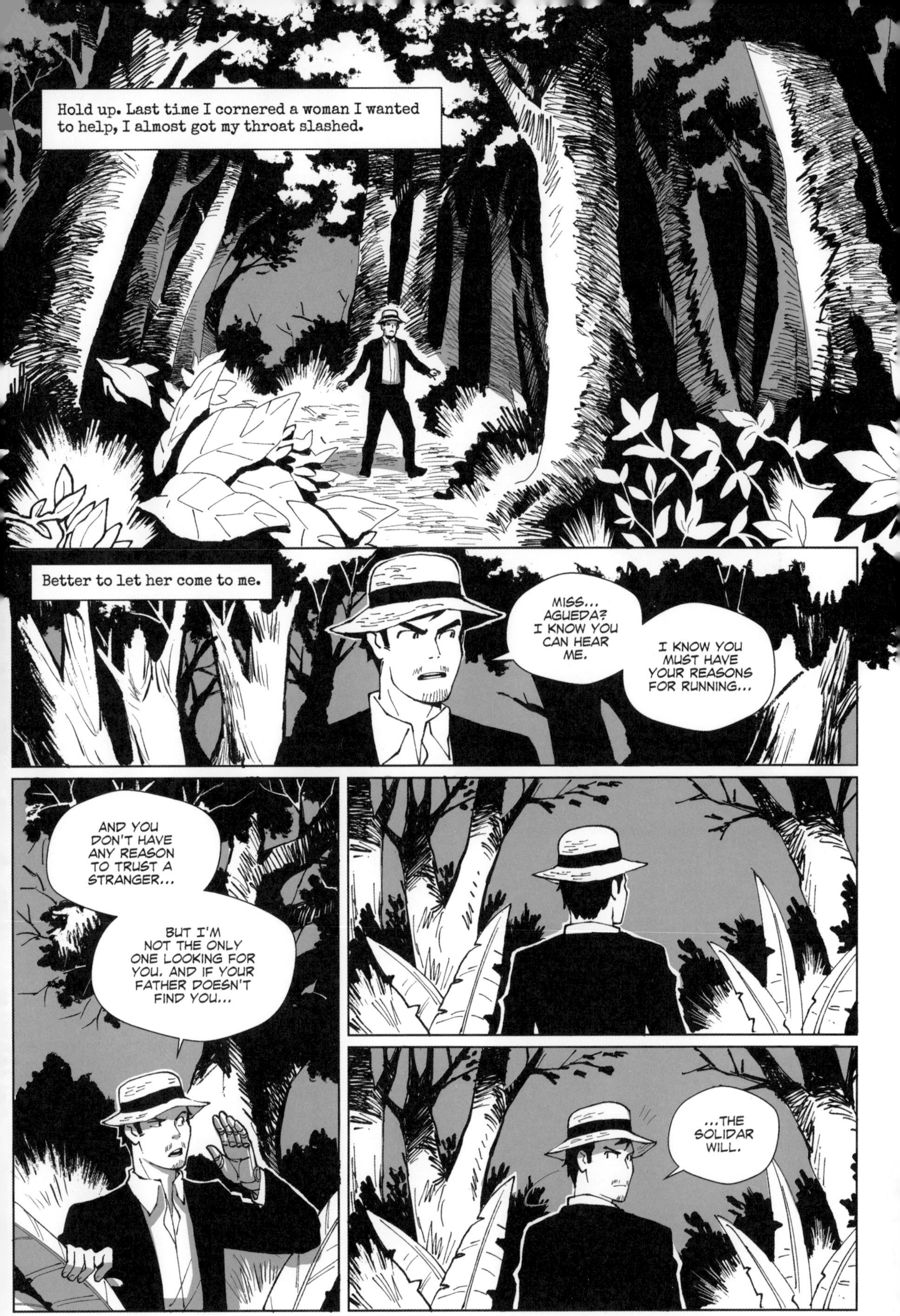
Hold up. Last time I cornered a woman I wanted to help, I almost got my throat slashed.
Better to let her come to me.
MISS... AGUEDA? I KNOW YOU CAN HEAR ME.
I KNOW YOU MUST HAVE YOUR REASONS FOR RUNNING...
AND YOU DON'T HAVE ANY REASON TO TRUST A STRANGER...
BUT I'M NOT THE ONLY ONE LOOKING FOR YOU. AND IF YOUR FATHER DOESN'T FIND YOU...
...THE SOLIDAR WILL.

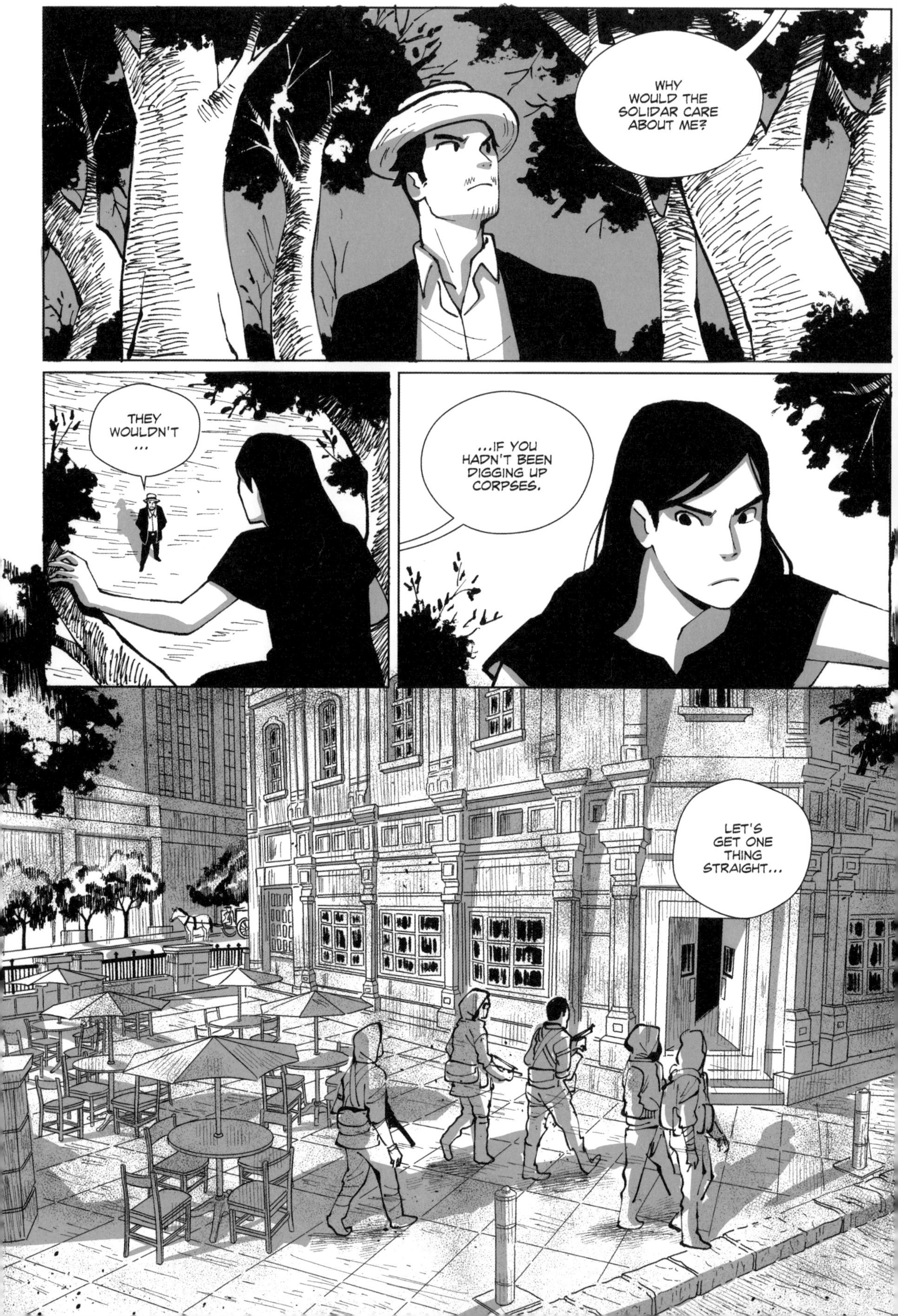
WHY WOULD THE SOLIDAR CARE ABOUT ME?
THEY WOULDN'T ...
...IF YOU HADN'T BEEN DIGGING UP CORPSES.
LET'S GET ONE THING STRAIGHT...

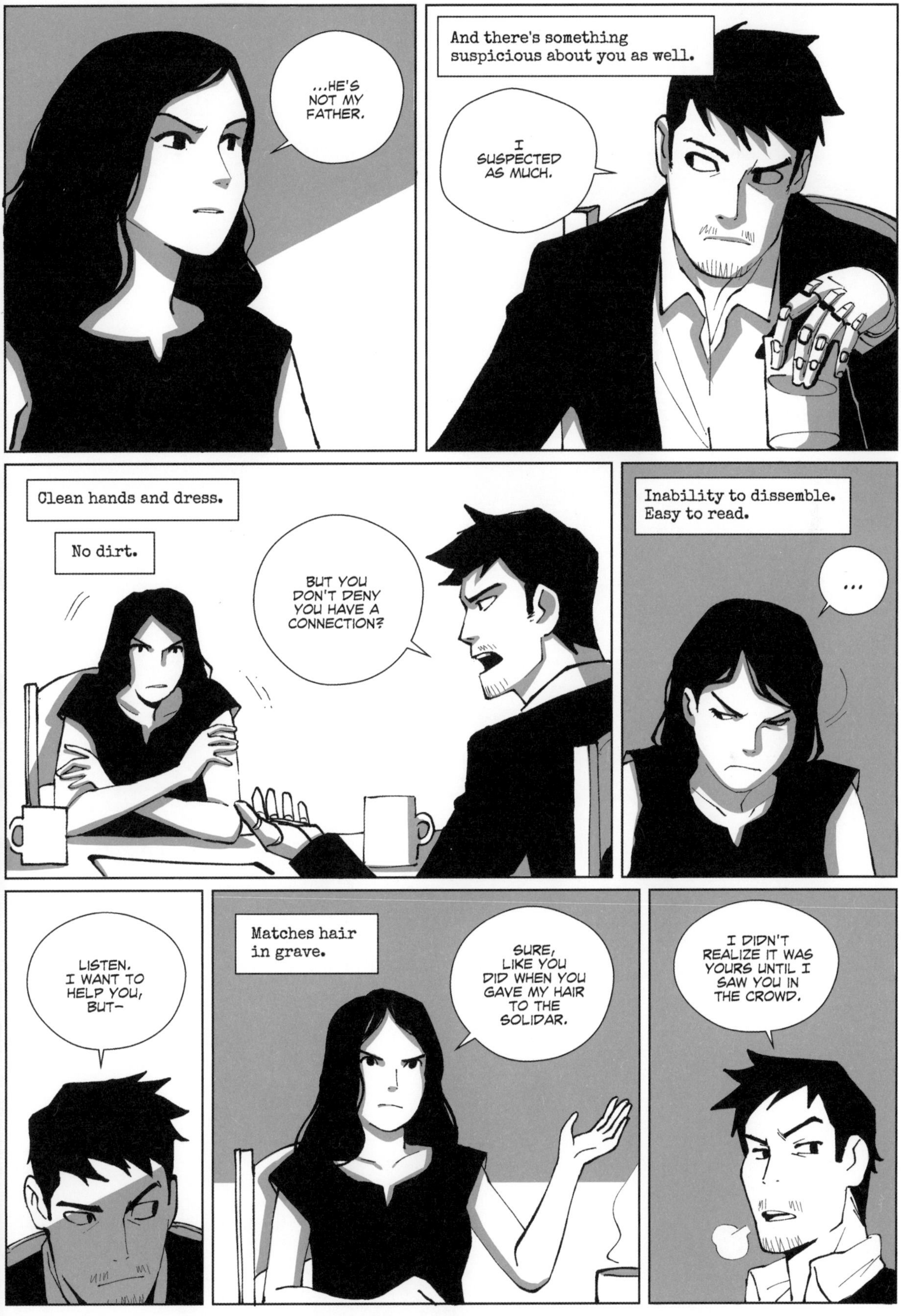
...HE'S NOT MY FATHER.
And there's something suspicious about you as well.
I SUSPECTED AS MUCH.
Clean hands and dress.
No dirt.
BUT YOU DON'T DENY YOU HAVE A CONNECTION?
Inability to dissemble. Easy to read.
...
LISTEN. I WANT TO HELP YOU, BUT-
Matches hair in grave.
SURE, LIKE YOU DID WHEN YOU GAVE MY HAIR TO THE SOLIDAR.
I DIDN'T REALIZE IT WAS YOURS UNTIL I SAW YOU IN THE CROWD.

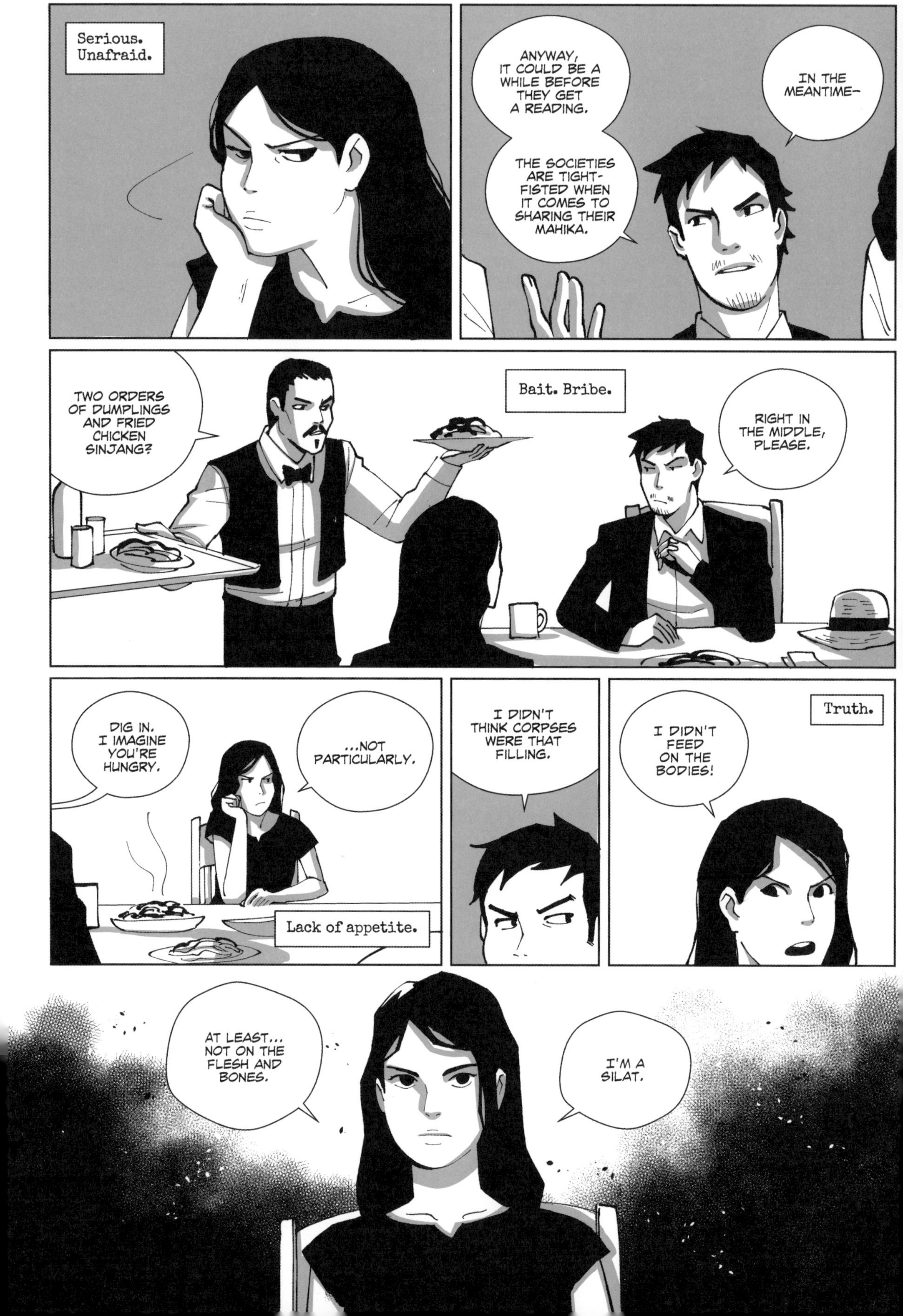
Serious. Unafraid.
ANYWAY, IT COULD BE A WHILE BEFORE THEY GET A READING.
THE SOCIETIES ARE TIGHT-FISTED WHEN IT COMES TO SHARING THEIR MAHIKA.
IN THE MEANTIME–
TWO ORDERS OF DUMPLINGS AND FRIED CHICKEN SINJANG?
Bait. Bribe.
RIGHT IN THE MIDDLE, PLEASE.
DIG IN. I IMAGINE YOU'RE HUNGRY.
...NOT PARTICULARLY.
Lack of appetite.
I DIDN'T THINK CORPSES WERE THAT FILLING.
Truth.
I DIDN'T FEED ON THE BODIES!
AT LEAST... NOT ON THE FLESH AND BONES.
I'M A SILAT.

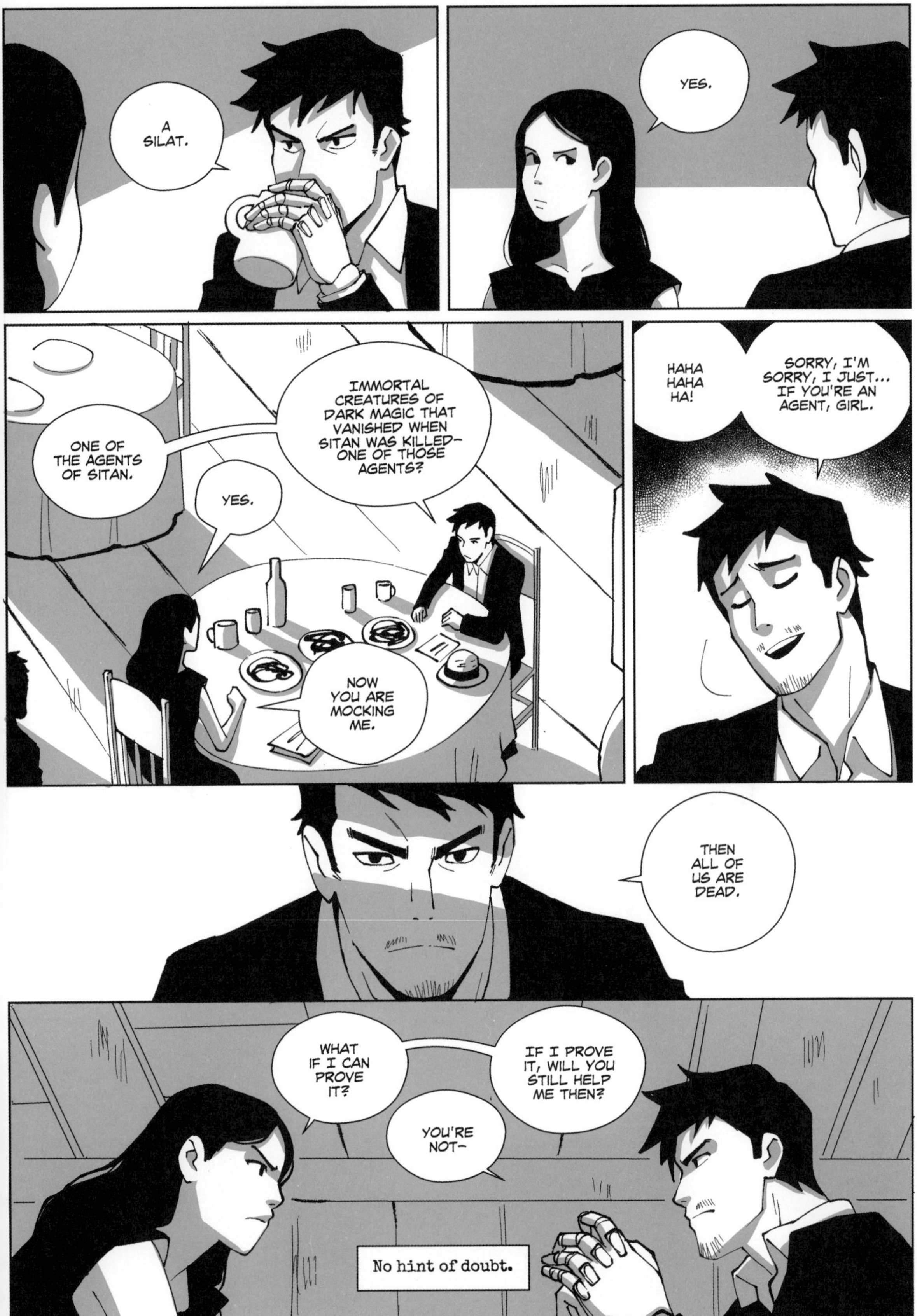
A SILAT.
YES.
ONE OF THE AGENTS OF SITAN.
IMMORTAL CREATURES OF DARK MAGIC THAT VANISHED WHEN SITAN WAS KILLED- ONE OF THOSE AGENTS?
YES.
NOW YOU ARE MOCKING ME.
HAHA HAHA HA!
SORRY, I'M SORRY, I JUST... IF YOU'RE AN AGENT, GIRL.
THEN ALL OF US ARE DEAD.
WHAT IF I CAN PROVE IT?
YOU'RE NOT-
IF I PROVE IT, WILL YOU STILL HELP ME THEN?
No hint of doubt.

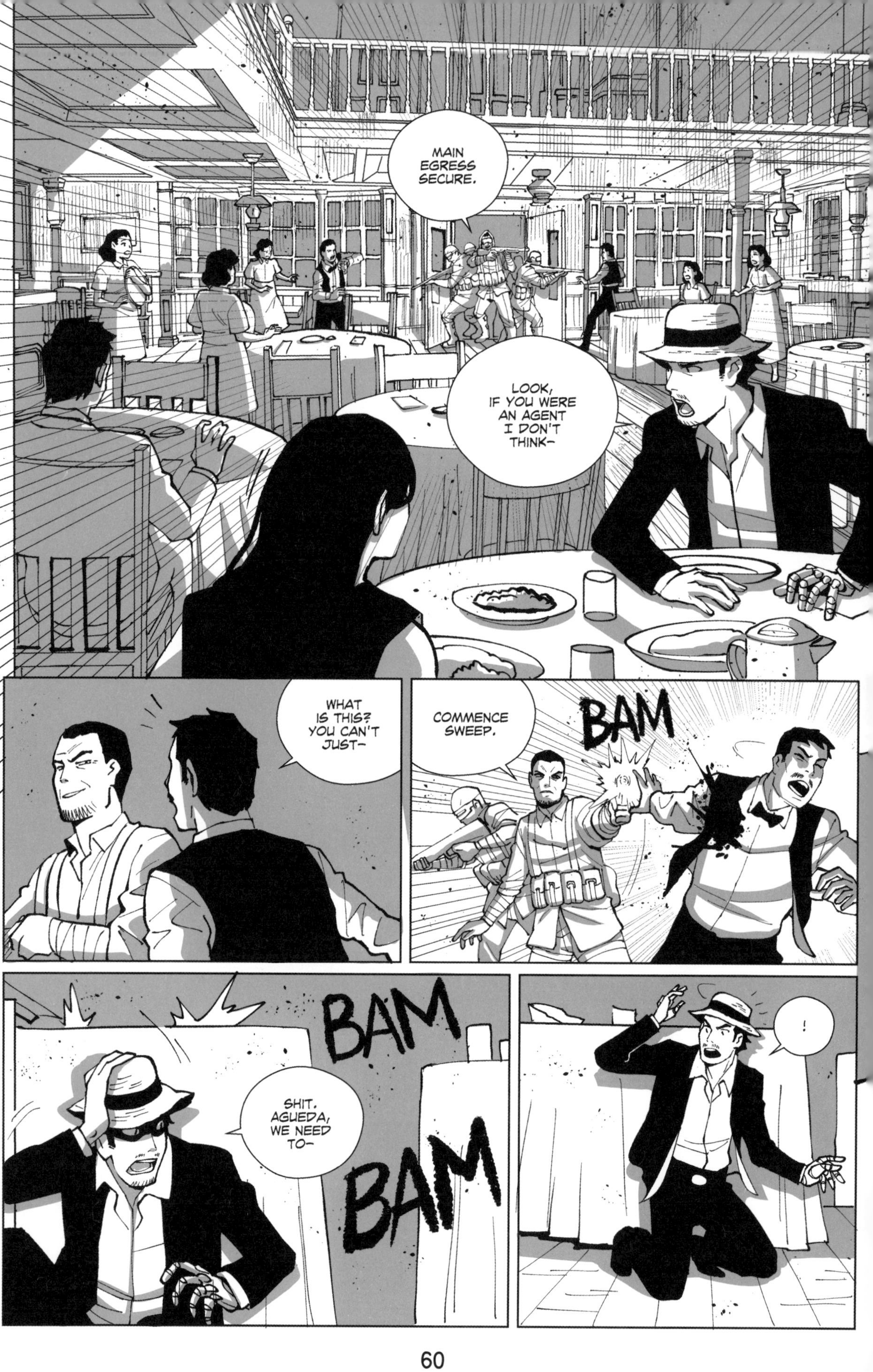
MAIN EGRESS SECURE.
LOOK, IF YOU WERE AN AGENT I DON'T THINK-
WHAT IS THIS? YOU CAN'T JUST-
COMMENCE SWEEP.
BAM
BAM
SHIT. AGUEDA, WE NEED TO-
BAM
!

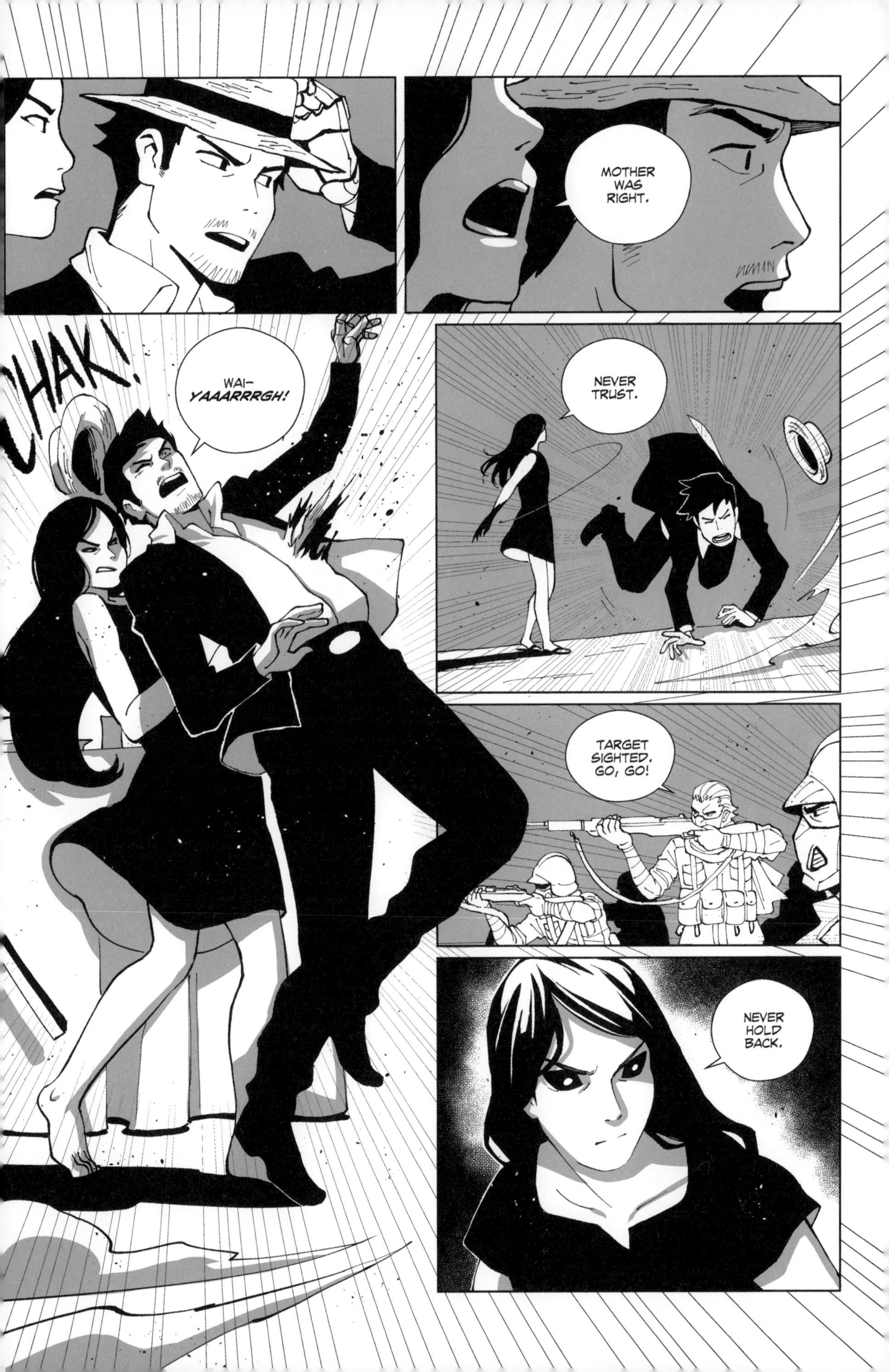

MOTHER WAS RIGHT.
CHAK!
WAI-YAAARRRGH!
NEVER TRUST.
TARGET SIGHTED. GO, GO!
NEVER HOLD BACK.

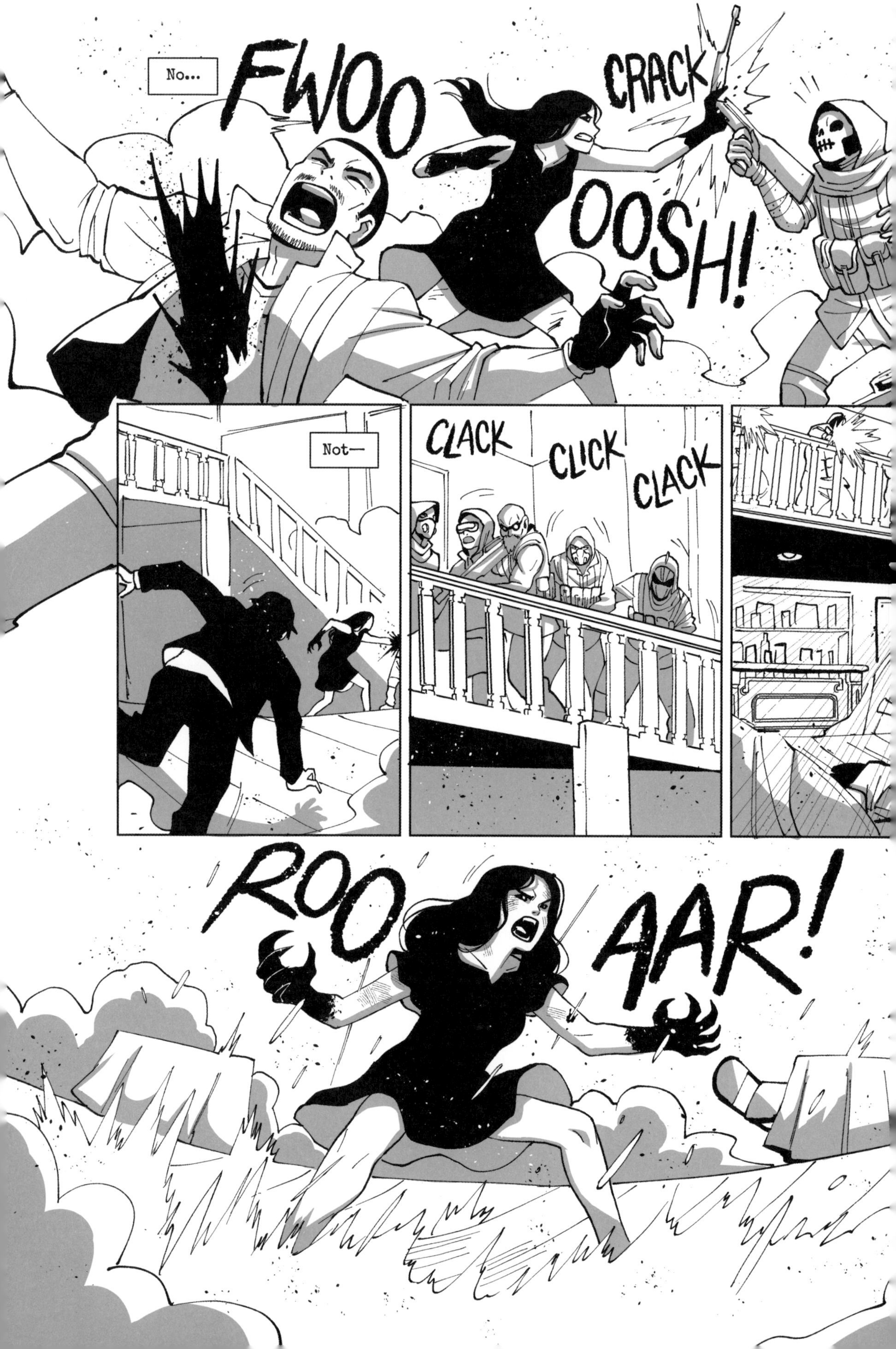
No...
FWOOOOSH!
CRACK
Not—
CLACK
CLICK
CLACK
ROOAAR!

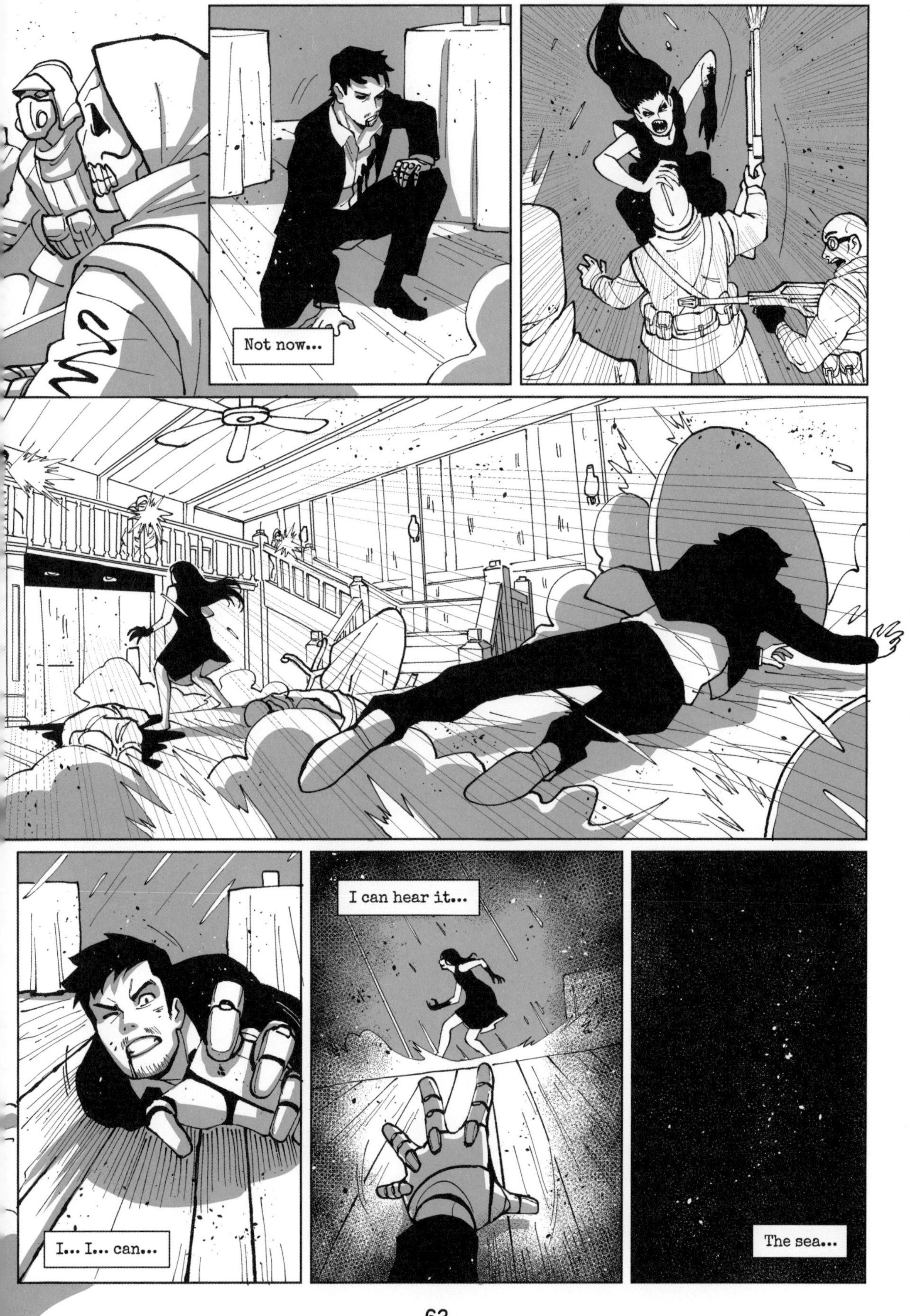
Not now...
I... I... can...
I can hear it...
The sea...

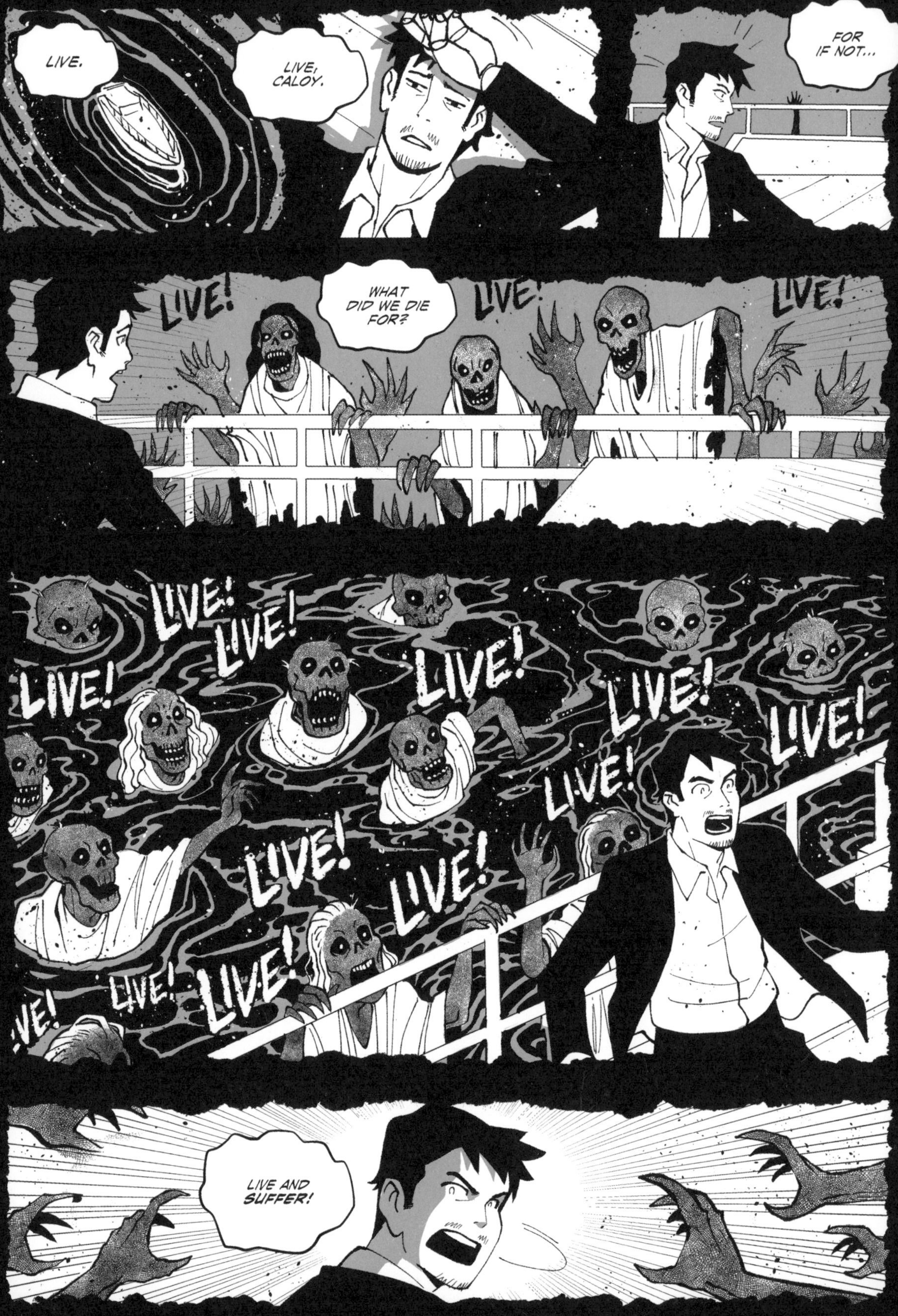
LIVE.
LIVE, CALOY.
FOR IF NOT...
LIVE!
WHAT DID WE DIE FOR?
LIVE!
LIVE!
LIVE!
LIVE!
LIVE!
LIVE!
LIVE!
LIVE!
LIVE!
LIVE!
LIVE!
LIVE!
LIVE!
LIVE!
LIVE AND SUFFER!

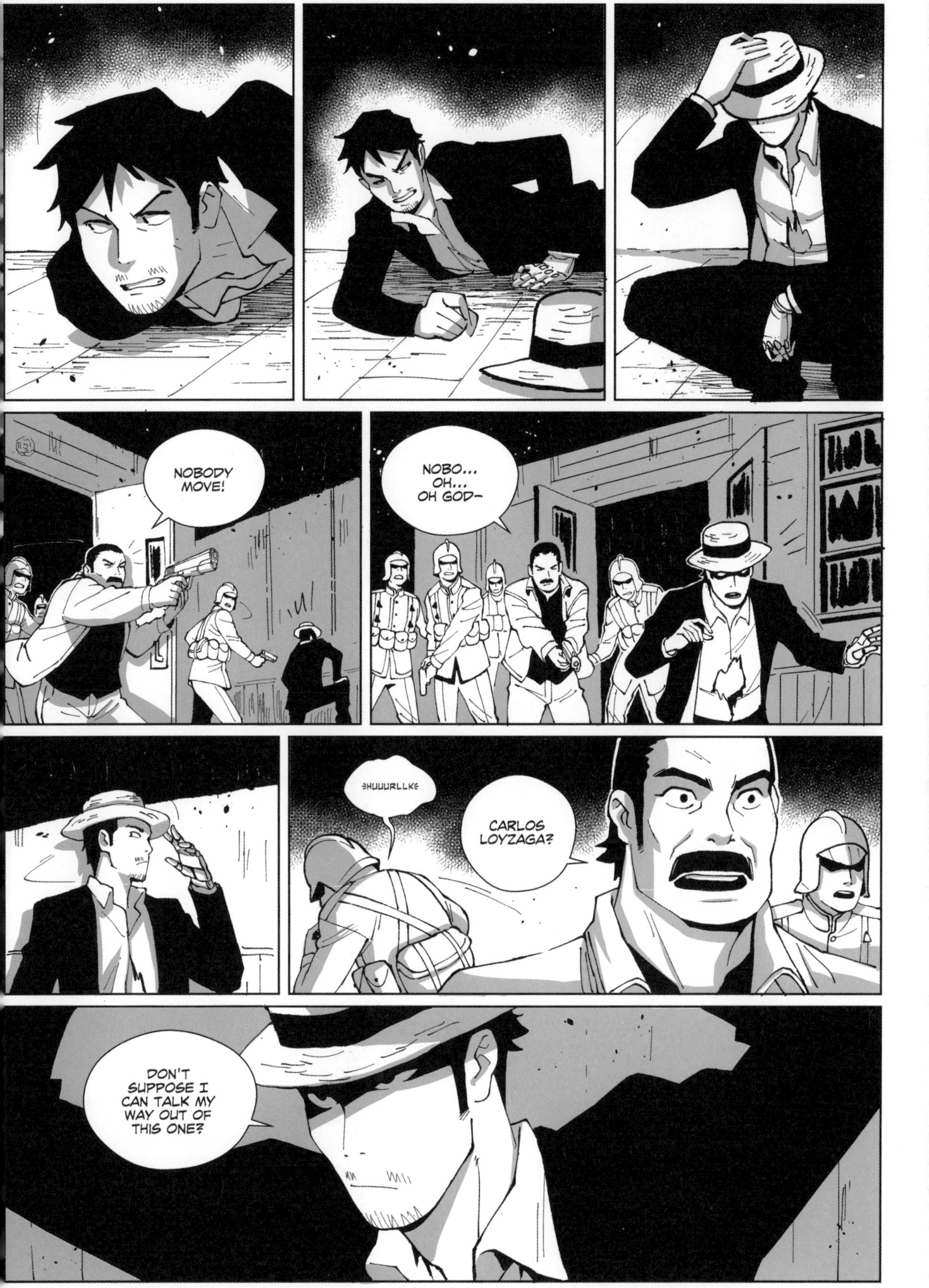

NOBODY MOVE!
NOBO... OH... OH GOD-
=HUUURLLK=
CARLOS LOYZAGA?
DON'T SUPPOSE I CAN TALK MY WAY OUT OF THIS ONE?

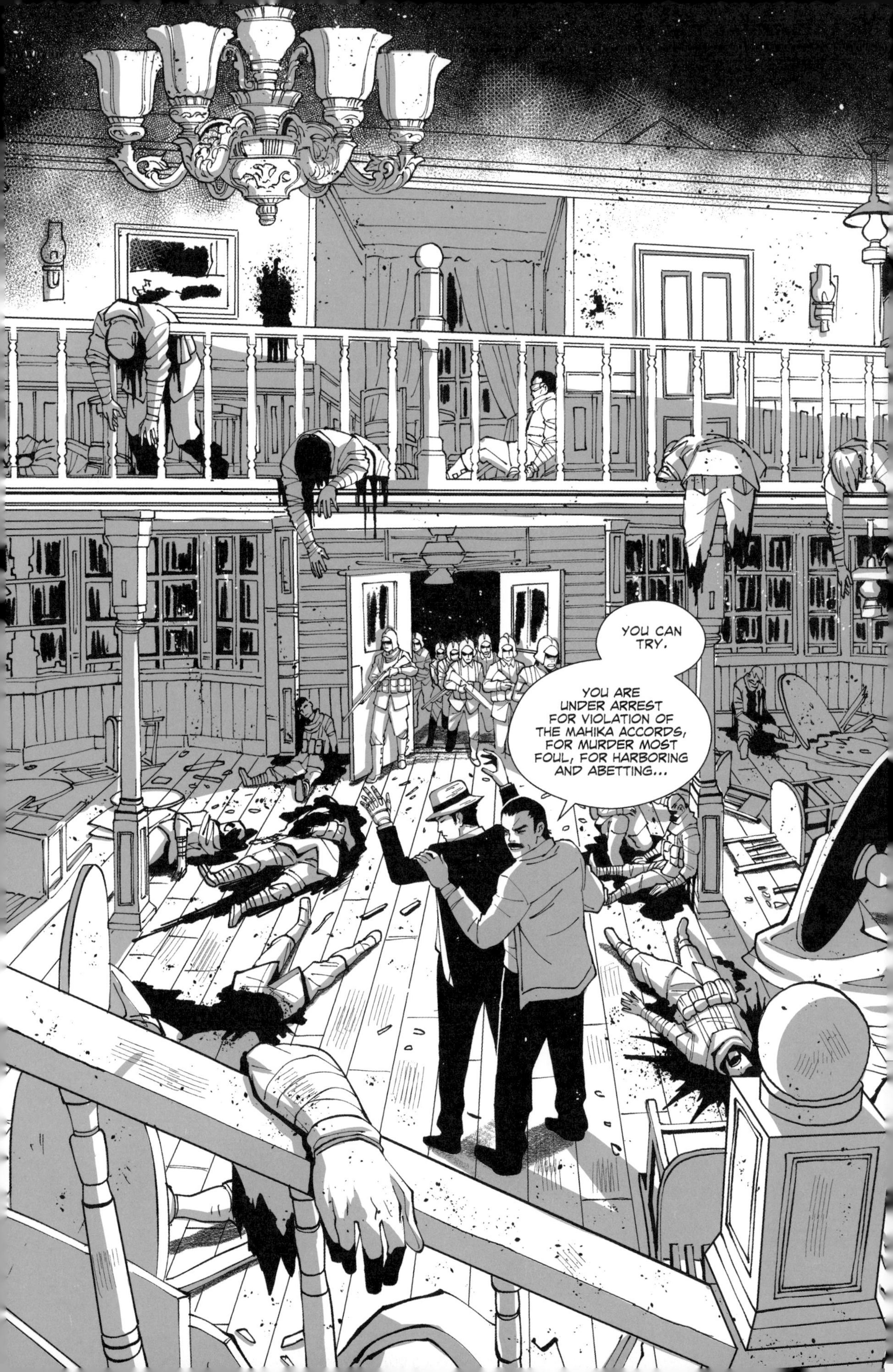
YOU CAN TRY.
YOU ARE UNDER ARREST FOR VIOLATION OF THE MAHIKA ACCORDS, FOR MURDER MOST FOUL, FOR HARBORING AND ABETTING...

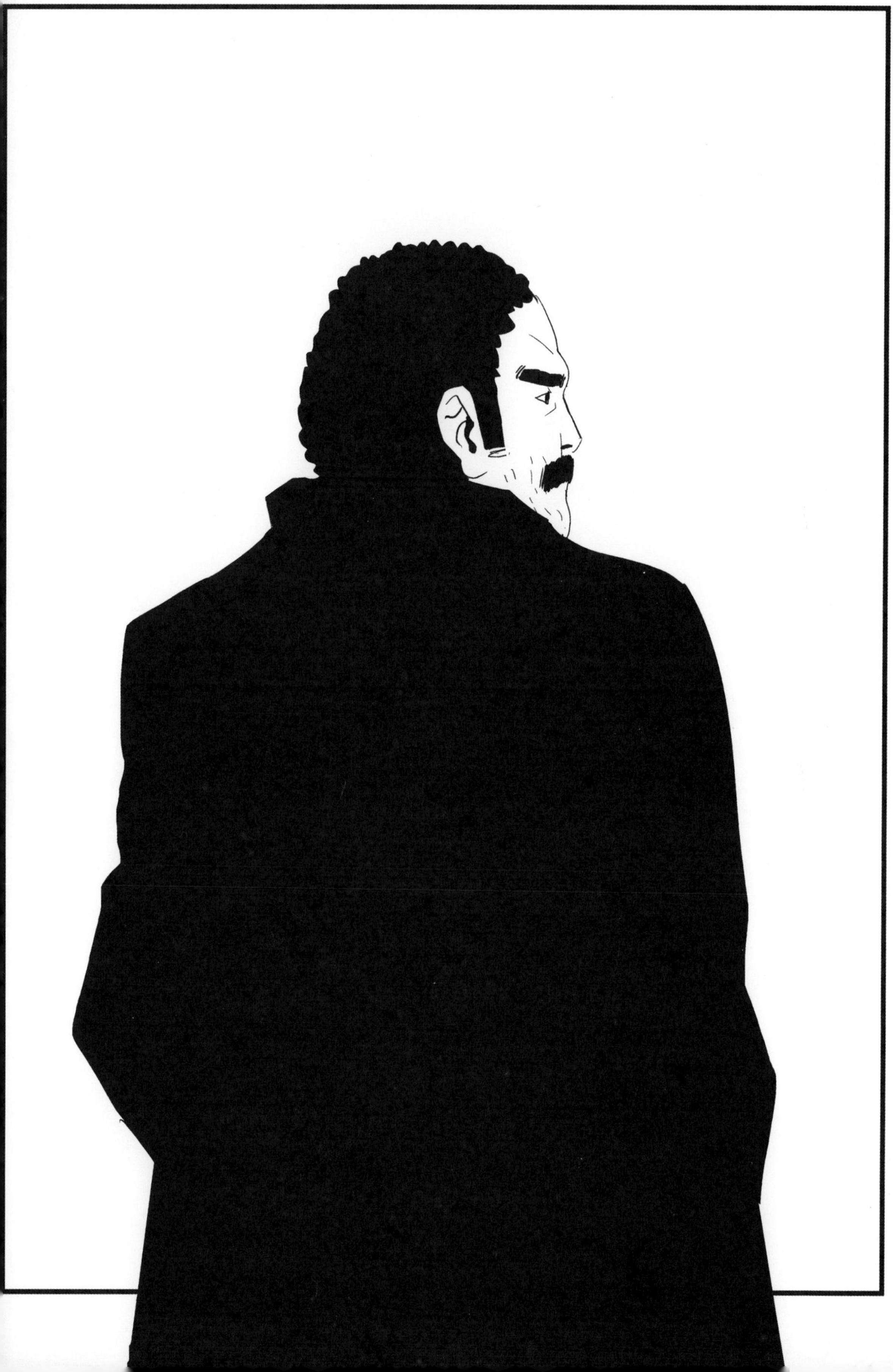

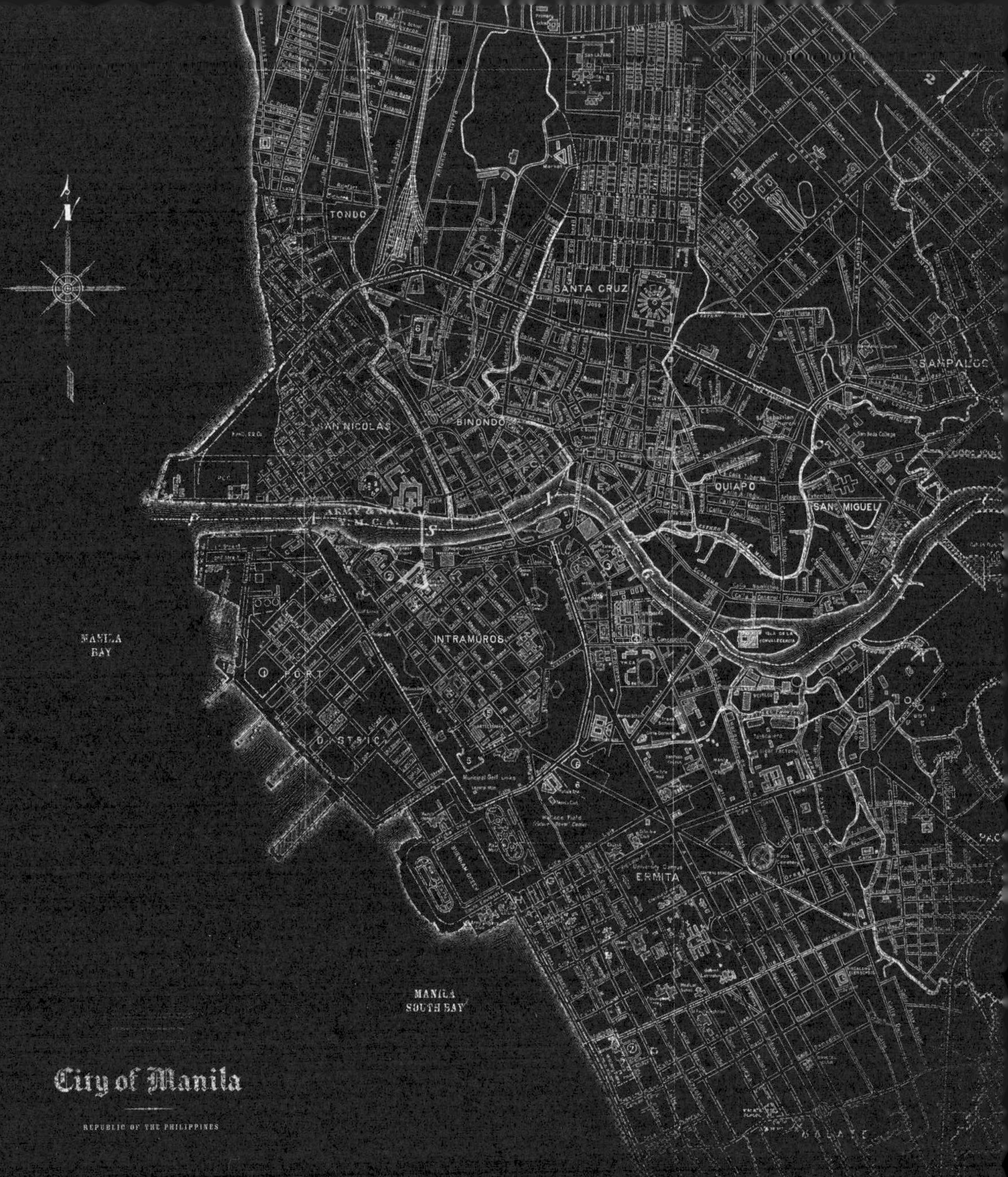
TONDO
SANTA CRUZ
SAMPALOC
SAN NICOLAS
BINONDO
QUIAPO
SAN MIGUEL
MANILA
BAY
INTRAMUROS
PORT
DISTRICT
ERMITA
MANILA
SOUTH BAY
City of Manila
REPUBLIC OF THE PHILIPPINES

THE CASE OF
THE CEMETERY GIRL

CHAPTER III

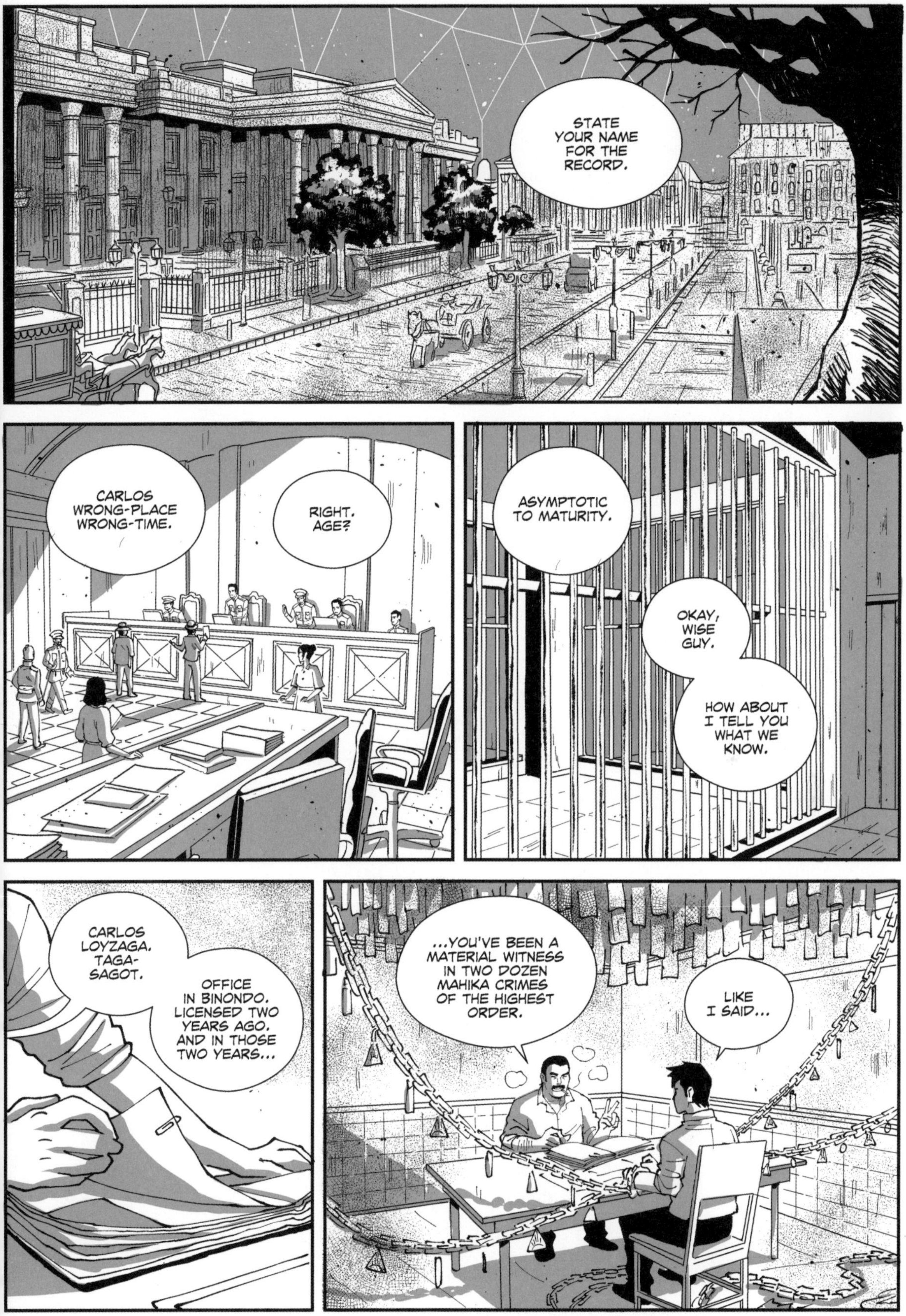
STATE YOUR NAME FOR THE RECORD.
CARLOS WRONG-PLACE WRONG-TIME.
RIGHT. AGE?
ASYMPTOTIC TO MATURITY.
OKAY, WISE GUY.
HOW ABOUT I TELL YOU WHAT WE KNOW.
CARLOS LOYZAGA. TAGA-SAGOT.
OFFICE IN BINONDO. LICENSED TWO YEARS AGO. AND IN THOSE TWO YEARS...
...YOU'VE BEEN A MATERIAL WITNESS IN TWO DOZEN MAHIKA CRIMES OF THE HIGHEST ORDER.
LIKE I SAID...

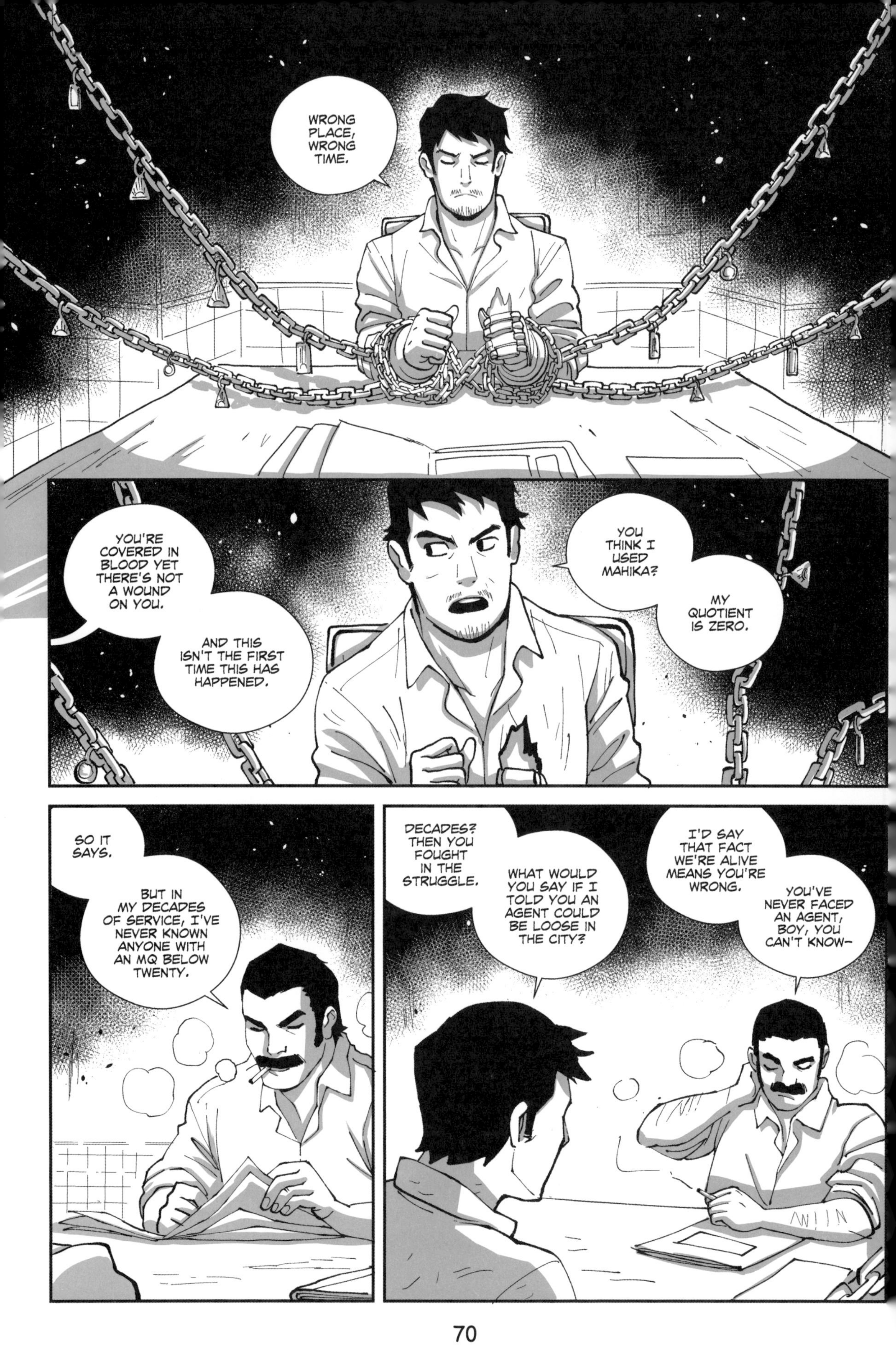
WRONG PLACE, WRONG TIME.
YOU'RE COVERED IN BLOOD YET THERE'S NOT A WOUND ON YOU.
AND THIS ISN'T THE FIRST TIME THIS HAS HAPPENED.
YOU THINK I USED MAHIKA?
MY QUOTIENT IS ZERO.
SO IT SAYS.
BUT IN MY DECADES OF SERVICE, I'VE NEVER KNOWN ANYONE WITH AN MQ BELOW TWENTY.
DECADES? THEN YOU FOUGHT IN THE STRUGGLE.
WHAT WOULD YOU SAY IF I TOLD YOU AN AGENT COULD BE LOOSE IN THE CITY?
I'D SAY THAT FACT WE'RE ALIVE MEANS YOU'RE WRONG.
YOU'VE NEVER FACED AN AGENT, BOY, YOU CAN'T KNOW–

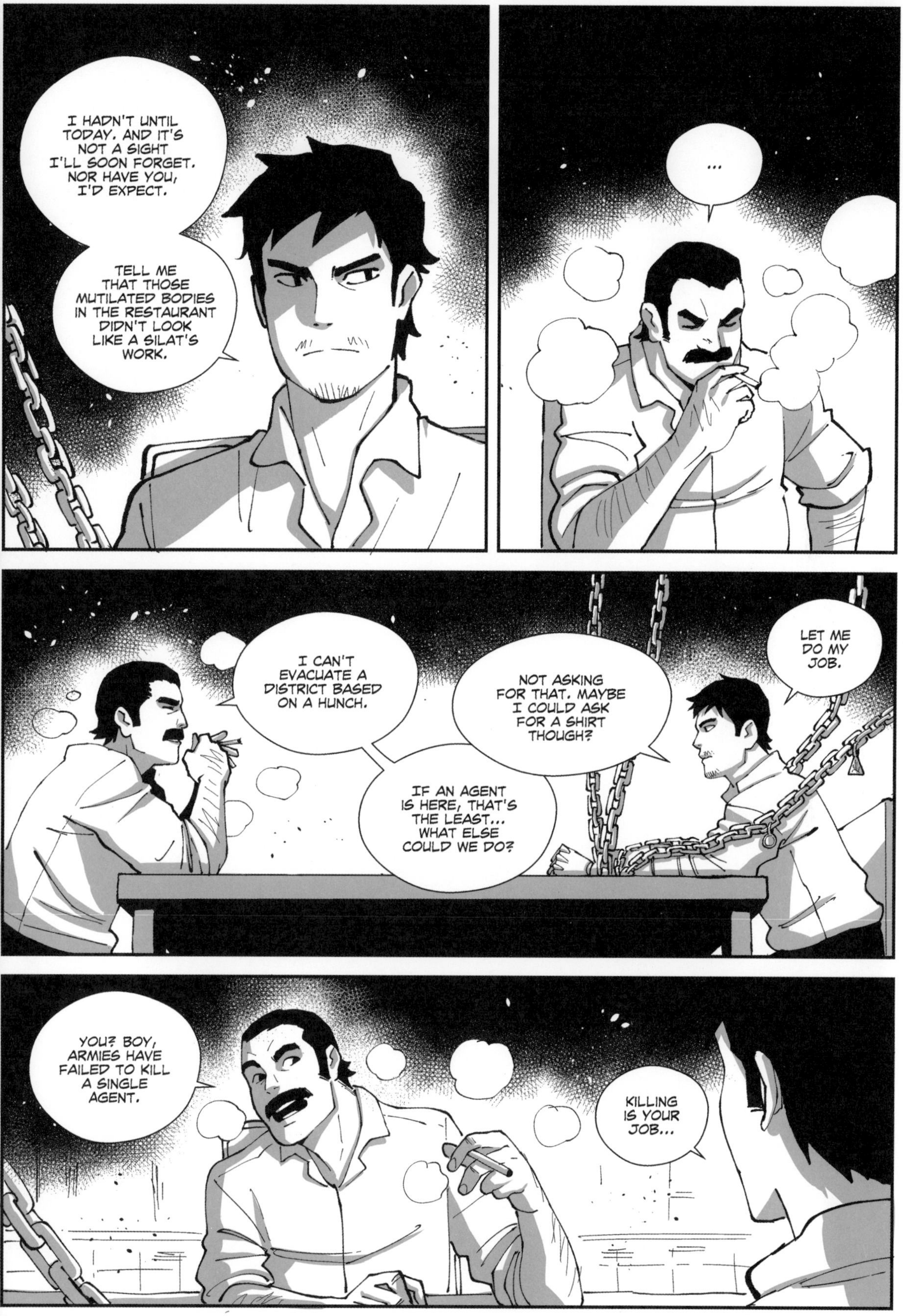
I HADN'T UNTIL TODAY. AND IT'S NOT A SIGHT I'LL SOON FORGET. NOR HAVE YOU, I'D EXPECT.
TELL ME THAT THOSE MUTILATED BODIES IN THE RESTAURANT DIDN'T LOOK LIKE A SILAT'S WORK.
...
I CAN'T EVACUATE A DISTRICT BASED ON A HUNCH.
NOT ASKING FOR THAT. MAYBE I COULD ASK FOR A SHIRT THOUGH?
LET ME DO MY JOB.
IF AN AGENT IS HERE, THAT'S THE LEAST... WHAT ELSE COULD WE DO?
YOU? BOY, ARMIES HAVE FAILED TO KILL A SINGLE AGENT.
KILLING IS YOUR JOB...

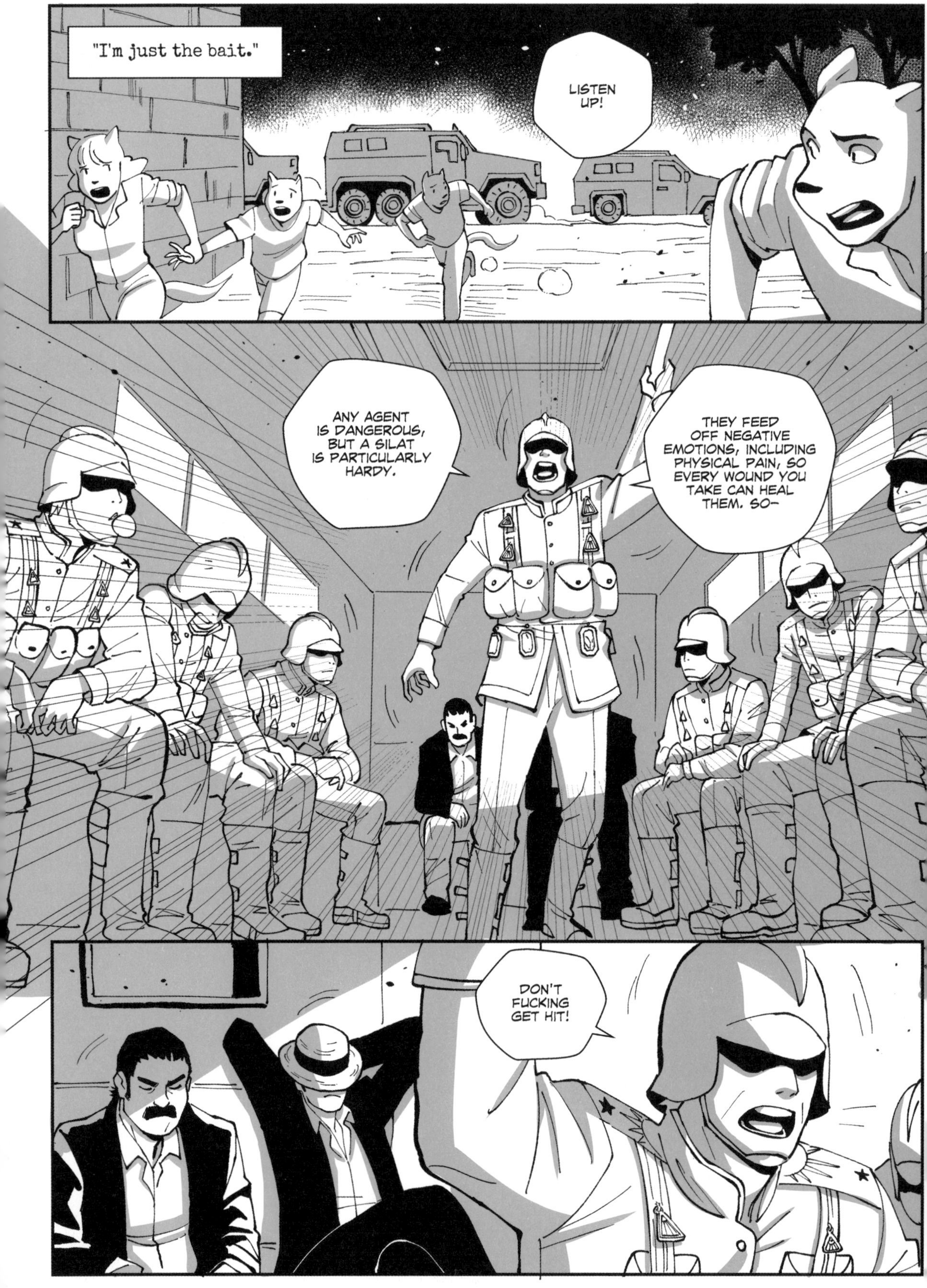
"I'm just the bait."
LISTEN UP!
ANY AGENT IS DANGEROUS, BUT A SILAT IS PARTICULARLY HARDY.
THEY FEED OFF NEGATIVE EMOTIONS, INCLUDING PHYSICAL PAIN, SO EVERY WOUND YOU TAKE CAN HEAL THEM. SO–
DON'T FUCKING GET HIT!

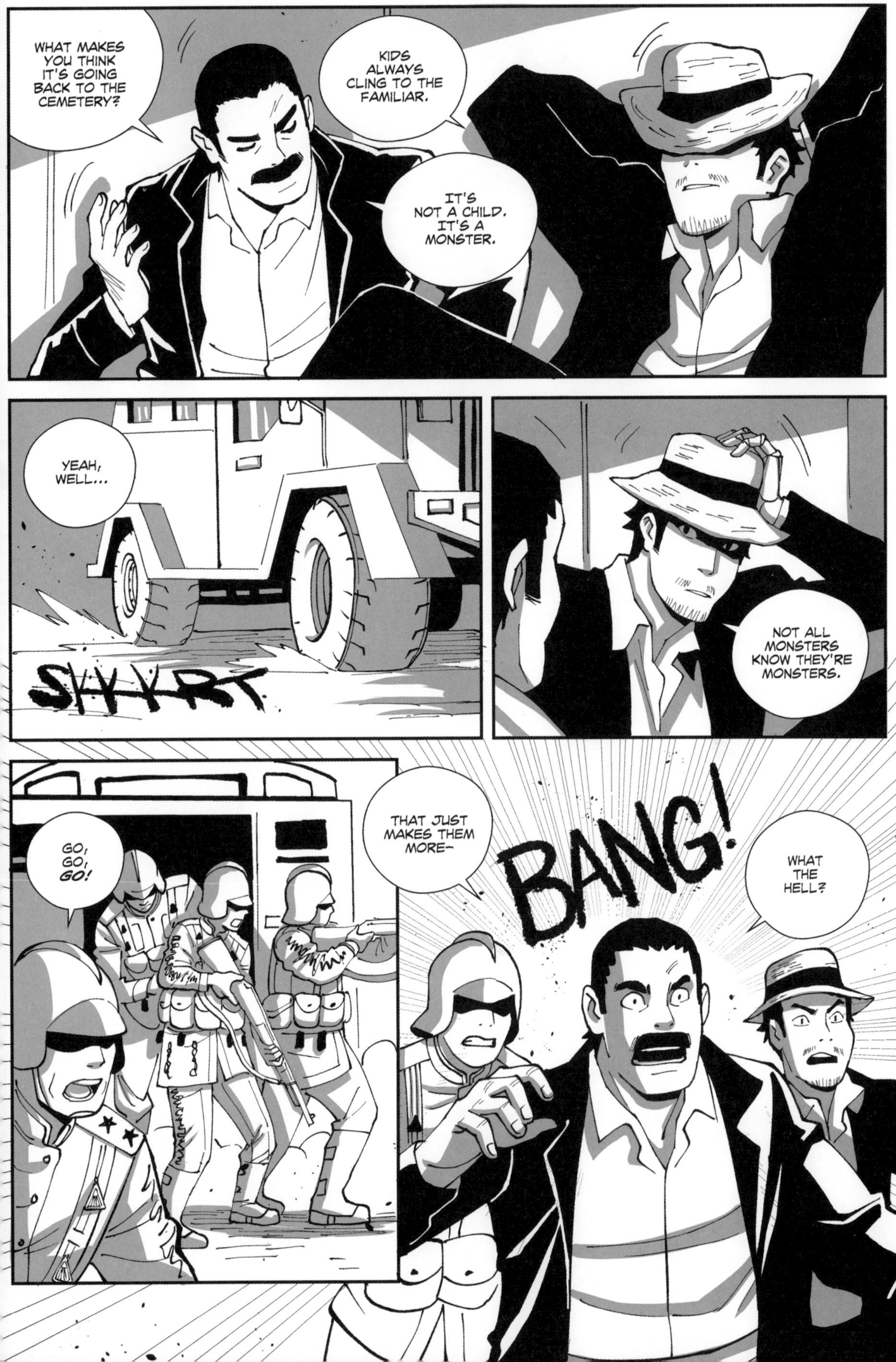
WHAT MAKES YOU THINK IT'S GOING BACK TO THE CEMETERY?
KIDS ALWAYS CLING TO THE FAMILIAR.
IT'S NOT A CHILD. IT'S A MONSTER.
YEAH, WELL...
SKKRT
NOT ALL MONSTERS KNOW THEY'RE MONSTERS.
GO, GO, GO!
THAT JUST MAKES THEM MORE–
BANG!
WHAT THE HELL?

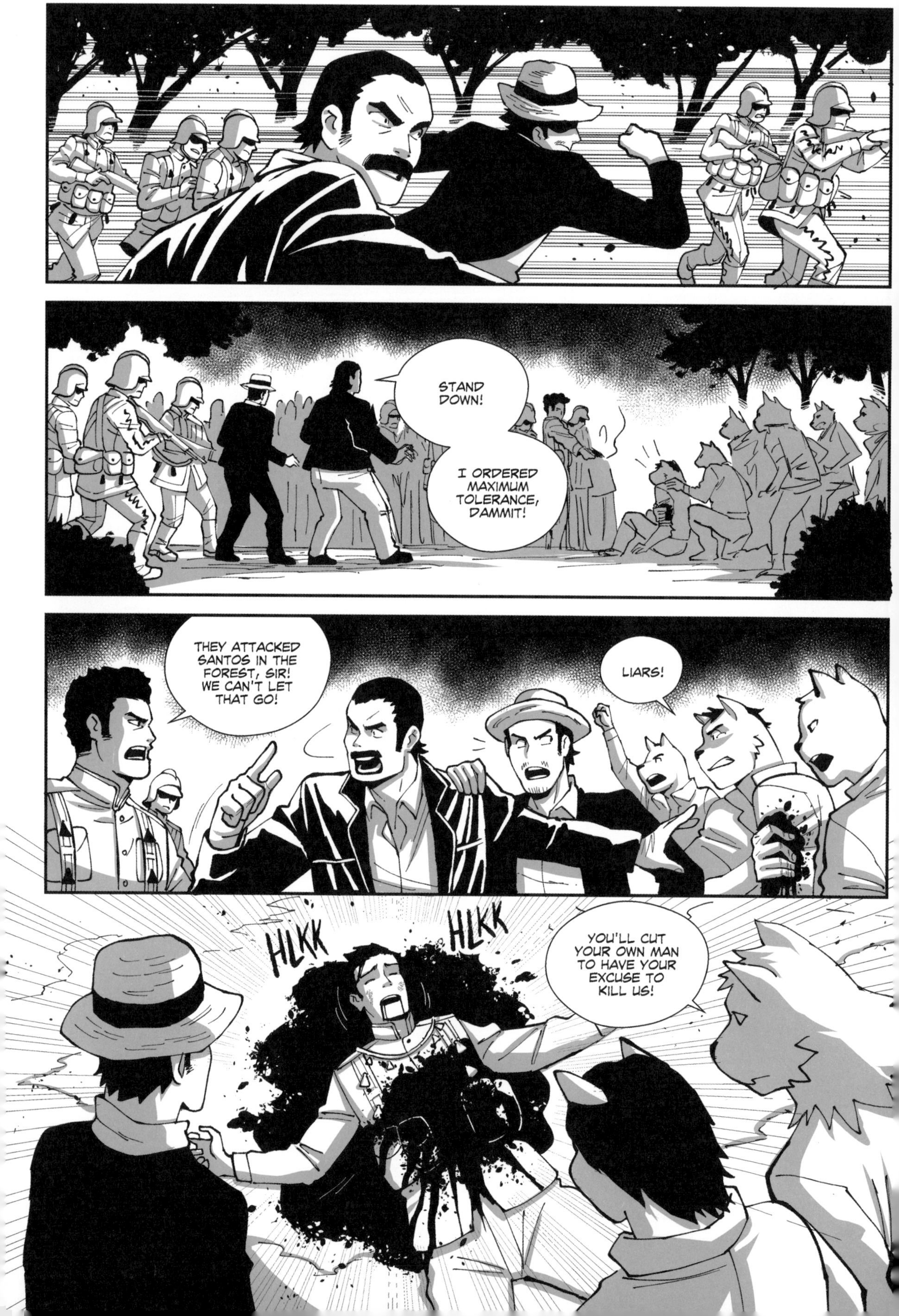
STAND DOWN!
I ORDERED MAXIMUM TOLERANCE, DAMMIT!
THEY ATTACKED SANTOS IN THE FOREST, SIR! WE CAN'T LET THAT GO!
LIARS!
HLKK
HLKK
YOU'LL CUT YOUR OWN MAN TO HAVE YOUR EXCUSE TO KILL US!

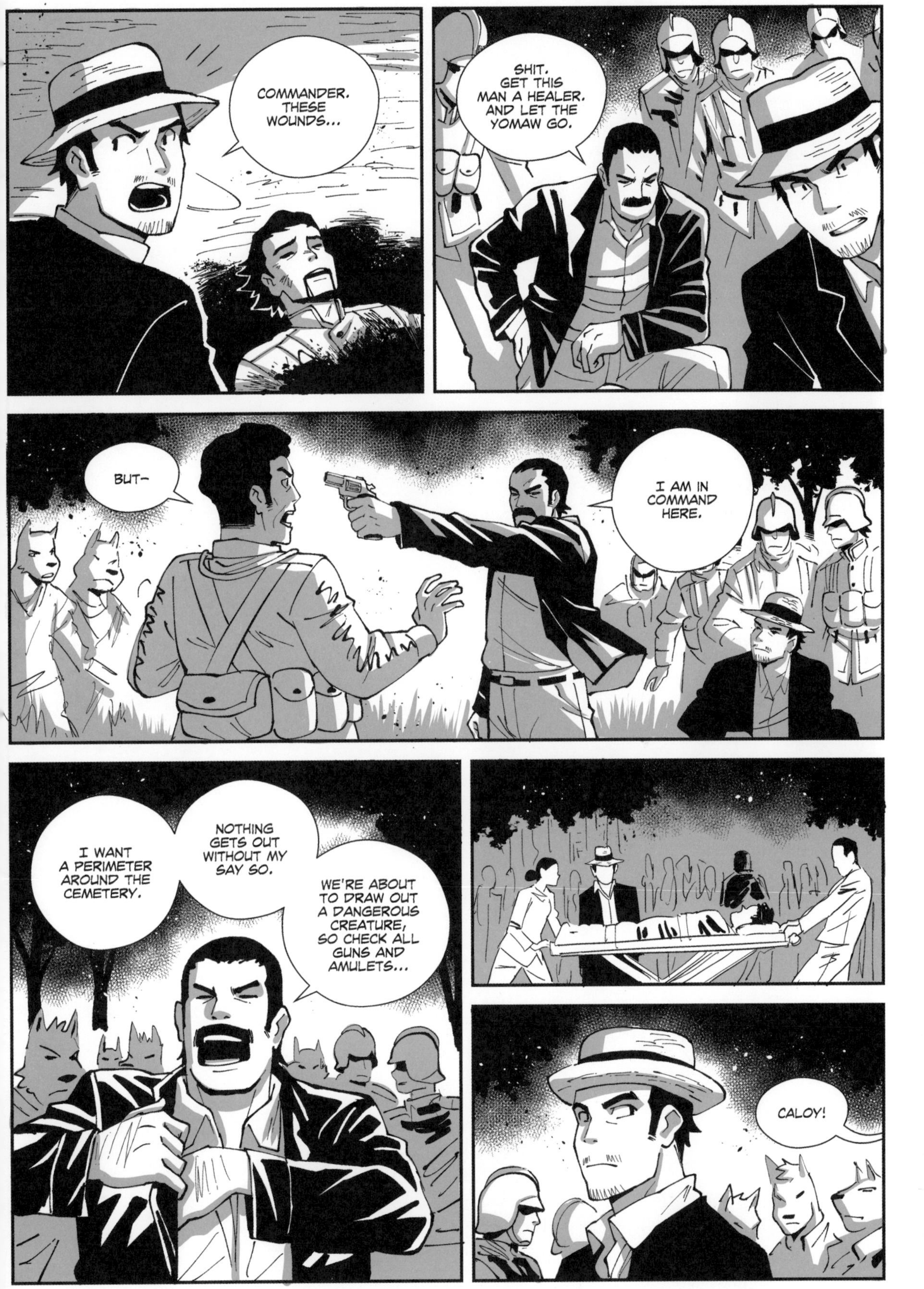
COMMANDER. THESE WOUNDS...
SHIT. GET THIS MAN A HEALER. AND LET THE YOMAW GO.
BUT-
I AM IN COMMAND HERE.
I WANT A PERIMETER AROUND THE CEMETERY.
NOTHING GETS OUT WITHOUT MY SAY SO.
WE'RE ABOUT TO DRAW OUT A DANGEROUS CREATURE, SO CHECK ALL GUNS AND AMULETS...
CALOY!

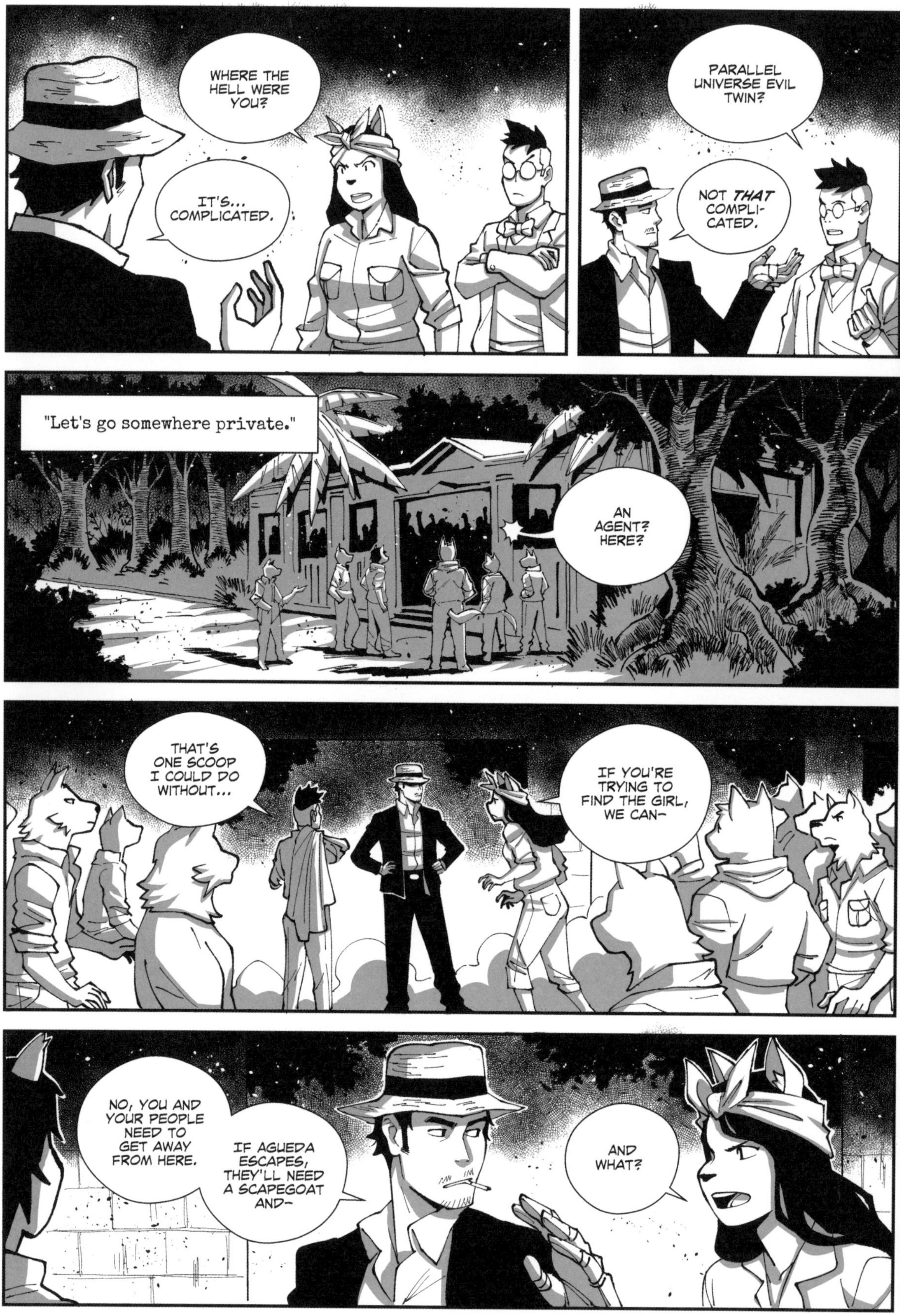
WHERE THE HELL WERE YOU?
IT'S... COMPLICATED.
PARALLEL UNIVERSE EVIL TWIN?
NOT *THAT* COMPLICATED.
"Let's go somewhere private."
AN AGENT? HERE?
THAT'S ONE SCOOP I COULD DO WITHOUT...
IF YOU'RE TRYING TO FIND THE GIRL, WE CAN-
NO, YOU AND YOUR PEOPLE NEED TO GET AWAY FROM HERE.
IF AGUEDA ESCAPES, THEY'LL NEED A SCAPEGOAT AND-
AND WHAT?

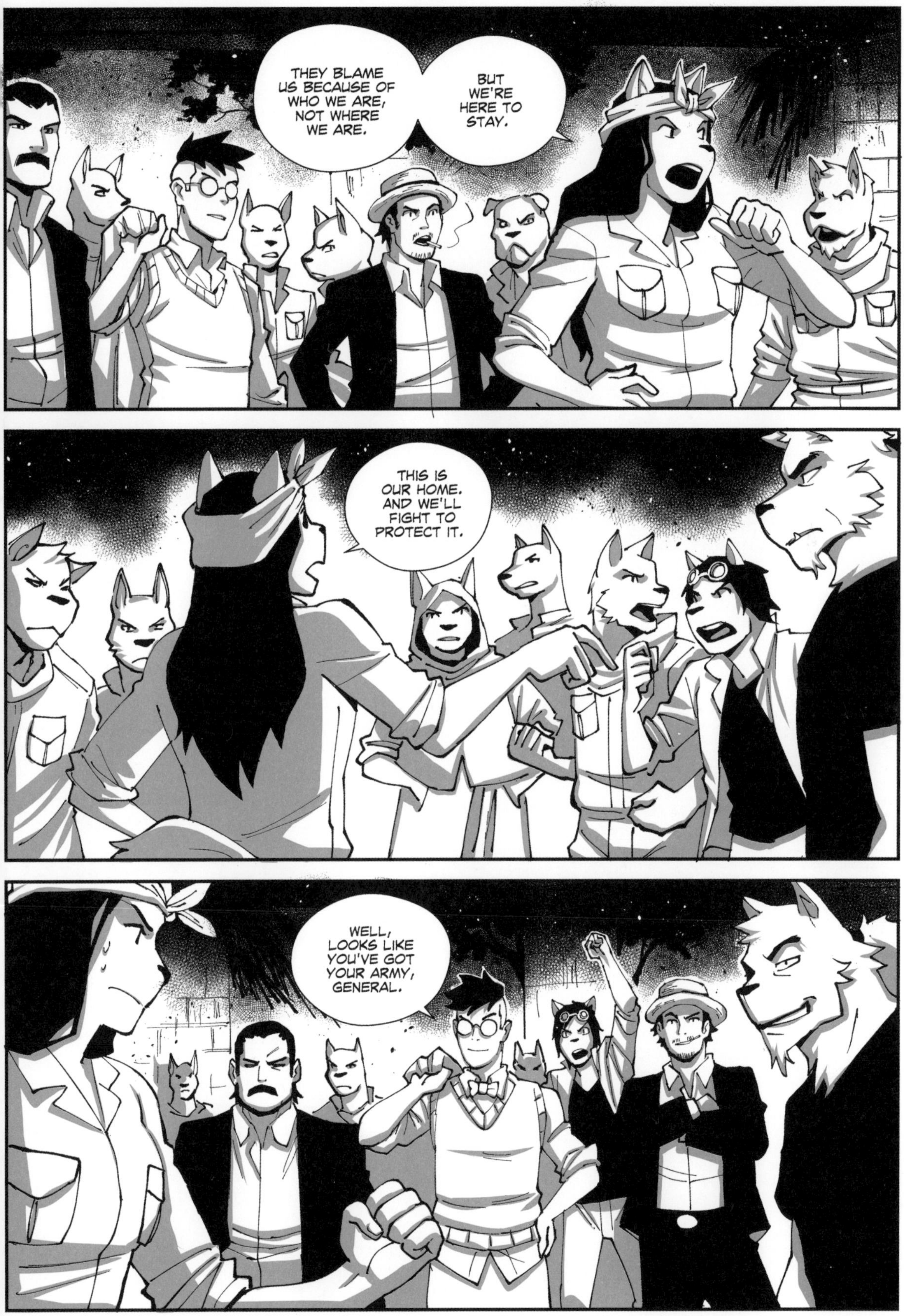
THEY BLAME US BECAUSE OF WHO WE ARE, NOT WHERE WE ARE.
BUT WE'RE HERE TO STAY.
THIS IS OUR HOME. AND WE'LL FIGHT TO PROTECT IT.
WELL, LOOKS LIKE YOU'VE GOT YOUR ARMY, GENERAL.

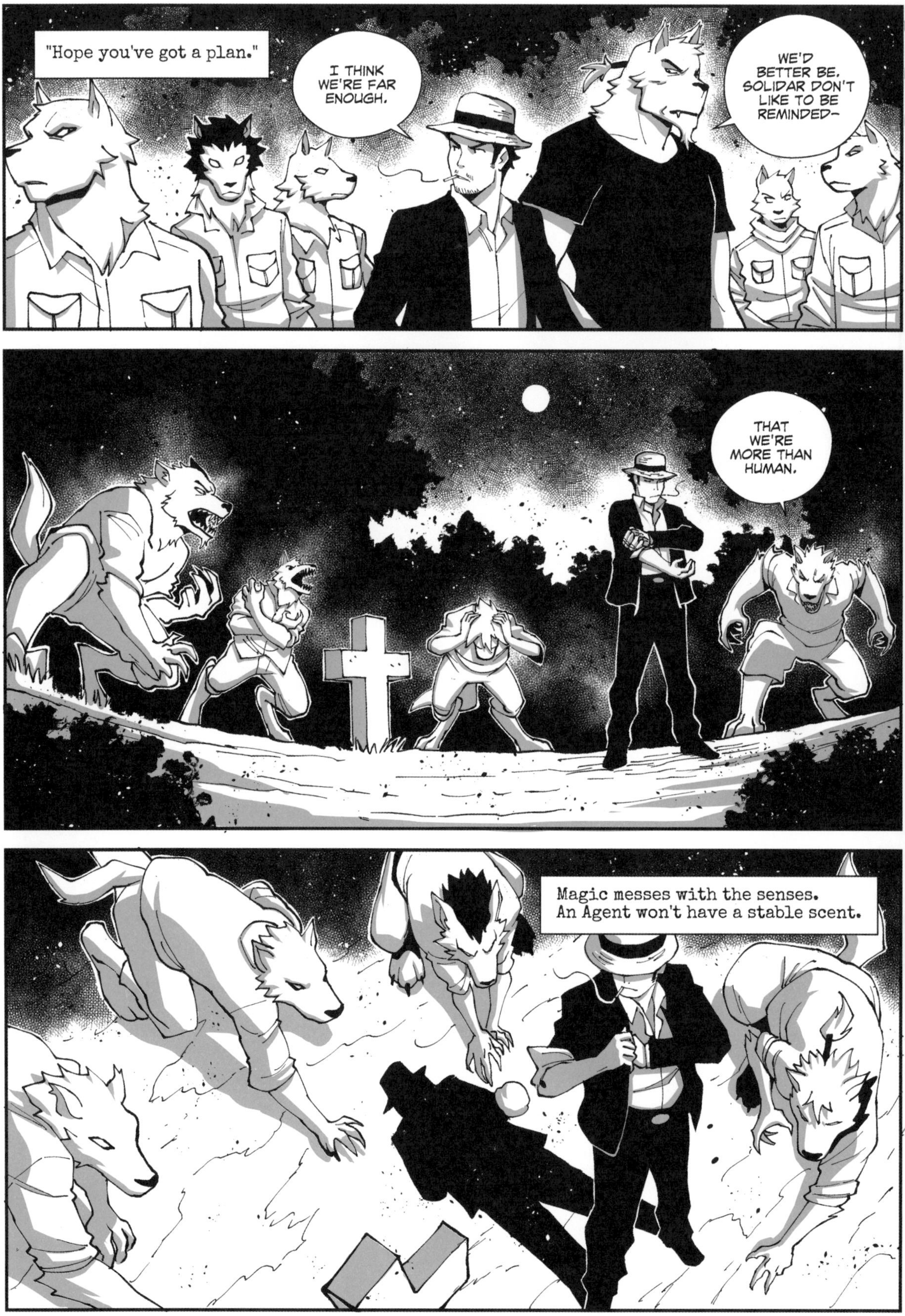
"Hope you've got a plan."
I THINK WE'RE FAR ENOUGH.
WE'D BETTER BE. SOLIDAR DON'T LIKE TO BE REMINDED–
THAT WE'RE MORE THAN HUMAN.
Magic messes with the senses. An Agent won't have a stable scent.

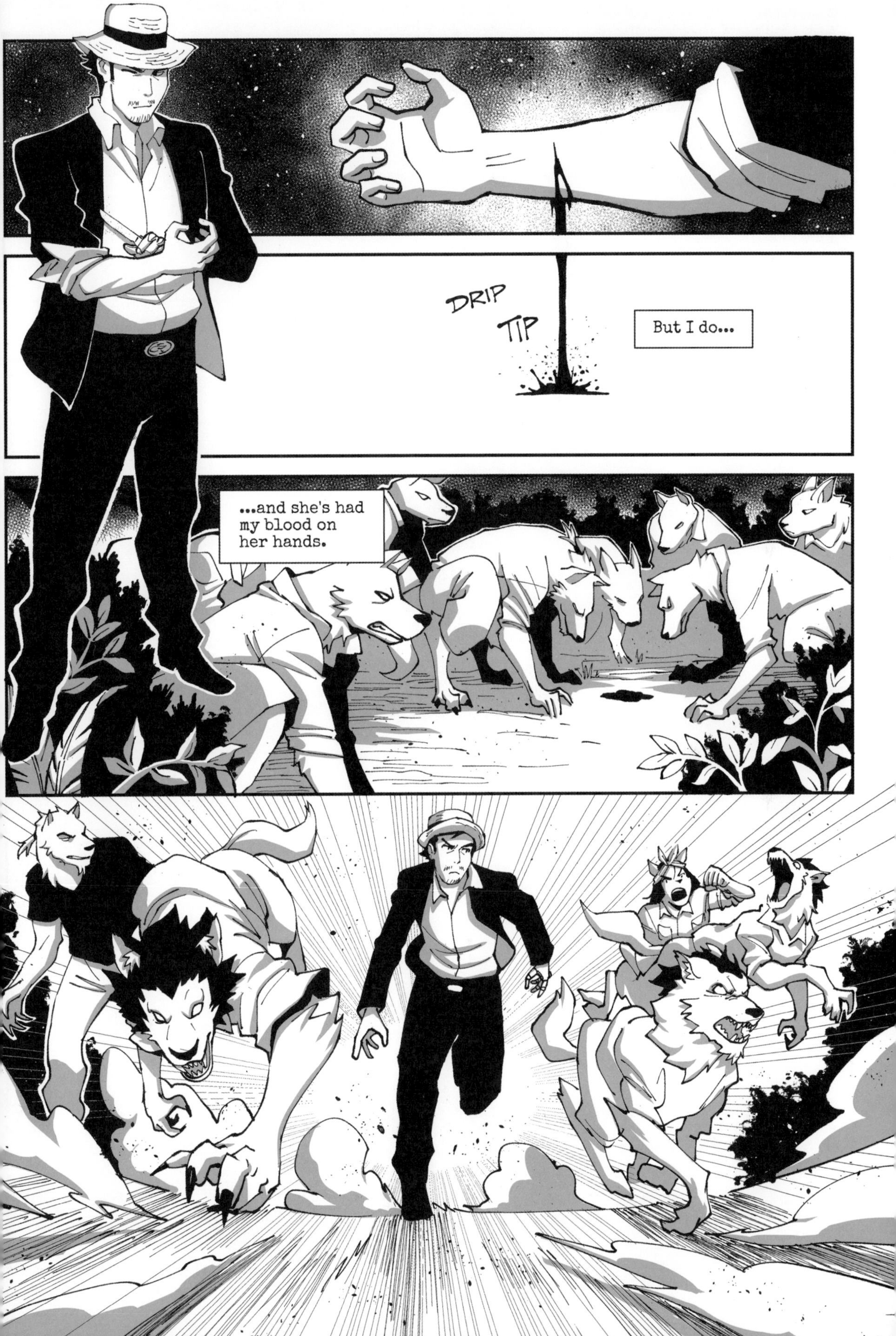
DRIP
TIP
But I do...
...and she's had my blood on her hands.

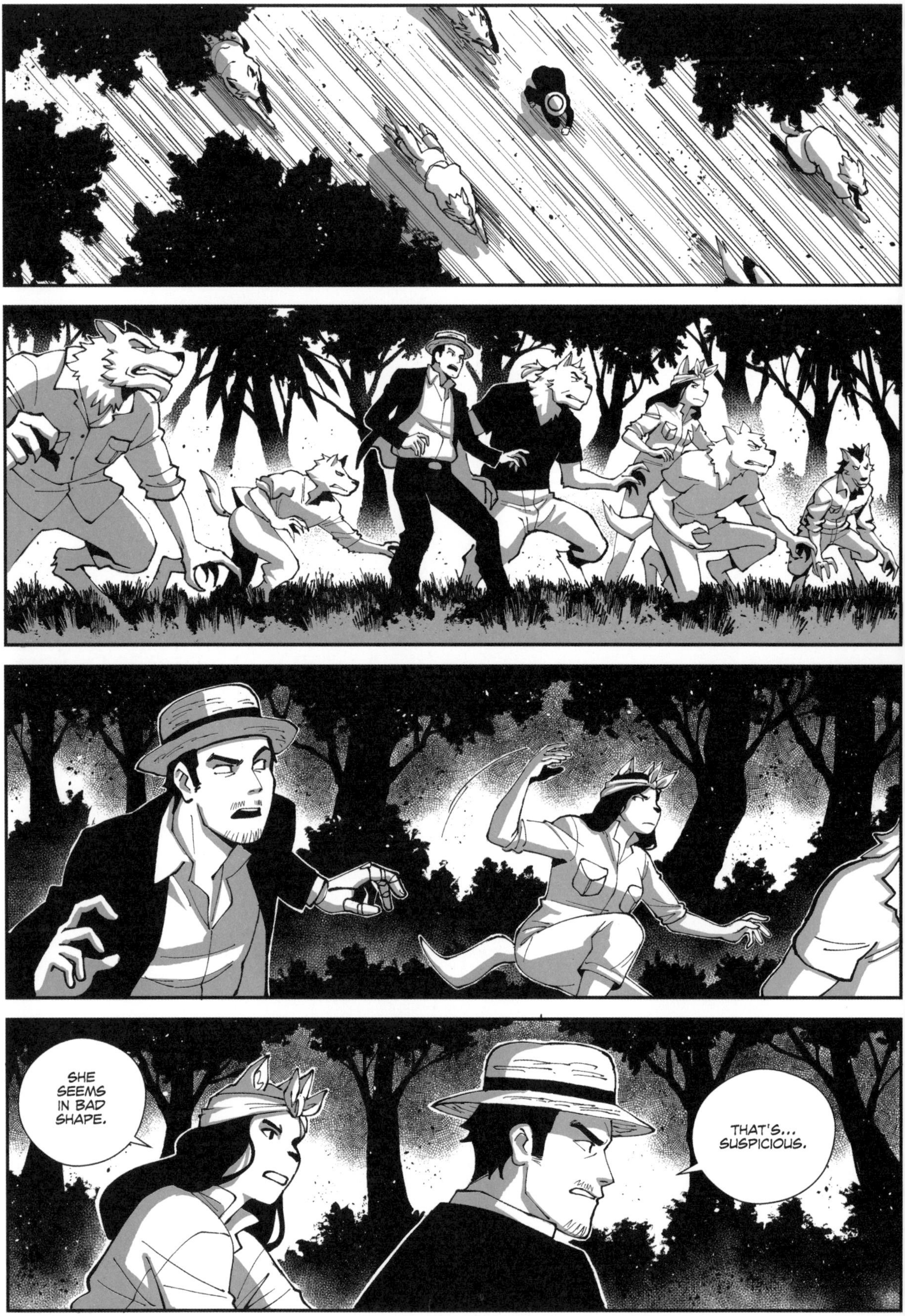
SHE SEEMS IN BAD SHAPE.
THAT'S... SUSPICIOUS.

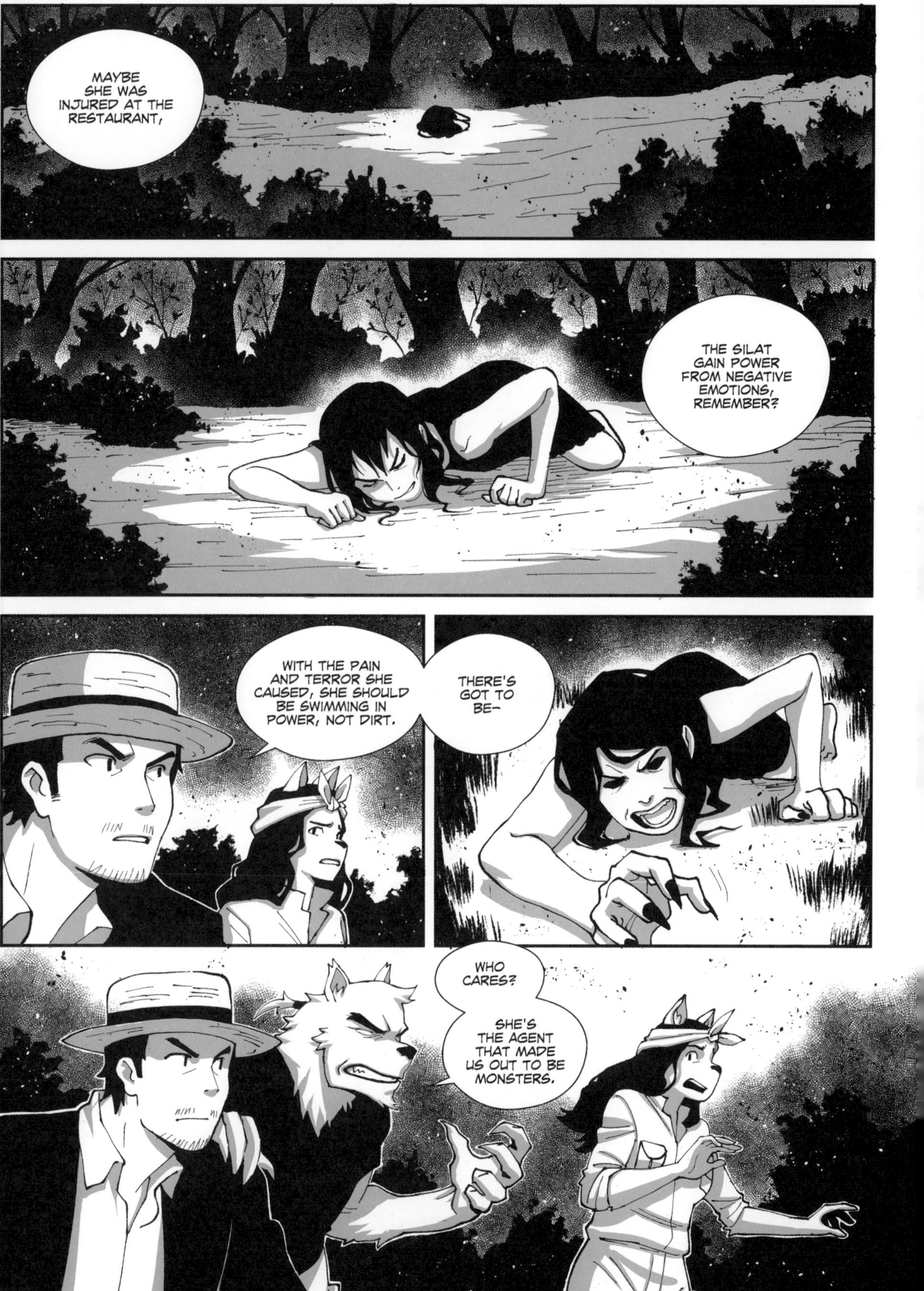
MAYBE SHE WAS INJURED AT THE RESTAURANT,
THE SILAT GAIN POWER FROM NEGATIVE EMOTIONS, REMEMBER?
WITH THE PAIN AND TERROR SHE CAUSED, SHE SHOULD BE SWIMMING IN POWER, NOT DIRT.
THERE'S GOT TO BE-
WHO CARES?
SHE'S THE AGENT THAT MADE US OUT TO BE MONSTERS.

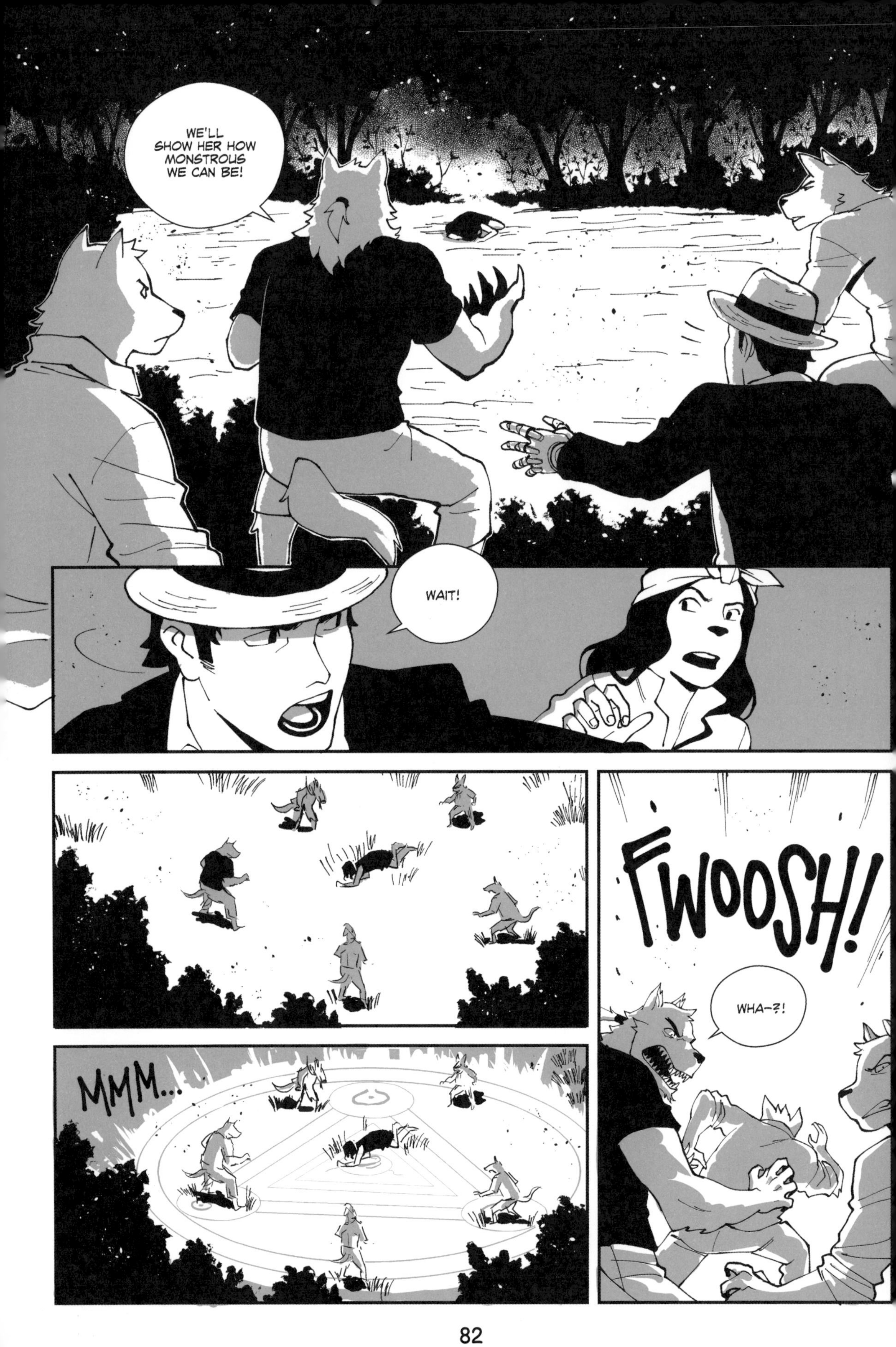
WE'LL SHOW HER HOW MONSTROUS WE CAN BE!
WAIT!
MMM...
FWOOSH!
WHA-?!

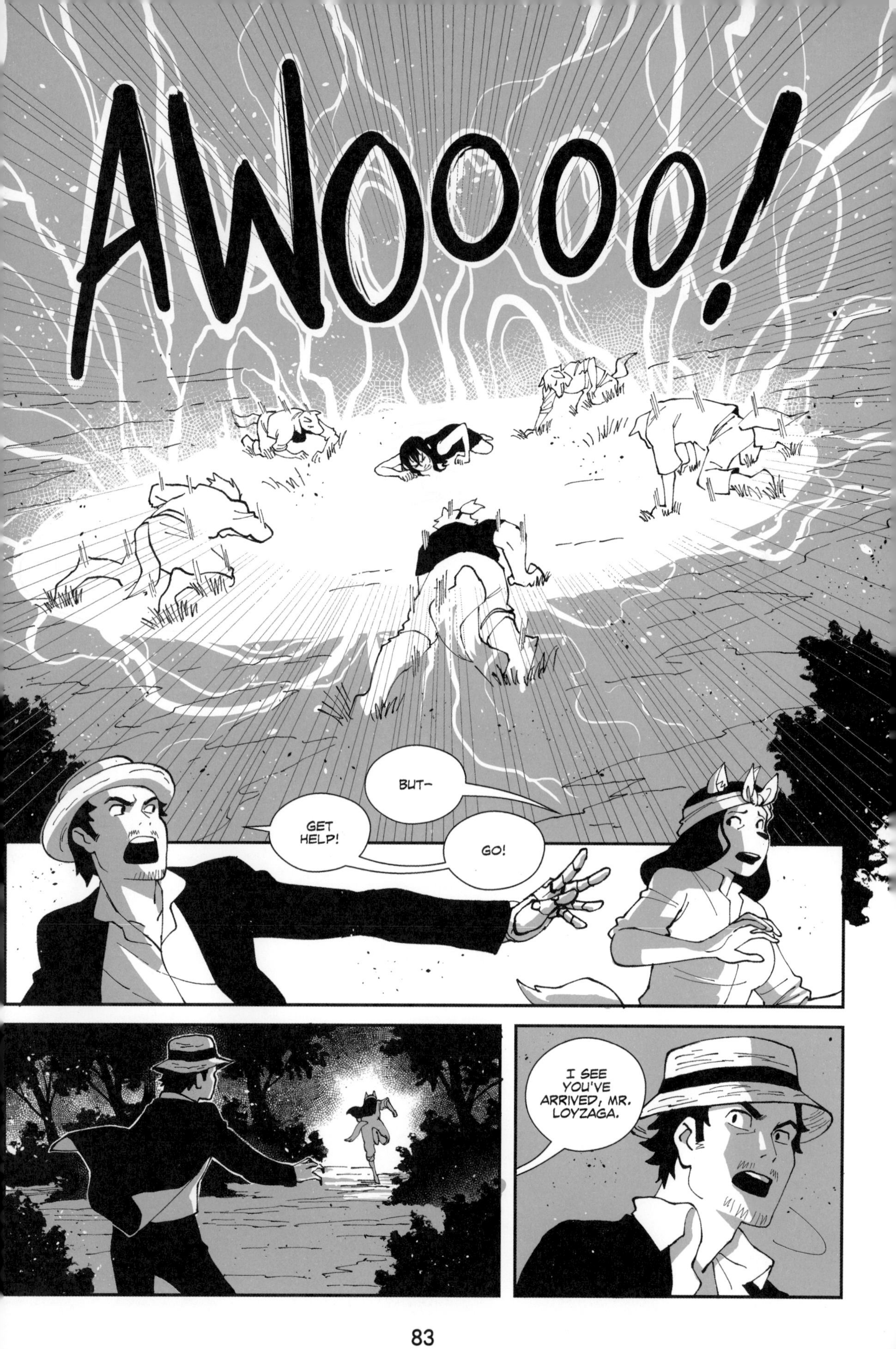
AWOOO!
BUT–
GET HELP!
GO!
I SEE YOU'VE ARRIVED, MR. LOYZAGA.

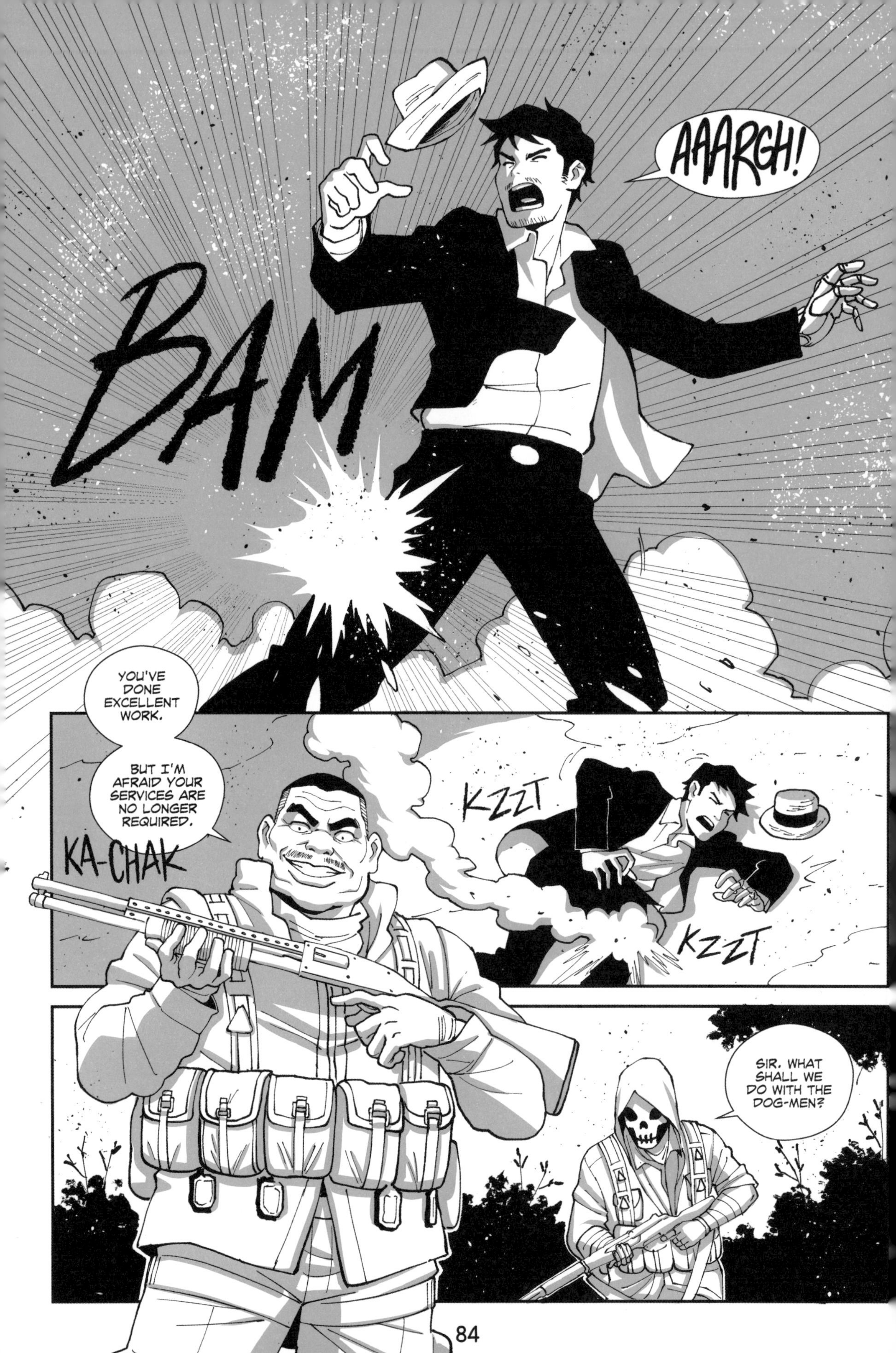
AAARGH!
BAM
YOU'VE DONE EXCELLENT WORK.
BUT I'M AFRAID YOUR SERVICES ARE NO LONGER REQUIRED.
KA-CHAK
KZZT
KZZT
SIR. WHAT SHALL WE DO WITH THE DOG-MEN?

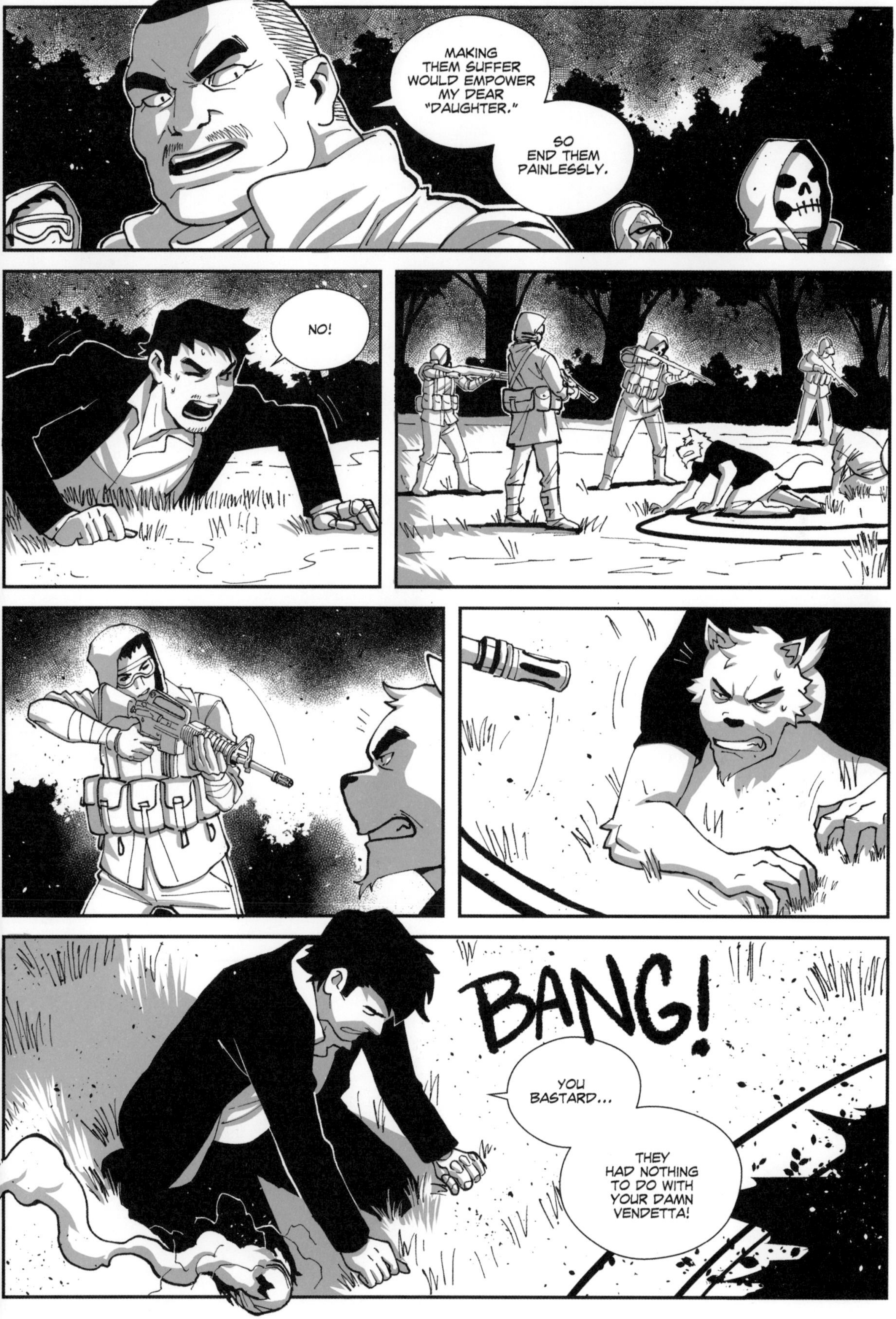
MAKING THEM SUFFER WOULD EMPOWER MY DEAR "DAUGHTER."
SO END THEM PAINLESSLY.
NO!
BANG!
YOU BASTARD...
THEY HAD NOTHING TO DO WITH YOUR DAMN VENDETTA!

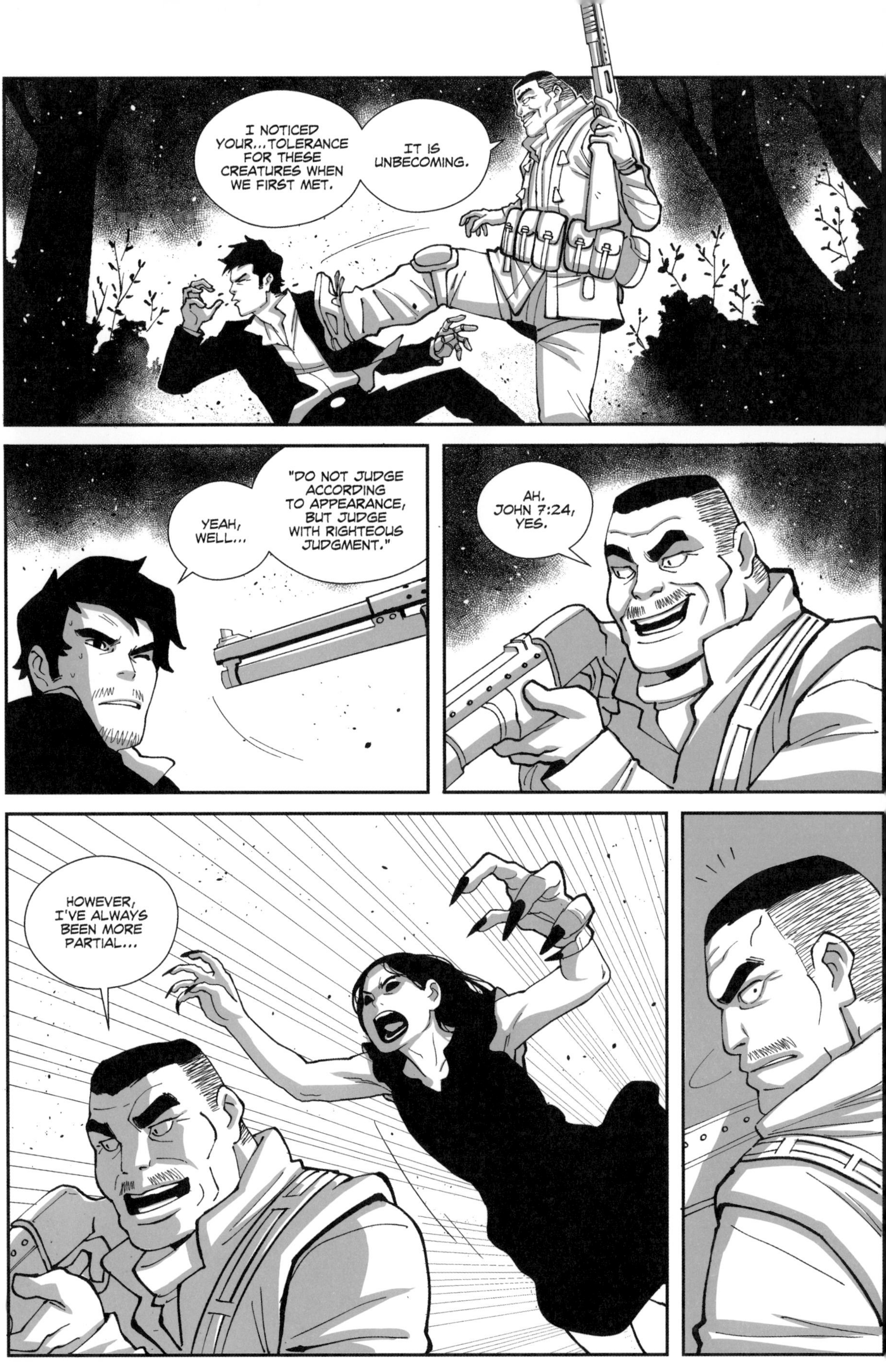
I NOTICED YOUR...TOLERANCE FOR THESE CREATURES WHEN WE FIRST MET.
IT IS UNBECOMING.
YEAH, WELL...
"DO NOT JUDGE ACCORDING TO APPEARANCE, BUT JUDGE WITH RIGHTEOUS JUDGMENT."
AH. JOHN 7:24, YES.
HOWEVER, I'VE ALWAYS BEEN MORE PARTIAL...

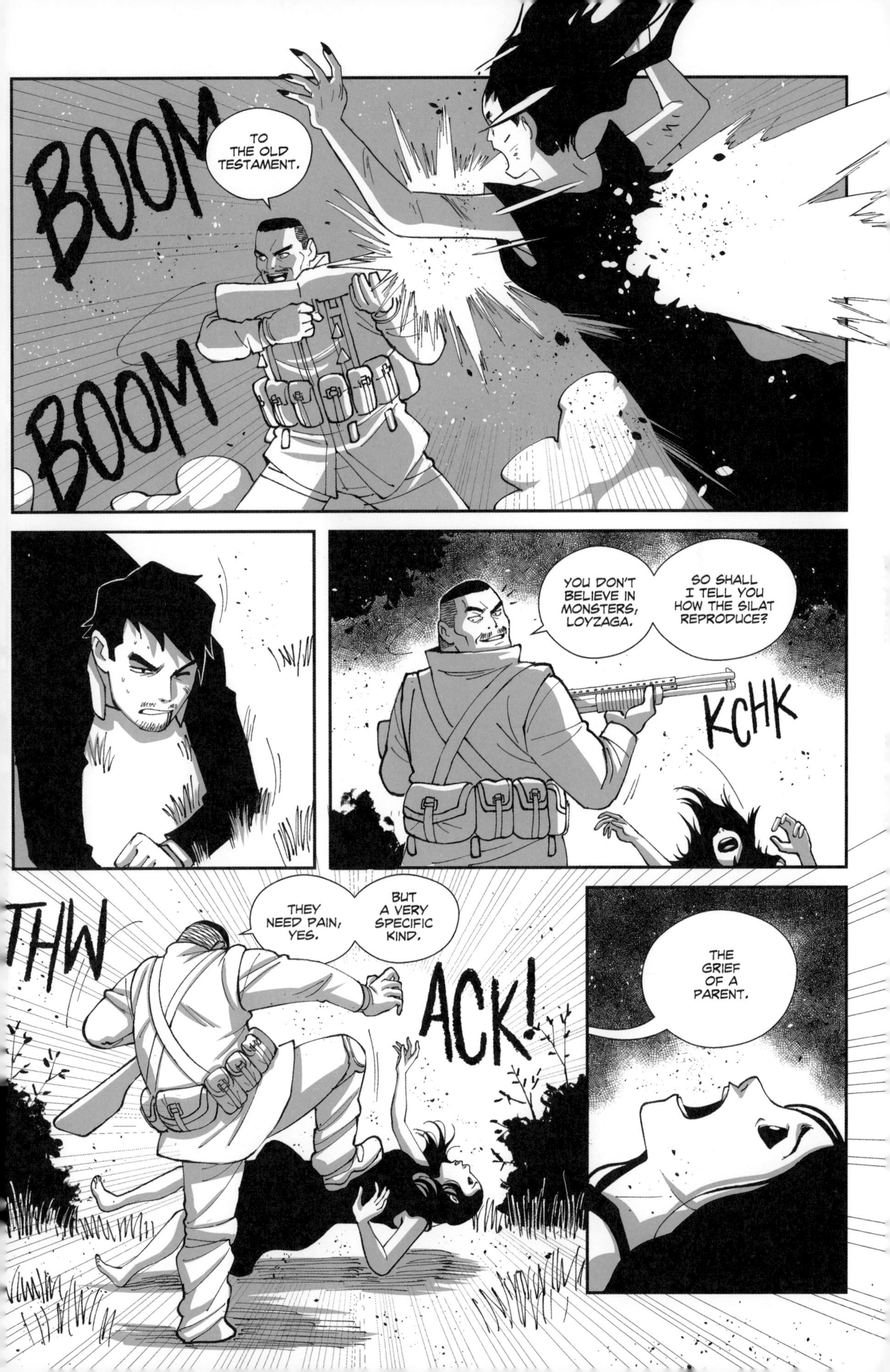
BOOM
TO THE OLD TESTAMENT.
BOOM
YOU DON'T BELIEVE IN MONSTERS, LOYZAGA.
SO SHALL I TELL YOU HOW THE SILAT REPRODUCE?
KCHK
THW
THEY NEED PAIN, YES.
BUT A VERY SPECIFIC KIND.
ACK!
THE GRIEF OF A PARENT.

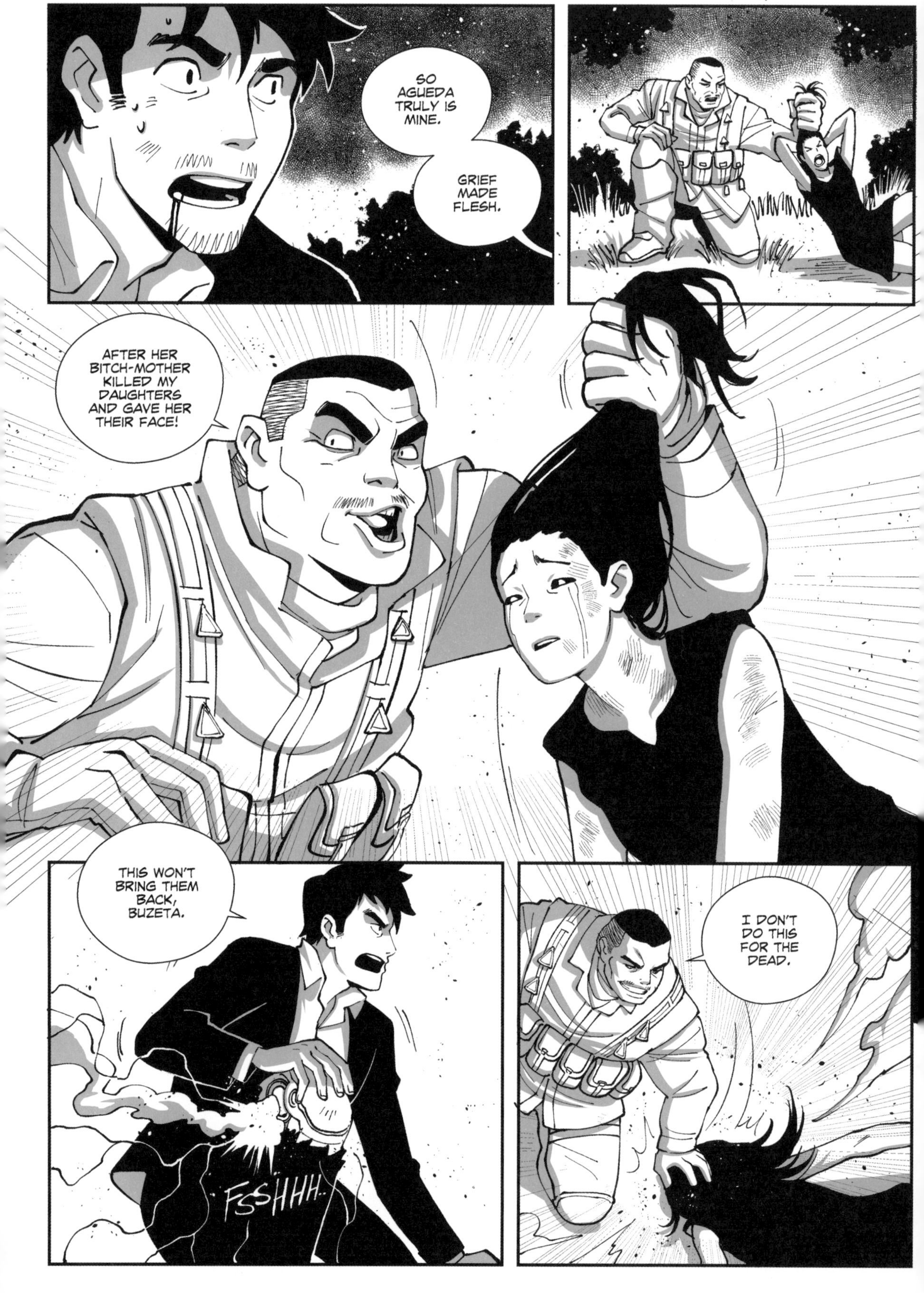
SO AGUEDA TRULY IS MINE.
GRIEF MADE FLESH.
AFTER HER BITCH-MOTHER KILLED MY DAUGHTERS AND GAVE HER THEIR FACE!
THIS WON'T BRING THEM BACK, BUZETA.
FSSHHH..
I DON'T DO THIS FOR THE DEAD.

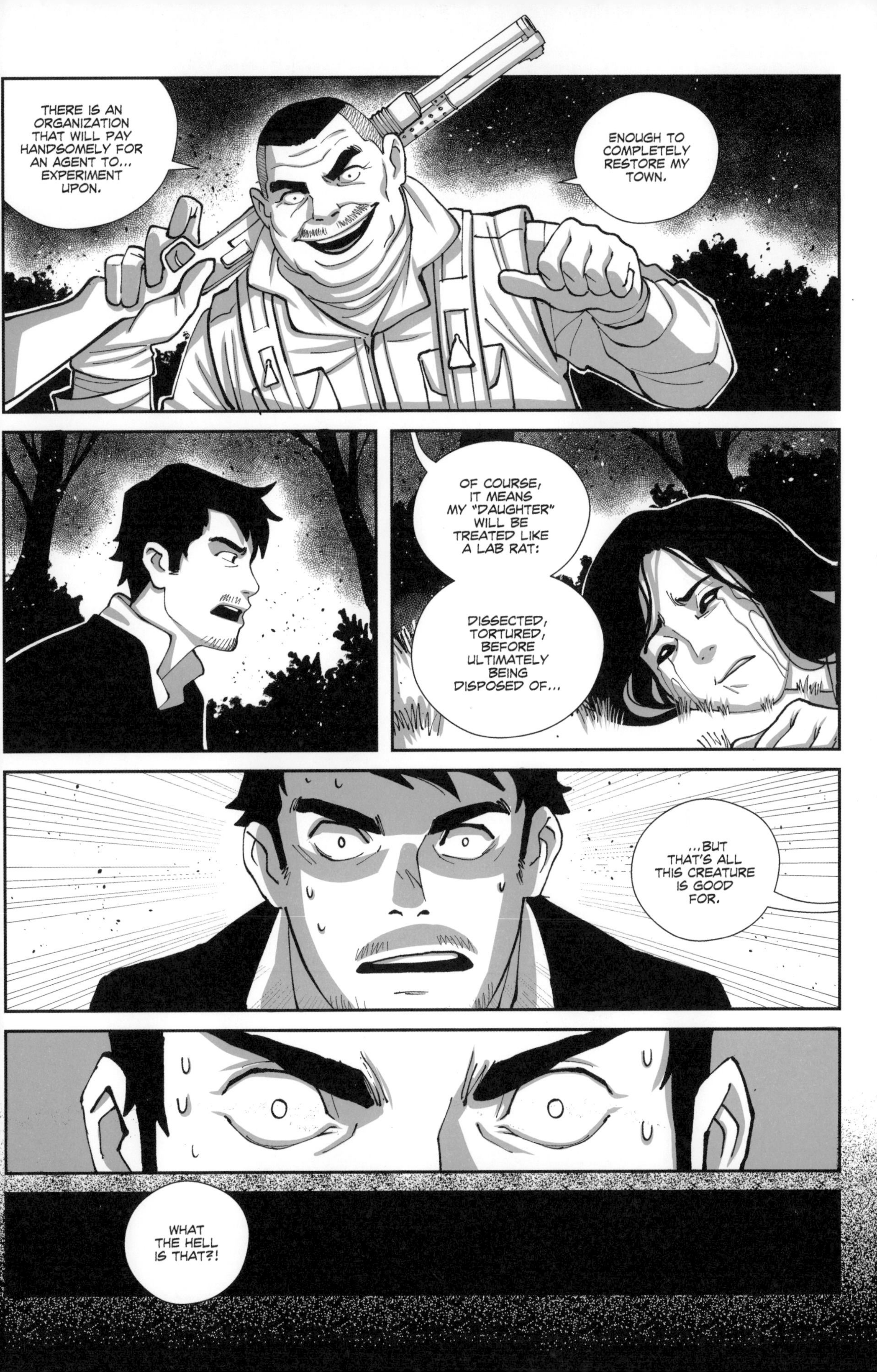
THERE IS AN ORGANIZATION THAT WILL PAY HANDSOMELY FOR AN AGENT TO... EXPERIMENT UPON.
ENOUGH TO COMPLETELY RESTORE MY TOWN.
OF COURSE, IT MEANS MY "DAUGHTER" WILL BE TREATED LIKE A LAB RAT:
DISSECTED, TORTURED, BEFORE ULTIMATELY BEING DISPOSED OF...
...BUT THAT'S ALL THIS CREATURE IS GOOD FOR.
WHAT THE HELL IS THAT?!

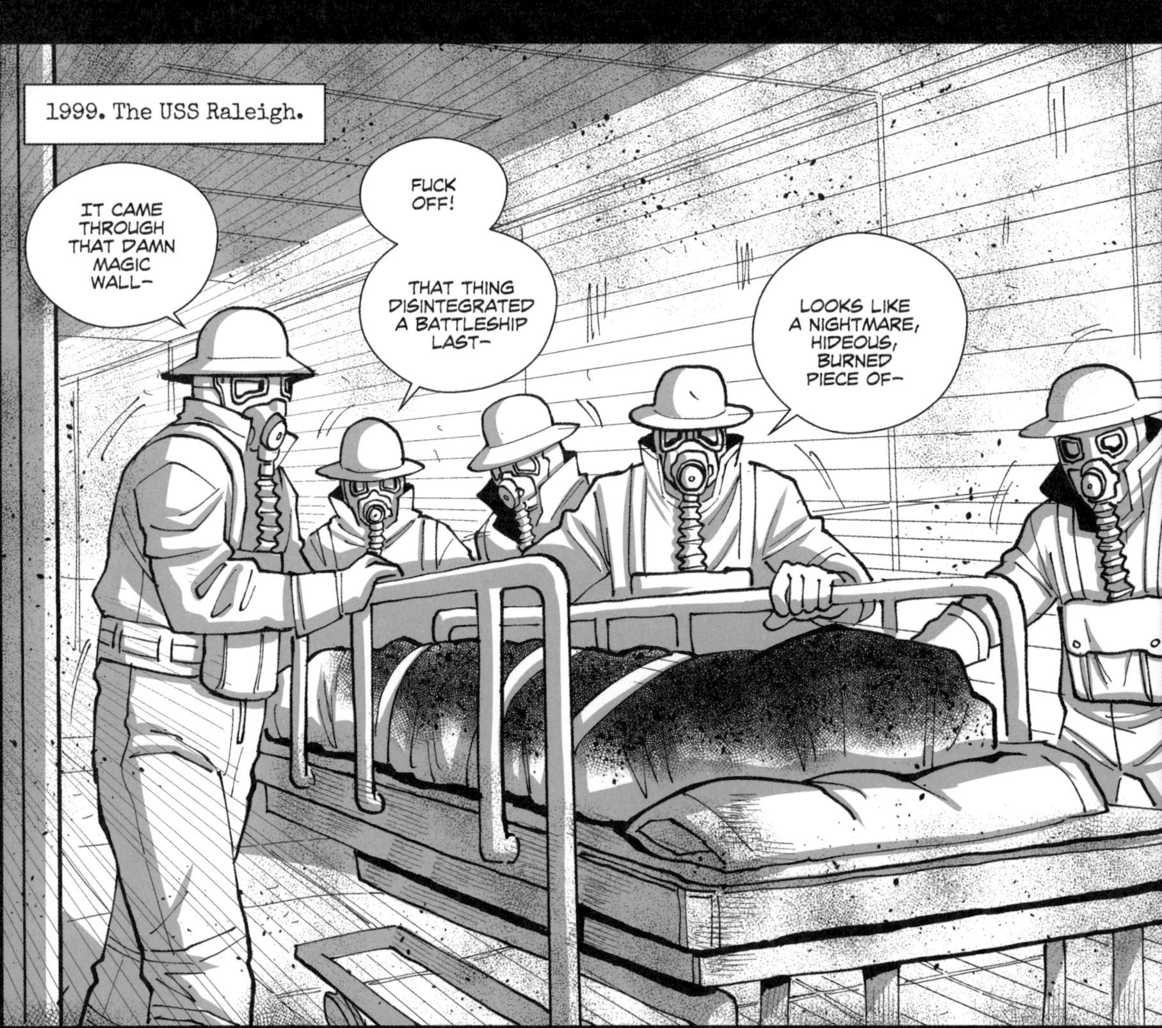
1999. The USS Raleigh.
IT CAME THROUGH THAT DAMN MAGIC WALL-
FUCK OFF!
THAT THING DISINTEGRATED A BATTLESHIP LAST-
LOOKS LIKE A NIGHTMARE, HIDEOUS, BURNED PIECE OF-

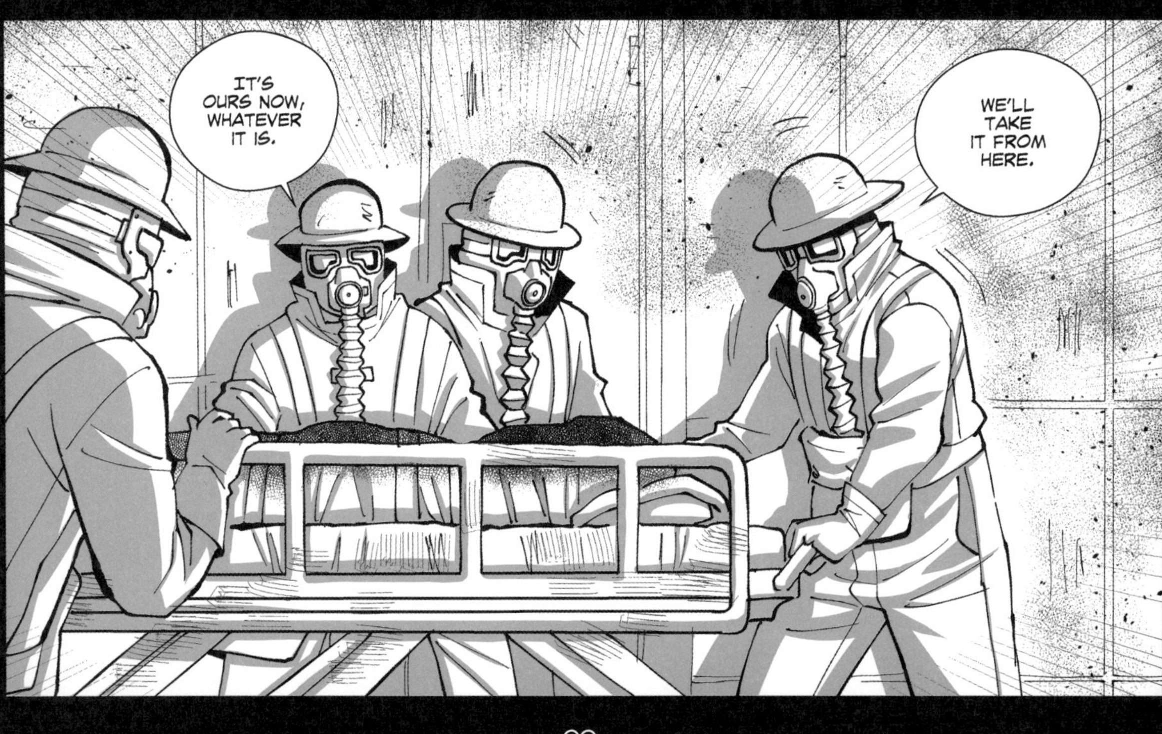
IT'S OURS NOW, WHATEVER IT IS.
WE'LL TAKE IT FROM HERE.

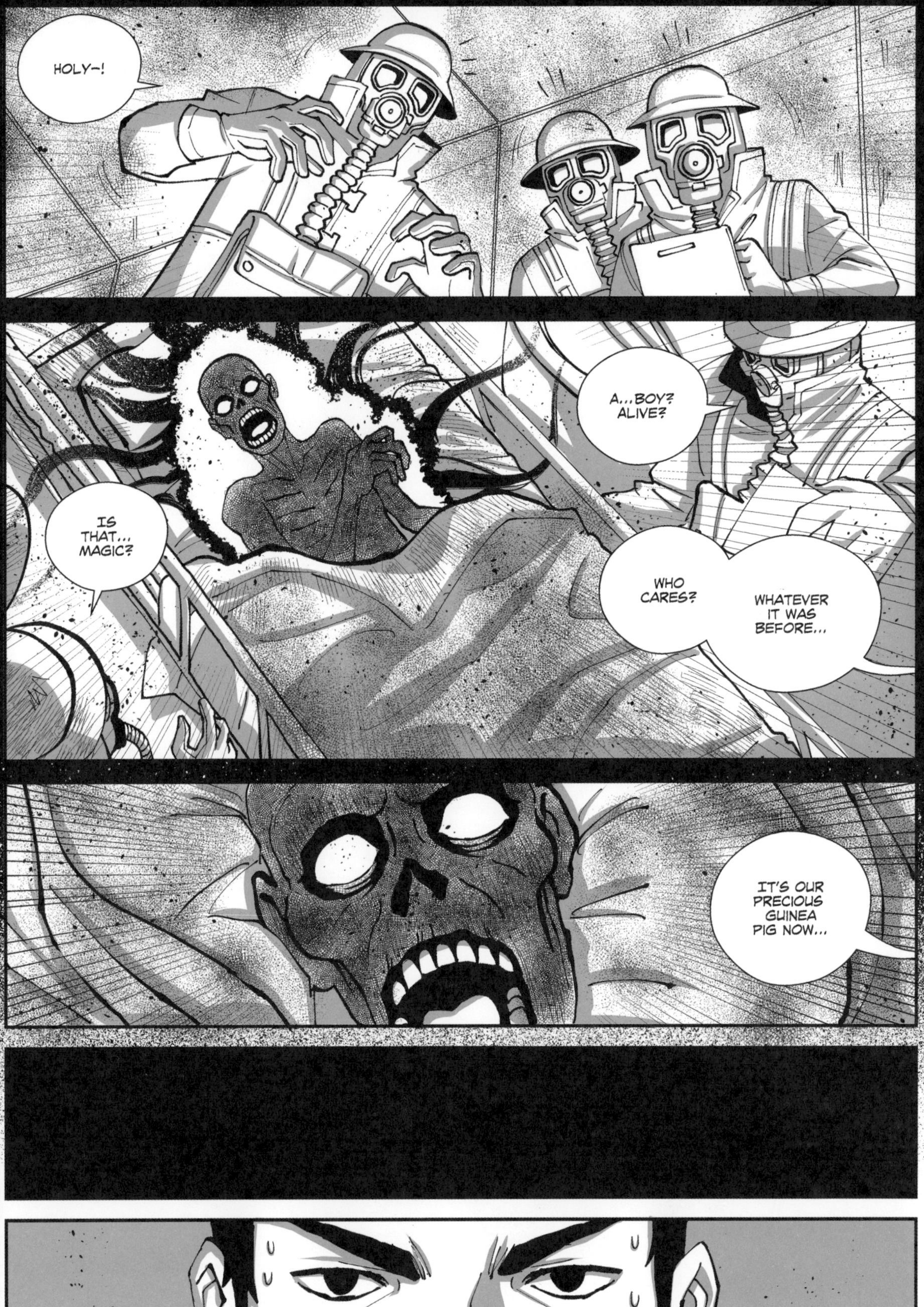
HOLY–!
A...BOY? ALIVE?
IS THAT... MAGIC?
WHO CARES?
WHATEVER IT WAS BEFORE...
IT'S OUR PRECIOUS GUINEA PIG NOW...

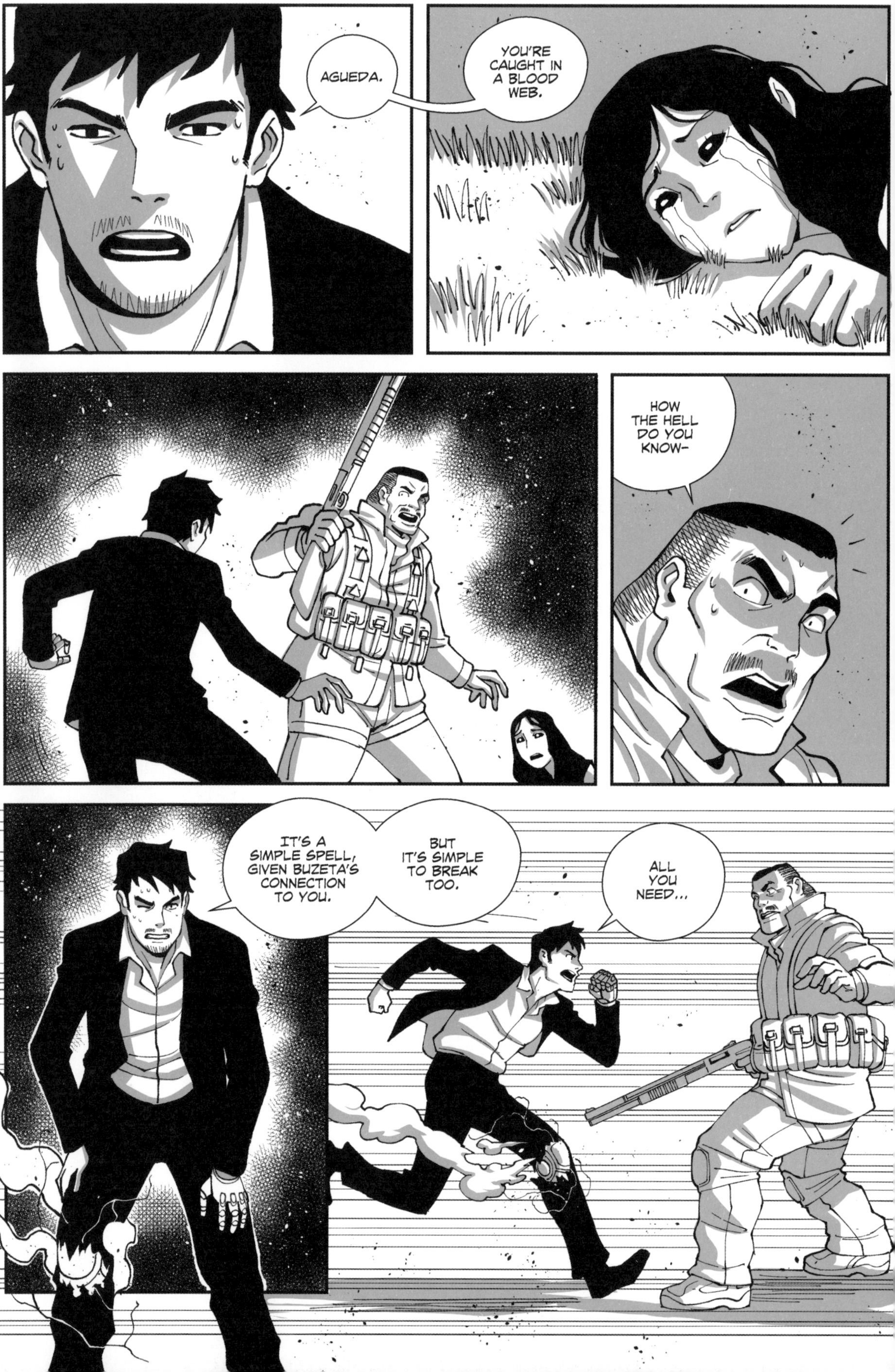
AGUEDA.
YOU'RE CAUGHT IN A BLOOD WEB.
HOW THE HELL DO YOU KNOW-
IT'S A SIMPLE SPELL, GIVEN BUZETA'S CONNECTION TO YOU.
BUT IT'S SIMPLE TO BREAK TOO.
ALL YOU NEED...

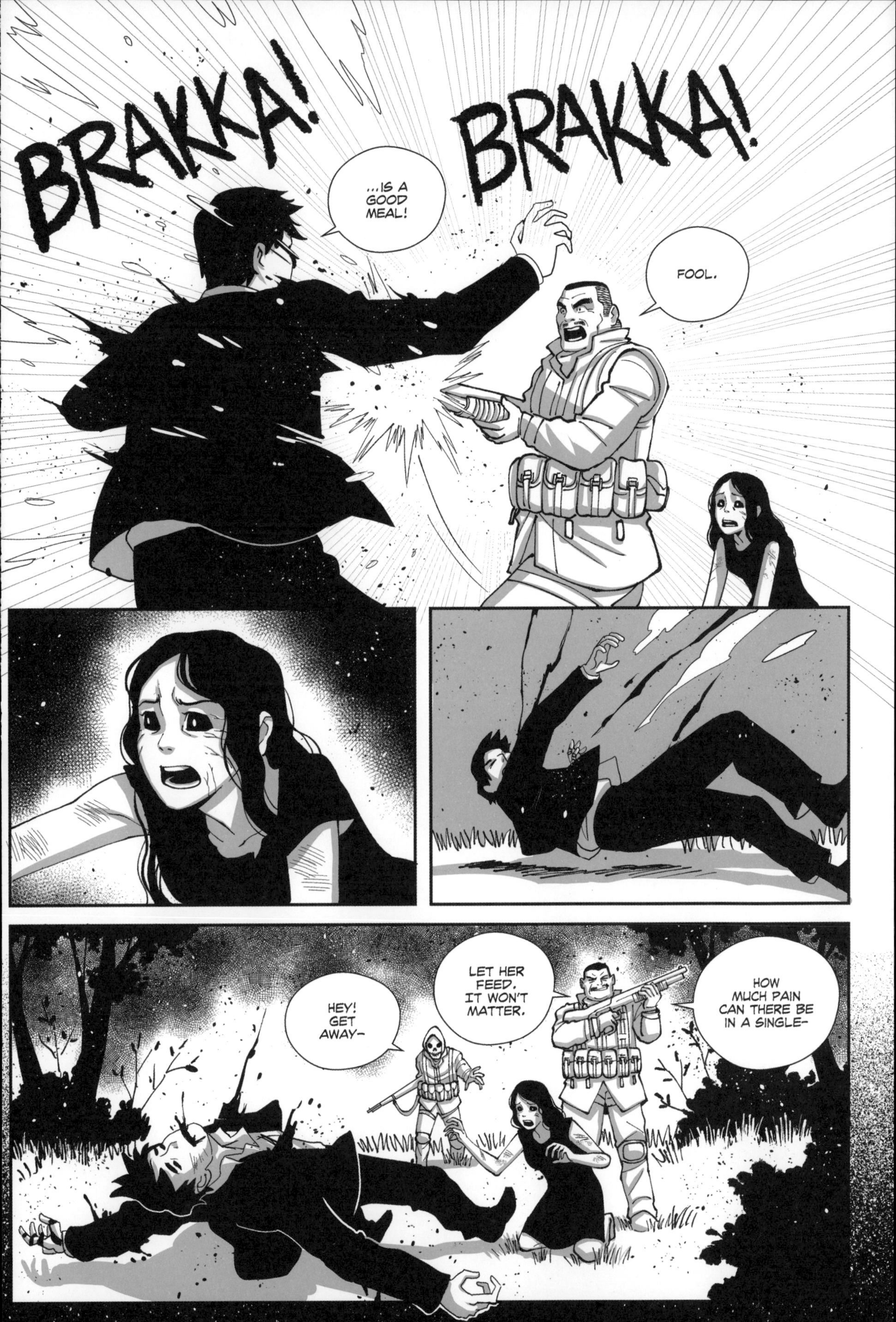
BRAKKA! BRAKKA!
...IS A GOOD MEAL!
FOOL.
HEY! GET AWAY-
LET HER FEED. IT WON'T MATTER.
HOW MUCH PAIN CAN THERE BE IN A SINGLE-

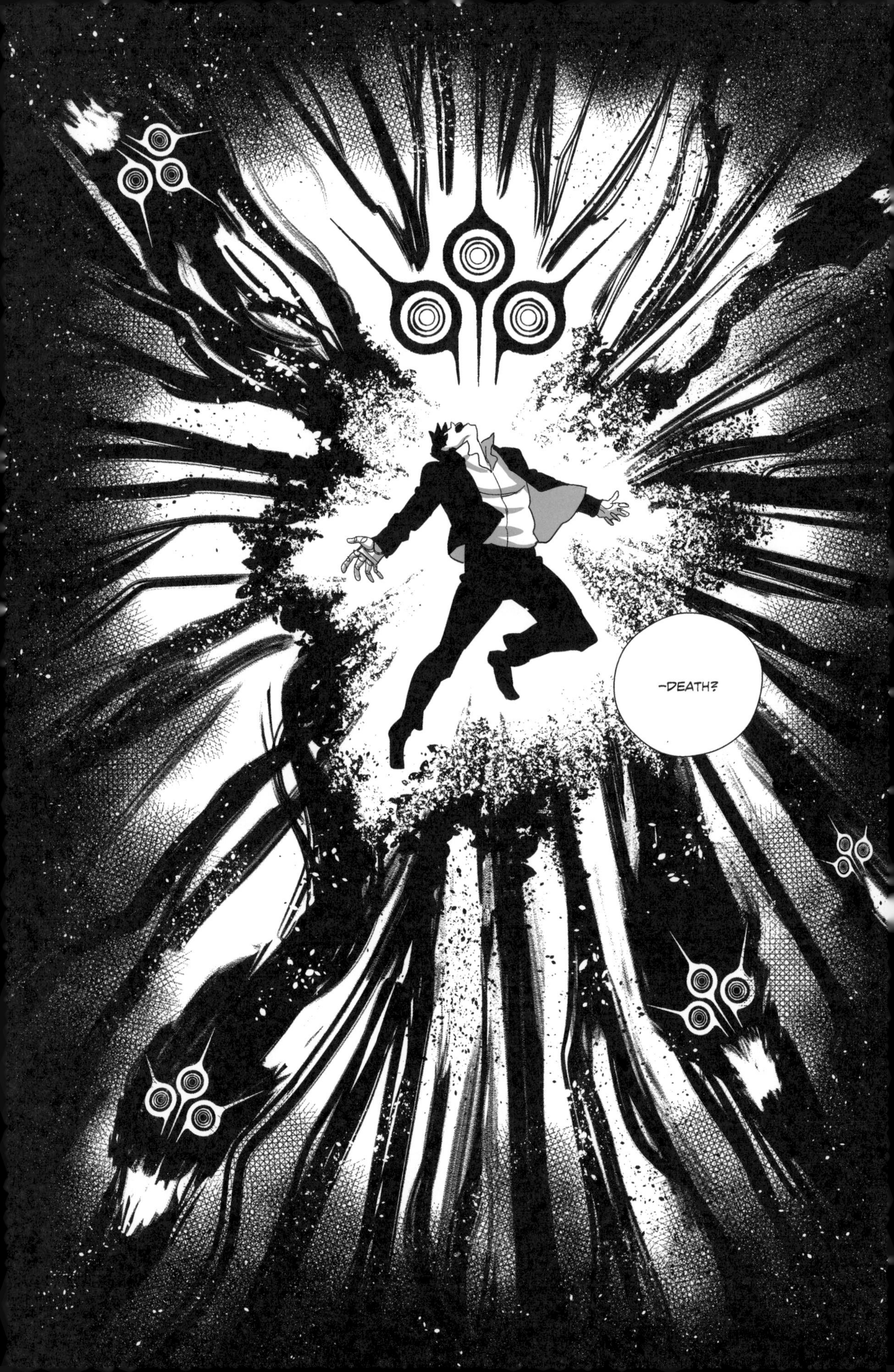
-DEATH?

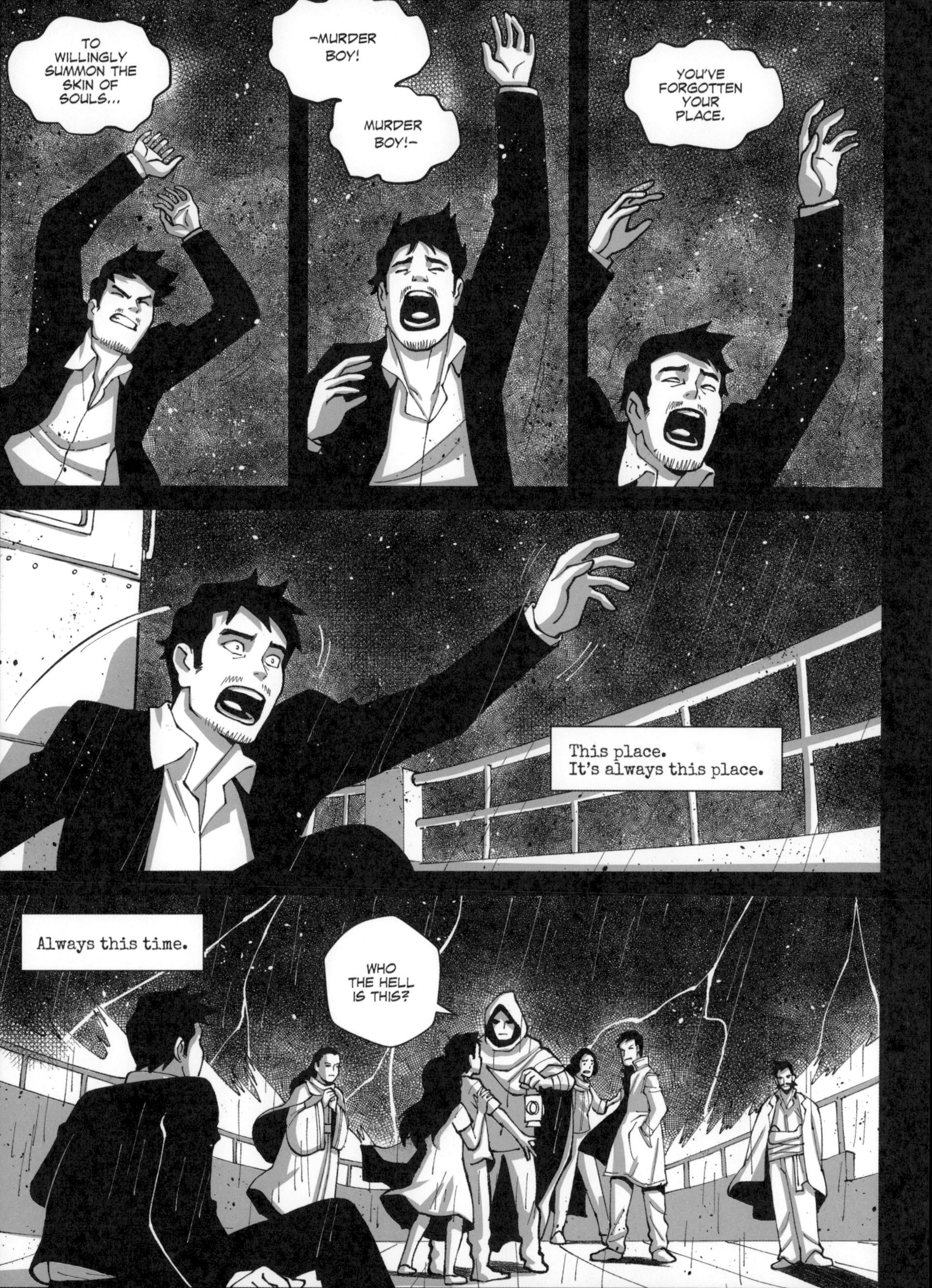
TO WILLINGLY SUMMON THE SKIN OF SOULS...
-MURDER BOY!
MURDER BOY!-
YOU'VE FORGOTTEN YOUR PLACE.
This place.
It's always this place.
Always this time.
WHO THE HELL IS THIS?

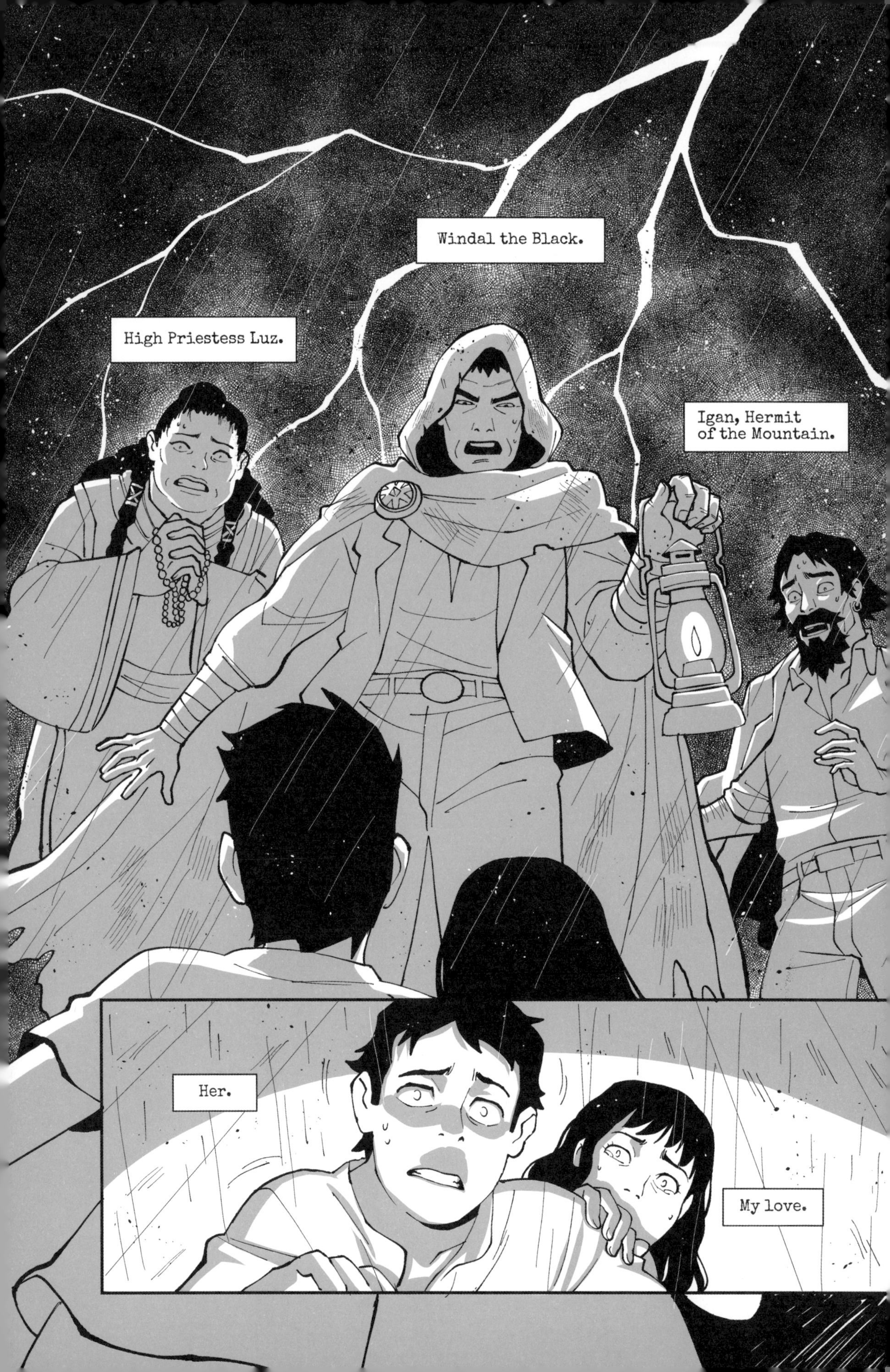
Windal the Black.
High Priestess Luz.
Igan, Hermit
of the Mountain.
Her.
My love.

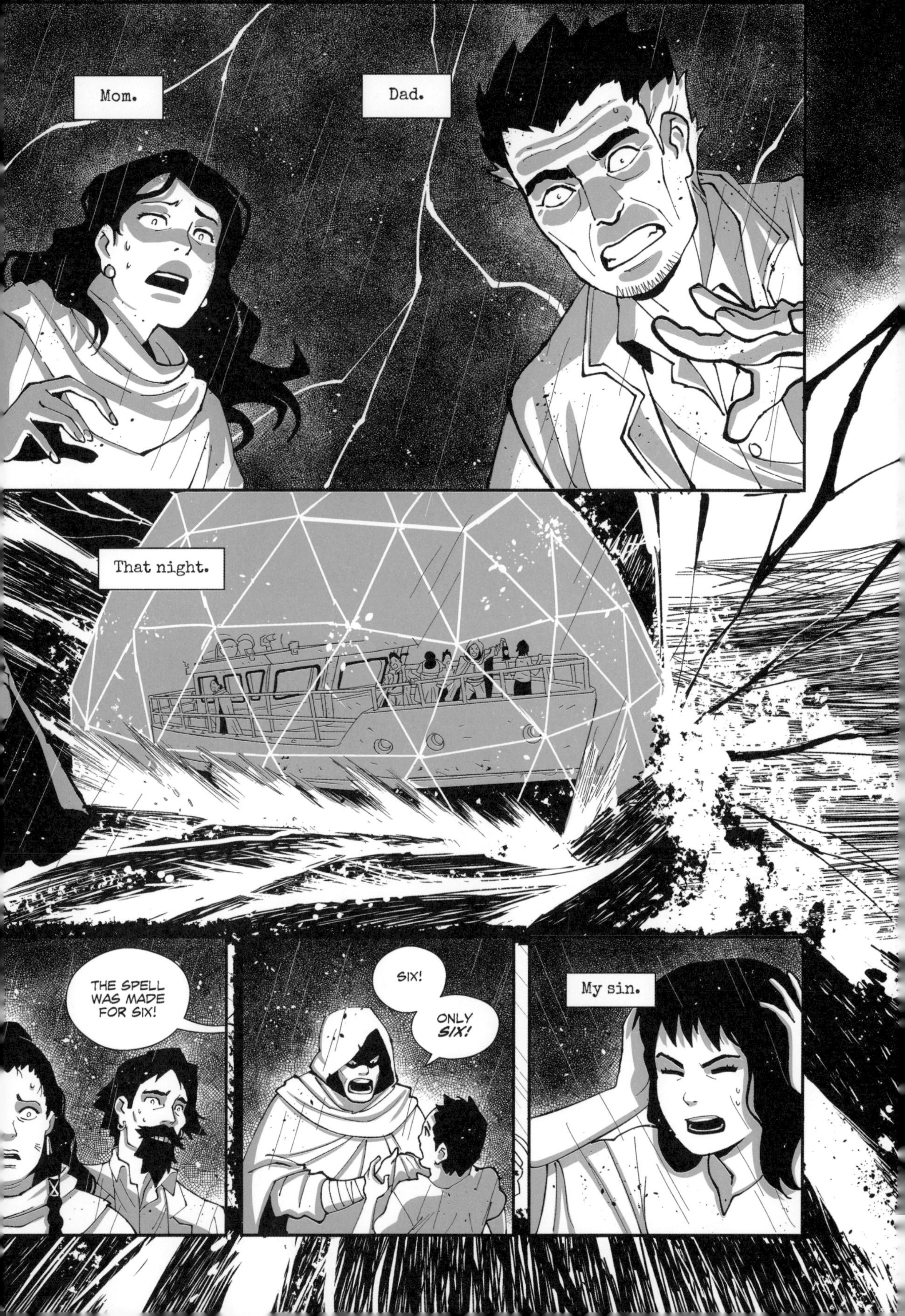
Mom.
Dad.
That night.
THE SPELL WAS MADE FOR SIX!
SIX!
ONLY SIX!
My sin.

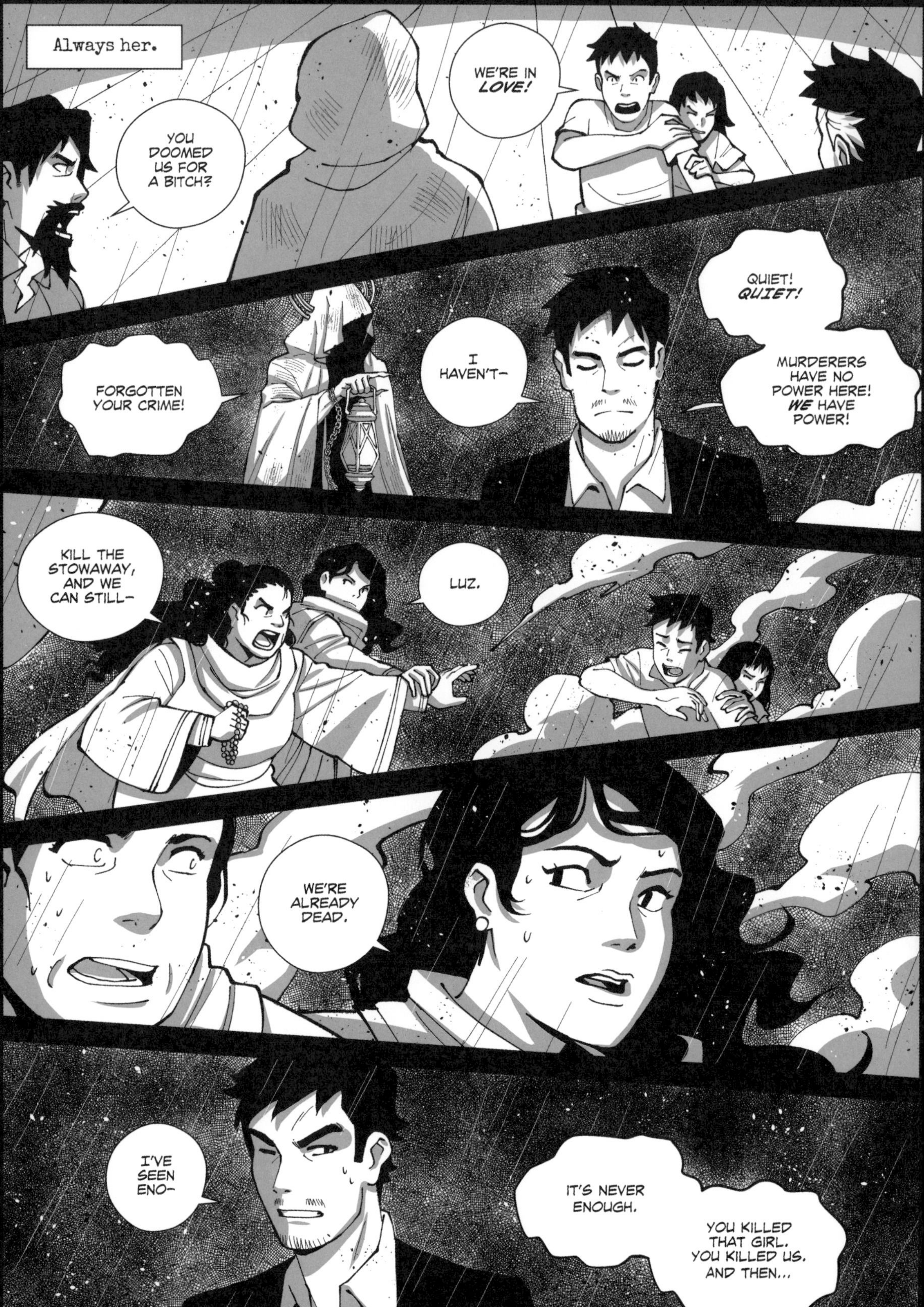
Always her.
YOU DOOMED US FOR A BITCH?
WE'RE IN LOVE!
FORGOTTEN YOUR CRIME!
I HAVEN'T-
QUIET! QUIET!
MURDERERS HAVE NO POWER HERE! WE HAVE POWER!
KILL THE STOWAWAY, AND WE CAN STILL-
LUZ.
WE'RE ALREADY DEAD.
I'VE SEEN ENO-
IT'S NEVER ENOUGH.
YOU KILLED THAT GIRL. YOU KILLED US. AND THEN...

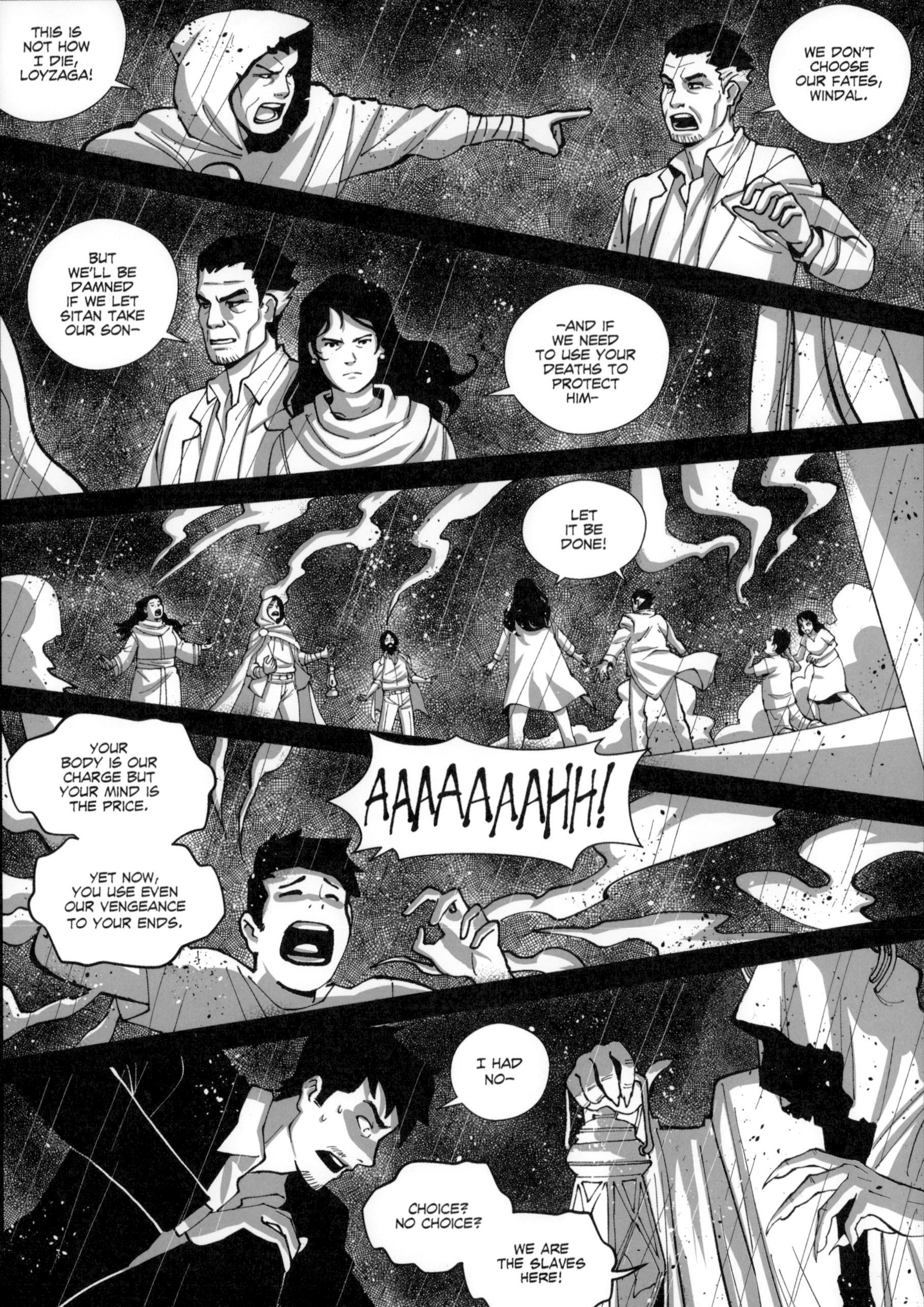
THIS IS NOT HOW I DIE, LOYZAGA!
WE DON'T CHOOSE OUR FATES, WINDAL.
BUT WE'LL BE DAMNED IF WE LET SITAN TAKE OUR SON-
-AND IF WE NEED TO USE YOUR DEATHS TO PROTECT HIM-
LET IT BE DONE!
YOUR BODY IS OUR CHARGE BUT YOUR MIND IS THE PRICE.
AAAAAAAHH!
YET NOW, YOU USE EVEN OUR VENGEANCE TO YOUR ENDS.
I HAD NO-
CHOICE? NO CHOICE?
WE ARE THE SLAVES HERE!

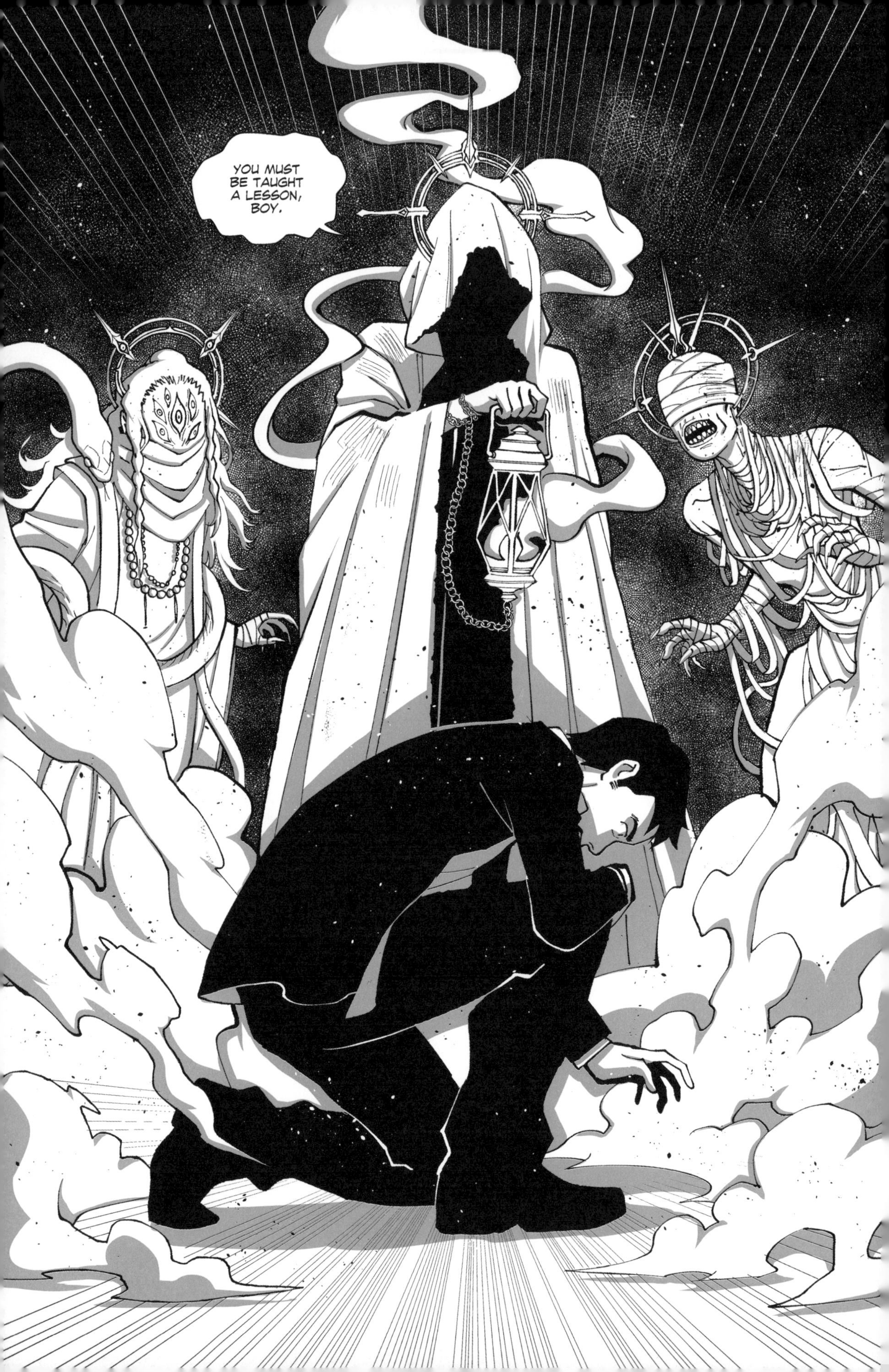
YOU MUST BE TAUGHT A LESSON, BOY.

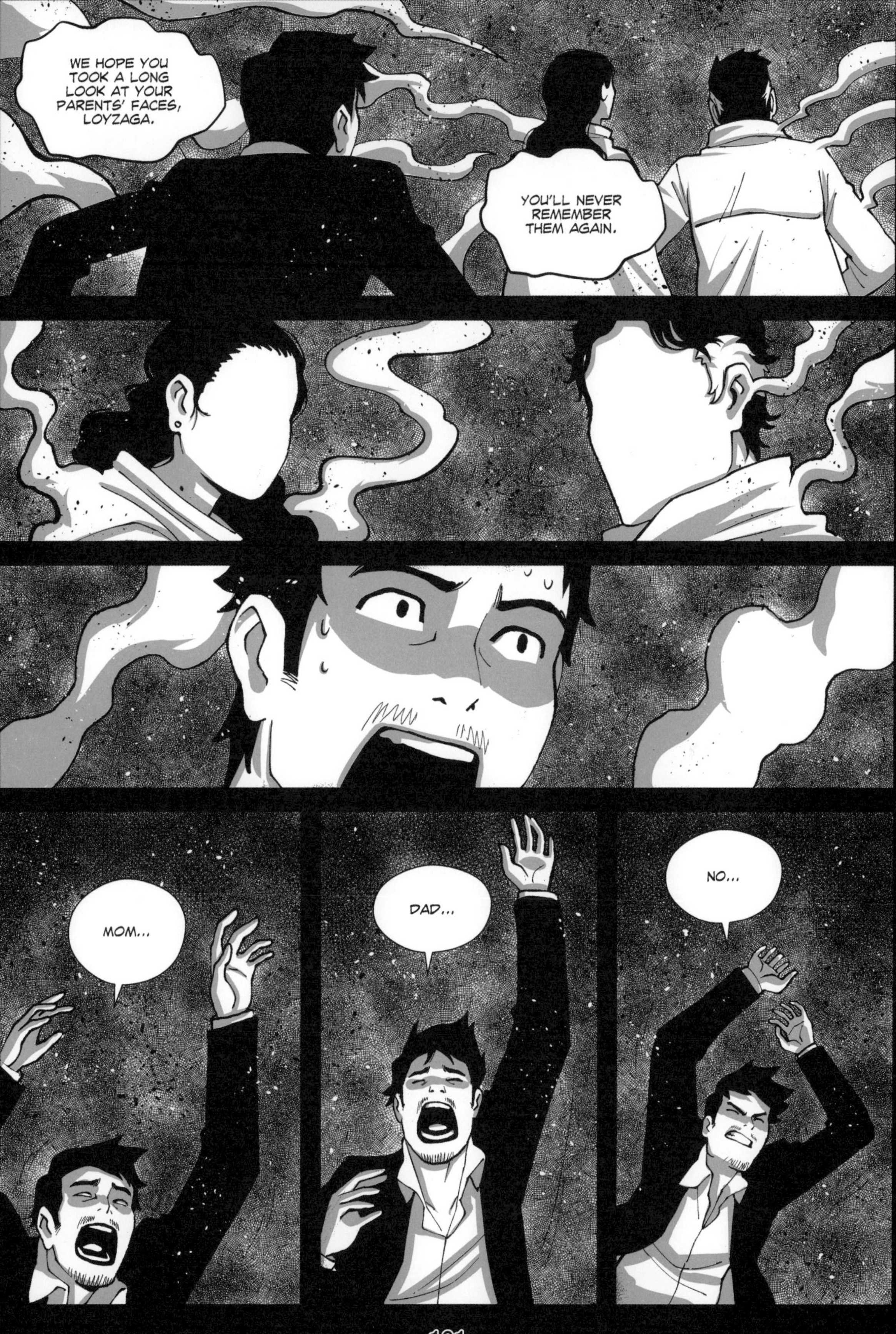
WE HOPE YOU TOOK A LONG LOOK AT YOUR PARENTS' FACES, LOYZAGA.
YOU'LL NEVER REMEMBER THEM AGAIN.
MOM...
DAD...
NO...

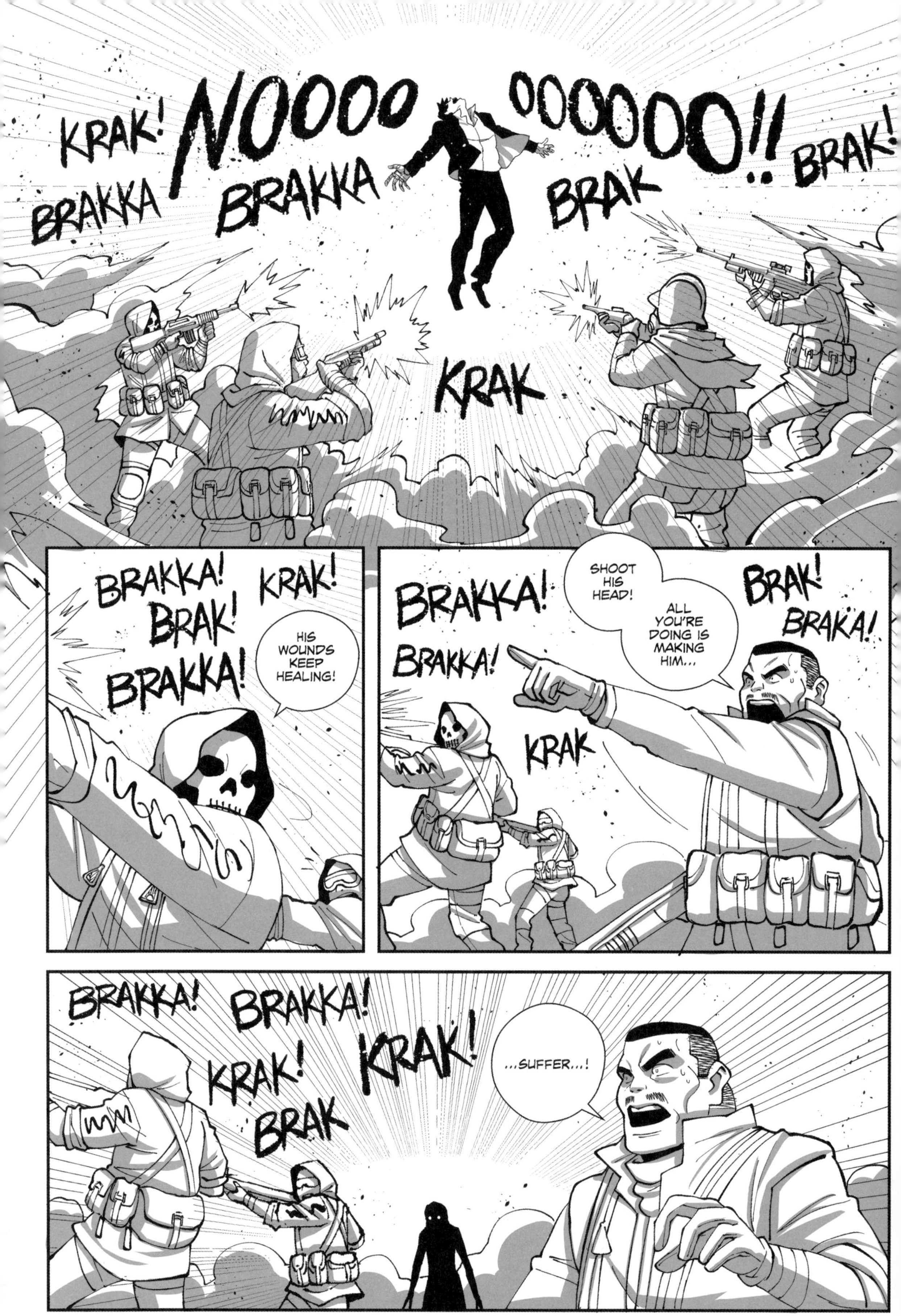
KRAK!
NOOOO OOOOOO!!
BRAK!
BRAKKA
BRAKKA
BRAK
KRAK
BRAKKA!
KRAK!
BRAK!
BRAKKA!
HIS WOUNDS KEEP HEALING!
BRAKKA!
SHOOT HIS HEAD!
BRAK!
BRAKA!
BRAKKA!
ALL YOU'RE DOING IS MAKING HIM...
KRAK
BRAKKA!
BRAKKA!
KRAK!
KRAK!
BRAK
...SUFFER...!

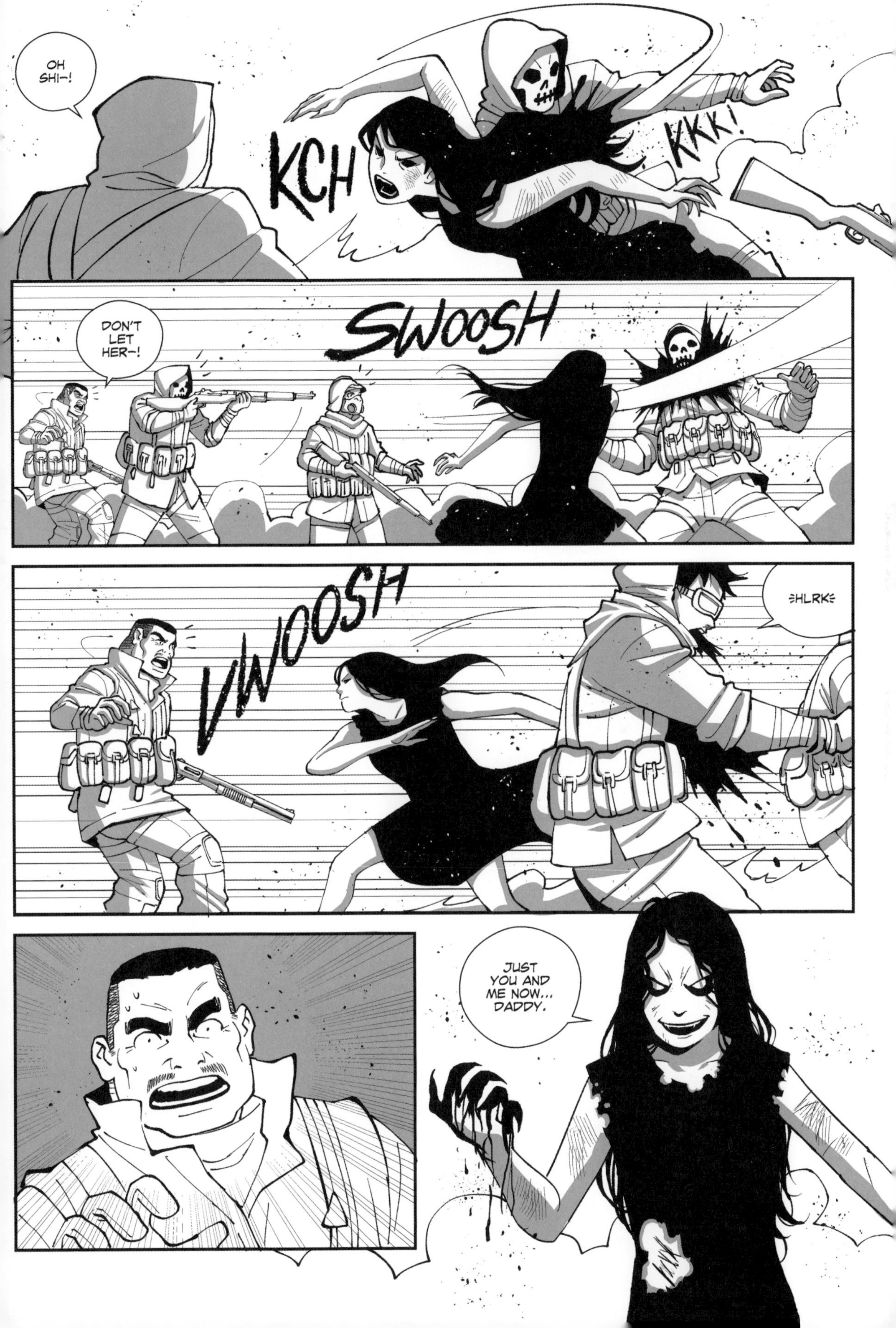
OH SHI--!
KCH
KKK!
DON'T LET HER--!
SWOOSH
VWOOSH
HLRK
JUST YOU AND ME NOW... DADDY.

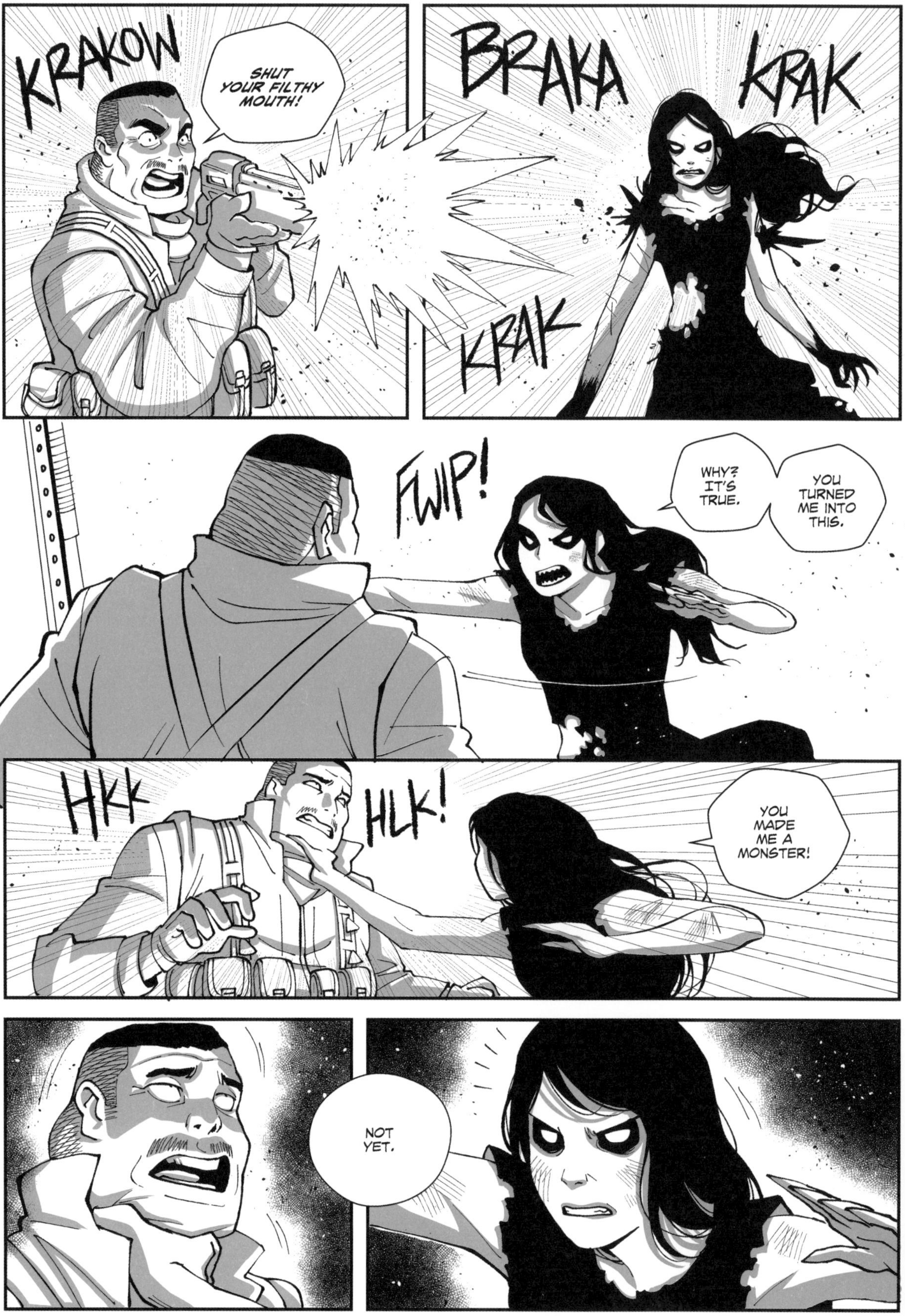
KRAKOW
SHUT YOUR FILTHY MOUTH!
BRAKA
KRAK
KRAK
FWIP!
WHY? IT'S TRUE.
YOU TURNED ME INTO THIS.
HKK
HLK!
YOU MADE ME A MONSTER!
NOT YET.

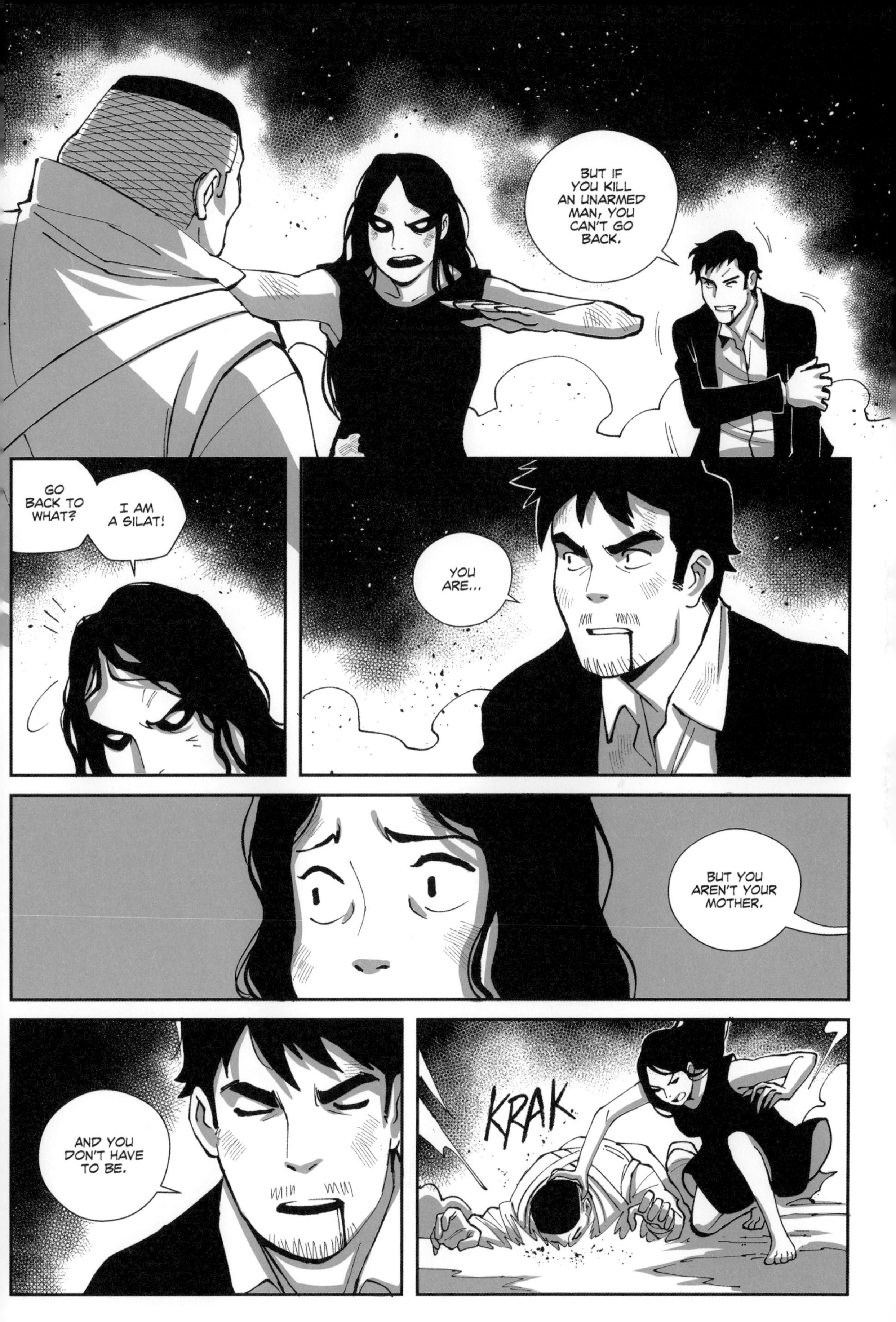

BUT IF YOU KILL AN UNARMED MAN, YOU CAN'T GO BACK.
GO BACK TO WHAT?
I AM A SILAT!
YOU ARE...
BUT YOU AREN'T YOUR MOTHER.
AND YOU DON'T HAVE TO BE.
KRAK

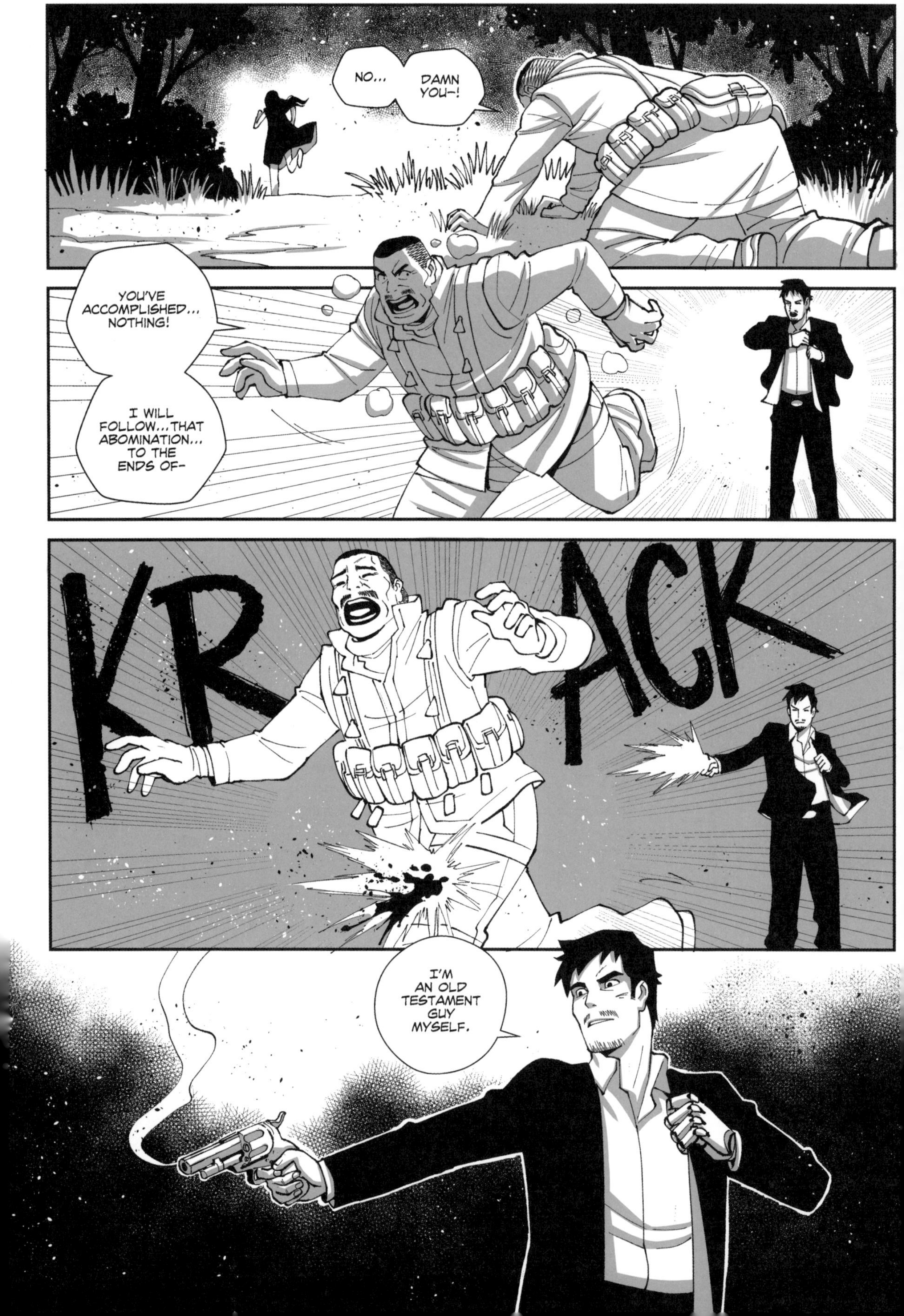
NO...
DAMN YOU-!
YOU'VE ACCOMPLISHED... NOTHING!
I WILL FOLLOW...THAT ABOMINATION... TO THE ENDS OF-
KRACK
I'M AN OLD TESTAMENT GUY MYSELF.

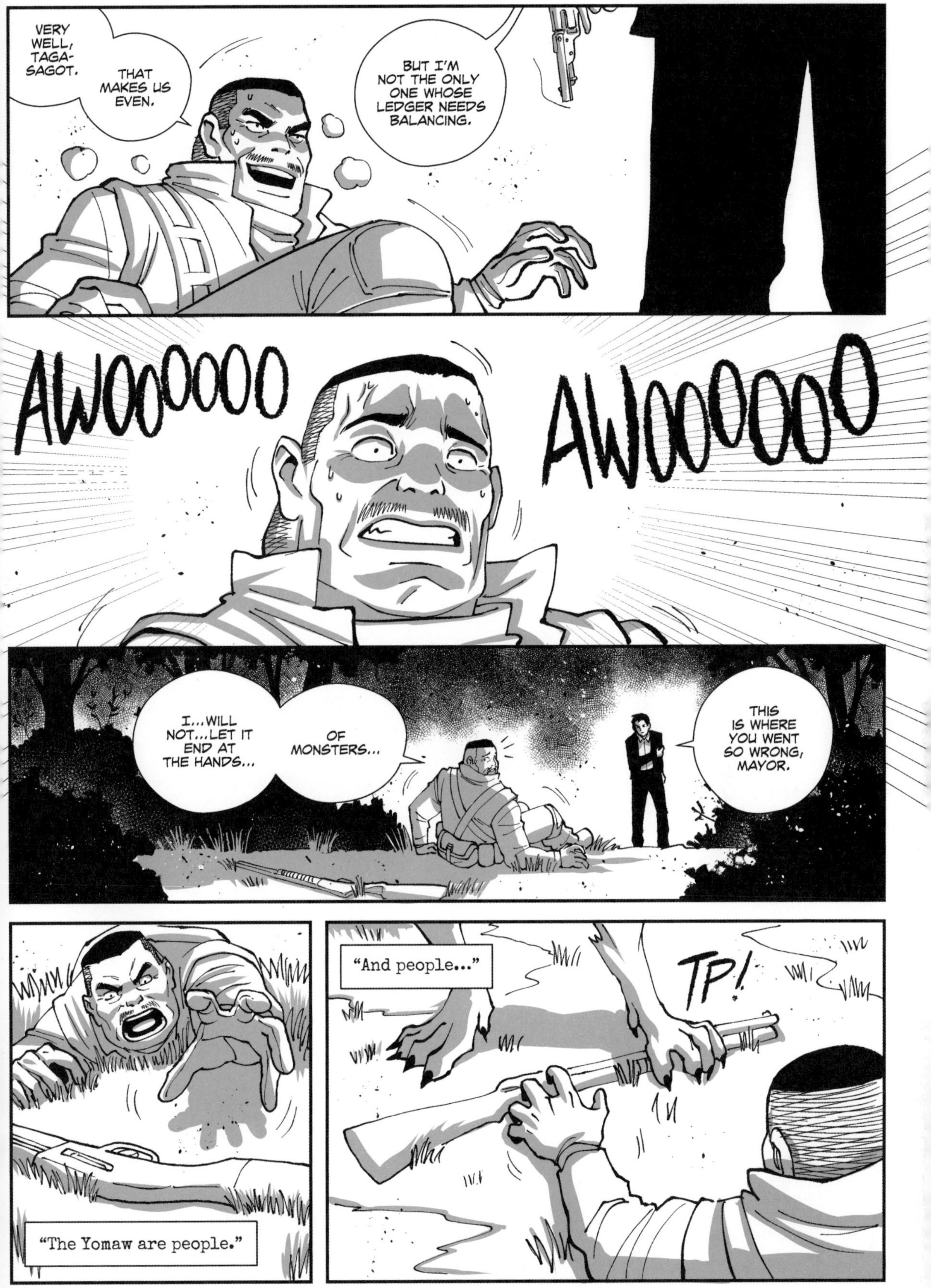
VERY WELL, TAGA-SAGOT.
THAT MAKES US EVEN.
BUT I'M NOT THE ONLY ONE WHOSE LEDGER NEEDS BALANCING.
AWOOOOOO
AWOOOOOO
I...WILL NOT...LET IT END AT THE HANDS...
OF MONSTERS...
THIS IS WHERE YOU WENT SO WRONG, MAYOR.
"The Yomaw are people."
"And people..."
TP!

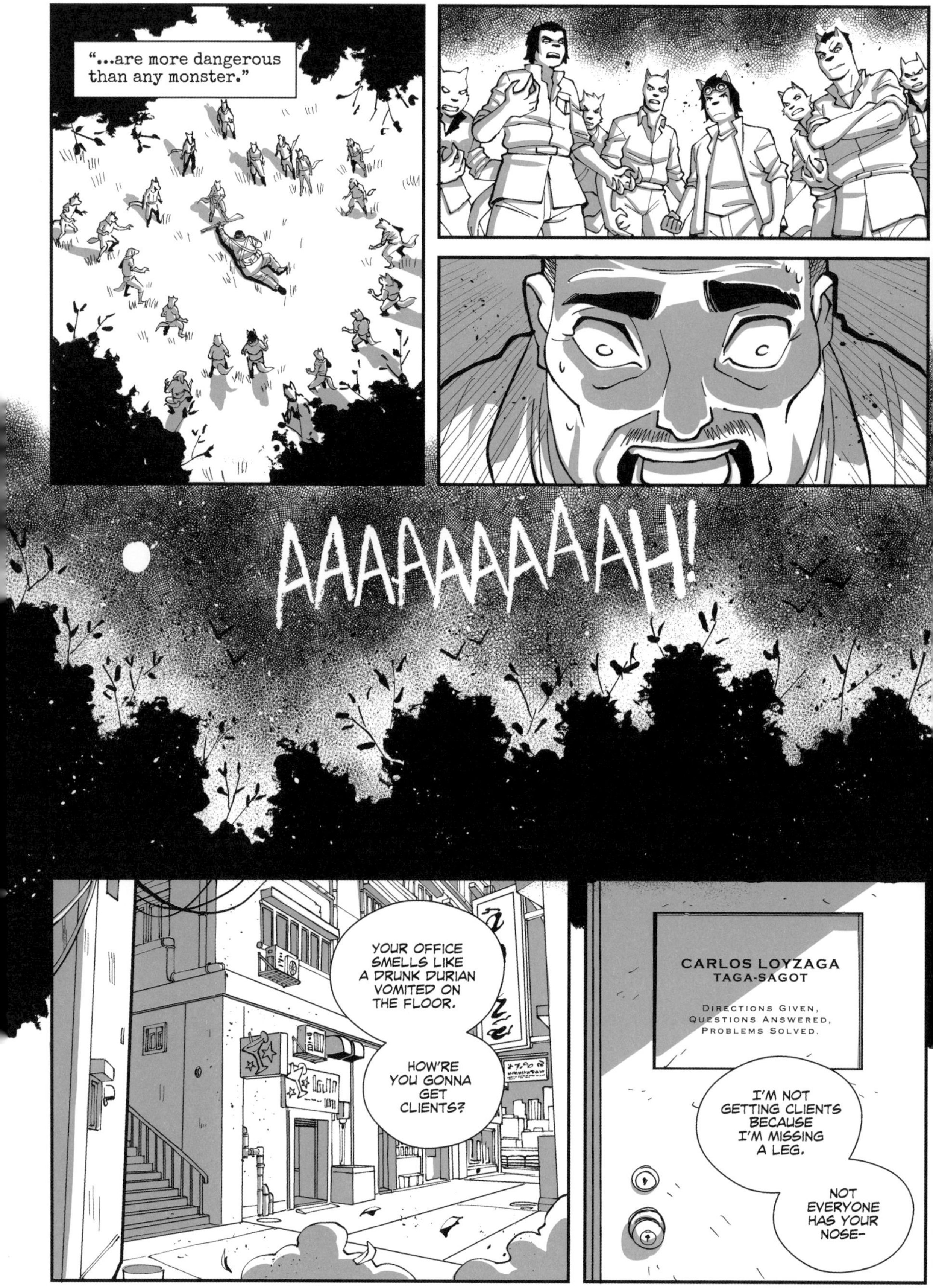
"...are more dangerous than any monster."
AAAAAAAAAAH!
YOUR OFFICE SMELLS LIKE A DRUNK DURIAN VOMITED ON THE FLOOR.
HOW'RE YOU GONNA GET CLIENTS?
CARLOS LOYZAGA
TAGA-SAGOT
Directions Given, Questions Answered, Problems Solved.
I'M NOT GETTING CLIENTS BECAUSE I'M MISSING A LEG.
NOT EVERYONE HAS YOUR NOSE-

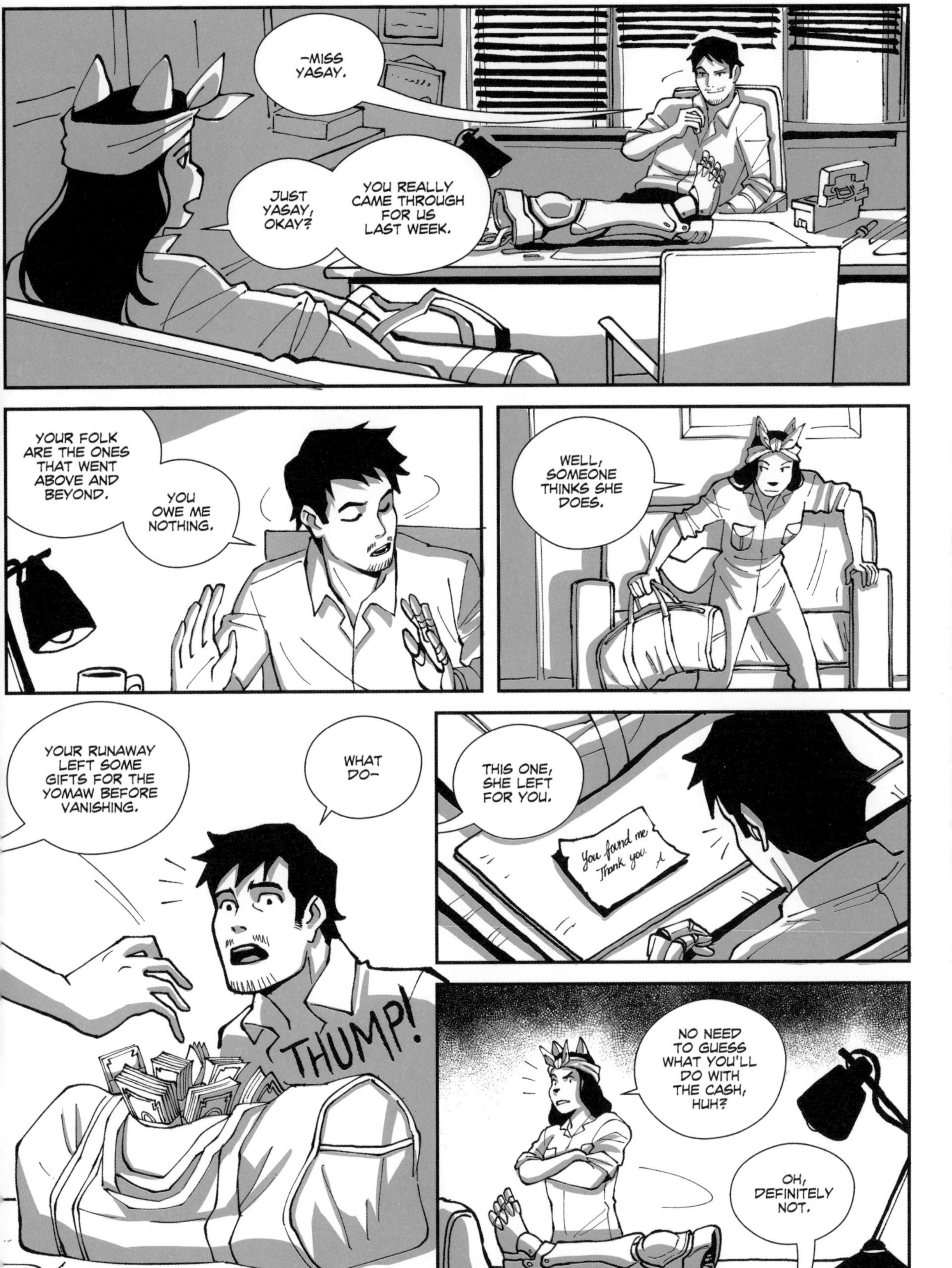
–MISS YASAY.
JUST YASAY, OKAY?
YOU REALLY CAME THROUGH FOR US LAST WEEK.
YOUR FOLK ARE THE ONES THAT WENT ABOVE AND BEYOND.
YOU OWE ME NOTHING.
WELL, SOMEONE THINKS SHE DOES.
YOUR RUNAWAY LEFT SOME GIFTS FOR THE YOMAW BEFORE VANISHING.
WHAT DO–
THUMP!
THIS ONE, SHE LEFT FOR YOU.
You found me Thank you. A
NO NEED TO GUESS WHAT YOU'LL DO WITH THE CASH, HUH?
OH, DEFINITELY NOT.

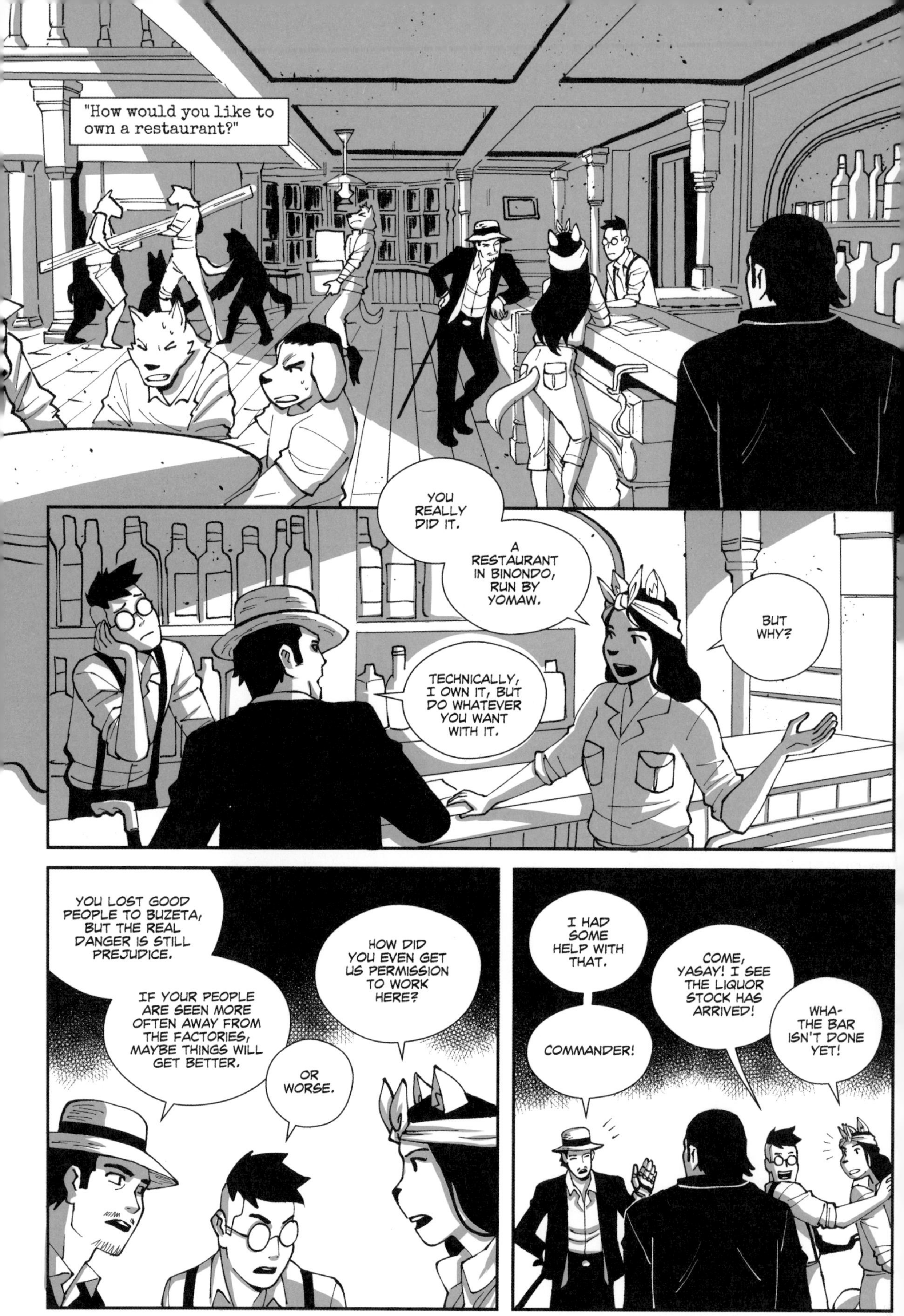
"How would you like to own a restaurant?"
YOU REALLY DID IT.
A RESTAURANT IN BINONDO, RUN BY YOMAW.
BUT WHY?
TECHNICALLY, I OWN IT, BUT DO WHATEVER YOU WANT WITH IT.
YOU LOST GOOD PEOPLE TO BUZETA, BUT THE REAL DANGER IS STILL PREJUDICE.
IF YOUR PEOPLE ARE SEEN MORE OFTEN AWAY FROM THE FACTORIES, MAYBE THINGS WILL GET BETTER.
OR WORSE.
HOW DID YOU EVEN GET US PERMISSION TO WORK HERE?
I HAD SOME HELP WITH THAT.
COMMANDER!
COME, YASAY! I SEE THE LIQUOR STOCK HAS ARRIVED!
WHA- THE BAR ISN'T DONE YET!

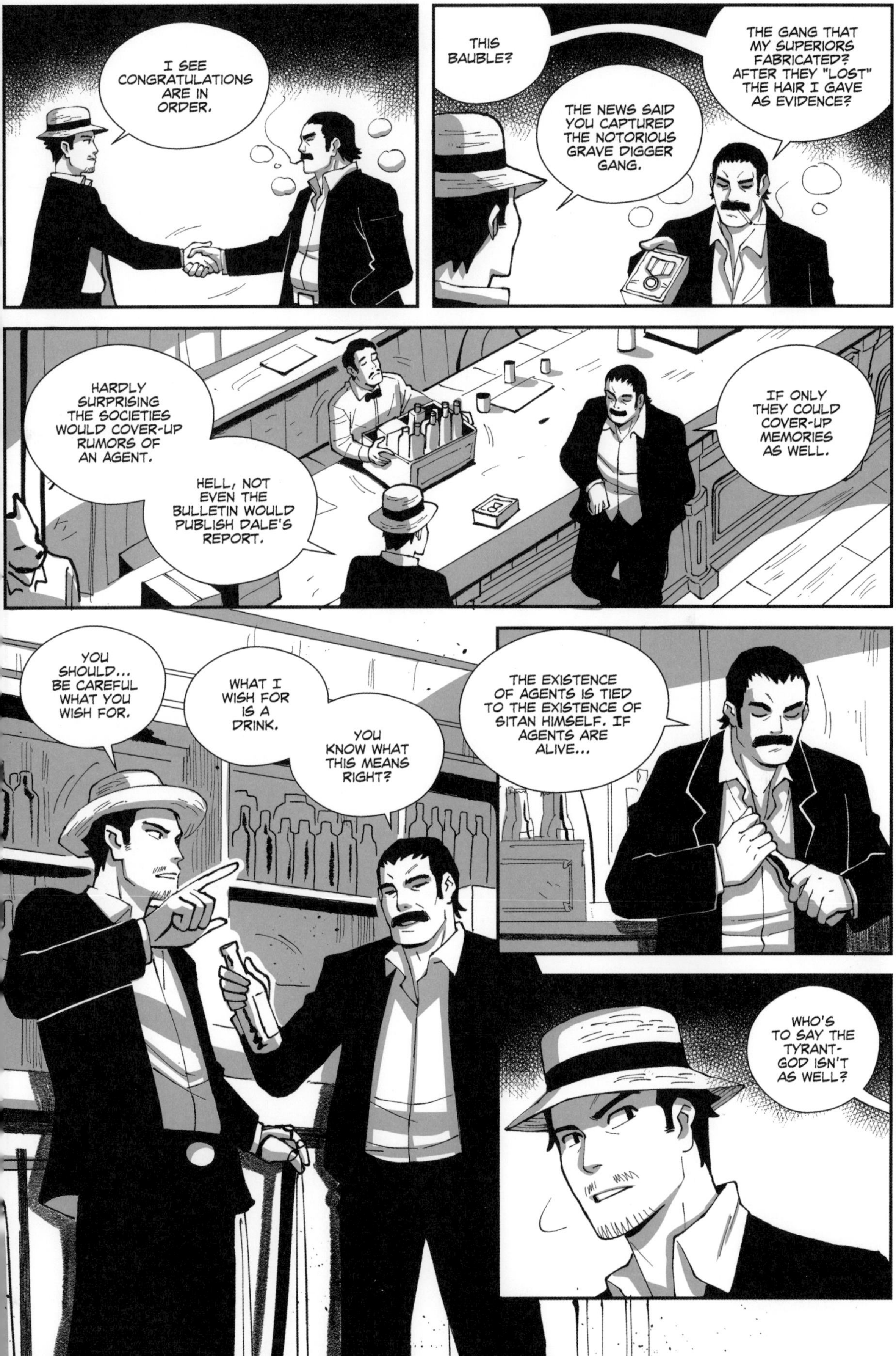
I SEE CONGRATULATIONS ARE IN ORDER.
THIS BAUBLE?
THE NEWS SAID YOU CAPTURED THE NOTORIOUS GRAVE DIGGER GANG.
THE GANG THAT MY SUPERIORS FABRICATED? AFTER THEY "LOST" THE HAIR I GAVE AS EVIDENCE?
HARDLY SURPRISING THE SOCIETIES WOULD COVER-UP RUMORS OF AN AGENT.
HELL, NOT EVEN THE BULLETIN WOULD PUBLISH DALE'S REPORT.
IF ONLY THEY COULD COVER-UP MEMORIES AS WELL.
YOU SHOULD... BE CAREFUL WHAT YOU WISH FOR.
WHAT I WISH FOR IS A DRINK.
YOU KNOW WHAT THIS MEANS RIGHT?
THE EXISTENCE OF AGENTS IS TIED TO THE EXISTENCE OF SITAN HIMSELF. IF AGENTS ARE ALIVE...
WHO'S TO SAY THE TYRANT-GOD ISN'T AS WELL?

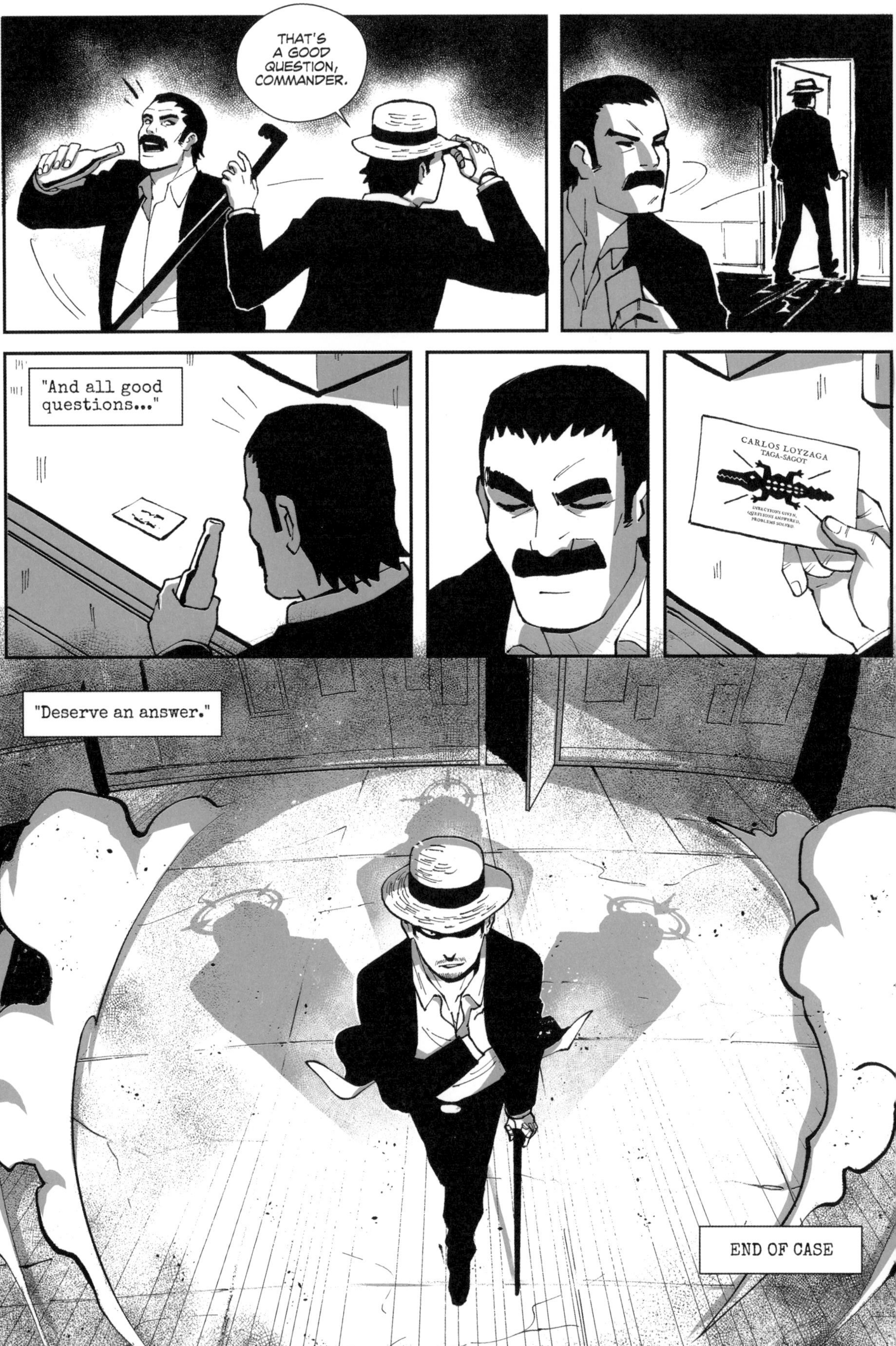
THAT'S A GOOD QUESTION, COMMANDER.
"And all good questions..."
CARLOS LOYZAGA
TAGA-SAGOT
DIRECTIONS GIVEN, QUESTIONS ANSWERED, PROBLEMS SOLVED.
"Deserve an answer."
END OF CASE